PENGUIN BOOKS

COLLECTED STORIES:
GABRIEL GARCÍA MÁRQUEZ

'Quite the nearest thing to pure sensual pleasure that prose can offer' *Daily Telegraph*

'A single sentence of García Márquez often has more meat to it than many whole novels' *Observer*

'Of all the living authors known to me, only one is undoubtedly touched by genius: Gabriel García Márquez' *Sunday Telegraph*

'A truly inspired storyteller' *New Statesman*

'An exquisite writer, wise, compassionate and extremely funny' *Sunday Telegraph*

'An imaginative writer of genius, the topmost pinnacle of an entire generation of Latin American novelists of cathedral-like proportions' *Guardian*

'One of this century's most evocative writers' Anne Tyler, *Chicago Sun-Times*

'García Márquez leaves an ineffaceable impression of magic, mystery and mastery' *Spectator*

'García Márquez is obsessed by death, by roses and by an ability to see life as if from just around the corner. He writes with power, using terrifying images. He fascinates utterly even while repelling and shocking' *Daily Telegraph*

'García Márquez is a retailer of wonders' *Sunday Times*

'No lover of fiction can fail to respond to the grace of Márquez's writing' *Sunday Telegraph*

'Márquez has insights and sympathies which he can project with the intensity of a reflecting mirror in a bright sun. He dazzles us with powerful effect' *New Statesman*

'The vigour and coherence of Márquez's vision, the brilliance and beauty of his imagery, the narrative tension . . . coursing through his pages . . . makes it difficult to put down' *Daily Telegraph*

'Sentence for sentence, there is hardly another writer in the world so generous with incidental pleasures' *Independent*

'Márquez is the master weaver of the real and the conjectured. His descriptive power astounds' *New Statesman*

'Underlying the marvellous wit, the inimitable humour and the superbly paced dialogue, there is the author's own anger, always controlled' *The Times*

'Every word and incident counts, everything hangs together, the work is a neatly perfect organism' *Financial Times*

ABOUT THE AUTHOR

Gabriel García Márquez was born in Aracataca, Colombia, in 1928. He studied at the University of Bogotá and later worked as a reporter for the Colombian newspaper *El Espectador* and as a foreign correspondent in Rome, Paris, Barcelona, Caracas and New York. He is the author of several novels and collections of stories, including *Eyes of a Blue Dog* (1947), *Leaf Storm* (1955), *No One Writes to the Colonel* (1958), *In Evil Hour* (1962), *Big Mama's Funeral* (1962), *One Hundred Years of Solitude* (1967), *Innocent Eréndira and Other Stories* (1972), *The Autumn of the Patriarch* (1975), *Chronicle of a Death Foretold* (1981), *Love in the Time of Cholera* (1985), *The General in His Labyrinth* (1989), *Strange Pilgrims* (1992) and *Of Love and Other Demons* (1994). His most recent book is the first volume of his autobiography, *Living to Tell the Tale*. Many of his books are published by Penguin. Gabriel García Márquez was awarded the Nobel Prize for Literature in 1982. He lives in Mexico City.

GABRIEL GARCÍA MÁRQUEZ

COLLECTED STORIES

TRANSLATED FROM THE SPANISH BY
GREGORY RABASSA AND J. S. BERNSTEIN

PENGUIN BOOKS

PENGUIN BOOKS

Published by the Penguin Group
Penguin Books Ltd, 80 Strand, London WC2R ORL, England
Penguin Group (USA) Inc., 375 Hudson Street, New York, New York 10014, USA
Penguin Group (Canada), 10 Alcorn Avenue, Toronto, Ontario, Canada M4V 3B2
(a division of Pearson Penguin Canada Inc.)
Penguin Ireland, 25 St Stephen's Green, Dublin 2, Ireland
(a division of Penguin Books Ltd)
Penguin Group (Australia), 250 Camberwell Road,
Camberwell, Victoria 3124, Australia (a division of Pearson Australia Group Pty Ltd)
Penguin Books India Pvt Ltd, 11 Community Centre, Panchsheel Park, New Delhi – 110 017, India
Penguin Group (NZ), cnr Airborne and Rosedale Roads, Albany,
Auckland 1310, New Zealand (a division of Pearson New Zealand Ltd)
Penguin Books (South Africa) (Pty) Ltd, 24 Sturdee Avenue, Rosebank 2196, South Africa

Penguin Books Ltd, Registered Offices: 80 Strand, London WC2R ORL, England

www.penguin.com

This collection first published by Jonathan Cape 1991
Published in Penguin Books 1996

16

Copyright © Gabriel García Márquez, 1954, 1961, 1972
English translations copyright © Harper & Row, Publishers, Inc., 1968, 1972, 1978
All rights reserved

The moral right of the author has been asserted

"Bitterness for Three Sleepwalkers" first appeared in *Translation*; "A Very Old Man with
Enormous Wings" in *New American Review*; "The Sea of Lost Time" in the *New Yorker*, "The
Handsomest Drowned Man in the World" in *Playboy*; "Death Constant Beyond Love" in
Atlantic Monthly; and Blacamán the Good, Vendor of Miracles" and "The Incredible Tale of
Innocent Eréndira and Her Heartless Grandmother" in *Esquire*

"Big Mama's Funeral" was originally published as "Los Funerales de la Mama Grande"
Copyright © by Universidad Veracruzana, Vera Cruz, Mexico

Printed in England by Clays Ltd, St Ives plc

Contents

PUBLISHER'S NOTE

These twenty-six stories by Gabriel García Márquez were
published in English in *No One Writes to the Colonel and
Other Stories* (1968), *Leaf Storm and Other Stories* (1972) and
Innocent Eréndira and Other Stories (1978). They are now
published in one volume in the chronological order of their
original publication in Spanish from the three volumes of short
stories *Eyes of a Blue Dog* (translated by Gregory Rabassa),
Big Mama's Funeral (translated by J. S. Bernstein), and *The
Incredible and Sad Tale of Innocent Eréndira and Her Heartless Grandmother* (translated by Gregory Rabassa).

Collected Stories

The Third Resignation

There was that noise again. That cold, cutting, vertical noise that he knew so well now; but it was coming to him now sharp and painful, as if he had become unaccustomed to it overnight.

It was spinning around inside his empty head, dull and biting. A beehive had risen up inside the four walls of his skull. It grew larger and larger with successive spirals, and it beat on him inside, making the stem of his spinal cord quiver with an irregular vibration, out of pitch with the sure rhythm of his body. Something had become unadapted in his human material structure; something that had functioned normally 'at other times' and now was hammering at his head from within with dry and hard blows made by the bones of a fleshless, skeletal hand, and it made him remember all the bitter sensations of life. He had the animal impulse to clench his fists and squeeze his temples, which sprouted blue and purple arteries with the firm pressure of his desperate pain. He would have liked to catch the noise that was piercing the moment with its sharp diamond point between the palms of his sensitive hands. The figure of a domestic cat made his muscles contract when he imagined it chasing through the tormented corners of his hot, fever-torn head. Now he would catch it. No. The noise had slippery fur, almost untouchable. But he was ready to catch it with his well-learned strategy and hold it long and tightly with all the strength of his desperation. He would not permit it to enter through his ear again, to come out through his mouth, through each one of his pores or his eyes, which rolled as it went through and remained blind, looking at the flight of the noise from the depths of the shattered darkness. He would not allow it to break its cut-glass crystals, its ice stars, against the interior wall of his cranium. That was what that noise was like: interminable, like a child beating his head against a concrete wall. Like all hard blows against nature's firm things. But if he could encircle it, isolate it, it would no longer torment him. Go and cut the variable figure from its own shadow. Grab it. Squeeze it, yes, once and for all now. Throw it onto the pavement with all his might and step on it ferociously until he could say, panting, that he had killed the noise that was tormenting him, that was driving him mad, and that was now stretched out on the ground like any ordinary thing, transformed into an integral death.

But it was impossible for him to squeeze his temples. His arms had been shortened on him and were now the limbs of a dwarf; small, chubby, adipose arms. He tried to shake his head. He shook it. The noise then appeared with greater force inside his skull, which had hardened, grown larger, felt itself more strongly attracted by gravity. The noise was heavy and hard. So heavy and hard that once he had caught and destroyed it, he would have the impression that he had plucked the petals off a lead flower.

He had heard the noise with the same insistence 'at other times.' He had heard it, for instance, on the day he had died for the first time. The time – when he saw a corpse – that he realized it was his own corpse. He looked at it and he touched it. He felt himself untouchable, unspatial, nonexistent. He really was a corpse and he could already feel the passage of death on his young and sickly body. The atmosphere had hardened all through the house, as if it had been filled with cement, and in the middle of that block – where objects had remained as when it had been an atmosphere of air – there he was, carefully placed inside a coffin of hard but transparent cement. 'That noise' had been in his head that time too. How distant and how cold the soles of his feet had felt there at the other end of the coffin, where they had placed a pillow, because the box was still too big for him and they had to adjust it, adapt the dead body to its new and last garment. They covered him with white and tied a handkerchief around his jaw; mortally handsome.

He was in his coffin, ready to be buried, and yet he knew that he wasn't dead. That if he tried to get up he could do it so easily. 'Spiritually,' at least. But it wasn't worth the trouble. Better to let himself die right there; die of 'death,' which was his illness. It had been some time since the doctor had said to his mother dryly:

'Madam, your child has a grave illness: he is dead. Nevertheless,' he went on, 'we shall do everything possible to keep him alive beyond death. We will succeed in making his organic functions continue through a complex system of autonutrition. Only the motor functions will be different, his spontaneous movements. We shall watch his life through growth, which, too, shall continue on in a normal fashion. It is simply "a living death." A real and true death . . . '

He remembered the words but in a confused way. Perhaps he had never heard them and it was the creation of his brain as his temperature rose during the crisis of typhoid fever.

While he was sinking into delirium. When he had read the tales of embalmed pharaohs. As his fever rose, he felt himself to be the protagonist. A kind of emptiness in his life had begun there. From then on he had been unable to distinguish, to remember what events were part of his delirium and what were part of his real life. That was why he doubted now. Perhaps the doctor had never mentioned that strange 'living death.' It was illogical, paradoxical, simply contradictory. And it made him suspect now that he really was dead. That he had been for eighteen years.

It was then – at the time of his death when he was seven years old – that his mother had had a small coffin made for him out of green wood; a child's coffin, but the doctor had ordered them to make a larger box, a box for a normal adult, because that one there might atrophy growth and he would develop into a deformed dead person or an abnormal living one. Or the detention of growth might impede his realizing that he was getting better. In view of that warning, his mother had a large coffin made for him, one for an adult corpse, and in it she placed three pillows at his feet so that he would fit it properly.

Soon he began to grow inside the box in such a way that every year they would remove some wool from the end pillow so as to give him room for growth. That was how he had spent half his life. Eighteen years. (He was twenty-five now.) And he had reached his normal, definitive height. The carpenter and the doctor had been mistaken in their calculations and had made the coffin two feet too long. They had thought he would have the stature of his father, who had been a half-savage giant. But that was not how it was. The only thing he had inherited from him was his thick beard. A thick, blue beard, which his mother was in the habit of arranging so as to give him a more decent appearance in his coffin. That beard bothered him terribly on hot days.

But there was something that worried him more than 'the noise!' It was the mice. Even as a child nothing in the world had worried him more, had produced more terror in him than mice. And it was precisely those disgusting animals who had been attracted by the smell of the candles that burned at his feet. They had already gnawed his clothes and he knew that soon they would start gnawing him, eating his body. One day he was able to see them: they were five shiny, slithery mice who had climbed up into the box by the table leg and were devouring him. By the time his mother noticed it there would be nothing left of him except rubble, his hard, cold bones. What produced even more horror in him was not exactly that the mice would eat him. After all, he could go on living with his skeleton. What tormented him was the innate terror he felt toward those small animals. His hair stood on end just thinking about those velvety creatures who ran all over his body, got into the folds of his skin, and brushed his lips with their icy paws. One of them climbed up to his eyelids and tried to gnaw at his cornea. He saw it, large and monstrous, in its desperate effort to bore through to his retina. He thought that it was a new death and surrendered completely to the imminence of vertigo.

He remembered that he had reached adulthood. He was twenty-five years old and that meant that he wouldn't grow any more. His features would become firm, serious. But when he was healthy he wouldn't be able to talk about his childhood. He hadn't had any. He had spent it dead.

His mother had taken rigorous care during the time between childhood and puberty. She was concerned about the perfect hygiene of the coffin and the room as a whole. She changed the flowers in the vases frequently and opened the windows every day so that the fresh air could come in. It was with great satisfaction that she examined the metric tape in those days, when after measuring him she would ascertain that he had grown several centimeters. She had the maternal satisfaction of seeing him alive. Still, she took care to avoid the presence of strangers in the house. After all, the existence of a corpse in family quarters over long years was disagreeable and mysterious. She was a woman of abnegation. But soon her optimism began to decline. During the last years, he saw her look at the metric tape with sadness. Her child was no longer growing. For the past few months the growth had not progressed a single millimeter. His mother knew that now it would be difficult to observe the presence of life in her beloved corpse. She had the fear that one morning she would find him 'really' dead, and perhaps because of that on the day in question he was able to observe that she approached his box discreetly and smelled his body. She had fallen into a crisis of pessimism. Of late she had neglected her attentions and no longer took the precaution of carrying the metric tape. She knew that he wasn't going to grow any more.

And he knew that now he was 'really' dead. He knew it because of that gentle tranquillity with which his organism had let itself be carried off. Everything had changed unseasonably. The imperceptible beats that only he could perceive had disappeared from his pulse now. He felt heavy, drawn by a reclaiming and potent force toward the primitive substance of the earth. The force of gravity seemed to attract him now with an irrevocable power. He was heavy, like a positive, undeniable corpse. But it was more restful that way. He didn't even have to breathe in order to live his death.

In an imaginary way, without touching himself, one by one he went over his members. There, on a hard pillow, was his head, turned a bit toward the left. He imagined his mouth slightly open because of the narrow strip of cold that filled his throat with hail. He had been chopped down like a twenty-five-year-old tree. Perhaps he had tried to close his mouth. The handkerchief that had held his jaw was loose. He was unable to get himself in place, compose himself, even to strike a pose to look like a decent corpse. His muscles, his members no longer responded as before, punctual to the call of the nervous system. He was no longer what he had been eighteen years before, a normal child who could move as he wished. He felt his fallen arms, fallen forever, tight against the cushioned sides of the coffin. His stomach hard, like the bark of a walnut tree. And beyond there were his legs, whole, exact, completing his perfect adult anatomy. His body rested heavily, but peacefully, with no discomfort whatever, as if the world had suddenly stopped and no one would break the silence, as if all the lungs of the earth had ceased breathing so as not to break the soft silence of the air. He felt as happy as a child face up on the thick, cool grass contemplating a high cloud flying off in the afternoon sky. He was happy, even though he knew he was dead, that he would rest forever in the box lined with artificial silk. He had great lucidity. It was not as before, after his first death, in which he felt dull, listless. The four candles they had placed around him, which were replaced every three months, had begun to go out again, just when they would be indispensable. He felt the closeness of the fresh, damp violets his mother had brought that morning. He felt it in the lilies, the roses. But all that terrible reality did not give him any anxiety. Quite the opposite, he was happy there, alone in his solitude. Would he feel fear afterward?

Who can say? It was hard to think about the moment when the hammer would pound the nails into the green wood and the coffin would creak under its certain hope of becoming a tree once more. His body, drawn now with greater force by the imperative of the earth, would remain tilted in a damp, claylike, soft depth and up there, four cubic yards above, the gravediggers' last blows would grow faint. No. He wouldn't feel fear there either. That would be the prolongation of his death, the most natural prolongation of his new state.

Not even a degree of heat would be left in his body, his medulla would have frozen forever and little ice stars would penetrate as deep as the marrow of his bones. How well he would grow used to his new life as a dead man! One day, however, he will feel his solid armor fall apart, and when he tries to name, review, each one of his members, he won't find them. He will feel that he doesn't have any definitive, exact form, and he will know with resignation that he has lost his perfect twenty-five-year-old anatomy and has been changed into a handful of shapeless dust, with no geometric definition.

The biblical dust of death. Perhaps then he will feel a slight nostalgia, the nostalgia of not being a formal, anatomical corpse, but, rather, an imaginary, abstract corpse, assembled only in the hazy memory of his kin. He will know then that he will rise up the capillary vessels of an apple tree and awaken, bitten by the hunger of a child on some autumn day. He will know – and that did sadden him – that he has lost his unity: that he is no longer even an ordinary dead man, a common corpse.

He had spent that last night in the solitary company of his own corpse.

But with the new day, with the penetration of the first rays of the lukewarm sun through the open window, he felt his skin softening. He observed it for a moment. Quiet, rigid. He let the air run over his body. There was no doubt about it: the 'smell' was there. During the night the corpse rot had begun to have its effects. His organism had begun to decompose, rot, like the bodies of all dead people. The 'smell' was undoubtedly, unmistakably, the smell of gamy meat, disappearing and then reappearing, more penetrating. His body was decomposing with the heat of the previous night. Yes. He was rotting. Within a few hours his mother would come to change the flowers and the stench of decomposed flesh would hit her from the threshold. Then they would take him away to sleep his second death among the other dead.

But suddenly fear struck him in the back like a dagger. Fear! Such a deep word, so meaningful! Now he really was afraid, with a true, 'physical' fear. What was its cause? He understood perfectly and it made his flesh creep: he probably wasn't dead. They'd put him there, in that box, which now seemed so perfectly soft, so cushioned, so terribly comfortable, and the phantom of fear opened the window of reality to him: They were going to bury him alive!

He couldn't be dead because he had an exact awareness of everything: of the life that was spinning and murmuring about him. Of the warm smell of heliotrope that came in through the open window and mingled with the other 'smell.' He was quite aware of the slow dripping of the water in the cistern. Of the cricket that had stayed in the corner and was still chirping, thinking that early morning was still there.

Everything denied his death. Everything except the 'smell.' But how could he know that the smell was his? Maybe his mother had forgotten to change the water in the vases the day before and the stems were rotting. Or maybe the mouse which the cat had dragged into his room had decomposed with the heat. No. The 'smell' couldn't be coming from his body.

A few moments before he had been happy with his death, because he had thought he was dead. Because a dead man can be happy with his irremediable situation. But a living person can't resign himself to being buried alive. Yet his members wouldn't respond to his call. He couldn't express himself and that was what caused his terror, the greatest terror of his life and of his death. They were going to bury him alive. He might be able to feel, be aware of the moment they nailed up the box. He would feel the emptiness of the body suspended across the shoulders of friends as his anguish and desperation grew with every step of the procession.

He will try to rise up in vain, to call with all his weakened forces, to pound inside the dark and narrow coffin so that they will know that he is still alive, that they are going to bury him alive. It would be useless. Even there his members would not respond to that urgent and last call of his nervous system.

He heard sounds in the next room. Could he have been asleep? Could all that life of a dead man have been a nightmare? But the sound of the dishes didn't go on. He became sad and maybe he was annoyed because of it. He would have wanted all the dishes in the world to break in one single crash right there beside him, to be awakened by an outside cause since his own will had failed.

But no. It wasn't a dream. He was sure that if it had been a dream his last intent to return to reality wouldn't have failed. He wouldn't wake up again. He felt the softness of the coffin, and the 'smell' had returned with greater strength now, with so much strength that he already doubted that it was his own smell. He would have liked to see his relatives there before he began to fall apart, and the spectacle of putrefying flesh would have produced a revulsion in them. The neighbors would flee in fright from the casket, holding a handkerchief to their mouths. They would spit. No. Not that. It would be better if they buried him. It would be better to get out of 'that' as soon as possible. Even he now wanted to be quit of his own corpse. Now he knew that he was truly dead, or, at least, inappreciably alive. What difference did it make? The 'smell' persisted in any case.

He would hear the last prayers with resignation, the last Latin mouthings and the acolytes' incompetent response. The cold of the cemetery, filled with dust and bones, would penetrate down even to his bones and dissipate the 'smell' a bit, perhaps. Perhaps – who knows! – the imminence of the moment will bring him out of that lethargy. When he feels himself swimming in his own sweat, in a viscous, thick water, as he had swum in the uterus of his mother before being born. Perhaps he is alive, then.

But most likely he is so resigned to dying now that he might well die of resignation.

The Other Side of Death

Without knowing why, he awoke with a start. A sharp smell of violets and formaldehyde, robust and broad, was coming from the other room, mingling with the aroma of the newly opened flowers sent out by the dawning garden. He tried to calm down, to recover the spirit he had suddenly lost in sleep. It must have been dawn now, because outside, in the garden, the sprinkler had begun to sing amidst the vegetables and the sky was blue through the open window. He looked about the shadowy room, trying to explain that sudden, unexpected awakening. He had the impression, the *physical* certainty, that someone had come in while he had been asleep. Yet he was alone, and the door, locked from the inside, showed no signs of violence. Up above the air over the window a morning star was awakening. He was quiet for a moment, as if trying to loosen the nervous tension that had pushed him to the surface of sleep, and closing his eyes, face up, he began to seek the broken thread of serenity again. His clustered blood broke up in his throat and beyond that, in his chest, his heart despaired robustly, marking, marking an accentuated and light rhythm as if it were coming from some headlong running. He reviewed the previous minutes in his mind. Maybe he'd had a strange dream. It might have been a nightmare. No. There was nothing particular, no reason for any start in 'that.'

They were traveling in a train – I remember it now – through a countryside – I've had this dream frequently – like a still life, sown with false, artificial trees bearing fruit of razors, scissors, and other diverse items – I remember now that I have to get my hair cut – barbershop instruments. He'd had that dream a lot of times but it had never produced that scare in him. There behind a tree was his brother, the other one, his twin, signaling – this happened to me somewhere in real life – for him to stop the train. Convinced of the futility of his message, he began to run after the coach until he fell, panting, his mouth full of froth. It was his absurd, irrational dream, of course, but there was no reason for it to have caused that restless awakening. He closed his eyes again, his temples still pounded by the current of blood that was rising firmly in him like a clenched fist. The train went into an arid, sterile, boring geography, and a pain he felt in his left leg made him turn his attention from the landscape. He observed that on his middle toe – I mustn't keep on wearing these tight shoes – he had a tumor. In a natural way, and as if he were used to it, he took a screwdriver out of his pocket and extracted the head of the tumor with it. He placed it carefully in a little blue box – can you see colors in dreams? – and he glimpsed, peeping out of the wound, the end of a greasy, yellow string. Without getting upset, as if he had expected that string to be there, he pulled on it slowly with careful precision. It was a long, very long tape, which came out by itself, with no discomfort or pain. A second later he lifted his eyes and saw that the railway coach had emptied out and that the only one left, in another compartment of the train, was his brother, dressed as a woman, in front of a mirror, trying to extract his left eye with a pair of scissors.

Actually, he was displeased with that dream, but he couldn't explain why it had altered his circulation, because on previous occasions when his nightmares had been hair-raising he had managed to maintain his calm. His hands felt cold. The smell of violets and formaldehyde persisted and became disagreeable, almost aggressive. With his eyes closed, trying to break the rising tempo of his breathing, he tried to find some trivial theme so he could sink into the dream that had been interrupted minutes before. He could think, for example, that in three hours I must go to the funeral parlor to cover the expenses. In the corner a wakeful cricket had raised its chirp and was filling the room with its sharp and cutting throat. The nervous tension began to recede slowly but effectively and he noticed once more the looseness, the laxity of his muscles. He felt that he had fallen on the soft and thick cushion while his body, light and weightless, had been run through by a sweet feeling of beatitude and fatigue and was losing consciousness of its own material structure, that heavy, earthy substance that defined it, placing it in an unmistakable and exact spot on the zoological scale and bearing a whole sum of systems, geometrically defined organs that lifted him up to the arbitrary hierarchy of rational animals. His eyelids, docile now, fell over his corneas in the same natural way with which his arms and legs mingled in a gathering of members that were slowly losing their independence, as if the whole organism had turned into one single, large, total organism, and he – the man – had abandoned his mortal roots so as to penetrate other, deeper and firmer, roots: the eternal roots of an integral and definitive dream. Outside, from the other side of the world, he could hear the cricket's song growing weaker until it disappeared from his senses, which had turned inward, submerging him in a new and uncomplicated notion of time and space, erasing the presence of that material world, physical and painful, full of insects and acrid smells of violets and formaldehyde.

Gently wrapped in the warm climate of a coveted serenity, he felt the lightness of his artificial and daily death. He sank into a loving geography, into an easy, ideal world, a world like one drawn by a child, with no algebraic equations, with no loving farewells, no force of gravity.

He wasn't exactly sure how long he'd been like that, between that noble surface of dreams and realities, but he did remember that suddenly, as if his throat had been cut by the slash of a knife, he'd given a start in bed and felt that his twin brother, his dead brother, was sitting on the edge of the bed.

Again, as before, his heart was a fist that rose up into his mouth and pushed him into a leap. The dawning light, the cricket that continued grinding the solitude with its little out-of-tune hand organ, the cool air that came up from the garden's universe, everything contributed to make him return to the real world once more. But this time he could understand what had caused his start. During the brief minutes of his dozing, and – I can see it now – during the whole night, when he had thought he'd had a peaceful, simple sleep, *with no thoughts*, his memory had been fixed on one single, constant, invariable image, an *autonomous* image that imposed itself on his thought in spite of the will and the resistance of the thought itself. Yes. Almost without his noticing it, 'that' thought had been overpowering him, filling him, completely inhabiting him, turning into a backdrop that was fixed there behind the other thoughts, giving support, the definitive vertebrae to the mental drama of his day and night. The idea of his twin brother's corpse had been firmly stuck in the whole center of his life. And now that they had left him there, in his parcel of land now, his eyelids fluttered by the rain, now *he was afraid* of him.

He never thought the blow would have been so strong. Through the partly opened window the smell entered again, mixed in now with a different smell, of damp earth, submerged bones, and his sense of smell came out to meet it joyfully, with the tremendous happiness of a bestial man. Many hours had already passed since the moment in which *he saw* it twisting like a badly wounded dog under the sheets, howling, biting out that last shout that filled his throat with salt, using his nails to try to break the pain that was climbing up *him*, along his back, to the roots of the tumor. He couldn't forget *his* thrashing like a dying animal, rebellious at the truth that had stopped in front of *him*, that had clasped *his* body with tenacity, with imperturbable constancy, something definitive, like death itself. He saw *him* during the last moments of *his* barbarous death throes. When he broke *his* nails against the walls, clawing at that last piece of life which was slipping away through his fingers, bleeding *him*, while the gangrene *was getting into him* through the side like an implacable woman. Then he saw *him* fall onto the messy bed, with a touch of resigned fatigue, sweating, as his froth-covered teeth drew a horrible, monstrous smile for the world out of him and death began to flow through his bones like a river of ashes.

It was then that I thought about the tumor that had ceased to pain in his stomach. I imagined it as round – now he felt the same sensation – swelling like an interior sun, unbearable like a yellow insect extending its vicious filaments towards the depths of the intestines. (He felt that his viscera had become dislocated inside him as before the imminence of a physio-logical necessity.) Maybe I'll have a tumor like his someday. At first it will be a small but growing sphere that will branch out, growing larger in my stomach like a fetus. I will probably feel it when it starts to take on motion, moving inward with the fury of a sleepwalking child, traveling through my intes-tines blindly – he put his hands on his stomach to contain the sharp pain – its anxious hands held out toward the shadows, looking for the warm matrix, the hospitable uterus that it is never to find; while its hundred feet of a fantastic animal will go on wrapping themselves up into a long and yellow umbili-cal cord. Yes. Maybe I – the stomach – like this brother who has just died, have a tumor at the root of my viscera. The smell that the garden had sent was returning now, strong, repugnant, enveloped in a nauseating stench. Time seemed to have stopped on the edge of dawn. The morning star had jelled on the glass while the neighboring room, where the corpse had been all the night before, was still exuding its strong formaldehyde message. It was, certainly, a different smell from that of the garden. This was a more anguished, a more specific smell than that mingled smell of unequal flowers. A smell that always, once it was known, was related to corpses. It was the glacial and exuberant smell left with him from the formic aldehyde of amphitheaters. He thought about the laboratory. He remembered the viscera preserved in abso-lute alcohol; the dissected birds. A rabbit saturated with formaldehyde has its flesh harden, it becomes dehydrated and loses its docile elasticity until it changes into a perpetual, eternalized rabbit. Formaldehyde. Where is this smell coming from? *The only way to contain rot.* If we men *had* formaldehyde in our veins *we would be* like the anatomical specimens submerged in absolute alcohol.

There outside he heard the beating of the increasing rain as it came hammering on the glass of the partly open window. A cool, joyful, and new air came in, loaded with dampness. The cold of his hands intensified, making him feel the presence of the formaldehyde in his arteries; as if the dampness of the courtyard had come into him down to the bones. Dampness. There's a lot of dampness 'there.' With a certain displeasure he thought about the winter nights when the rain will pass through the grass and the dampness will come to rest on his brother's side, circulate through his body like a concrete current. It seemed to him that the dead had need of a different circulatory system that hurled them toward another irremediable and final death. At the moment he didn't want it to rain any more, he wanted summer to be an eternal, dominant season. Because of his thoughts, he was displeased by the persistence of that damp clatter on the glass. He wanted the clay of cemeteries to be dry, always dry, because it made him restless to think that after two weeks, when the dampness begins to run through the marrow, there would no longer be another man equal, exactly equal to him under the ground.

Yes. *They* were twin brothers, exact, whom no one could distinguish at first sight. Before, when they both were living their separate lives, they were nothing but *two twin brothers*, simple and apart like two different men. *Spiritually* there was no common factor between them. But now, when rigidity, the terrible reality, was climbing up along his back like an invertebrate animal, something had dissolved in his integral atmosphere, something that sounded like an emptiness, as if a precipice had opened up at his side, or as if his body had suddenly been sliced in two by an axe; not that exact, anatomical body under a perfect geometrical definition; not that physical body that now felt fear; another body, rather, that was coming from beyond his, that had been sunken with him in the liquid night of the maternal womb and was climbing up with him through the branches of an ancient genealogy; that was with him in the blood of his four pairs of great-grandparents and that came from way back, from the beginning of the world, sustaining with its weight, with its mysterious presence, the whole universal balance. It might be that he had been in the blood of Isaac and Rebecca, that it was his other brother who had been born shackled to his heel and who came tumbling along generation after generation, night after night, from kiss to kiss, from love to love, descending through arteries and testicles until he arrived, as on a night voyage at the womb of his recent mother. The mysterious ancestral itinerary was being presented to him now as painful and true, now that the equilibrium had been broken and the equation definitively solved. He knew that something was lacking for his personal harmony, his formal and everyday integrity: *Jacob had been irremediably freed from his ankles!*

During the days when his brother was ill he hadn't had this feeling, because the emaciated face, transfigured by fever and pain, with the grown beard, had been quite different from his.

Once he was motionless, lying out on top of his total death, a barber was called to 'arrange' the corpse. He was present, leaning tightly against the wall, when the man dressed in white arrived bearing the clean instruments of his profession … With the precision of a master he covered the dead man's beard with lather – the frothy mouth: that was how I saw him before he died – and slowly, as one who goes about revealing a tremendous secret, he began to shave him. It was then that he was assaulted by 'that' terrible idea. As the pale and earthen face of his twin brother emerged under the passage of the razor, he had the feeling that the corpse there was not *a thing* that was alien to him but was made from his same earthy substance, that it was his own repetition … He had the strange feeling that his kin had extracted his image from the mirror, the one he saw reflected in the glass when he shaved. Now that image, which used to respond to every movement of his, had gained independence. He had watched it being shaved other times, every morning. But now he was witnessing the dramatic experience of another man's taking the beard off the image in his mirror, his own physical presence unneeded. He had the certainty, the assurance, that if he had gone over to a mirror at that moment he would have found it blank, even though physics had no precise explanation for the phenomenon. It was an awareness of splitting in two! His double was a corpse! Desperate, trying to react, he touched the firm wall that rose up in him by touch, a kind of current of security. The barber finished his work and with the tip of his scissors closed the corpse's eyelids. Night left him trembling inside, with the irrevocable solitude of the plucked corpse. That was how exact they were. Two identical brothers, disquietingly repeated.

It was then, as he observed how intimately joined those two natures were, that it occurred to him that something extraordinary, something unexpected, was going to happen. He imagined that the separation of the two bodies in space was just appearance, while in reality the two of them had a single, total nature. Maybe when organic decomposition reaches the dead one, he, the living one, will begin to decay also within his animated world.

He could hear the rain beating more strongly on the panes and the cricket suddenly snapped his string. His hands were now intensely cold with a long, dehumanized coldness. The smell of formaldehyde, stronger now, made him think about the possibility of reaching the rottenness that his twin brother was communicating to him from there, from his frozen hole in the ground. That's absurd! Maybe the phenomenon is the opposite: the influence must be exercised by the one who remained with life, with his energy, with his vital cell! Maybe – on this level – he and his brother, too, will remain intact, sustaining a balance between life and death as they defend themselves against putrefaction. But who can be sure of it? Wasn't it just as possible that the buried brother would remain incorruptible while rottenness would invade the living one with all its blue octopuses?

He thought that the last hypothesis was the most probable and resigned himself to wait for the arrival of his tremendous hour. His flesh had become soft, adipose, and he thought he could feel a blue substance covering him all over. He sniffed down below for the coming of his own bodily odors, but only the formaldehyde from the next room agitated his olfactory membranes with an icy, unmistakable shudder. Nothing worried him after that. The cricket in its corner tried to start its ballad up again while a thick, exact drop began to run along the ceiling in the very center of the room. He heard it drop without surprise because he knew that the wood was old in that spot, but he imagined that drop, formed from cool, good, friendly water, coming from the sky, from a better life, one that was broader and not so full of idiotic phenomena like love or digestion or twinship. Maybe that drop would fill the room in the space of an hour or in a thousand years and would dissolve that mortal armor, that vain substance, which perhaps – why not? – between brief instants would be nothing but a sticky mixture of albumen and whey. Everything was equal now. Only his own death came between him and his grave. Resigned, he listened to the drop, thick, heavy, exact, as it dripped in the other world, in the mistaken and absurd world of rational creatures.

Eva Is Inside Her Cat

All of a sudden she noticed that her beauty had fallen all apart on her, that it had begun to pain her physically like a tumor or a cancer. She still remembered the weight of the privilege she had borne over her body during adolescence, which she had dropped now – who knows where? – with the weariness of resignation, with the final gesture of a declining creature. It was impossible to bear that burden any longer. She had to drop that useless attribute of her personality somewhere; as she turned a corner, somewhere in the outskirts. Or leave it behind on the coat-rack of a second-rate restaurant like some old useless coat. She was tired of being the center of attention, of being under siege from men's long looks. At night, when insomnia stuck its pins into her eyes, she would have liked to be an ordinary woman, without any special attraction. Everything was hostile to her within the four walls of her room. Desperate, she could feel her vigil spreading out under her skin, into her head, pushing the fever upward toward the roots of her hair. It was as if her arteries had become peopled with hot, tiny insects who, with the approach of dawn, awoke each day and ran about on their moving feet in a rending subcutaneous adventure in that place of clay made fruit where her anatomical beauty had found its home. In vain she struggled to chase those terrible creatures away. She couldn't. They were part of her own organism. They'd been there, alive, since much before her physical existence. They came from the heart of her father, who had fed them painfully during his nights of desperate solitude. Or maybe they had poured into her arteries through the cord that linked her to her mother ever since the beginning of the world. There was no doubt that those insects had not been born spontaneously inside her body. She knew that they came from back there, that all who bore her surname had to bear them, had to suffer them as she did when insomnia held unconquerable sway until dawn. It was those very insects who painted that bitter expression, that unconsolable sadness on the faces of her forebears. She had seen them looking out of their extinguished existence, out of their ancient portraits, victims of that same anguish. She still remembered the disquieting face of the great-grandmother who, from her aged canvas, begged for a minute of rest, a second of peace from those insects who there, in the channels of her blood, kept on martyrizing her, pitilessly beautifying her. No. Those insects didn't belong to her. They came, transmitted from generation to generation, sustaining with their tiny armor all the prestige of a select caste, a painfully select group. Those insects had been born in the womb of the first woman who had had a beautiful daughter. But it was necessary, urgent, to put a stop to that heritage. Someone must renounce the eternal transmission of that artificial beauty. It was no good for women of her breed to admire themselves as they came back from their mirrors if during the night those creatures did their slow, effective, ceaseless work with a constancy of centuries. It was no longer beauty, it was a sickness that had to be halted, that had to be cut off in some bold and radical way.

She still remembered the endless hours spent on that bed sown with hot needles. Those nights when she tried to speed time along so that with the arrival of daylight the beasts would stop hurting her. What good was beauty like that? Night after night, sunken in her desperation, she thought it would have been better for her to have been an ordinary woman, or a man. But that useless virtue was denied her, fed by insects of remote origin who were hastening the irrevocable arrival of her death. Maybe she would have been happy if she had had the same lack of grace, that same desolate ugliness, as her

Czechoslovakian friend who had a dog's name. She would have been better off ugly, so that she could sleep peacefully like any other Christian.

She cursed her ancestors. They were to blame for her insomnia. They had transmitted that exact, invariable beauty, as if after death mothers shook and renewed their heads in order to graft them onto the trunks of their daughters. It was as if the same head, a single head, had been continuously transmitted, with the same ears, the same nose, the identical mouth, with its weighty intelligence, to all the women who were to receive it irremediably like a painful inheritance of beauty. It was there, in the transmission of the head, that the eternal microbe that came through across generations had been accentuated, had taken on personality, strength, until it became an invincible being, an incurable illness, which upon reaching her after having passed through a complicated process of judgment, could no longer be borne and was bitter and painful ... just like a tumor or a cancer.

It was during those hours of wakefulness that she remembered the things disagreeable to her fine sensibility. She remembered the objects that made up the sentimental universe where, as in a chemical stew, those microbes of despair had been cultivated. During those nights, with her big round eyes open and frightened, she bore the weight of the darkness that fell upon her temples like molten lead. Everything was asleep around her. And from her corner, in order to bring on sleep, she tried to go back over her childhood memories.

But that remembering always ended with a terror of the unknown. Always, after wandering through the dark corners of the house, her thoughts would find themselves face to face with fear. Then the struggle would begin. The real struggle against three unmovable enemies. She would never – no, she would never – be able to shake the fear from her head. She would have to bear it as it clutched at her throat. And all just to live in that ancient mansion, to sleep alone in that corner, away from the rest of the world.

Her thoughts always went down along the damp, dark

passageways, shaking the dry cobweb-covered dust off the portraits. That disturbing and fearsome dust that fell from above, from the place where the bones of her ancestors were falling apart. Invariably she remembered the 'boy.' She imagined him there, sleepwalking under the grass in the courtyard beside the orange tree, a handful of wet earth in his mouth. She seemed to see him in his clay depths, digging upward with his nails, his teeth, fleeing the cold that bit into his back, looking for the exit into the courtyard through that small tunnel where they had placed him along with the snails. In winter she would hear him weeping with his tiny sob, mud-covered, drenched with rain. She imagined him intact. Just as they had left him five years before in that water-filled hole. She couldn't think of him as having decomposed. On the contrary, he was probably most handsome sailing along in that thick water as on a voyage with no escape. Or she saw him alive but frightened, afraid of feeling himself alone, buried in such a somber courtyard. She herself had been against their leaving him there, under the orange tree, so close to the house. She was afraid of him. She knew that on nights when insomnia hounded her he would sense it. He would come back along the wide corridors to ask her to stay with him, ask her to defend him against those other insects, who were eating at the roots of his violets. He would come back to have her let him sleep beside her as he did when he was alive. She was afraid of feeling him beside her again after he had leaped over the wall of death. She was afraid of stealing those hands that the 'boy' would always keep closed to warm up his little piece of ice. She wished, after she saw him turned into cement, like the statue of fear fallen in the mud, she wished that they would take him far away so that she wouldn't remember him at night. And yet they had left him there, where he was imperturbable now, wretched, feeding his blood with the mud of earthworms. And she had to resign herself to seeing him return from the depths of his shadows. Because always, invariably, when she lay awake she began to think about the 'boy,' who must be calling her from his piece of earth to help him flee that absurd death.

But now, in her new life, temporal and spaceless, she was more tranquil. She knew that outside her world there, everything would keep going on with the same rhythm as before; that her room would still be sunken in early-morning darkness, and her things, her furniture, her thirteen favorite books, all in place. And that on her unoccupied bed, the body aroma that filled the void of what had been a whole woman was only now beginning to evaporate. But how could 'that' happen? How could she, after being a beautiful woman, her blood peopled by insects, pursued by the fear of the total night, have the immense, wakeful nightmare now of entering a strange, unknown world where all dimensions had been eliminated? She remembered. That night – the night of her passage – had been colder than usual and she was alone in the house, martyrized by insomnia. No one disturbed the silence, and the smell that came from the garden was a smell of fear. Sweat broke out on her body as if the blood in her arteries were pouring out its cargo of insects. She wanted someone to pass by on the street, someone who would shout, would shatter that halted atmosphere. For something to move in nature, for the earth to move around the sun again. But it was useless. There was no waking up even for those imbecilic men who had fallen asleep under her ear, inside the pillow. She, too, was motionless. The walls gave off a strong smell of fresh paint, that thick, grand smell that you don't smell with your nose but with your stomach. And on the table the single clock, pounding on the silence with its mortal machinery. 'Time ... oh, time!' she sighed, remembering death. And there in the courtyard, under the orange tree, the 'boy' was still weeping with his tiny sob from the other world.

She took refuge in all her beliefs. Why didn't it dawn right then and there or why didn't she die once and for all? She had never thought that beauty would cost her so many sacrifices. At that moment – as usual – it still pained her on top of her fear. And underneath her fear those implacable insects were still martyrizing her. Death had squeezed her into life like a spider, biting her in a rage, ready to make her succumb. But the final moment was taking its time. Her hands, those hands that men squeezed like imbeciles with manifest animal nervousness, were motionless, paralyzed by fear, by that irrational terror that came from within, with no motive, just from knowing that she was abandoned in that ancient house. She tried to react and couldn't. Fear had absorbed her completely and remained there, fixed, tenacious, almost corporeal, as if it were some invisible person who had made up his mind not to leave her room. And the most upsetting part was that the fear had no justification at all, that it was a unique fear, without any reason, a fear just because.

The saliva had grown thick on her tongue. That hard gum that stuck to her palate and flowed because she was unable to contain it was bothersome between her teeth. It was a desire that was quite different from thirst. A superior desire that she was feeling for the first time in her life. For a moment she forgot about her beauty, her insomnia, and her irrational fear. She didn't recognize herself. For an instant she thought that the microbes had left her body. She felt that they'd come out stuck to her saliva. Yes, that was all very fine. It was fine that the insects no longer occupied her and that she could sleep now, but she had to find a way to dissolve that resin that dulled her tongue. If she could only get to the pantry and ... But what was she thinking about? She gave a start of surprise. She'd never felt 'that desire.' The urgency of the acidity had debilitated her, rendering useless the discipline that she had faithfully followed for so many years ever since the day they had buried the 'boy.' It was foolish, but she felt revulsion about eating an orange. She knew that the 'boy' had climbed up to the orange blossoms and that the fruit of next autumn would be swollen with his flesh, cooled by the coolness of his death. No. She couldn't eat them. She knew that under every orange tree in the world there was a boy buried, sweetening the fruit with the lime of his bones. Nevertheless, she had to eat an orange now. It was the only thing for that gum that was smothering her. It was foolishness to think that the 'boy' was inside a fruit. She would take advantage of that moment in which beauty had stopped paining her to get to the pantry. But wasn't that strange? It was the first time in her life that she'd felt a real urge to eat an orange. She became happy, happy. Oh, what pleasure! Eating an orange. She didn't know why, but she'd never had such a demanding desire. She would get up, happy to be a normal woman again, singing merrily until she got to the pantry, singing merrily like a new woman, newborn. She would even get to the courtyard and ...

Her memory was suddenly cut off. She remembered that she had tried to get up and that she was no longer in her bed, that her body had disappeared, that her thirteen favorite books were no longer there, that she was no longer she, now that she was bodiless, floating, drifting over an absolute nothingness, changed into an amorphous dot, tiny, lacking direction. She was unable to pinpoint what had happened. She was confused. She just had the sensation that someone had pushed her into space from the top of a precipice. She felt changed into an abstract, imaginary being. She felt changed into an incorporeal woman, something like her suddenly having entered that high and unknown world of pure spirits.

She was afraid again. But it was a different fear from what she had felt a moment before. It was no longer the fear of the 'boy''s weeping. It was a terror of the strange, of what was mysterious and unknown in her new world. And to think that all of it had happened so innocently, with so much naïveté on her part. What would she tell her mother when she told her what had happened when she got home? She began to think about how alarmed the neighbors would be when they opened the door to her bedroom and discovered that the bed was empty, that the locks had not been touched, that no one had been able to enter or to leave, and that, nonetheless, she wasn't there. She imagined her mother's desperate movements as she searched through the room, conjecturing, wondering 'what could have become of that girl?' The scene was clear to her. The neighbors would arrive and begin to weave comments together – some of them malicious – concerning her disappearance. Each would think according to his own and particular way of thinking. Each would try to offer the most logical explanation, the most acceptable, at least, while her mother would run along all the corridors in the big house, desperate, calling her by name.

And there she would be. She would contemplate the moment, detail by detail, from a corner, from the ceiling, from the chinks in the wall, from anywhere; from the best angle, shielded by her bodiless state, in her spacelessness. It bothered her, thinking about it. Now she realized her mistake. She wouldn't be able to give any explanation, clear anything up, console anybody. No living being could be informed of her transformation. Now – perhaps the only time that she needed them – she wouldn't have a mouth, arms, so that everybody could know that she was there, in her corner, separated from the three-dimensional world by an unbridgeable distance. In her new life she was isolated, completely prevented from grasping emotions. But at every moment something was vibrating in her, a shudder that ran through her, overwhelming her, making her aware of that other physical universe that moved outside her world. She couldn't hear, she couldn't see, but she *knew* about that sound and that sight. And there, in the heights of her superior world, she began to know that an environment of anguish surrounded her.

Just a moment before – according to our temporal world – she had made the passage, so that only now was she beginning to know the peculiarities, the characteristics, of her new world. Around her an absolute, radical darkness spun. How long would that darkness last? Would she have to get used to it for eternity? Her anguish grew from her concentration as she saw herself sunken in that thick impenetrable fog: could she be in limbo? She shuddered. She remembered everything she had heard about limbo. If she really was there, floating beside her were other pure spirits, those of children who had died without baptism, who had been dying for a thousand years. In the darkness she tried to find next to her those beings who must have been much purer, ever so much simpler, than she. Completely isolated from the physical world, condemned to a sleepwalking and eternal life. Maybe the 'boy' was there looking for an exit that would lead him to his body.

But no. Why should she be in limbo? Had she died, perhaps? No. It was simply a change in state, a normal passage from the physical world to an easier, uncomplicated world, where all dimensions had been eliminated.

Now she would not have to bear those subterranean insects. Her beauty had collapsed on her. Now, in that elemental situation, she could be happy. Although – oh! – not completely happy, because now her greatest desire, the desire to eat an orange, had become impossible. It was the only thing that might have caused her still to want to be in her first life. To be able to satisfy the urgency of the acidity that still persisted after the passage. She tried to orient herself so as to reach the pantry and feel, if nothing else, the cool and sour company of the oranges. It was then that she discovered a new characteristic of her world: she was everywhere in the house, in the courtyard, on the roof, even in the 'boy''s orange tree. She was in the whole physical world there beyond. And yet she was nowhere. She became upset again. She had lost control over herself. Now she was under a superior will, she was a useless being, absurd, good for nothing. Without knowing why, she began to feel sad. She almost began to feel nostalgia for her beauty: for the beauty that had foolishly ruined her.

But one supreme idea reanimated her. Hadn't she heard, perhaps, that pure spirits can penetrate any body at will? After all, what harm was there in trying? She attempted to remember what inhabitant of the house could be put to the proof. If she could fulfill her aim she would be satisfied: she could eat the orange. She remembered. At that time the servants were usually not there. Her mother still hadn't arrived. But the need to eat an orange, joined now to the curiosity of seeing herself incarnate in a body different from her own, obliged her to act at once. And yet there was no one there in whom she could incarnate herself. It was a desolating bit of reason: there was nobody in the house. She would have to live eternally isolated from the outside world, in her undimensional world, unable to eat the first orange. And all because of a foolish thing. It would have been better to go on bearing up for a few more years under that hostile beauty and not wipe herself out forever, making herself useless, like a conquered beast. But it was too late.

She was going to withdraw, disappointed, into a distant region of the universe, to a place where she could forget all her earthly desires. But something made her suddenly hold back. The promise of a better future had opened up in her unknown region. Yes, there was someone in the house in whom she could reincarnate herself: the cat! Then she hesitated. It was difficult to resign herself to live inside an animal. She would have soft, white fur, and a great energy for a leap would probably be concentrated in her muscles. And she would feel her eyes glow in the dark like two green coals. And she would have white, sharp teeth to smile at her mother from her feline heart with a broad and good animal smile. But no! It couldn't be. She imagined herself quickly inside the body of the cat, running through the corridors of the house once more, managing four uncomfortable legs, and that tail would move on its own, without rhythm, alien to her will. What would life look like through those green and luminous eyes? At night she would go to mew at the sky so that it would not pour its moonlit cement down on the face of the 'boy,' who would be on his back drinking in the dew. Maybe in her status as a cat she would also feel fear. And maybe, in the end, she would be unable to eat the orange with that carnivorous mouth. A coldness that came from right then and there, born of the very roots of her spirit, quivered in her memory. No. It was impossible to incarnate herself in the cat. She was afraid of one day feeling in her palate, in her throat, in all her quadruped organism, the irrevocable desire to eat a mouse. Probably when her spirit began to inhabit the cat's body she would no longer feel any desire to eat an orange but the repugnant and urgent desire to eat a mouse. She shuddered on thinking about it, caught between her teeth after the chase. She felt it struggling in its last attempts at escape, trying to free itself to get back to its hole again. No. Anything but that. It was preferable to stay there for eternity, in that distant and mysterious world of pure spirits.

But it was difficult to resign herself to live forgotten forever. Why did she have to feel the desire to eat a mouse? Who would rule in that synthesis of woman and cat? Would the primitive animal instinct of the body rule, or the pure will of the woman? The answer was crystal clear. There was no reason to be afraid. She would incarnate herself in the cat and would eat her desired orange. Besides, she would be a strange being, a cat with the intelligence of a beautiful woman. She would be the center of all attention . . . It was then, for the first time, that she understood that above all her virtues what was in command was the vanity of a metaphysical woman.

Like an insect on the alert which raises its antennae, she put her energy to work throughout the house in search of the cat. It must still be on top of the stove at that time, dreaming that it would wake up with a sprig of heliotrope between its teeth. But it wasn't there. She looked for it again, but she could no longer find the stove. The kitchen wasn't the same. The corners of the house were strange to her; they were no longer those dark corners full of cobwebs. The cat was nowhere to be found. She looked on the roof, in the trees, in the drains, under the bed, in the pantry. She found everything confused. Where she expected to find the portraits of her ancestors again, she found only a bottle of arsenic. From there on she found arsenic all through the house, but the cat had disappeared. The house was no longer the same as before. What had happened to her things? Why were her thirteen favorite books now covered with a thick coat of arsenic? She remembered the orange tree in the courtyard. She looked for it, and tried to find the 'boy' again in his pit of water. But the orange tree wasn't in its place and the 'boy' was nothing now but a handful of arsenic mixed with ashes underneath a heavy concrete platform. Now she really was going to sleep. Everything was different. And the house had a strong smell of arsenic that beat on her nostrils as if from the depths of a pharmacy.

Only then did she understand that three thousand years had passed since the day she had had a desire to eat the first orange.

Bitterness
for Three Sleepwalkers

Now we had her there, abandoned in a corner of the house. Someone told us, before we brought her things – her clothes which smelled of newly cut wood, her weightless shoes for the mud – that she would be unable to get used to that slow life, with no sweet tastes, no attraction except that harsh, wattled solitude, always pressing on her back. Someone told us – and a lot of time had passed before we remembered it – that she had also had a childhood. Maybe we didn't believe it then. But now, seeing her sitting in the corner with her frightened eyes and a finger placed on her lips, maybe we accepted the fact that she'd had a childhood once, that once she'd had a touch that was sensitive to the anticipatory coolness of the rain, and that she always carried an unexpected shadow in profile to her body.

All this – and much more – we believed that afternoon when we realized that above her fearsome subworld she was completely human. We found it out suddenly, as if a glass had been broken inside, when she began to give off anguished shouts; she began to call each one of us by name, speaking amidst tears until we sat down beside her; we began to sing and clap hands as if our shouting could put the scattered pieces of glass back together. Only then were we able to believe that at one time she had had a childhood. It was as if her shouts were like a revelation somehow; as if they had a lot of remembered tree and deep river about them. When she got up, she leaned over a little and, still without covering her face with her apron, still without blowing her nose, and still with tears, she told us:

'I'll never smile again.'

We went out into the courtyard, the three of us, not talking: maybe we thought we carried common thoughts. Maybe we thought it would be best not to turn on the lights in the house. She wanted to be alone – maybe – sitting in the dark corner, weaving the final braid which seemed to be the only thing that would survive her passage toward the beast.

Outside, in the courtyard, sunk in the deep vapor of the insects, we sat down to think about her. We'd done it so many times before. We might have said that we were doing what we'd been doing every day of our lives.

Yet it was different that night: she'd said that she would never smile again, and we, who knew her so well, were certain that the nightmare had become the truth. Sitting in a triangle, we imagined her there inside, abstract, incapacitated, unable even to hear the innumerable clocks that measured the marked and minute rhythm with which she was changing into dust. 'If we only had the courage at least to wish for her death,' we thought in a chorus. But we wanted her like that: ugly and glacial, like a mean contribution to our hidden defects.

We'd been adults since before, since a long time back. She, however, was the oldest in the house. That same night she had been able to be there, sitting with us, feeling the measured throbbing of the stars, surrounded by healthy sons. She would have been the respectable lady of the house if she had been the wife of a solid citizen or the concubine of a punctual man. But she became accustomed to living in only one dimension, like a straight line, perhaps because her vices or her virtues could not be seen in profile. We'd known that for many years now. We weren't even surprised one morning, after getting up, when we found her face down in the courtyard, biting the earth in a hard, ecstatic way. Then she smiled, looked at us again; she had fallen out of the second-story window onto the hard clay of the courtyard and had remained there, stiff and concrete, face down on the damp clay. But later we learned that the only thing she had kept intact was her fear of distances, a natural fright upon facing space. We lifted her up by the shoulders. She wasn't as hard as she had seemed to us at first. On the contrary, her organs were loose, detached from her will, like a lukewarm corpse that hadn't begun to stiffen.

Her eyes were open, her mouth was dirty with that earth that already must have had a taste of sepulchral sediment for her when we turned her face up to the sun, and it was as if we had placed her in front of a mirror. She looked at us all with a dull, sexless expression that gave us – holding her in my arms now – the measure of her absence. Someone told us she was dead; and afterward she remained smiling with that cold and quiet smile that she wore at night when she moved about the house awake. She said she didn't know how she got to the courtyard. She said that she'd felt quite warm, that she'd been listening to a cricket, penetrating, sharp, which seemed – so she said – about to knock down the wall of her room, and that she had set herself to remembering Sunday's prayers, with her cheek tight against the cement floor.

We knew, however, that she couldn't remember any prayer, for we discovered later that she'd lost the notion of time when she said she'd fallen asleep holding up the inside of the wall that the cricket was pushing on from outside and that she was fast asleep when someone, taking her by the shoulders, moved the wall aside and laid her down with her face to the sun.

That night we knew, sitting in the courtyard, that she would never smile again. Perhaps her inexpressive seriousness pained us in anticipation, her dark and willful living in a corner. It pained us deeply, as we were pained the day we saw her sit down in the corner where she was now; and we heard her say that she wasn't going to wander through the house any more. At first we couldn't believe her. We'd seen her for months on end going through the rooms at all hours, her head hard and her shoulders drooping, never stopping, never growing tired. At night we would hear her thick body noise moving between two darknesses, and we would lie awake in bed many times hearing her stealthy walking, following her all through the house with our ears. Once she told us that she had seen the cricket inside the mirror glass, sunken, submerged in the solid transparency, and that it had crossed through the glass surface to reach her. We really didn't know what she was trying to tell us, but we could all see that her clothes were wet, sticking to her body, as if she had just come out of a cistern. Without trying to explain the phenomenon, we decided to do away with the insects in the house: destroy the objects that obsessed her.

We had the walls cleaned; we ordered them to chop down the plants in the courtyard and it was as if we had cleansed the silence of the night of bits of trash. But we no longer heard her walking, nor did we hear her talking about crickets any more, until the day when, after the last meal, she remained looking at us, she sat down on the cement floor, still looking at us, and said: 'I'm going to stay here, sitting down,' and we shuddered, because we could see that she had begun to look like something already almost completely like death.

That had been a long time ago and we had even grown used to seeing her there, sitting, her braid always half wound, as if she had become dissolved in her solitude and, even though she was there to be seen, had lost her natural faculty of being present. That's why we now knew that she would never smile again; because she had said so in the same convinced and certain way in which she had told us once that she would never walk again. It was as if we were certain that she would tell us later: 'I'll never see again,' or maybe 'I'll never hear again,' and we knew that she was sufficiently human to go along willing the elimination of her vital functions and that spontaneously she would go about ending herself, sense by sense, until one day we would find her leaning against the wall, as if she had fallen asleep for the first time in her life. Perhaps there was still a lot of time left for that, but the three of us, sitting in the courtyard, would have liked to hear her sharp and sudden broken-glass weeping that night, at least to give us the illusion that a baby . . . a girl baby had been born in the house. In order to believe that she had been born renewed.

Dialogue with the Mirror

The man who had had the room before, after having slept the sleep of the just for hours on end, oblivious to the worries and unrest of the recent early morning, awoke when the day was well advanced and the sounds of the city completely invaded the air of the half-opened room. He must have thought – since no other state of mind occupied him – about the thick preoccupation of death, about his full, round fear, about the piece of earth – clay of himself – that his brother must have had under his tongue. But the joyful sun that clarified the garden drew his attention toward another life, which was more ordinary, more earthly, and perhaps less true than his fearsome interior existence. Toward his life as an ordinary man, a daily animal, which made him remember – without relying on his nervous system, his changeable liver – the irremediable impossibility of sleeping like a bourgeois. He thought – and there, surely, there was something of bourgeois mathematics in the tongue-twisting figures – of the financial riddles of the office.

Eight-twelve. I will certainly be late. He ran the tips of his fingers over his cheek. The harsh skin, sown with stumps, passed the feeling of the hard hairs through his digital antennae. Then, with the palm of his half-opened hand, he felt his distracted face carefully, with the serene tranquillity of a surgeon who knows the nucleus of the tumor, and from the bland surface toward the inside the hard substance of a truth rose up, one that on occasion had turned him white with anguish. There, under his fingertips – and after the fingertips, bone against bone – his irrevocable anatomical condition held an order of compositions buried, a tight universe of weaves, of lesser worlds, which bore him along, raising his fleshy armor toward a height less enduring than the natural and final position of his bones.

Yes. Against the pillow, his head sunken in the soft material, his body falling into the repose of his organs, life had a horizontal taste, a better accommodation to its own principles. He knew that with the minimum effort of closing his eyes, the long, fatiguing task awaiting him would begin to be resolved in a climate that was becoming uncomplicated, without compromises with either time or space: with no need, when he reached it, for the chemical adventure that made up his body to suffer the slightest impairment. On the contrary, like that, with his eyes closed, there was a total economy of vital resources, an absolute absence of organic wear. His body, sunk in the water of dreams, could move, live, evolve toward other forms of existence where his real world would have, as its intimate necessity, an identical – if not greater – density of motion with which the necessity of living would remain completely satisfied without any detriment to his physical integrity. Much easier – then – would be the chore of living with beings, things, acting, nevertheless, in exactly the same way as in the real world. The chores of shaving, taking the bus, solving equations at the office would be simple and uncomplicated in his dream and would produce in him the same inner satisfaction in the end.

Yes. It was better doing it in that artificial way, as he was already doing; looking in the lighted room for the direction of the mirror. As he would have kept on doing if at that instant a heavy machine, brutal and absurd, had not ruptured the lukewarm substance of his incipient dream. Returning now to the conventional world, the problem certainly took on greater characteristics of seriousness. Nonetheless, the curious theory that had just inspired softness in him had turned him toward a region of understanding, and from within his man-body he felt the displacement of the mouth to the side in an expression which must have been an involuntary smile. 'Having to shave when I have to be over the books in twenty minutes. Bath eight minutes, five if I hurry, breakfast seven. Unpleasant old sausages. Mabel's shop: provisions, hardware, drugs, liquors; it's like somebody's box; I've forgotten the name. (The bus breaks down on Tuesdays, seven minutes late.) Pendora. No: Peldora. That's not it. A half hour in all. There's no time. I forgot the name, a word with everything in it. Pedora. It begins with *P*.'

With his bathrobe on, in front of the wash basin now, a sleepy face, hair uncombed and no shave, he receives a bored look from the mirror. A quick shudder catches him with a cold thread as he discovers his own dead brother, newly arisen, in that image. The same tired face, the same look that was still not fully awake.

A new movement sent the mirror a quantity of light destined to bring out a pleasant expression, but the simultaneous return of that light brought back to him – going against his plans – a grotesque grimace. Water. The hot flow has opened up torrential, exuberant, and the wave of white, thick steam is interposed between him and the glass. In that way – taking advantage of the interruption with a quick movement – he manages to make an adjustment with his own time and with the time inside the quicksilver.

He rose above the leather strop, filling the mirror with pointed ears, cold metal; and the cloud – breaking up now – shows him the other face again, hazy with physical complications, mathematical laws with which geometry was attempting volume in a new way, a concrete formula for light. There, opposite him, was the face, with a pulse, with throbs of its own presence, transfigured into an expression which was simultaneously a smile and mocking seriousness, appearing in the damp glass which the condensation of vapor had left clean.

He smiled. (It smiled.) He showed – to himself – his tongue. (It showed – to the real one – its tongue.) The one in the mirror had a pasty, yellow tongue: 'Your stomach is upset,' he diagnosed (a wordless expression) with a grimace. He smiled again. (It smiled again.) But now he could see that there was something stupid, artificial, and false in the smile that was returned to him. He smoothed his hair (it smoothed its hair) with his right hand (left hand), returning the bashful smile at once (and disappearing). He was surprised at his own behavior, standing in front of the mirror and making faces like an idiot. Nevertheless, he thought that everybody behaved the same way in front of a mirror and his indignation was greater then with the certainty that since the world was idiotic, he was only rendering tribute to vulgarity. Eight-seventeen.

He knew that he would have to hurry if he didn't want to be fired from the agency. From that agency that for some time now had been changed into the starting point of his singular daily funeral cortege.

The shaving cream, in contact with the brush, had now raised a bluish whiteness that brought him back from his worries. It was the moment in which the suds came up through his body, through the network of arteries, and facilitated the functioning of his whole vital mechanism. . . . Thus, returning to normality, it seemed more comfortable to search his soaped-up brain for the word he wanted to compare Mabel's shop with. Peldora. Mabel's junk shop. Paldora. Provisions or drugs. Or everything at the same time: Pendora.

There were enough suds in the mug. But he kept on rubbing the brush, almost with passion. The childish spectacle of the bubbles gave him the clear joy of a big child as it crept up into his heart, heavy and hard, like cheap liquor. A new effort in search of the syllable would have been sufficient then for the word to burst forth, ripe and brutal; for it to come to the surface in that thick, murky water of his flighty memory. But that time, as on other occasions, the scattered, detached pieces of a single system would not adjust themselves exactly in order to gain organic totality, and he was ready to give up the word forever: Pendora!

And now it was time to desist in that useless search, because – they both raised their eyes, which met – his twin brother, with his frothy brush, had begun to cover his chin with blue-white coolness, letting his left hand move – he imitated him with the right – with smoothness and precision, until the delineated zone had been covered. He glanced away, and the geometry of the hands on the clock showed itself to him, intent on the solution of a new theorem of anguish: eight-eighteen. He was moving too slowly. So that with the firm aim of finishing quickly, he gripped the razor as the horn handle obeyed the mobility of his little finger.

Calculating that in three minutes the task would be done, he raised his right arm (left arm) to the level of his right ear (left ear), making the observation along the way that nothing should turn out to be as difficult as shaving oneself the way the image in the mirror was doing. From that he had derived a whole series of very complicated calculations with an aim to verifying the speed of the light which, *almost* simultaneously, was making the trip back and forth and reproducing that movement. But the aesthete in him, after a struggle approximately equal to the square root of the velocity he might have found, overcame the mathematician and the artist's thoughts went toward the movements of the blade that greenblue-whited with the various touches of the light. Rapidly – and the mathematician and the aesthete were at peace now – he brought the edge down along the right cheek (left cheek) to the meridian of the lip and observed with satisfaction that the left cheek on the image showed clean between its edges of lather.

He had still not shaken the blade clean when a smokiness loaded with the bitter smell of roasting meat began to arrive from the kitchen. He felt the quiver under his tongue and the torrent of easy, thin saliva that filled his mouth with the energetic taste of hot fat. Fried kidneys. There was finally a change in Mabel's damned store. Pendora. Not that either. The sound of the gland in the midst of the sauce broke in his ear with a memory of hammering rain, which was, in effect, the same from the recent early dawn. Therefore he mustn't forget his galoshes and his raincoat. Kidneys in gravy. No doubt about it.

Of all his senses none deserved as much mistrust as smell. But even beyond his five senses and even when that feast was nothing more than a bit of optimism on the part of his pituitary, the need to finish as soon as possible was at that moment the most urgent need of his five senses. With precision and deftness – the mathematician and the artist showed their teeth – he brought the razor backward (forward) and forward (backward) up to the corner of his mouth to the right (left), while with his left hand (right hand) he smoothed the skin, facilitating in that way the passage of the metal edge, from front (back) to back (front), and up (up) and down, finishing – both panting – the simultaneous work.

But precisely upon finishing, when he was giving the last touches to his left cheek with his right hand, he managed to see his own elbow against the mirror. He saw it, large, strange, unknown, and observed with surprise that above the elbow, other eyes equally large and equally unknown were searching wildly for the direction of the blade. Someone is trying to hang my brother. A powerful arm. Blood! The same thing always happens when I'm in a hurry.

On his face he sought the corresponding place; but his finger was clean and his touch showed no solution of continuity. He gave a start. There were no wounds on his skin, but there in the mirror the other one was bleeding slightly. And inside him the annoyance that last night's upset would be repeated became his truth again, a consciousness of unfolding. But there was the chin (round: identical faces). Those hairs on the mole needed the tip of the razor.

He thought he had observed a cloud of worry haze over the hasty expression of his image. Could it be possible, due to the great rapidity with which he was shaving – and the mathematician took complete charge of the situation – that the velocity of light was unable to cover the distance in order to record all the movements? Could he, in his haste, have got ahead of the image in the mirror and finished the job one motion ahead of it? Or could it have been possible – and the artist, after a brief struggle, managed to dislodge the mathematician – that the image had taken on its own life and had resolved – by living in an uncomplicated time – to finish more slowly than its external subject?

Visibly preoccupied, he turned the hot-water faucet on and felt the rise of the warm, thick steam, while the splashing of his face in the fresh water filled his ears with a guttural sound. On his skin, the pleasant harshness of the freshly laundered towel made him breathe in the deep satisfaction of a hygienic animal. Pandora! That's the word: Pandora.

He looked at the towel with surprise and closed his eyes, disconcerted, while there in the mirror, a face just like his contemplated him with large, stupid eyes and the face was crossed by a crimson thread.

He opened his eyes and smiled (it smiled). Nothing mattered to him any more. Mabel's store is a Pandora's box.

The hot smell of the kidneys in gravy honored his nostrils, with greater urgency now. And he felt satisfaction – positive satisfaction – that a large dog had begun to wag its tail inside his soul.

Eyes of a Blue Dog

Then she looked at me. I thought that she was looking at me for the first time. But then, when she turned around behind the lamp and I kept feeling her slippery and oily look in back of me, over my shoulder, I understood that it was I who was looking at her for the first time. I lit a cigarette. I took a drag on the harsh, strong smoke, before spinning in the chair, balancing on one of the rear legs. After that I saw her there, as if she'd been standing beside the lamp looking at me every night. For a few brief minutes that's all we did: look at each other. I looked from the chair, balancing on one of the rear legs. She stood, with a long and quiet hand on the lamp, looking at me. I saw her eyelids lighted up as on every night. It was then that I remembered the usual thing, when I said to her: 'Eyes of a blue dog.' Without taking her hand off the lamp she said to me: 'That. We'll never forget that.' She left the orbit, sighing: 'Eyes of a blue dog. I've written it everywhere.'

I saw her walk over to the dressing table. I watched her appear in the circular glass of the mirror looking at me now at the end of a back and forth of mathematical light. I watched her keep on looking at me with her great hot-coal eyes: looking at me while she opened the little box covered with pink mother of pearl. I saw her powder her nose. When she finished, she closed the box, stood up again, and walked over to the lamp once more, saying: 'I'm afraid that someone is dreaming about this room and revealing my secrets.' And over the flame she held the same long and tremulous hand that she had been warming before sitting down at the mirror. And she said: 'You don't feel the cold.' And I said to her: 'Sometimes.' And she said to me: 'You must feel it now.' And then I understood why I couldn't have been alone in the seat. It was the cold that had been giving me the certainty of my solitude. 'Now I feel it,' I said. 'And it's strange because the night is quiet. Maybe the sheet fell off.' She didn't answer. Again she began to move toward the mirror and I turned again in the chair, keeping my back to her. Without seeing her, I knew what she was doing. I knew that she was sitting in front of the mirror again, seeing my back, which had had time to reach the depths of the mirror and be caught by her look, which had also had just enough time to reach the depths and return – before the hand had time to start the second turn – until her lips were anointed now with crimson, from the first turn of her hand in front of the mirror. I saw, opposite me, the smooth wall, which was like another blind mirror in which I couldn't see her – sitting behind me – but could imagine her where she probably was as if a mirror had been hung in place of the wall. 'I see you,' I told her. And on the wall I saw what was as if she had raised her eyes and had seen me with my back turned toward her from the chair, in the depths of the mirror, my face turned toward the wall. Then I saw her lower her eyes again and remain with her eyes always on her brassiere, not talking. And I said to her again: 'I see you.' And she raised her eyes from her brassiere again. 'That's impossible,' she said. I asked her why. And she, with her eyes quiet and on her brassiere again: 'Because your face is turned toward the wall.' Then I spun the chair around. I had the cigarette clenched in my mouth. When I stayed facing the mirror she was back by the lamp. Now she had her hands open over the flame, like the two wings of a hen, toasting herself, and with her face shaded by her own fingers. 'I think I'm going to catch cold,' she said. 'This must be a city of ice.' She turned her face to profile and her skin, from copper to red, suddenly became sad. 'Do something about it,' she said. And she began to get undressed, item by item, starting at the top with the brassiere. I told her: 'I'm going to turn back to the wall.' She said: 'No. In any case, you'll see me the way you did when your back was turned.' And no sooner had she said it than she was almost completely undressed, with the flame licking her long copper skin. 'I've always wanted to see you like that, with the skin of your belly full of deep pits, as if you'd been beaten.' And before I realized that my words had become clumsy at the sight of her nakedness, she became motionless, warming herself on the globe of the lamp, and she said: 'Sometimes I think I'm made of metal.' She was silent for an instant. The position of her hands over the flame varied slightly. I said: 'Sometimes, in other dreams, I've thought you were only a little bronze statue in the corner of some museum. Maybe that's why you're cold.' And she said: 'Sometimes, when I sleep on my heart, I can feel my body growing hollow and my skin is like plate. Then, when the blood beats inside me, it's as if someone were calling by knocking on my stomach and I can feel my own copper sound in the bed. It's like – what do you call it – laminated metal.' She drew closer to the lamp. 'I would have liked to hear you,' I said. And she said: 'If we find each other sometime, put your ear to my ribs when I sleep on the left side and you'll hear me echoing. I've always wanted you to do it sometime.' I heard her breathe heavily as she talked. And she said that for years she'd done nothing different. Her life had been dedicated to finding me in reality, through that identifying phrase: 'Eyes of a blue dog.' And she went along the street saying it aloud, as a way of telling the only person who could have understood her:

'I'm the one who comes into your dreams every night and tells you: "Eyes of a blue dog."' And she said that she went into restaurants and before ordering said to the waiters: 'Eyes of a blue dog.' But the waiters bowed reverently, without remembering ever having said that in their dreams. Then she would write on the napkins and scratch on the varnish of the tables with a knife: 'Eyes of a blue dog.' And on the steamed-up windows of hotels, stations, all public buildings, she would write with her forefinger: 'Eyes of a blue dog.' She said that once she went into a drugstore and noticed the same smell that she had smelled in her room one night after having dreamed about me. 'He must be near,' she thought, seeing the clean, new tiles of the drugstore. Then she went over to the clerk and said to him: 'I always dream about a man who says to me: "Eyes of a blue dog."' And she said the clerk had looked at her eyes and told her: 'As a matter of fact, miss, you do have eyes like that.' And she said to him: 'I have to find the man who told me those very words in my dreams.' And the clerk started to laugh and moved to the other end of the counter. She kept on seeing the clean tile and smelling the odor. And she opened her purse and on the tiles, with her crimson lipstick, she wrote in red letters: 'Eyes of a blue dog.' The clerk came back from where he had been. He told her: 'Madam, you have dirtied the tiles.' He gave her a damp cloth, saying: 'Clean it up.' And she said, still by the lamp, that she had spent the whole afternoon on all fours, washing the tiles and saying: 'Eyes of a blue dog,' until people gathered at the door and said she was crazy.

Now, when she finished speaking, I remained in the corner, sitting, rocking in the chair. 'Every day I try to remember the phrase with which I am to find you,' I said. 'Now I don't think I'll forget it tomorrow. Still, I've always said the same thing and when I wake up I've always forgotten what the words I can find you with are.' And she said: 'You invented them yourself on the first day.' And I said to her: 'I invented them because I saw your eyes of ash. But I never remember the next morning.' And she, with clenched fists, beside the lamp, breathed deeply: 'If you could at least remember now what city I've been writing it in.'

Her tightened teeth gleamed over the flame. 'I'd like to touch you now,' I said. She raised the face that had been looking at the light; she raised her look, burning, roasting, too, just like her, like her hands, and I felt that she saw me, in the corner where I was sitting, rocking in the chair. 'You'd never told me that,' she said. 'I tell you now and it's the truth,' I said. From the other side of the lamp she asked for a cigarette. The butt had disappeared between my fingers. I'd forgotten that I was smoking. She said: 'I don't know why I can't remember where I wrote it.' And I said to her: 'For the same reason that tomorrow I won't be able to remember the words.' And she said sadly: 'No. It's just that sometimes I think that I've dreamed that too.' I stood up and walked toward the lamp. She was a little beyond, and I kept on walking with the cigarettes and matches in my hand, which would not go beyond the lamp. I held the cigarette out to her. She squeezed it between her lips and leaned over to reach the flame before I had time to light the match. 'In some city in the world, on all the walls, those words have to appear in writing: "Eyes of a blue dog,"' I said. 'If I remembered them tomorrow I could find you.' She raised her head again and now the lighted coal was between her lips. 'Eyes of a blue dog,' she sighed, remembered, with the cigarette drooping over her chin and one eye half closed. Then she sucked in the smoke with the cigarette between her fingers and exclaimed: 'This is something else now. I'm warming up.' And she said it with her voice a little lukewarm and fleeting, as if she hadn't really said it, but as if she had written it on a piece of paper and had brought the paper close to the flame while I read: 'I'm warming,' and she had continued with the paper between her thumb and forefinger, turning it around as it was being consumed and I had just read ' ... up,' before the paper was completely consumed and dropped all wrinkled to the floor, diminished, converted into light ash dust. 'That's better,' I said. 'Sometimes it frightens me to see you that way. Trembling beside a lamp.'

We had been seeing each other for several years. Sometimes, when we were already together, somebody would drop a spoon outside and we would wake up. Little by little we'd been coming to understand that our friendship was subordinated to things, to the simplest of happenings. Our meetings always ended that way, with the fall of a spoon early in the morning.

Now, next to the lamp, she was looking at me. I remembered that she had also looked at me in that way in the past, from that remote dream where I made the chair spin on its back legs and remained facing a strange woman with ashen eyes. It was in that dream that I asked her for the first time: 'Who are you?' And she said to me: 'I don't remember.' I said to her: 'But I think we've seen each other before.' And she said, indifferently: 'I think I dreamed about you once, about this same room.' And I told her: 'That's it. I'm beginning to remember now.' And she said: 'How strange. It's certain that we've met in other dreams.'

She took two drags on the cigarette. I was still standing, facing the lamp, when suddenly I kept looking at her. I looked her up and down and she was still copper; no longer hard and cold metal, but yellow, soft, malleable copper. 'I'd like to touch you,' I said again. And she said: 'You'll ruin everything.' I said: 'It doesn't matter now. All we have to do is turn the pillow over in order to meet again.' And I held my hand out over the lamp. She didn't move. 'You'll ruin everything,' she said again before I could touch her. 'Maybe, if you come around behind the lamp, we'd wake up frightened in who knows what part of the world.' But I insisted: 'It doesn't matter.' And she said: 'If we turned over the pillow, we'd meet again. But when you wake up you'll have forgotten.' I began to move toward the corner. She stayed behind, warming her hands over the flame. And I still wasn't beside the chair when I heard her say behind me: 'When I wake up at midnight, I keep turning in bed, with the fringe of the pillow burning my knee, and repeating until dawn: "Eyes of a blue dog."'

Then I remained with my face toward the wall. 'It's already dawning,' I said without looking at her. 'When it struck two I was awake and that was a long time back.' I went to the door. When I had the knob in my hand, I heard her voice again, the same, invariable. 'Don't open that door,' she said. 'The hallway is full of difficult dreams.' And I asked her: 'How do you know?' And she told me: 'Because I was there a moment ago and I had to come back when I discovered I was sleeping on my heart.' I had the door half opened. I moved it a little and a cold, thin breeze brought me the fresh smell of vegetable earth, damp fields. She spoke again. I gave the turn, still moving the door, mounted on silent hinges, and I told her: 'I don't think there's any hallway outside here. I'm getting the smell of country.' And she, a little distant, told me: 'I know that better than you. What's happening is that there's a woman outside dreaming about the country.' She crossed her arms over the flame. She continued speaking: 'It's that woman who always wanted to have a house in the country and was never able to leave the city.' I remembered having seen the woman in some previous dream, but I knew, with the door ajar now, that within half an hour I would have to go down for breakfast. And I said: 'In any case, I have to leave here in order to wake up.'

Outside the wind fluttered for an instant, then remained quiet, and the breathing of someone sleeping who had just turned over in bed could be heard. The wind from the fields had ceased. There were no more smells. 'Tomorrow I'll recognize you from that,' I said. 'I'll recognize you when on the street I see a woman writing "Eyes of a blue dog" on the walls.' And she, with a sad smile – which was already a smile of surrender to the impossible, the unreachable – said: 'Yet you won't remember anything during the day.' And she put her hands back over the lamp, her features darkened by a bitter cloud. 'You're the only man who doesn't remember anything of what he's dreamed after he wakes up.' ▪

The Woman Who Came
at Six O'Clock

The swinging door opened. At that hour there was nobody in José's restaurant. It had just struck six and the man knew that the regular customers wouldn't begin to arrive until six-thirty. His clientele was so conservative and regular that the clock hadn't finished striking six when a woman entered, as on every day at that hour, and sat down on the stool without saying anything. She had an unlighted cigarette tight between her lips.

'Hello, queen,' José said when he saw her sit down. Then he went to the other end of the counter, wiping the streaked surface with a dry rag. Whenever anyone came into the restaurant José did the same thing. Even with the woman, with whom he'd almost come to acquire a degree of intimacy, the fat and ruddy restaurant owner put on his daily comedy of a hard-working man. He spoke from the other end of the counter.

'What do you want today?' he said.

'First of all I want to teach you how to be a gentleman,' the woman said. She was sitting at the end of the stools, her elbows on the counter, the extinguished cigarette between her lips. When she spoke, she tightened her mouth so that José would notice the unlighted cigarette.

'I didn't notice,' José said.

'You still haven't learned to notice anything,' said the woman.

The man left the cloth on the counter, walked to the dark cupboards which smelled of tar and dusty wood, and came back immediately with the matches. The woman leaned over to get the light that was burning in the man's rustic, hairy hands. José saw the woman's lush hair, all greased with cheap, thick Vaseline. He saw her uncovered shoulder above the flowered brassiere. He saw the beginning of her twilight breast when the woman raised her head, the lighted butt between her lips now.

'You're beautiful tonight, queen,' José said.

'Stop your nonsense,' the woman said. 'Don't think that's going to help me pay you.'

'That's not what I meant, queen,' José said. 'I'll bet your lunch didn't agree with you today.'

The woman sucked in the first drag of thick smoke, crossed her arms, her elbows still on the counter, and remained looking at the street through the wide restaurant window. She had a melancholy expression. A bored and vulgar melancholy.

'I'll fix you a good steak,' José said.

'I still haven't got any money,' the woman said.

'You haven't had any money for three months and I always fix you something good,' José said.

'Today's different,' said the woman somberly, still looking out at the street.

'Every day's the same,' José said. 'Every day the clock says six, then you come in and say you're hungry as a dog and then I fix you something good. The only difference is this: today you didn't say you were as hungry as a dog but that today is different.'

'And it's true,' the woman said. She turned to look at the man, who was at the other end of the counter checking the refrigerator. She examined him for two or three seconds. Then she looked at the clock over the cupboard. It was three minutes after six. 'It's true, José. Today is different,' she said. She let the smoke out and kept on talking with crisp, impassioned words. 'I didn't come at six today, that's why it's different, José.'

The man looked at the clock.

'I'll cut off my arm if that clock is one minute slow,' he said.

'That's not it, José. I didn't come at six o'clock today,' the woman said.

'It just struck six, queen,' José said. 'When you came in it was just finishing.'

'I've got a quarter of an hour that says I've been here,' the woman said.

José went over to where she was. He put his great puffy face up to the woman while he tugged on one of his eyelids with his index finger.

'Blow on me here,' he said.

The woman threw her head back. She was serious, annoyed, softened, beautified by a cloud of sadness and fatigue.

'Stop your foolishness, José. You know I haven't had a drink for six months.'

'Tell it to somebody else,' he said, 'not to me. I'll bet you've had a pint or two at least.'

'I had a couple of drinks with a friend,' she said.

'Oh, now I understand,' José said.

'There's nothing to understand,' the woman said. 'I've been here for a quarter of an hour.'

The man shrugged his shoulders.

'Well, if that's the way you want it, you've got a quarter of an hour that says you've been here,' he said. 'After all, what difference does it make, ten minutes this way, ten minutes that way?'

'It makes a difference, José,' the woman said. And she stretched her arms over the glass counter with an air of careless abandon. She said: 'And it isn't that I wanted it that way; it's just that I've been here for a quarter of an hour.' She looked at the clock again and corrected herself: 'What am I saying – it's been twenty minutes.'

'O.K., queen,' the man said. 'I'd give you a whole day and the night that goes with it just to see you happy.'

During all this time José had been moving about behind the counter, changing things, taking something from one place and putting it in another. He was playing his role.

'I want to see you happy,' he repeated. He stopped suddenly, turning to where the woman was. 'Do you know that I love you very much?'

The woman looked at him coldly.

'Ye-e-es . . . ? What a discovery, José. Do you think I'd go with you even for a million pesos?'

'I didn't mean that, queen,' José said. 'I repeat, I bet your lunch didn't agree with you.'

'That's not why I said it,' the woman said. And her voice became less indolent. 'No woman could stand a weight like yours, even for a million pesos.'

José blushed. He turned his back to the woman and began to dust the bottles on the shelves. He spoke without turning his head.

'You're unbearable today, queen. I think the best thing is for you to eat your steak and go home to bed.'

'I'm not hungry,' the woman said. She stayed looking out at the street again, watching the passers-by of the dusking city. For an instant there was a murky silence in the restaurant. A peacefulness broken only by José's fiddling about in the cupboard. Suddenly the woman stopped looking out into the street and spoke with a tender, soft, different voice.

'Do you really love me, Pepillo?'

'I do,' José said dryly, not looking at her.

'In spite of what I've said to you?' the woman asked.

'What did you say to me?' José asked, still without any inflection in his voice, still without looking at her.

'That business about a million pesos,' the woman said.

'I'd already forgotten,' José said.

'So do you love me?' the woman asked.

'Yes,' said José.

There was a pause. José kept moving about, his face turned towards the cabinets, still not looking at the woman. She blew out another mouthful of smoke, rested her bust on the counter, and then, cautiously roguishly, biting her tongue before saying it, as if speaking on tiptoe:

'Even if you didn't go to bed with me?' she asked.

And only then did José turn to look at her.

'I love you so much that I wouldn't go to bed with you,' he said. Then he walked over to where she was. He stood looking into her face, his powerful arms leaning on the counter in front of her, looking into her eyes. He said: 'I love you so much that every night I'd kill the man who goes with you.'

At the first instant the woman seemed perplexed. Then she looked at the man attentively, with a wavering expression of compassion and mockery. Then she had a moment of brief disconcerted silence. And then she laughed noisily.

'You're jealous, José. That's wild, you're jealous!'

José blushed again with frank, almost shameful timidity, as might have happened to a child who'd revealed all his secrets all of a sudden. He said:

'This afternoon you don't seem to understand anything, queen.' And he wiped himself with the rag. He said:

'This bad life is brutalizing you.'

But now the woman had changed her expression.

'So, then,' she said. And she looked into his eyes again, with a strange glow in her look, confused and challenging at the same time.

'So you're not jealous.'

'In a way I am,' José said. 'But it's not the way you think.'

He loosened his collar and continued wiping himself, drying his throat with the cloth.

'So?' the woman asked.

'The fact is I love you so much that I don't like your doing it,' José said.

'What?' the woman asked.

'This business of going with a different man every day,' José said.

'Would you really kill him to stop him from going with me?' the woman asked.

'Not to stop him from going with you, no,' José said. 'I'd kill him because he *went* with you.'

'It's the same thing,' the woman said.

The conversation had reached an exciting density. The woman was speaking in a soft, low, fascinated voice. Her face was almost stuck up against the man's healthy, peaceful face, as he stood motionless, as if bewitched by the vapor of the words.

'That's true,' José said.

'So,' the woman said, and reached out her hand to stroke the man's rough arm. With the other she tossed away her butt. 'So you're capable of killing a man?'

'For what I told you, yes,' José said. And his voice took on an almost dramatic stress.

The woman broke into convulsive laughter, with an obvious mocking intent.

'How awful, José. How awful,' she said, still laughing. 'José killing a man. Who would have known that behind the fat and sanctimonious man who never makes me pay, who cooks me a steak every day and has fun talking to me until I find a man, there lurks a murderer. How awful, José! You scare me!'

José was confused. Maybe he felt a little indignation. Maybe, when the woman started laughing, he felt defrauded.

'You're drunk, silly,' he said. 'Go get some sleep. You don't even feel like eating anything.'

But the woman had stopped laughing now and was serious again, pensive, leaning on the counter. She watched the man go away. She saw him open the refrigerator and close it again without taking anything out. Then she saw him move to the other end of the counter. She watched him polish the shining glass, the same as in the beginning. Then the woman spoke again with the tender and soft tone of when she said: 'Do you really love me, Pepillo?'

'José,' she said.

The man didn't look at her.

'José!'

'Go home and sleep,' José said. 'And take a bath before you go to bed so you can sleep it off.'

'Seriously, José,' the woman said. 'I'm not drunk.'

'Then you've turned stupid,' José said.

'Come here, I've got to talk to you,' the woman said.

The man came over stumbling, halfway between pleasure and mistrust.

'Come closer!'

He stood in front of the woman again. She leaned forward, grabbed him by the hair, but with a gesture of obvious tenderness.

'Tell me again what you said at the start,' she said.

'What do you mean?' José asked. He was trying to look at her with his head turned away, held by the hair.

'That you'd kill a man who went to bed with me,' the woman said.

'I'd kill a man who went to bed with you, queen. That's right,' José said.

The woman let him go.

'In that case you'd defend me if I killed him, right?' she asked affirmatively, pushing José's enormous pig head with a movement of brutal coquettishness. The man didn't answer anything. He smiled.

'Answer me, José,' the woman said. 'Would you defend me if I killed him?'

'That depends,' José said. 'You know it's not as easy as you say.'

'The police wouldn't believe anyone more than you,' the woman said.

José smiled, honored, satisfied. The woman leaned over toward him again, over the counter.

'It's true, José. I'm willing to bet that you've never told a lie in your life,' she said.

'You won't get anywhere this way,' José said.

'Just the same,' the woman said. 'The police know you and they'll believe anything without asking you twice.'

José began pounding on the counter opposite her, not knowing what to say. The woman looked out at the street again. Then she looked at the clock and modified the tone of her voice, as if she were interested in finishing the conversation before the first customers arrived.

'Would you tell a lie for me, José?' she asked. 'Seriously.'

And then José looked at her again, sharply, deeply, as if a tremendous idea had come pounding up in his head. An idea that had entered through one ear, spun about for a moment, vague, confused, and gone out through the other, leaving behind only a warm vestige of terror.

'What have you got yourself into, queen?' José asked. He leaned forward, his arms folded over the counter again. The woman caught the strong and ammonia-smelling vapor of his breathing, which had become difficult because of the pressure that the counter was exercising on the man's stomach.

'This is really serious, queen. What have you got yourself into?' he asked.

The woman made her head spin in the opposite direction.

'Nothing,' she said. 'I was just talking to amuse myself.'

Then she looked at him again.

'Do you know you may not have to kill anybody?'

'I never thought about killing anybody,' José said, distressed.

'No, man,' the woman said. 'I mean nobody goes to bed with me.'

'Oh!' José said. 'Now you're talking straight out. I always thought you had no need to prowl around. I'll make a bet that if you drop all this I'll give you the biggest steak I've got every day, free.'

'Thank you, José,' the woman said. 'But that's not why. It's because I *can't* go to bed with anyone any more.'

'You're getting things all confused again,' José said. He was becoming impatient.

'I'm not getting anything confused,' the woman said. She stretched out on the seat and José saw her flat, sad breasts underneath her brassiere.

'Tomorrow I'm going away and I promise you I won't come back and bother you ever again. I promise you I'll never go to bed with anyone.'

'Where'd you pick up that fever?' José asked.

'I decided just a minute ago,' the woman said. 'Just a minute ago I realized it's a dirty business.'

José grabbed the cloth again and started to clean the glass in front of her. He spoke without looking at her.

He said:

'Of course, the way you do it it's a dirty business. You should have known that a long time ago.'

'I was getting to know it a long time ago,' the woman said, 'but I was only convinced of it just a little while ago. Men disgust me.'

José smiled. He raised his head to look at her, still smiling, but he saw her concentrated, perplexed, talking with her shoulders raised, twirling on the stool with a taciturn expression, her face gilded by premature autumnal grain.

'Don't you think they ought to lay off a woman who kills a man because after she's been with him she feels disgust with him and everyone who's been with her?'

'There's no reason to go that far,' José said, moved, a thread of pity in his voice.

'What if the woman tells the man he disgusts her while she watches him get dressed because she remembers that she's been rolling around with him all afternoon and feels that neither soap nor sponge can get his smell off her?'

'That all goes away, queen,' José said, a little indifferent now, polishing the counter. 'There's no reason to kill him. Just let him go.'

But the woman kept on talking, and her voice was a uniform, flowing, passionate current.

'But what if the woman tells him he disgusts her and the man stops getting dressed and runs over to her again, kisses her again, does . . .?'

'No decent man would ever do that,' José says.

'What if he does?' the woman asks, with exasperating anxiety. 'What if the man isn't decent and does it and then the woman feels that he disgusts her so much that she could die, and she knows that the only way to end it all is to stick a knife in under him?'

'That's terrible,' José said. 'Luckily there's no man who would do what you say.'

'Well,' the woman said, completely exasperated now. 'What if he did? Suppose he did.'

'In any case it's not that bad,' José said. He kept on cleaning the counter without changing position, less intent on the conversation now.

The woman pounded the counter with her knuckles. She became affirmative, emphatic.

'You're a savage, José,' she said. 'You don't understand anything.' She grabbed him firmly by the sleeve. 'Come on, tell me that the woman should kill him.'

'O.K.,' José said with a conciliatory bias. 'It's all probably just the way you say it is.'

'Isn't that self-defense?' the woman asked, grabbing him by the sleeve.

Then José gave her a lukewarm and pleasant look.

'Almost, almost,' he said. And he winked at her, with an expression that was at the same time a cordial comprehension and a fearful compromise of complicity. But the woman was serious. She let go of him.

'Would you tell a lie to defend a woman who does that?' she asked.

'That depends,' said José.

'Depends on what?' the woman asked.

'Depends on the woman,' said José.

'Suppose it's a woman you love a lot,' the woman said. 'Not to be with her, but like you say, you love her a lot.'

'O.K., anything you say, queen,' José said, relaxed, bored.

He'd gone off again. He'd looked at the clock. He'd seen that it was going on half-past six. He'd thought that in a few minutes the restaurant would be filling up with people and maybe that was why he began to polish the glass with greater effort, looking at the street through the window. The woman stayed on her stool, silent, concentrating, watching the man's movements with an air of declining sadness. Watching him as a lamp about to go out might have looked at a man. Suddenly, without reacting, she spoke again with the unctuous voice of servitude.

'José!'

The man looked at her with a thick, sad tenderness, like a maternal ox. He didn't look at her to hear her, just to look at her, to know that she was there, waiting for a look that had no reason to be one of protection or solidarity. Just the look of a plaything.

'I told you I was leaving tomorrow and you didn't say anything,' the woman said.

'Yes,' José said. 'You didn't tell me where.'

'Out there,' the woman said. 'Where there aren't any men who want to sleep with somebody.'

José smiled again.

'Are you really going away?' he asked, as if becoming aware of life, quickly changing the expression on his face.

'That depends on you,' the woman said. 'If you know enough to say what time I got here, I'll go away tomorrow and I'll never get mixed up in this again. Would you like that?'

José gave an affirmative nod, smiling and concrete. The woman leaned over to where he was.

'If I come back here someday I'll get jealous when I find another woman talking to you, at this time and on this same stool.'

'If you come back here you'll have to bring me something,' José said.

'I promise you that I'll look everywhere for the tame bear, bring him to you,' the woman said.

José smiled and waved the cloth through the air that separated him from the woman, as if he were cleaning an invisible pane of glass. The woman smiled too, with an expression of cordiality and coquetry now. Then the man went away, polishing the glass to the other end of the counter.

'What, then?' José said without looking at her.

'Will you really tell anyone who asks you that I got here at a quarter to six?' the woman said.

'What for?' José said, still without looking at her now, as if he had barely heard her.

'That doesn't matter,' the woman said. 'The thing is that you do it.'

José then saw the first customer come in through the swinging door and walk over to a corner table. He looked at the clock. It was six-thirty on the dot.

'O.K., queen,' he said distractedly. 'Anything you say. I always do whatever you want.'

'Well,' the woman said. 'Start cooking my steak, then.'

The man went to the refrigerator, took out a plate with a piece of meat on it, and left it on the table. Then he lighted the stove.

'I'm going to cook you a good farewell steak, queen,' he said.

'Thank you, Pepillo,' the woman said.

She remained thoughtful as if suddenly she had become sunken in a strange subworld peopled with muddy, unknown forms. Across the counter she couldn't hear the noise that the raw meat made when it fell into the burning grease. Afterward she didn't hear the dry and bubbling crackle as José turned the flank over in the frying pan and the succulent smell of the marinated meat by measured moments saturated the air of the restaurant. She remained like that, concentrated, reconcentrated, until she raised her head again, blinking as if she were coming back out of a momentary death. Then she saw the man beside the stove, lighted up by the happy, rising fire.

'Pepillo.'

'What!'

'What are you thinking about?' the woman asked.

'I was wondering whether you could find the little windup bear someplace,' José said.

'Of course I can,' the woman said. 'But what I want is for you to give me everything I asked for as a going-away present.'

José looked at her from the stove.

'How often have I got to tell you?' he said. 'Do you want something besides the best steak I've got?'

'Yes,' the woman said.

'What is it?' José asked.

'I want another quarter of an hour.'

José drew back and looked at the clock. Then he looked at the customer, who was still silent, waiting in the corner, and finally at the meat roasting in the pan. Only then did he speak.

'I really don't understand, queen,' he said.

'Don't be foolish, José,' the woman said. 'Just remember that I've been here since five-thirty.'

Nabo

THE BLACK MAN WHO MADE
THE ANGELS WAIT . . .

Nabo was lying face down in the hay. He felt the smell of a urinated stable rubbing on his body. On his brown and shiny skin he felt the warm embers of the last horses, but he couldn't feel the skin. Nabo couldn't feel anything. It was as if he'd gone to sleep with the last blow of the horseshoe on his forehead and now that was the only feeling he had. He opened his eyes. He closed them again and then was quiet, stretched out, stiff, as he had been all afternoon, feeling himself growing without time, until someone behind him said: 'Come on, Nabo. You've slept enough already.' He turned over and didn't see the horses; the door was closed. Nabo must have imagined that the animals were somewhere in the darkness in spite of the fact that he couldn't hear their impatient stamping. He imagined that the person speaking to him was doing it from outside the stable, because the door was closed from inside and barred. Once more the voice behind him said: 'That's right, Nabo, you've slept enough already. You've been asleep for almost three days.' Only then did Nabo open his eyes completely and remember: 'I'm here because a horse kicked me.'

He didn't know what hour he was living. The days had been left behind. It was as if someone had passed a damp sponge over those remote Saturday nights when he used to go to the town square. He forgot about the white shirt. He forgot that he had a green hat made of green straw and dark pants. He forgot that he didn't have any shoes. Nabo would go to the square on Saturday nights and sit in a corner, silent, not to listen to the music but to watch the black man. Every Saturday he saw him. The Negro wore horn-rimmed glasses, tied to his ears, and he played the saxophone at one of the rear music stands. Nabo saw the black man but the black man didn't see Nabo. At least, if someone had known that Nabo went to the square on Saturday nights to see the Negro and had asked him (not now, because he couldn't remember) whether the black man had ever seen him, Nabo would have said no. It was the only thing he did after currying the horses: watch the black man.

One Saturday the Negro wasn't at his place in the band. Nabo probably thought at first that he wasn't going to play anymore in the public concerts in spite of the fact that the music stand was there. Although for that reason precisely, the fact that the music stand was there, he thought later that the Negro would be back the following Saturday. But on the following Saturday he wasn't back and the music stand wasn't in its place.

Nabo rolled onto one side and he saw the man talking to him. At first he didn't recognize him, blotted out by the darkness of the stable. The man was sitting on a jutting beam, talking and patting his knees. 'A horse kicked me,' Nabo said again, trying to recognize the man. 'That's right,' the man said. 'The horses aren't here now and we're waiting for you in the choir.' Nabo shook his head. He still hadn't begun to think, but now he thought he'd seen the man somewhere. Nabo didn't understand, but he didn't find it strange either that someone should say that to him, because every day while he curried the horses he invented songs to distract them. Then he would sing the same songs he sang to the horses in the living room to distract the mute girl. When he was singing if someone had told him that he was taking him to a choir, it wouldn't have surprised him. Now he was surprised even less because he didn't understand. He was fatigued, dulled, brutish. 'I want to know where the horses are,' he said. And the man said: 'I already told you, the horses aren't here. All we're interested in is to get a voice like yours.' And perhaps, face down in the hay, Nabo heard, but he couldn't distinguish the pain that the horseshoe had left on his forehead from his other disordered sensations. He turned his head on the hay and fell asleep.

Nabo still went to the square for two or three weeks in spite of the fact that the Negro was no longer in the band. Perhaps someone would have answered him if Nabo had asked what had happened to the black man. But he didn't ask and kept on going to the concerts until another man with another saxophone came to take the Negro's spot. Then Nabo was convinced that the Negro wouldn't be back and he decided not to return to the square. When he awoke he thought he had slept a very short time. The smell of damp hay still burned in his nose. The darkness was still there before his eyes, surrounding him. And the man was still in the corner. The obscure and peaceful voice of the man who patted his knees, saying: 'We're waiting for you, Nabo. You've been asleep for almost two years and you refuse to get up.' Then Nabo closed his eyes again. He opened them again, kept looking at the corner, and saw the man once more, disoriented, perplexed. Only then did he recognize him.

If the people in the house had known what Nabo was doing on the square on Saturday nights, they probably would have thought that when he stopped going he did so because now he had music at home. That was when we brought the gramophone to amuse the girl. Since it needed someone to wind it up all day, it seemed most natural that that person should be Nabo. He could do it when he didn't have to take care of the horses. The girl remained seated, listening to records. Sometimes, when the music was playing, the girl would get out of her chair, still looking at the wall, drooling, and would drag herself to the veranda. Nabo would lift the needle and start to sing. In the beginning, when he first came to the house and we asked him what he could do, Nabo said that he could sing. But that didn't interest anyone. What we needed was a boy to curry the horses. Nabo stayed, but he kept on singing, as if we had hired him to sing and the business of currying the horses was only a distraction that made the work easier. That went on for more than a year, until those of us in the house grew used to the idea that the girl would never be able to walk, would never recognize anyone, would always be the little dead and lonely girl who listened to the gramophone looking coldly at the wall until we lifted her out of her chair and took her to her room. Then she ceased to pain us, but Nabo was still faithful, punctual, cranking the gramophone. That was during the time when Nabo was still going to the square on Saturday nights. One day, when the boy was in the stable, someone beside the gramophone said: 'Nabo!' We were on the veranda, not concerned about something no one could have said. But when we heard it a second time: 'Nabo!' we raised our heads and asked 'Who's with the girl?' And someone said: 'I didn't see anyone come in.' And another said: 'I'm sure I heard a voice calling Nabo.' But when we went to look all we found was the girl on the floor, leaning against the wall.

Nabo came back early and went to bed. It was the following Saturday that he didn't return to the square because the Negro had been replaced. And three weeks later, on a Monday, the gramophone began to play while Nabo was in the stable. No one worried at first. Only later, when we saw the black boy coming, singing and still dripping from the water of the horses, did we ask him: 'How'd you get out?' He said: 'Through the door. I've been in the stable since noon.' 'The gramophone's playing. Can't you hear it?' we asked him. And Nabo said he could. And we asked him: 'Who wound it up?' And he, shrugging his shoulders: 'The girl. She's been winding it for a long time now.'

That was the way things were until the day we found him lying face down on the hay, locked in the stable and with the edge of the horseshoe encrusted on his forehead. When we picked him up by the shoulders, Nabo said: 'I'm here because a horse kicked me.' But no one was interested in what he might have said. We were interested in his cold, dead eyes and mouth full of green froth. He spent the whole night weeping, burning with fever, delirious, talking about the comb that he'd lost in the hay in the stable. That was the first day. On the following day, when he opened his eyes and said: 'I'm thirsty,' and we brought him water, he drank it all down in one swallow and twice asked for a little more. We asked him how he felt and he said: 'I feel as if a horse had kicked me.' And he kept on talking all day and all night. And finally he sat up in bed, pointed up with his forefinger, and said that the galloping of the horses had kept him awake all night. But he'd had no fever since the night before. He was no longer delirious, but he kept on talking until they put a handkerchief in his mouth. Then Nabo began to sing behind the handkerchief, saying that next to his ear he could hear the breathing of the blind horses looking for water on top of the closed door. When we took out the handkerchief so that he could eat something, he turned toward the wall and we all thought that he'd fallen asleep and it was even possible that he had fallen asleep for a while. But when he awoke he was no longer on the bed. His feet were tied and his hands were tied to a brace beam in the room. Trussed up, Nabo began to sing.

When he recognized him, Nabo said to the man: 'I've seen you before.' And the man said: 'Every Saturday you used to watch me in the square.' And Nabo said: 'That's right, but I thought I saw you and you didn't see me.' And the man said: 'I never saw you, but later on, when I stopped coming, I felt as if someone had stopped watching me on Saturdays.' And Nabo said: 'You never came back, but I kept on going for three or four weeks.' And the man, still not moving, patting himself on the knees: 'I couldn't go back to the square even though it was the only thing that was worth anything.' Nabo tried to sit up, shook his head in the hay, and still he heard the cold, obstinate voice, until he no longer had time even to know that he was falling asleep again. Always, ever since the horse had kicked him, that happened. And he always heard the voice: 'We're waiting for you, Nabo. There's no longer any way to measure the time you've been asleep.'

Four weeks after the Negro had stopped coming to the band, Nabo was combing the tail of one of the horses. He'd never done that. He would just curry them and sing in the meantime. But on Wednesday he'd gone to the market and had seen a comb and had said to himself: 'That comb is for combing the horses' tails.' That was when the whole thing happened with the horse that gave him a kick and left him all mixed up for the rest of his life, ten or fifteen years before. Somebody in the house said: 'It would have been better if he'd died that day and hadn't gone on like this, all through, talking nonsense for the rest of his life.' But no one had seen him again ever since the day we locked him up. Only we knew that he was there, locked up in the room, and since then the girl hadn't moved the gramophone again. But in the house we had very little interest in knowing about it. We'd locked him up as if he were a horse, as if the kick had passed the sluggishness on to him and encrusted on his forehead was all the stupidity of horses: animalness. And we left him isolated within four walls as if we'd decided he should die of imprisonment because we weren't cold-blooded enough to kill him in any other way. Fourteen years passed like that until one of the children grew up and said he had the urge to see his face. And he opened the door.

Nabo saw the man again. 'A horse kicked me,' he said. And the man said: 'You've been saying that for centuries and in the meantime we've been waiting for you in the choir.' Nabo shook his head again, sank his wounded forehead into the hay once more, and thought he suddenly remembered how things had happened. 'It was the first time I ever combed a horse's tail,' he said. And the man said: 'We wanted it that way so you would come and sing in the choir.' And Nabo said: 'I shouldn't have bought the comb.' And the man said: 'You would have come across it in any case. We'd decided that you'd find the comb and comb the horses' tails.' And Nabo said: 'I'd never stood behind them before.' And the man, still tranquil, still not showing impatience: 'But you did stand there and the horse kicked you. It was the only way for you to come to the choir.' And the conversation, implacable, daily, went on until someone in the house said: 'It must be fifteen years since anyone opened that door.' The girl (she hadn't grown, she was over thirty and was beginning to get sad in her eyelids) was sitting looking at the wall when they opened the door. She turned her face in the other direction, sniffing. And when they closed the door, they said again: 'Nabo's peaceful. There's nothing moving inside anymore. One of these days he'll die and we won't be able to tell except for the smell.' And someone said: 'We can tell by the food. He's never stopped eating. He's fine like that, locked up with no one to bother him. He gets good light from the rear side.' And things stayed like that; except that the girl kept on looking toward the door, sniffing the warm fumes that filtered through the cracks. She stayed like that until early in the morning, when we heard a metallic sound in the living room and we remembered that it was the same sound that had been heard fifteen years before when Nabo was winding the gramophone. We got up, lighted the lamp, and heard the first measures of the forgotten song; the sad song that had been dead on the records for such a long time. The sound kept on, more and more strained, until a dry sound was heard at the instant we reached the living room, and we could still hear the record playing and saw the girl in the corner beside the gramophone, looking at the wall and holding up the crank. We didn't say anything, but went back to our rooms remembering that someone had told us some-time that the girl knew how to crank the gramophone. Thinking that, we stayed awake, listening to the worn little tune from the record that was still spinning on what was left of the broken spring.

The day before, when they opened the door, it smelled of biological waste, of a dead body. The one who had opened it shouted: 'Nabo! Nabo!' But nobody answered from inside. Beside the opening was the empty plate. Three times a day the plate was put under the door and three times a day the plate came out again with no food on it. That was how we knew that Nabo was alive. But by no other means. There was no more moving inside, no more singing. And it must have been after they closed the door that Nabo said to the man: 'I can't go to the choir.' And the man asked why. And Nabo said: 'Because I haven't got any shoes.' And the man, raising his feet, said: 'That doesn't matter. Nobody wear shoes here.' And Nabo saw the hard, yellow soles of the bare feet the man was holding up. 'I've been waiting for you here for an eternity,' the man said. 'The horse only kicked me a moment ago,' Nabo said. 'Now I'll throw a little water on my face and take them out for a walk.' And the man said: 'The horses don't need you anymore. There aren't any more horses. You're the one who should come with us.' And Nabo said: 'The horses should have been here.' He got up a little, sank his hands into the hay while the man said: 'They haven't had anyone to look after them for fifteen years.' But Nabo was scratching the ground under the hay, saying: 'The comb must still be here.' And the man said: 'They closed up the stable fifteen years ago. It's full of rubbish now.' And Nabo said: 'Rubbish doesn't collect in one afternoon. Until I find the comb I won't move out of here.'

On the following day, after they'd fastened the door again, they heard the difficult movements inside once more. No one moved afterward. No one said anything again when the first creaks were heard and the door began to give way under unusual pressure. Inside something like the panting of a penned animal was heard. Finally the groan of rusty hinges was heard as they broke when Nabo shook his head again. 'Until I find the comb, I won't go to the choir,' he said. 'It must be around here somewhere.' And he dug in the hay, breaking it, scratching the ground, until the man said: 'All right Nabo. If the only thing you're waiting for to come to the choir is to find the comb, go look for it.' He leaned forward, his face darkened by a patient haughtiness. He put his hands against the barrier and said: 'Go ahead Nabo. I'll see that nobody stops you.'

And then the door gave way and the huge bestial Negro with the harsh scar marked on his forehead (in spite of the fact that fifteen years had passed) came out stumbling over the furniture, his fists raised and menacing, still with the rope they had tied him with fifteen years before (when he was a little black boy who looked after the horses); and (before reaching the courtyard) he passed by the girl, who remained seated, the crank of the gramophone still in her hand since the night before (when she saw the unchained black force she remembered something that at one time must have been a word) and he reached the courtyard (before finding the stable), after having knocked down the living-room mirror with his shoulder, but without seeing the girl (neither beside the gramophone nor in the mirror), and he stood with his face to the sun, his eyes closed, blind (while inside the noise of the broken mirror was still going on), and he ran aimlessly, like a blindfolded horse instinctively looking for the stable door that fifteen years of imprisonment had erased from his memory but not from his instincts (since that remote day when he had combed the horse's tail and was left befuddled for the rest of his life), and leaving behind catastrophe, dissolution, and chaos like a blindfolded bull in a roomful of lamps, he reached the back yard (still without finding the stable), and scratched on the ground with the tempestuous fury with which he had knocked down the mirror, thinking perhaps that by scratching on the ground he could make the smell of mare's urine rise up again, until he finally reached the stable doors and pushed them too soon, falling inside on his face, in his death agony perhaps, but still confused by that fierce animalness that a half-second before had prevented him from hearing the girl, who raised the crank when she heard him pass and remembered, drooling, but without moving from the chair, without moving her mouth but twirling the crank of the gramophone in the air, remembered the only word she had ever learned to say in her life, and shouted it from the living room: 'Nabo! Nabo!'

Someone Has Been
Disarranging These Roses

Since it's Sunday and it's stopped raining, I think I'll take a bouquet of roses to my grave. Red and white roses, the kind that she grows to decorate altars and wreaths. The morning has been saddened by the taciturn and overwhelming winter that has set me to remembering the knoll where the townspeople abandon their dead. It's a bare, treeless place, swept only by the providential crumbs that return after the wind has passed. Now that it's stopped raining and the noonday sun has probably hardened the soapy slope, I should be able to reach the grave where my child's body rests, mingled now, dispersed among snails and roots.

She is prostrate before her saints. She's remained abstracted since I stopped moving in the room, when I failed in the first attempt to reach the altar and pick the brightest and freshest roses. Maybe I could have done it today, but the little lamp blinked and she, recovered from her ecstasy, raised her head and looked toward the corner where the chair is. She must have thought: 'It's the wind again,' because it's true that something creaked beside the altar and the room rocked for an instant, as if the level of the stagnant memories in it for so long had shifted. Then I understood that I would have to wait for another occasion to get the roses because she was still awake, looking at the chair, and she would have heard the sound of my hands beside her face. Now I've got to wait until she leaves the room in a moment and goes to the one next door to sleep her measured and invariable Sunday siesta. Maybe then I can leave with the roses and be back before she returns to this room and remains looking at the chair.

Last Sunday was more difficult. I had to wait almost two hours for her to fall into ecstasy. She seemed restless, preoccupied, as if she had been tormented by the certainty that her solitude in the house had suddenly become less intense. She took several turns about the room with the bouquet of roses before leaving it on the altar. Then she went out into the hallway, turned in, and went to the next room. I knew that she was looking for the lamp. And later, when she passed by the door again and I saw her in the light of the hall with her dark little jacket and her pink stockings, it seemed to me now that she was still the girl who forty years ago had leaned over my bed in that same room and said: 'Now that they've put in the toothpicks your eyes are open and hard.' She was just the same, as if time hadn't passed since that remote August afternoon when the women brought her into the room and showed her the corpse and told her: 'Weep, he was like a brother to you,' and she leaned against the wall, weeping, obeying, still soaked from the rain.

For three or four Sundays now I've been trying to get to where the roses are, but she's been vigilant in front of the altar, keeping watch over the roses with a frightened diligence that I hadn't known in her during the twenty years she's been living in the house. Last Sunday, when she went out to get the lamp, I managed to put a bouquet of the best roses together. At no moment had I been closer to fulfilling my desires. But when I was getting ready to return to the chair, I heard her steps in the corridor again. I rearranged the roses on the altar quickly and then I saw her appear in the doorway with the lamp held high.

She was wearing her dark little jacket and the pink stockings, but on her face there was something like the phosphorescence of a revelation. She didn't seem then to be the woman who for twenty years has been growing roses in the garden, but the same child who on that August afternoon had been brought into the next room so that she could change her clothes and who was coming back now with a lamp, fat and grown old, forty years later.

My shoes still have the hard crust of clay that had formed on them that afternoon in spite of the fact that they've been drying beside the extinguished stove for forty years. One day I went to get them. That was after they'd closed up the doors, taken down the bread and the sprig of aloe from the entrance-way, and taken away the furniture. All the furniture except for the chair in the corner which has served me as a seat all this time. I knew that the shoes had been set to dry and they didn't even remember them when they abandoned the house. That's why I went to get them.

She returned many years later. So much time had passed that the smell of musk in the room had blended in with the smell of the dust, with the dry and tiny breath of the insects. I was alone in the house, sitting in the corner, waiting. And I had learned to make out the sound of rotting wood, the flutter of the air becoming old in the closed bedrooms. That was when she came. She had stood in the door with a suitcase in her hand, wearing a green hat and the same little cotton jacket that she hadn't taken off ever since then. She was still a girl. She hadn't begun to get fat and her ankles didn't swell under her stockings as they do now. I was covered with dust and cobwebs when she opened the door, and, somewhere in the room, the cricket who'd been singing for twenty years fell silent. But in spite of that, in spite of the cobwebs and the dust, the sudden reluctance of the cricket and the new age of the new arrival, I recognized in her the girl who on that stormy August afternoon had gone with me to collect nests in the stable. Just the way she was, standing in the doorway with the suitcase in her hand and her green hat on, she looked as if she were suddenly going to shout, say the same thing she'd said when they found me face up on the hay-covered stable floor still grasping the railing of the broken stairs. When she opened the door wide the hinges creaked and the dust from the ceiling fell in clumps, as if someone had started hammering on the ridge of the roof, then she paused on the threshold, coming halfway into the room after, and with the voice of someone calling a sleeping person she said: 'Boy! Boy!' And I remained still in the chair, rigid, with my feet stretched out.

I thought she had come only to see the room, but she continued living in the house. She aired out the room and it was as if she had opened her suitcase and her old smell of musk had come from it. The others had taken the furniture and clothing away in trunks. She had taken away only the smells of the room, and twenty years later she brought them back again, put them in their place, and rebuilt the little altar, just the way it was before. Her presence alone was enough to restore what the implacable industry of time had destroyed. Since then she has eaten and slept in the room next door, but she spends the day in this one, conversing silently with the saints. In the afternoons she sits in the rocker next to the door and mends clothing. And when someone comes for a bouquet of roses, she puts the money in the corner of the kerchief that she ties to her belt and invariably says: 'Pick the ones on the right, those on the left are for the saints.'

That's the way she's been for twenty years, in the rocker, darning her things, rocking, looking at the chair as if now she weren't taking care of the boy with whom she had shared her childhood afternoons but the invalid grandson who has been sitting here in the corner ever since the time his grandmother was five years old.

It's possible that now, when she lowers her head again, I can approach the roses. If I can manage to do so I'll go to the knoll, lay them on the grave, and come back to my chair to wait for the day when she won't return to the room and the sounds will cease in all the rooms.

On that day there'll be a change in all this, because I'll have to leave the house again in order to tell someone that the rose woman, the one who lives in the tumble-down house, is in need of four men to take her to the knoll. Then I'll be alone forever in the room. But, on the other hand, she'll be satisfied. Because on that day she'll learn that it wasn't the invisible wind that came to her altar every Sunday and disarranged the roses.

The Night of the Curlews

We were sitting, the three of us, around the table, when someone put a coin in the slot and the Wurlitzer played once more the record that had been going all night. The rest happened so fast that we didn't have time to think. It happened before we could remember where we were, before we could get back our sense of location. One of us reached his hand out over the counter, groping (we couldn't see the hand, we heard it), bumped into a glass, and then was still, with both hands resting on the hard surface. Then the three of us looked for ourselves in the darkness and found ourselves there, in the joints of the thirty fingers piled up on the counter. One of us said:

'Let's go.'

And we stood up as if nothing had happened. We still hadn't had time to get upset.

In the hallway, as we passed, we heard the nearby music spinning out at us. We caught the smell of sad women sitting and waiting. We felt the prolonged emptiness of the hall before us while we walked toward the door, before the other smell came out to greet us, the sour smell of the woman sitting by the door. We said:

'We're leaving.'

The woman didn't answer anything. We heard the creak of a rocking chair, rising up as she stood. We heard the footsteps on the loose board and the return of the woman again, when the hinges creaked once more and the door closed behind us.

We turned around. Right there, behind us, there was a

harsh, cutting breeze of an invisible dawn, and a voice that said:

'Get out of the way. I'm coming through with this.'

We moved back. And the voice spoke again:

'You're still against the door.'

And only then, when we'd moved to all sides and had found the voice everywhere, did we say:

'We can't get out of here. The curlews have pecked out our eyes.'

Then we heard several doors open. One of us let go of the other hands and we heard him dragging along in the darkness, weaving, bumping into the things that surrounded us. He spoke from somewhere in the darkness.

'We must be close,' he said. 'There's a smell of piled-up trunks around here.'

We felt the contact of his hands again. We leaned against the wall and another voice passed by then, but in the opposite direction.

'They might be coffins,' one of us said.

The one who had dragged himself into the corner and was breathing beside us now said:

'They're trunks. Ever since I was little I've been able to tell the smell of stored clothing.'

Then we moved in that direction. The ground was soft and smooth, fine earth that had been walked on. Someone held out a hand. We felt the contact with long, live skin, but we no longer felt the wall opposite.

'This is a woman,' we said.

The other one, the one who had spoken of trunks, said:

'I think she's asleep.'

The body shook under our hands, trembled, we felt it slip away, not as if it had got out of our reach, but as if it had ceased to exist. Still, after an instant in which we remained motionless, stiffened, leaning against each other's shoulders, we heard her voice.

'Who's there?' it said.

'It's us,' we replied without moving.

The movement of the bed could be heard, the creaking and the shuffling of feet looking for slippers in the darkness. Then we pictured the seated woman, looking at us as when she still hadn't awakened completely.

'What are you doing here?' she asked.

And we answered:

'We don't know. The curlews pecked out our eyes.'

The voice said that she'd heard something about that. That the newspapers had said that three men had been drinking in a courtyard where there were five or six curlews. Seven curlews. One of the men began singing like a curlew, imitating them.

'The worst was that he was an hour behind,' she said. 'That was when the birds jumped on the table and pecked out their eyes.'

She said that's what the newspapers had said, but nobody had believed them. We said:

'If people had gone there, they'd have seen the curlews.'

And the woman said:

'They did. The courtyard was full of people the next day, but the woman had already taken the curlews somewhere else.'

When we turned around, the woman stopped speaking. There was the wall again. By just turning around we would find the wall. Around us, surrounding us, there was always a wall. One let go of our hands again. We heard him crawling again, smelling the ground, saying:

'Now I don't know where the trunks are. I think we're somewhere else now.'

And we said:

'Come here. Somebody's here next to us.'

We heard him come close. We felt him stand up beside us and again his warm breath hit us in the face.

'Reach out that way,' we told him. 'There's someone we know there.'

He must have reached out, he must have moved toward the place we indicated, because an instant later he came back to tell us:

'I think it's a boy.'

And we told him:

'Fine. Ask him if he knows us.'

He asked the question. We heard the apathetic and simple voice of the boy, who said:

'Yes, I know you. You're the three men whose eyes were pecked out by the curlews.'

Then an adult voice spoke. The voice of a woman who seemed to be behind a closed door, saying:

'You're talking to yourself again.'

And the child's voice, unconcerned, said:

'No. The men who had their eyes pecked out by the curlews are here again.'

There was a sound of hinges and then the adult voice, closer than the first time.

'Take them home,' she said.

And the boy said:

'I don't know where they live.'

And the adult voice said:

'Don't be mean. Everybody knows where they live ever since the night the curlews pecked their eyes out.'

Then she went on in a different tone, as if she were speaking to us:

'What happened is that nobody wanted to believe it and they say it was a fake item made up by the papers to boost their circulation. No one has seen the curlews.'

And he said:

'But nobody would believe me if I led them along the street.'

We didn't move. We were still, leaning against the wall, listening to her. And the woman said:

'If this one wants to take you it's different. After all, nobody would pay much attention to what a boy says.'

The child's voice cut in:

'If I go out onto the street with them and they say that they're the men who had their eyes pecked out by the curlews, the boys will throw stones at me. Everybody on the street says it couldn't have happened.'

There was a moment of silence. Then the door closed again and the boy spoke:

'Besides, I'm reading *Terry and the Pirates* right now.'

Someone said in our ear:

'I'll convince him.'

He crawled over to where the voice was.

'I like it,' he said. 'At least tell us what happened to Terry this week.'

He's trying to gain his confidence, we thought. But the boy said:

'That doesn't interest me. The only thing I like are the colors.'

'Terry's in a maze,' we said.

And the boy said:

'That was Friday. Today's Sunday and what I like are the colors,' and he said it with a cold, dispassionate, indifferent voice.

When the other one came back, we said:

'We've been lost for almost three days and we haven't had a moment's rest.'

And one said:

'All right. Let's rest awhile, but without letting go of each other's hands.'

We sat down. An invisible sun began to warm us on the shoulders. But not even the presence of the sun interested us. We felt it there, everywhere, having already lost the notion of distance, time, direction. Several voices passed.

'The curlews pecked out our eyes,' we said.

And one of the voices said:

'These here took the newspapers seriously.'

The voices disappeared. And we kept on sitting, like that, shoulder to shoulder, waiting, in that passing of voices, in that passing of images, for a smell or a voice that was known to us to pass. The sun was above our heads, still warming us. Then someone said:

'Let's go toward the wall again.'

And the others, motionless, their heads lifted toward the

invisible light:

'Not yet. Let's just wait till the sun begins to burn us on the face.'

Monologue of Isabel
Watching It Rain in Macondo

Winter fell one Sunday when people were coming out of church. Saturday night had been suffocating. But even on Sunday morning nobody thought it would rain. After mass, before we women had time to find the catches on our parasols, a thick, dark wind blew, which with one broad, round swirl swept away the dust and hard tinder of May. Someone next to me said: 'It's a water wind.' And I knew it even before then. From the moment we came out onto the church steps I felt shaken by a slimy feeling in my stomach. The men ran to the nearby houses with one hand on their hats and a handkerchief in the other, protecting themselves against the wind and the dust storm. Then it rained. And the sky was a gray, jellyish substance that flapped its wings a hand away from our heads.

During the rest of the morning my stepmother and I were sitting by the railing, happy that the rain would revive the thirsty rosemary and nard in the flowerpots after seven months of intense summer and scorching dust. At noon the reverberation of the earth stopped and a smell of turned earth, of awakened and renovated vegetation mingled with the cool and healthful odor of the rain in the rosemary. My father said at lunchtime: 'When it rains in May, it's a sign that there'll be good tides.' Smiling, crossed by the luminous thread of the new season, my stepmother told me: 'That's what I heard in the sermon.' And my father smiled. And he ate with a good appetite and even let his food digest leisurely beside the railing, silent, his eyes closed, but not sleeping, as if to think that he was dreaming while awake.

It rained all afternoon in a single tone. In the uniform and peaceful intensity you could hear the water fall, the way it is when you travel all afternoon on a train. But without our noticing it, the rain was penetrating too deeply into our senses. Early Monday morning, when we closed the door to avoid the cutting, icy draft that blew in from the courtyard, our senses had been filled with rain. And on Monday morning they had overflowed. My stepmother and I went back to look at the garden. The harsh gray earth of May had been changed overnight into a dark, sticky substance like cheap soap. A trickle of water began to run off the flowerpots. 'I think they had more than enough water during the night,' my stepmother said. And I noticed that she had stopped smiling and that her joy of the previous day had changed during the night into a lax and tedious seriousness. 'I think you're right,' I said. 'It would be better to have the Indians put them on the veranda until it stops raining.' And that was what they did, while the rain grew like an immense tree over the other trees. My father occupied the same spot where he had been on Sunday afternoon, but he didn't talk about the rain. He said: 'I must have slept poorly last night because I woke up with a stiff back.' And he stayed there, sitting by the railing with his feet on a chair and his head turned toward the empty garden. Only at dusk, after he had turned down lunch, did he say: 'It looks as if it will never clear.' And I remembered the months of heat. I remembered August, those long and awesome siestas in which we dropped down to die under the weight of the hour, our clothes sticking to our bodies, hearing outside the insistent and dull buzzing of the hour that never passed. I saw the washed-down walls, the joints of the beams all puffed up by the water. I saw the small garden, empty for the first time, and the jasmine bush against the wall, faithful to the memory of my mother. I saw my father sitting in a rocker, his painful vertebrae resting on a pillow and his sad eyes lost in the labyrinth of the rain. I remembered the August nights in whose wondrous silence nothing could be heard except the millenary sound that the earth makes as it spins on its rusty, unoiled axis. Suddenly I felt overcome by an overwhelming sadness.

It rained all Monday, just like Sunday. But now it seemed to be raining in another way, because something different and bitter was going on in my heart. At dusk a voice beside my chair said: 'This rain is a bore.' Without turning to look, I recognized Martín's voice. I knew that he was speaking in the next chair, with the same cold and awesome expression that hadn't varied, not even after that gloomy December dawn when he started being my husband. Five months had passed since then. Now I was going to have a child. And Martín was there beside me saying that the rain bored him. 'Not a bore,' I said. 'It seems terribly sad to me, with the empty garden and those poor trees that can't come in from the courtyard.' Then I turned to look at him and Martín was no longer there. It was only a voice that was saying to me: 'It doesn't look as if it will ever clear,' and when I looked toward the voice I found only the empty chair.

On Tuesday morning we found a cow in the garden. It looked like a clay promontory in its hard and rebellious immobility, its hooves sunken in the mud and its head bent over. During the morning the Indians tried to drive it away with sticks and stones. But the cow stayed there, imperturbable in the garden, hard, inviolable, its hooves still sunken in the mud and its huge head humiliated by the rain. The Indians harassed it until my father's patient tolerance came to its defense. 'Leave her alone,' he said. 'She'll leave the way she came.'

At sundown on Tuesday the water tightened and hurt, like a shroud over the heart. The coolness of the first morning began to change into a hot and sticky humidity. The temperature was neither cold nor hot; it was the temperature of a fever chill. Feet sweated inside shoes. It was hard to say what was more disagreeable, bare skin or the contact of clothing on skin. All activity had ceased in the house. We sat on the veranda but we no longer watched the rain as we did on the first day. We no longer felt it falling. We no longer saw anything except the outline of the trees in the mist, with a sad and desolate sunset which left on your lips the same taste with which you awaken after having dreamed about a stranger. I knew that it was Tuesday and I remembered the twins of Saint Jerome, the blind girls who came to the house every week to sing us simple songs, saddened by the bitter and unprotected prodigy of their voices. Above the rain I heard the blind twins' little song and I imagined them at home, huddling, waiting for the rain to stop so they could go out and sing. The twins of Saint Jerome wouldn't come that day, I thought, nor would the beggar woman be on the veranda after siesta, asking, as on every Tuesday, for the eternal branch of lemon balm.

That day we lost track of meals. At siesta time my step-mother served a plate of tasteless soup and a piece of stale bread. But actually we hadn't eaten since sunset on Monday and I think that from then on we stopped thinking. We were paralyzed, drugged by the rain, given over to the collapse of nature with a peaceful and resigned attitude. Only the cow was moving in the afternoon. Suddenly a deep noise shook her insides and her hooves sank into the mud with greater force. Then she stood motionless for half an hour, as if she were already dead but could not fall down because the habit of being alive prevented her, the habit of remaining in one position in the rain, until the habit grew weaker than her body. Then she doubled her front legs (her dark and shiny haunches still raised in a last agonized effort) and sank her drooling snout into the mud, finally surrendering to the weight of her own matter in a silent, gradual, and dignified ceremony of total downfall. 'She got that far,' someone said behind me. And I turned to look and on the threshold I saw the Tuesday beggar woman who had come through the storm to ask for the branch of lemon balm.

Perhaps on Wednesday I might have grown accustomed to that overwhelming atmosphere if on going to the living room I hadn't found the table pushed against the wall, the furniture piled on top of it, and on the other side, on a parapet prepared during the night, trunks and boxes of household utensils. The spectacle produced a terrible feeling of emptiness in me. Something had happened during the night. The house was in disarray; the Guajiro Indians, shirtless and barefoot, with their pants rolled up to their knees, were carrying the furniture into the dining room. In the men's expression, in the very diligence with which they were working, one could see the cruelty of their frustrated rebellion, of their necessary and humiliating inferiority in the rain. I moved without direction, without will. I felt changed into a desolate meadow sown with algae and lichens, with soft, sticky toadstools, fertilized by the repugnant plants of dampness and shadows. I was in the living room contemplating the desert spectacle of the piled-up furniture when I heard my stepmother's voice warning me from her room that I might catch pneumonia. Only then did I realize that the water was up to my ankles, that the house was flooded, the floor covered by a thick surface of viscous, dead water.

On Wednesday noon it still hadn't finished dawning. And before three o'clock in the afternoon night had come on completely ahead of time and sickly, with the same slow, monotonous, and pitiless rhythm of the rain in the courtyard. It was a premature dusk, soft and lugubrious, growing in the midst of the silence of the Guajiros, who were squatting on the chairs against the walls, defeated and impotent against the disturbance of nature. That was when news began to arrive from outside. No one brought it to the house. It simply arrived, precise, individualized, as if led by the liquid clay that ran through the streets and dragged household items along, things and more things, the leftovers of a remote catastrophe, rubbish and dead animals. Events that took place on Sunday, when the rain was still the announcement of a providential season, took two days to be known at our house. And on Wednesday the news arrived as if impelled by the very inner dynamism of the storm. It was learned then that the church was flooded and its collapse expected. Someone who had no reason to know said that night: 'The train hasn't been able to cross the bridge since Monday. It seems that the river carried away the tracks.' And it was learned that a sick woman had disappeared from her bed and had been found that afternoon floating in the courtyard.

Terrified, possessed by the fright and the deluge, I sat down in the rocker with my legs tucked up and my eyes fixed on the damp darkness full of hazy foreboding. My stepmother appeared in the doorway with the lamp held high and her head erect. She looked like a family ghost before whom I felt no fear whatever because I myself shared her supernatural condition. She came over to where I was. She still held her head high and the lamp in the air, and she splashed through the water on the veranda. 'Now we have to pray,' she said. And I noticed her dry and wrinkled face, as if she had just left her tomb or as if she had been made of some substance different from human matter. She was across from me with her rosary in her hand saying: 'Now we have to pray. The water broke open the tombs and now the poor dead are floating in the cemetery.'

I may have slept a little that night when I awoke with a start because of a sour and penetrating smell like that of decomposing bodies. I gave a strong shake to Martín, who was snoring beside me. 'Don't you notice it?' I asked him. And he said: 'What?' And I said: 'The smell. It must be the dead people floating along the streets.' I was terrified by that idea, but Martín turned to the wall and with a husky and sleepy voice said: 'That's something you made up. Pregnant women are always imagining things.'

At dawn on Thursday the smells stopped, the sense of distance was lost. The notion of time, upset since the day before, disappeared completely. Then there was no Thursday. What should have been Thursday was a physical, jellylike thing that could have been parted with the hands in order to look into Friday. There were no men or women there. My stepmother, my father, the Indians were adipose and improbable bodies that moved in the marsh of winter. My father said to me: 'Don't move away from here until you're told what to do,' and his voice was distant and indirect and didn't seem to be perceived by the ear but by touch, which was the only sense that remained active.

But my father didn't return: he got lost in the weather. So when night came I called my stepmother to tell her to accompany me to my bedroom. I had a peaceful and serene sleep, which lasted all through the night. On the following day the atmosphere was still the same, colorless, odorless, and without any temperature. As soon as I awoke I jumped into a chair and remained there without moving, because something told me that there was still a region of my consciousness that hadn't awakened completely. Then I heard the train whistle. The prolonged and sad whistle of the train fleeing the storm. *It must have cleared somewhere*, I thought, and a voice behind me seemed to answer my thought. 'Where?' it said. 'Who's there?' I asked looking. And I saw my stepmother with a long thin arm in the direction of the wall. 'It's me,' she said. And I asked her: 'Can you hear it?' And she said yes, maybe it had cleared on the outskirts and they'd repaired the tracks. Then she gave me a tray with some steaming breakfast. It smelled of garlic sauce and boiled butter. It was a plate of soup. Disconcerted, I asked my stepmother what time it was. And she, calmly, with a voice that tasted of prostrated resignation, said: 'It must be around two-thirty. The train isn't late after all this.' I said: 'Two-thirty! How could I have slept so long!' And she said: 'You haven't slept very long. It can't be more than three o'clock.' And I, trembling, feeling the plate slip through my fingers: 'Two-thirty on Friday,' I said. And she, monstrously tranquil: 'Two-thirty on Thursday, child. *Still* two-thirty on Thursday.'

I don't know how long I was sunken in that somnambulism where the senses lose their value. I only know that after many uncountable hours I heard a voice in the next room. A voice that said: 'Now you can roll the bed to this side.' It was a tired voice, but not the voice of a sick person, rather that of a convalescent. Then I heard the sound of the bricks in the water. I remained rigid before I realized that I was in a horizontal position. Then I felt the immense emptiness. I felt the wavering and violent silence of the house, the incredible immobility that affected everything. And suddenly I felt my heart turned into a frozen stone. *I'm dead*, I thought. *My God, I'm dead*. I gave a jump in the bed. I shouted: 'Ada! Ada!' Martín's unpleasant voice answered me from the other side. 'They can't hear you, they're already outside by now.' Only then did I realize that it had cleared and that all around us a silence stretched out, a tranquillity, a mysterious and deep beatitude, a perfect state which must have been very much like death. Then footsteps could be heard on the veranda. A clear and completely living voice was heard. Then a cool breeze shook the panel of the door, made the doorknob squeak, and a solid and monumental body, like a ripe fruit, fell deeply into the cistern in the courtyard. Something in the air revealed the presence of an invisible person who was smiling in the darkness. *Good Lord*, I thought then, confused by the mixup in time. *It wouldn't surprise me now if they were coming to call me to go to last Sunday's mass.*

Tuesday Siesta

The train emerged from the quivering tunnel of sandy rocks, began to cross the symmetrical, interminable banana plantations, and the air became humid and they couldn't feel the sea breeze any more. A stifling blast of smoke came in the car window. On the narrow road parallel to the railway there were oxcarts loaded with green bunches of bananas. Beyond the road, in uncultivated spaces set at odd intervals there were offices with electric fans, red-brick buildings, and residences with chairs and little white tables on the terraces among dusty palm trees and rosebushes. It was eleven in the morning, and the heat had not yet begun.

'You'd better close the window,' the woman said. 'Your hair will get full of soot.'

The girl tried to, but the shade wouldn't move because of the rust.

They were the only passengers in the lone third-class car. Since the smoke of the locomotive kept coming through the window, the girl left her seat and put down the only things they had with them: a plastic sack with some things to eat and a bouquet of flowers wrapped in newspaper. She sat on the opposite seat, away from the window, facing her mother. They were both in severe and poor mourning clothes.

The girl was twelve years old, and it was the first time she'd ever been on a train. The woman seemed too old to be her mother, because of the blue veins on her eyelids and her small, soft, and shapeless body, in a dress cut like a cassock. She was riding with her spinal column braced firmly against the back of the seat, and held a peeling patent-leather handbag in her lap with both hands. She bore the conscientious serenity of someone accustomed to poverty.

By twelve the heat had begun. The train stopped for ten minutes to take on water at a station where there was no town. Outside, in the mysterious silence of the plantations, the shadows seemed clean. But the still air inside the car smelled like untanned leather. The train did not pick up speed. It stopped at two identical towns with wooden houses painted bright colors. The woman's head nodded and she sank into sleep. The girl took off her shoes. Then she went to the washroom to put the bouquet of flowers in some water.

When she came back to her seat, her mother was waiting to eat. She gave her a piece of cheese, half a corn-meal pancake, and a cookie, and took an equal portion out of the plastic sack for herself. While they ate, the train crossed an iron bridge very slowly and passed a town just like the ones before, except that in this one there was a crowd in the plaza. A band was playing a lively tune under the oppressive sun. At the other side of town the plantations ended in a plain which was cracked from the drought.

The woman stopped eating.

'Put on your shoes,' she said.

The girl looked outside. She saw nothing but the deserted plain, where the train began to pick up speed again, but she put the last piece of cookie into the sack and quickly put on her shoes. The woman gave her a comb.

'Comb your hair,' she said.

The train whistle began to blow while the girl was combing her hair. The woman dried the sweat from her neck and wiped the oil from her face with her fingers. When the girl stopped combing, the train was passing the outlying houses of a town larger but sadder than the earlier ones.

'If you feel like doing anything, do it now,' said the woman. 'Later, don't take a drink anywhere even if you're dying of thirst. Above all, no crying.'

The girl nodded her head. A dry, burning wind came in the

window, together with the locomotive's whistle and the clatter of the old cars. The woman folded the plastic bag with the rest of the food and put it in the handbag. For a moment a complete picture of the town, on that bright August Tuesday, shone in the window. The girl wrapped the flowers in the soaking-wet newspapers, moved a little farther away from the window, and stared at her mother. She received a pleasant expression in return. The train began to whistle and slowed down. A moment later it stopped.

There was no one at the station. On the other side of the street, on the sidewalk shaded by the almond trees, only the pool hall was open. The town was floating in the heat. The woman and the girl got off the train and crossed the abandoned station – the tiles split apart by the grass growing up between – and over to the shady side of the street.

It was almost two. At that hour, weighted down by drowsiness, the town was taking a siesta. The stores, the town offices, the public school were closed at eleven, and didn't reopen until a little before four, when the train went back. Only the hotel across from the station, with its bar and pool hall, and the telegraph office at one side of the plaza stayed open. The houses, most of them built on the banana company's model, had their doors locked from inside and their blinds drawn. In some of them it was so hot that the residents ate lunch in the patio. Others leaned a chair against the wall, in the shade of the almond trees, and took their siesta right out in the street.

Keeping to the protective shade of the almond trees, the woman and the girl entered the town without disturbing the siesta. They went directly to the parish house. The woman scratched the metal grating on the door with her fingernail, waited a moment, and scratched again. An electric fan was humming inside. They did not hear the steps. They hardly heard the slight creaking of a door, and immediately a cautious voice, right next to the metal grating: 'Who is it?' The woman tried to see through the grating.

'I need a priest,' she said.

'He's sleeping now.'

'It's an emergency,' the woman insisted.

Her voice showed a calm determination.

The door was opened a little way, noiselessly, and a plump, older woman appeared, with very pale skin and hair the color of iron. Her eyes seemed too small behind her thick eyeglasses.

'Come in,' she said, and opened the door all the way.

They entered a room permeated with an old smell of flowers. The woman of the house led them to a wooden bench and signaled them to sit down. The girl did so, but her mother remained standing, absent-mindedly, with both hands clutching the handbag. No noise could be heard above the electric fan.

The woman of the house reappeared at the door at the far end of the room. 'He says you should come back after three,' she said in a very low voice. 'He just lay down five minutes ago.'

'The train leaves at three-thirty,' said the woman.

It was a brief and self-assured reply, but her voice remained pleasant, full of undertones. The woman of the house smiled for the first time.

'All right,' she said.

When the far door closed again, the woman sat down next to her daughter. The narrow waiting room was poor, neat, and clean. On the other side of the wooden railing which divided the room, there was a worktable, a plain one with an oilcloth cover, and on top of the table a primitive typewriter next to a vase of flowers. The parish records were beyond. You could see that it was an office kept in order by a spinster.

The far door opened and this time the priest appeared, cleaning his glasses with a handkerchief. Only when he put them on was it evident that he was the brother of the woman who had opened the door.

'How can I help you?' he asked.

'The keys to the cemetery,' said the woman.

The girl was seated with the flowers in her lap and her feet crossed under the bench. The priest looked at her, then looked at the woman, and then through the wire mesh of the window at the bright, cloudless sky.

'In this heat,' he said. 'You could have waited until the sun went down.'

The woman moved her head silently. The priest crossed to the other side of the railing, took out of the cabinet a notebook covered in oilcloth, a wooden penholder, and an inkwell, and sat down at the table. There was more than enough hair on his hands to account for what was missing on his head.

'Which grave are you going to visit?' he asked

'Carlos Centeno's,' said the woman.

'Who?'

'Carlos Centeno,' the woman repeated.

The priest still did not understand.

'He's the thief who was killed here last week,' said the woman in the same tone of voice. 'I am his mother.'

The priest scrutinized her. She stared at him with quiet self-control, and the Father blushed. He lowered his head and began to write. As he filled the page, he asked the woman to identify herself, and she replied unhesitatingly, with precise details, as if she were reading them. The Father began to sweat. The girl unhooked the buckle of her left shoe, slipped her heel out of it, and rested it on the bench rail. She did the same with the right one.

It had all started the Monday of the previous week, at three in the morning, a few blocks from there. Rebecca, a lonely widow who lived in a house full of odds and ends, heard above the sound of the drizzling rain someone trying to force the front door from outside. She got up, rummaged around in her closet for an ancient revolver that no one had fired since the days of Colonel Aureliano Buendía, and went into the living room without turning on the lights. Orienting herself not so much by the noise at the lock as by a terror developed in her by twenty-eight years of loneliness, she fixed in her imagination not only the spot where the door was but also the exact height of the lock. She clutched the weapon with both hands, closed her eyes, and squeezed the trigger. It was the first time in her life that she had fired a gun. Immediately after the explosion, she could hear nothing except the murmur of the drizzle on the galvanized roof. Then she heard a little metallic bump on the cement porch, and a very low voice, pleasant but terribly exhausted: 'Ah, Mother.' The man they found dead in front of the house in the morning, his nose blown to bits, wore a flannel shirt with colored stripes, everyday pants with a rope for a belt, and was barefoot. No one in town knew him.

'So his name was Carlos Centeno,' murmured the Father when he finished writing.

'Centeno Ayala,' said the woman. 'He was my only boy.'

The priest went back to the cabinet. Two big rusty keys hung on the inside of the door; the girl imagined, as the mother had when she was a girl and as the priest himself must have imagined at some time, that they were Saint Peter's keys. He took them down, put them on the open notebook on the railing and pointed with his forefinger to a place on the page he had just written, looking at the woman.

'Sign here.'

The woman scribbled her name, holding the handbag under her arm. The girl picked up the flowers, came to the railing shuffling her feet, and watched her mother attentively.

The priest sighed.

'Didn't you ever try to get him on the right track?'

The woman answered when she finished signing.

'He was a very good man.'

The priest looked first at the woman and then at the girl, and realized with a kind of pious amazement that they were not about to cry. The woman continued in the same tone:

'I told him never to steal anything that anyone needed to eat, and he minded me. On the other hand, before, when he used to box, he used to spend three days in bed, exhausted from being punched.'

'All his teeth had to be pulled out,' interrupted the girl.

'That's right,' the woman agreed. 'Every mouthful I ate those days tasted of the beatings my son got on Saturday nights.'

'God's will is inscrutable,' said the Father.

But he said it without much conviction, partly because experience had made him a little skeptical and partly because of the heat. He suggested that they cover their heads to guard against sunstroke. Yawning, and now almost completely asleep, he gave them instructions about how to find Carlos Centeno's grave. When they came back, they didn't have to knock. They should put the key under the door; and in the same place, if they could, they should put an offering for the Church. The woman listened to his directions with great attention, but thanked him without smiling.

The Father had noticed that there was someone looking inside, his nose pressed against the metal grating, even before he opened the door to the street. Outside was a group of children. When the door was opened wide, the children scattered. Ordinarily, at that hour there was no one in the street. Now there were not only children. There were groups of people under the almond trees. The Father scanned the street swimming in the heat and then he understood. Softly, he closed the door again.

'Wait a moment,' he said without looking at the woman.

His sister appeared at the far door with a black jacket over her nightshirt and her hair down over her shoulders. She looked silently at the Father.

'What was it?' he asked.

'The people have noticed,' murmured his sister.

'You'd better go out by the door to the patio,' said the Father.

'It's the same there,' said his sister. 'Everybody is at the windows.'

The woman seemed not to have understood until then. She tried to look into the street through the metal grating. Then she took the bouquet of flowers from the girl and began to move toward the door. The girl followed her.

'Wait until the sun goes down,' said the Father.

'You'll melt,' said his sister, motionless at the back of the room. 'Wait and I'll lend you a parasol.'

'Thank you,' replied the woman. 'We're all right this way.' She took the girl by the hand and went into the street.

One of These Days

Monday dawned warm and rainless, Aurelio Escovar, a dentist without a degree, and a very early riser, opened his office at six. He took some false teeth, still mounted in their plaster mold, out of the glass case and put on the table a fistful of instruments which he arranged in size order, as if they were on display. He wore a collarless striped shirt, closed at the neck with a golden stud, and pants held up by suspenders. He was erect and skinny, with a look that rarely corresponded to the situation, the way deaf people have of looking.

When he had things arranged on the table, he pulled the drill toward the dental chair and sat down to polish the false teeth. He seemed not to be thinking about what he was doing, but worked steadily, pumping the drill with his feet, even when he didn't need it.

After eight he stopped for a while to look at the sky through the window, and he saw two pensive buzzards who were drying themselves in the sun on the ridgepole of the house next door. He went on working with the idea that before lunch it would rain again. The shrill voice of his eleven-year-old son interrupted his concentration.

'Papá.'

'What?'

'The Mayor wants to know if you'll pull his tooth.'

'Tell him I'm not here.'

He was polishing a gold tooth. He held it at arm's length, and examined it with his eyes half closed. His son shouted again from the little waiting room.

'He says you are, too, because he can hear you.'

The dentist kept examining the tooth. Only when he had put it on the table with the finished work did he say: 'So much the better.'

He operated the drill again. He took several pieces of a bridge out of a cardboard box where he kept the things he still had to do and began to polish the gold.

'Papá.'

'What?'

He still hadn't changed his expression.

'He says if you don't take out his tooth, he'll shoot you.'

Without hurrying, with an extremely tranquil movement, he stopped pedaling the drill, pushed it away from the chair, and pulled the lower drawer of the table all the way out. There was a revolver. 'O.K.,' he said. 'Tell him to come and shoot me.'

He rolled the chair over opposite the door, his hand resting on the edge of the drawer. The Mayor appeared at the door. He had shaved the left side of his face, but the other side, swollen and in pain, had a five-day-old beard. The dentist saw many nights of desperation in his dull eyes. He closed the drawer with his fingertips and said softly:

'Sit down.'

'Good morning,' said the Mayor.

'Morning,' said the dentist.

While the instruments were boiling, the Mayor leaned his skull on the headrest of the chair and felt better. His breath was icy. It was a poor office: an old wooden chair, the pedal drill, a glass case with ceramic bottles. Opposite the chair was a window with a shoulder-high cloth curtain. When he felt the dentist approach, the Mayor braced his heels and opened his mouth.

Aurelio Escovar turned his head toward the light. After inspecting the infected tooth, he closed the Mayor's jaw with a cautious pressure of his fingers.

'It has to be without anesthesia,' he said.

'Why?'

'Because you have an abscess.'

The Mayor looked him in the eye. 'All right,' he said, and tried to smile. The dentist did not return the smile. He brought the basin of sterilized instruments to the worktable and took them out of the water with a pair of cold tweezers, still without hurrying. Then he pushed the spittoon with the tip of his shoe, and went to wash his hands in the washbasin. He did all this without looking at the Mayor. But the Mayor didn't take his eyes off him.

It was a lower wisdom tooth. The dentist spread his feet and grasped the tooth with the hot forceps. The Mayor seized the arms of the chair, braced his feet with all his strength, and felt an icy void in his kidneys, but didn't make a sound. The dentist moved only his wrist. Without rancor, rather with a bitter tenderness, he said:

'Now you'll pay for our twenty dead men.'

The Mayor felt the crunch of bones in his jaw, and his eyes filled with tears. But he didn't breathe until he felt the tooth come out. Then he saw it through his tears. It seemed so foreign to his pain that he failed to understand his torture of the five previous nights.

Bent over the spittoon, sweating, panting, he unbuttoned his tunic and reached for the handkerchief in his pants pocket. The dentist gave him a clean cloth.

'Dry your tears,' he said.

The Mayor did. He was trembling. While the dentist washed his hands, he saw the crumbling ceiling and a dusty spider web with spider's eggs and dead insects. The dentist returned, drying his hands. 'Go to bed,' he said, 'and gargle with salt water.' The Mayor stood up, said goodbye with a casual military salute, and walked toward the door, stretching his legs, without buttoning up his tunic.

'Send the bill,' he said.

'To you or the town?'

The mayor didn't look at him. He closed the door and said through the screen:

'It's the same damn thing.'

There Are No Thieves
In This Town

Damaso came back to the room at the crack of dawn. Ana, his wife, six months pregnant, was waiting for him seated on the bed, dressed and with her shoes on. The oil lamp began to go out. Damaso realized that his wife had been waiting for him every minute through the whole night, and even now, at that moment when she could see him in front of her, was waiting still. He made a quieting gesture which she didn't reply to. She fixed her frightened eyes on the bundle of red cloth which he carried in his hand, pressed her lips together, and began to tremble. Damaso caught her by the chemise with a silent violence. He exhaled a bitter odor.

Ana let him lift her almost up in the air. Then she threw all the weight of her body forward, crying against her husband's red-striped flannel shirt, and clutched him around the kidneys until she managed to calm down.

'I fell asleep sitting up,' she said. 'Suddenly the door opened and you were pushed into the room, drenched with blood.'

Damaso held her at arm's length without saying anything. He set her down on the bed again. Then he put the bundle in her lap and went out to urinate in the patio. She untied the string and saw that there were three billiard balls, two white ones and a red one, dull and very worn from use.

When he returned to the room, Damaso found her in deep thought.

'And what good is this?' Ana asked.

He shrugged his shoulders.

'To play billiards.'

He tied the bundle up again and put it, together with the homemade skeleton key, the flashlight, and the knife, in the bottom of the trunk. Ana lay down facing the wall without taking off her clothes. Damaso took off only his pants. Stretched out in bed, smoking in the darkness, he tried to recognize some trace of his adventure in the scattered rustlings of the dawn, until he realized that his wife was awake.

'What are you thinking about?'

'Nothing,' she said.

Her voice, ordinarily a low contralto, seemed thicker because of her rancor. Damaso took one last puff on the cigarette and stubbed out the butt on the earthen floor.

'There was nothing else.' He sighed. 'I was inside about an hour.'

'They might have shot you,' she said.

Damaso trembled. 'Damn you,' he said, rapping the wooden bedframe with his knuckles. He felt around on the floor for his cigarettes and matches.

'You have the feelings of a donkey,' Ana said. 'You should have remembered that I was here, unable to sleep, thinking that you were being brought home dead every time there was a noise in the street.' She added with a sigh:

'And all that just to end up with three billiard balls.'

'There was nothing but twenty-five cents in the drawer.'

'Then you shouldn't have taken anything.'

'The hard part was getting in,' said Damaso. 'I couldn't come back empty-handed.'

'You could have taken anything else.'

'There was nothing else,' said Damaso.

'No place has as many things as the pool hall.'

'So it would seem,' said Damaso. 'But then, when you are inside there, you start to look at the things and to search all over, and you realize that there's nothing that's worth anything.'

She was silent for a long time. Damaso imagined her with her eyes open, trying to find some object of value in the darkness of memory.

'Perhaps,' she said.

Damaso lit up again. The alcohol was leaving him, in concentric waves, and he assumed once more the weight, the volume, and the responsibility of his limbs. 'There was a cat there,' he said. 'An enormous white cat.' Ana turned around, pressed her swollen belly against her husband's, and put her leg between his knees. She smelled of onion.

'Were you very frightened?'

'Me?'

'You,' said Ana. 'They say men get frightened too.'

He felt her smile, and he smiled. 'A little,' he said. 'I had to piss so bad I couldn't stand it.' He let himself be kissed without kissing her back. Then, conscious of the risks, but without regretting it, as if evoking the memories of a trip, he told her the details of his adventure.

She spoke after a long silence.

'It was crazy.'

'It's all a question of starting,' said Damaso, closing his eyes. 'Besides, it didn't turn out so bad for a first attempt.'

The sun's heat was late in coming. When Damaso woke up, his wife had been up for a while. He put his head under the faucet in the patio and held it there a few minutes until he was fully awake. The room was part of a gallery of similar and separate rooms, with a common patio crossed by clotheslines. Against the back wall, separated from the patio by a tin partition, Ana had set up a portable stove for cooking and for heating her irons, and a little table for eating and ironing. When she saw her husband approach, she put the ironed clothes to one side and took the irons off the stove so she could heat the coffee. She was older than he, with very pale skin, and her movements had the gentle efficiency of people who are used to reality.

Through the fog of his headache, Damaso realized that his wife wanted to tell him something with her look. Until then, he hadn't paid any attention to the voices in the patio.

'They haven't been talking about anything else all morning,' murmured Ana, giving him his coffee. 'The men went over there a little while ago.'

Damaso saw for himself that the men and children had disappeared from the patio. While he drank his coffee, he silently followed the conversation of the women who were hanging their clothes in the sun. Finally he lit a cigarette and left the kitchen.

'Teresa,' he called.

A girl with her clothes wet, plastered to her body, replied to his call. 'Be careful,' murmured Ana. The girl came over.

'What's going on?' asked Damaso.

'Someone got into the pool hall and walked off with everything,' the girl said.

She seemed to know all the details. She explained how they had taken the place apart, piece by piece, and had even carried off the billiard table. She spoke with such conviction that Damaso could not believe it wasn't true.

'Shit,' he said, coming back to the kitchen.

Ana began to sing between clenched teeth. Damaso leaned a chair against the patio wall, trying to repress his anxiety. Three months before, when he had turned twenty, the line of his mustache, cared for not only with a secret sense of sacrifice but also with a certain tenderness, had added a touch of maturity to his pockmarked face. Since then he had felt like an adult. But this morning, with the memories of the night before floating in the swamp of his headache, he could not find where to begin to live.

When she finished ironing, Ana put the clean clothes into two equal piles and got ready to go out.

'Don't be gone long,' said Damaso.

'The usual.'

He followed her into the room. 'I left your plaid shirt there,' Ana said. 'You'd better not wear the striped one again.' She confronted her husband's clear cat's eyes.

'We don't know if anyone saw you.'

Damaso dried the sweat from his hands on his pants.

'No one saw me.'

'We don't know,' Ana repeated. She was carrying a bundle of clothes in each arm. 'Besides, its better for you not to go out. Wait until I take a little stroll around there as if I weren't interested.'

In town people were talking of nothing else. Ana had to listen to the details of the same event several times, in different and contradictory versions. When she finished delivering the clothes, instead of going to the market as she did every Saturday, she went straight to the plaza.

She found fewer people in front of the pool hall than she had imagined. Some men were talking in the shade of the almond trees. The Syrians had put away their colored cloth for lunch, and the stores seemed to be dozing under the canvas awnings. A man was sleeping sprawled in a rocking chair, with his lips and legs wide apart, in the hotel lobby. Everything was paralyzed in the noonday heat.

Ana continued along by the pool hall, and when she passed the empty lot opposite the docks, she found the crowd. Then she remembered something Damaso had told her, which everybody knew but which only the real customers of the place could have remembered: the rear door of the pool hall faced the empty lot. A moment later, folding her arms over her belly, she mingled with the crowd, her eyes fixed on the door that had been forced. The lock was intact but one of the staples had been pulled out like a tooth. For a moment Ana regarded the damage caused by that solitary and modest effort and thought about her husband with a feeling of pity.

'Who was it?' she asked

She didn't dare look around.

They answered her, 'No one knows. They say it was a stranger.'

'It had to be,' said a woman behind her. 'There are no thieves in *this* town. Everybody knows everybody else.'

Ana turned her head. 'That's right,' she said smiling. She was covered with sweat. There was a very old man next to her with wrinkles on the back of his neck.

'Did they take everything?' she asked.

'Two hundred pesos, and the billiard balls,' the old man said. He looked at her with unusual interest. 'Pretty soon we'll have to sleep with our eyes open.'

Ana looked away. 'That's right,' she said again. She put a cloth over her head, moving off, without being able to avoid the impression that the old man was still looking at her.

For a quarter of an hour the crowd jammed into the empty lot behaved respectfully, as if there were a dead person behind the broken door. Then it became agitated, turned around, and spilled out into the plaza.

The owner of the pool hall was at the front door, with the Mayor and two policemen. Short and rotund, his pants held up only by the pressure of his stomach, and with eyeglasses like those that children make, the owner seemed endowed with an overwhelming dignity.

The crowd surrounded him. Leaning against the wall, Ana listened to his report until the crowd began to disperse. Then, sweltering in the heat, she returned to her room in the middle of a noisy demonstration by the neighbors.

Stretched out in bed, Damaso had asked himself many times how Ana had managed to wait for him the night before without smoking. When he saw her enter, smiling, taking from her head the cloth covered with sweat, he squashed the almost unsmoked cigarette on the earthen floor, in the middle of a line of butts, and waited with increased anxiety.

'Well?'

Ana kneeled next to the bed.

'Well, besides being a thief, you're a liar,' she said.

'Why?'

'Because you told me there was nothing in the drawer.'

Damaso frowned.

'There was nothing.'

'There were two hundred pesos,' said Ana.

'That's a lie,' he replied raising his voice. Sitting up in bed he regained his confidential tone. 'There was only twenty-five cents.'

He convinced her. 'He's an old crook,' said Damaso,

clenching his fists. 'He's looking for me to smash his face in.'
Ana laughed out loud.

'Don't be stupid.'

He ended up laughing, too. While he was shaving, his wife
told him what she had been able to find out. The police were
looking for a stranger. 'They say he arrived Thursday and that
they saw him last night walking around the docks,' she said.
'They say they can't find him anywhere.' Damaso thought
about the stranger whom he'd never seen; for an instant he
was really convinced, and suspected him.

'He may have gone away,' said Ana.

As always, Damaso needed three hours to get dressed. First
came the precise trimming of his mustache. Then his bath
under the faucet in the patio. With an interest which nothing
had diminished since the night she saw him for the first time,
Ana followed step by step the laborious process of his
combing his hair. When she saw him looking at himself in the
mirror before he went out, with his red plaid shirt on, Ana felt
old and sloppy. Damaso jabbed at her with the agility of a
professional boxer. She caught him by the wrists.

'Do you have any money?'

'I'm rich,' answered Damaso in good humor. 'I've got the
two hundred pesos.'

Ana turned toward the wall, took a roll of bills out of her
bosom, and gave a peso to her husband, saying:

'Take it, Valentino.'

That night Damaso was in the plaza with a group of his
friends. The people who came in from the country with things
to sell at Sunday's market were putting up their awnings amid
the stands which sold French fries and lottery tickets, and
from early evening on you could hear them snoring. Damaso's
friends didn't seem any more interested in the theft at the pool
hall than in the radio broadcast of the baseball championship,
which they couldn't hear that night because the pool hall was
closed. Talking about baseball, they went to the movie
without previously deciding to or finding out about what was
playing.

They were showing a movie with Cantinflas. In the first row of the balcony Damaso laughed shamelessly. He felt as if he were convalescing from his emotions. It was a pleasant June night, and in the empty stretches when you could see only the haze of the projector, the silence of the stars weighed in upon the roofless theater.

All at once the images on the screen went dim and there was a clatter at the back of the orchestra. In the sudden brightness, Damaso felt discovered, accused, and tried to run. But immediately he saw the audience in the orchestra paralyzed, and a policeman, his belt rolled around his fist, ferociously beating a man with the heavy copper buckle. He was a gigantic Negro. The women began to scream, and the policeman who was beating the Negro shouted over the women, 'Thief! Thief!' The Negro rolled between the row of chairs, chased by two policemen who struck at his kidneys until they managed to grab him from behind. Then the one who had thrashed him tied his elbows behind his back with a strap, and the three of them pushed him toward the door. The thing happened so quickly that Damaso understood what had happened only when the Negro passed next to him, his shirt torn and his face smeared with a mixture of dust, sweat, and blood, sobbing, 'Murderers, murderers.' Then they turned on the projector and the film continued.

Damaso didn't laugh again. He saw snatches of a disconnected story, chain-smoking, until the lights went on and the spectators looked at each other as if they were frightened by reality. 'That was good!' someone beside him exclaimed. Damaso didn't look at him.

'Cantinflas is very good,' he said.

The current of people carried him to the door. The food hawkers, loaded with baskets, were going home. It was after eleven, but there were a lot of people in the street waiting for them to come out of the movie to find out about the Negro's capture.

That night Damaso entered the room so cautiously that when Ana, who was half asleep, noticed him, he was smoking his second cigarette, stretched out in bed.

'The food is on the stove,' she said.

'I'm not hungry,' said Damaso.

Ana sighed. 'I dreamed that Nora was making puppets out of butter,' she said, still without waking up. Suddenly she realized that she had fallen asleep without intending to, and turned toward Damaso, dazed, rubbing her eyes.

'They caught the stranger,' she said.

Damaso waited before he spoke.

'Who said?'

'They caught him at the movie,' said Ana. 'Everyone is over there.'

She related a distorted version of the arrest. Damaso didn't correct her.

'Poor man.' Ana sighed.

'Why poor?' protested Damaso heatedly. 'So you would rather have me be the one in the trap.'

She knew him too well to reply. She sensed him smoking, breathing like an asthmatic, until the first light of dawn. Then she felt him out of bed, turning the room upside down in some obscure pursuit which seemed to depend on touch rather than sight. Then she felt him scraping the floor under the bed for more than fifteen minutes, and then she felt him undress in the darkness, trying not to make a noise, without realizing that she hadn't stopped helping him for a second by making him think she was asleep. Something stirred in her most primitive instincts. Ana knew then that Damaso had been at the movie, and understood why he had just buried the billiard balls under the bed.

The pool hall opened on Monday and was invaded by a hot-headed clientele. The billiard table had been covered with a purple cloth which gave the place a funereal air. A sign was tacked on the wall: 'NO BALLS, NO BILLIARDS.' People came in to read the sign as if it were news. Some stood before it for a long time, rereading it with impenetrable devotion.

Damaso was among the first customers. He had spent a part of his life on the benches set aside for the spectators, and he was there from the moment the doors opened. It was as difficult but as spontaneous as a condolence call. He gave the owner a pat on the back, from across the counter, and said:

'What a pain, Roque.'

The owner shook his head with a pained little smile, sighing. 'That's right,' he said. And he continued waiting on the customers while Damaso, settled on one of the counter stools, regarded the ghostly table under its purple shroud.

'How strange,' he said.

'That's right,' agreed a man on the next stool. 'It looks like we're in Holy Week.'

When the majority of customers went to eat lunch, Damaso put a coin in the jukebox and picked a Mexican ballad whose position on the selector he knew by heart. Roque was moving tables and chairs to the back of the hall.

'What are you doing?' asked Damaso.

'I'm setting up for cards,' replied Roque. 'I have to do something until the balls come.'

Moving almost hesitantly with a chair in each hand, he looked like a recent widower.

'When are they coming?' Damaso asked.

'Within a month, I hope.'

'By then the others will have reappeared,' said Damaso.

Roque observed the row of little tables with satisfaction. 'They won't show up,' he said, drying his forehead with his sleeve. 'They've been starving the Negro since Saturday and he doesn't want to tell where they are.' He measured Damaso through his glasses blurred with sweat.

'I'm sure he threw them into the river.'

Damaso bit his lips.

'And the two hundred pesos?'

'Them either,' said Roque. 'They only found thirty on him.'

They looked each other in the eye. Damaso could not have explained his impression that the look established between him and Roque a relationship of complicity. That afternoon, from the lavatory, Ana saw him come home dancing like a boxer. She followed him into the room.

'All settled,' said Damaso. 'The old man is so resigned that he ordered new balls. Now it's just a question of waiting until they all forget.'

'And the Negro?'

'That's nothing,' said Damaso, shrugging his shoulders. 'If they don't find the balls they'll have to let him go.'

After the meal, they sat outside the front door and were talking to the neighbors until the loudspeaker at the movie went off. When they went to bed, Damaso was excited.

'A terrific job just occurred to me,' he said.

Ana realized that he'd been mulling over the idea since dusk.

'I'll go from town to town,' Damaso went on. 'I'll steal the billiard balls in one and I'll sell them in the next. Every town has a pool hall.'

'Until they shoot you.'

'Shoot, what kind of shoot?' he said. 'You only see that in the movies.' Planted in the middle of the room, he was choking on his own enthusiasm. Ana began to get undressed, seemingly indifferent, but in reality listening to him with compassionate attention.

'I'm going to buy a row of suits,' said Damaso, pointing with his forefinger at an imaginary closet the length of the wall. 'From here to there. And also fifty pairs of shoes.'

'God willing,' said Ana.

Damaso fixed her with a serious look.

'You're not interested in my affairs,' he said.

'They are very far away from me,' said Ana. She put out the lamp, lay down next to the wall, and added with definite bitterness, 'When you're thirty I'll be forty-seven.'

'Don't be silly,' said Damaso.

He felt his pockets for the matches. 'You won't have to wrestle with any more clothes, either,' he said, a little baffled. Ana gave him a light. She looked at the flame until the match went out, and threw it down. Stretched out in bed Damaso kept talking.

'Do you know what billiard balls are made of?'

Ana didn't answer.

'Out of elephant tusks,' he went on. 'They are so hard to find that it takes a month for them to come. Can you imagine?'

'Go to sleep,' interrupted Ana. 'I have to get up at five.'

Damaso had returned to his natural state. He spent the morning in bed smoking, and after the siesta he began to get ready to go out. At night he listened to the radio broadcast of the baseball championship in the pool hall. He had the ability to forget his projects with as much enthusiasm as he needed to think them up.

'Do you have any money?' he asked his wife on Saturday.

'Eleven pesos,' she answered, adding softly, 'It's the rent.'

'I'll make a deal with you.'

'What?'

'Lend them to me.'

'We have to pay the rent.'

'We'll pay it later.'

Ana shook her head. Damaso grabbed her by the wrist and prevented her from getting up from the table where they had just eaten breakfast.

'It's just for a few days,' he said, petting her arm with distracted tenderness. 'When I sell the balls we'll have enough cash for everything.'

Ana didn't yield.

That night Damaso took her to the movie and didn't take his hand off her shoulder even while he was talking with his friends during intermission. They saw snatches of the movie. When it was over, Damaso was impatient.

'Then I'll have to rob the money,' he said.

Ana shrugged her shoulders. 'I'll club the first person I find,' said Damaso, pushing her through the crowd leaving the movie. 'Then they'll take me to jail for murder.' Ana smiled inwardly. But she remained firm. The following morning, after a stormy night, Damaso got dressed with visible and ominous haste. He passed close to his wife and growled:

'I'm never coming back.'

Ana could not hold back a slight tremor.

'Have a good trip!' she shouted.

After he slammed the door, an empty and endless Sunday began for Damaso. The shiny crockery in the public market, and the brightly dressed women who, with their children, were leaving eight-o'clock Mass, lent a happy note to the plaza, but the air was beginning to stiffen with heat.

He spent the day in the pool hall. A group of men played cards in the morning, and before lunch there was a brief rush of customers. But it was obvious that the establishment had lost its attractiveness. Only at dusk, when the baseball program went on, did it recover a little of its old animation.

After they closed the hall, Damaso found himself with no place to go, in the plaza which now seemed drained. He went down the street parallel to the harbor, following the sound of some happy, distant music. At the end of the street there was an enormous, empty dance hall, decked out in faded paper garlands, and at the back of the hall a band on a wooden platform. A suffocating smell of makeup floated within.

Damaso sat at the counter. When the piece ended, the boy who played the cymbals in the band collected coins among the men who had been dancing. A girl left her partner in the middle of the floor and approached Damaso.

'What's new, Valentino?'

Damaso offered her a seat beside him. The bartender, face powdered and with a carnation on his ear, asked in falsetto:

'What will you have?'

The girl turned toward Damaso.

'What are we drinking?'

'Nothing.'

'It's my treat.'

'That's not it,' said Damaso. 'I'm hungry.'

'Pity,' sighed the bartender. 'With those eyes.'

They went into the dining room at the back of the hall. By the shape of her body, the girl seemed too young, but the crust of powder and rouge, and the lipstick on her lips, made it hard to know her real age. After they ate, Damaso followed her to the room at the back of a dark patio where they could hear the breathing of sleeping animals. The bed was occupied by an infant covered with colored rags. The girl put the rags in a wooden box, laid the infant inside, and then put the box on the floor.

'The mice will eat him,' said Damaso.

'No, they don't,' she said.

She changed her red dress for another with a lower neckline, with big yellow flowers.

'Who is the father?' Damaso asked.

'I haven't the slightest idea,' she said. And then, from the doorway, 'I'll be right back.'

He heard her lock the door. He smoked several cigarettes, stretched out on his back and with his clothes on. The bed-springs vibrated in time to the bass drum. He didn't know at what point he fell asleep. When he awoke, the room seemed bigger in the music's absence.

The girl was getting undressed beside the bed.

'What time is it?'

'Around four,' she said. 'Did the child cry?'

'I don't think so,' said Damaso.

The girl lay down very close to him, scrutinizing him with her eyes turned slightly away while she unbuttoned his shirt. Damaso realized that she had been drinking heavily. He tried to put out the light.

'Leave it on,' she said. 'I love to look in your eyes.'

From dawn on, the room filled with rural noises. The child cried. The girl took him into bed and nursed him, humming a three-note song, until they all fell asleep. Damaso didn't notice that the girl woke up around seven, left the room, and came back without the child.

'Everybody is going down to the harbor,' she said.

Damaso felt as if he hadn't slept more than an hour the whole night.

'What for?'

'To see the Negro who stole the balls,' she said. 'They're taking him away today.'

Damaso lit a cigarette.

'Poor man.' The girl sighed.

'Why poor?' said Damaso. 'Nobody made him into a thief.'

The girl thought for a moment with her head on his chest. In a very low voice she said:

'It wasn't him.'

'Who said?'

'I know it,' she said. 'The night they broke into the pool hall, the Negro was with Gloria, and he spent the whole next day in her room, until around nighttime. Then they came to say they had arrested him in the movie.'

'Gloria can tell the police.'

'The Negro told them that,' she said. 'The Mayor went to Gloria's, turned the room upside down, and said he was going to take her to jail as an accomplice. Finally, it was settled for twenty pesos.'

Damaso got up before eight.

'Stay here,' the girl said. 'I'm going to kill a chicken for lunch.'

Damaso shook the comb into the palm of his hand before putting it in his back pocket. 'I can't,' he said, drawing the girl to him by the wrists. She had washed her face, and she was really very young, with two big black eyes which gave her a helpless look. She held him around the waist.

'Stay here,' she insisted.

'Forever?'

She blushed slightly and drew back.

'Joker,' she said.

Ana was exhausted that morning. But the town's excitement was contagious. Faster than usual, she collected the clothing to wash that week, and went to the harbor to witness the departure of the Negro. An impatient crowd was waiting next to the launches which were ready to shove off. Damaso was there.

Ana prodded him in the kidneys with her forefingers.

'What are you doing here?' asked Damaso, startled.

'I came to see you off,' said Ana.

Damaso rapped on a lamppost with his knuckles.

'Damn you,' he said.

After lighting a cigarette, he threw the empty pack into the river. Ana took another out of her chemise and put it in his shirt pocket. Damaso smiled for the first time.

'You never learn,' he said.

Ana went 'Ha, ha.'

A little later they put the Negro on board. They took him through the middle of the plaza, his wrists tied behind his back with a rope held by a policeman. Two other policemen armed with rifles walked beside him. He was shirtless, his lower lip split open, and one eyebrow swollen, like a boxer. He avoided the crowd's looks with passive dignity. At the door of the pool hall, where the greater part of the crowd had gathered to witness both ends of the show, the owner watched him pass moving his head silently. The rest observed him with a sort of eagerness.

The launch cast off at once. The Negro was on deck, tied hand and foot to an oil drum. When the launch turned around in the middle of the river and whistled for the last time, the Negro's back shone.

'Poor man,' whispered Ana.

'Criminals,' someone near her said. 'A human being can't stand so much sun.'

Damaso located the voice coming from an extraordinarily fat woman, and he began to move toward the plaza. 'You talk too much,' he hissed in Ana's ear. 'Now all you have to do is to shout the whole story.' She accompanied him to the door of the pool hall.

'At least go home and change,' she said when she left him. 'You look like a beggar.'

The event had brought an excited group to the hall. Trying to serve them all, Roque was waiting on several tables at once. Damaso waited until he passed next to him.

'Would you like some help?'

Roque put half a dozen bottles of beer in front of him with glasses upended on the necks.

'Thanks, son.'

Damaso took the bottles to the tables. He took several orders, and kept on taking and bringing bottles until the customers left for lunch. Early in the morning, when he returned to the room, Ana realized that he had been drinking. She took his hand and put it on her belly.

'Feel here,' she said. 'Don't you feel it?'

Damaso gave no sign of enthusiasm.

'He's kicking now,' said Ana. 'He spends all night giving me little kicks inside.'

But he didn't react. Concentrating on himself, he went out very early the next day and didn't return until midnight. A week passed that way. For the few moments he spent in the house, smoking in bed, he avoided conversation. Ana intensified her attentions. On one particular occasion, at the beginning of their life together, he had behaved in the same way, and then she had not known him well enough not to bother him. Astride her in bed, Damaso had punched her and made her bleed.

This time she waited. At night she put a pack of cigarettes next to the lamp, knowing that he could stand hunger and thirst but not the need to smoke. At last, in the middle of July, Damaso returned to the room at dusk. Ana became nervous, thinking that he must be very confused to come looking for her at that hour. They ate in silence. But before going to bed Damaso was dazed and gentle, and out of the blue he said:

'I want to leave.'

'Where to?'

'Anywhere.'

Ana looked around the room. The magazine covers which she herself had cut out and pasted to the walls until they were completely covered with pictures of movie stars were faded and colorless. She had lost count of the men who, from being looked at so much from the bed, had disappeared gradually and taken those colors with them.

'You're bored with me,' she said.

'It's not that,' said Damaso. 'It's this town.'

'It's like every other town.'

'I can't sell the balls,' said Damaso.

'Leave the balls alone,' said Ana. 'As long as God gives me the strength to wrestle with the laundry you won't have to go around taking chances.' And after a pause she added softly:

'I don't know how that business ever occurred to you.'

Damaso finished his cigarette before speaking.

'It was so easy that I can't understand how it never occurred to anyone else,' he said.

'For the money,' admitted Ana. 'But no one would have been stupid enough to steal the balls.'

'I did it without thinking,' Damaso said. 'I was leaving when I saw them behind the counter in their little box, and I thought that it was all too much work to come away emptyhanded.'

'That was your mistake,' said Ana.

Damaso felt relieved. 'And meanwhile the new ones haven't come,' he said. 'They sent word that now they're more expensive, and Roque said he canceled the order.' He lit another cigarette, and while he spoke, he felt that his heart was being freed from some dark preoccupation.

He told her that the owner had decided to sell the pool table. It wasn't worth much. The cloth, torn by the clumsy tricks of learners, had been repaired with different-colored squares and the whole piece needed to be replaced. Meanwhile the hall's customers, who had grown old with billiards, now had no other amusement than the broadcasts of the baseball championship.

'So,' Damaso finished, 'without wanting to, we hurt the whole town.'

'For nothing,' said Ana.

'Next week the championship is over,' said Damaso.

'And that's not the worst of it,' said Ana. 'The worst is the Negro.'

Lying against his shoulder, as in the early days, she knew

what her husband was thinking. She waited until he finished the cigarette. Then, with a cautious voice, she said:

'Damaso.'

'What's the matter?'

'Return them.'

He lit another cigarette.

'That's what I've been thinking for days,' he said. 'But the bitch of it is that I can't figure out how.'

So they decided to leave the balls in a public place. Then Ana thought that while that would solve the problem of the pool hall, it would leave the problem of the Negro unsettled. The police could interpret the find in many ways, without absolving him. Nor did she forget the possibility that the balls might be found by someone who, instead of returning them, would keep them to sell them.

'Well, as long as the thing is going to be done,' concluded Ana, 'it's better to do it right.'

They dug up the balls. Ana wrapped them in newspapers, taking care that the wrapping should not reveal the shape of the contents, and she put them in the trunk.

'We have to wait for the right occasion,' she said.

But they spent weeks waiting for the right occasion. The night of August 20th – two months after the robbery – Damaso found Roque seated behind the counter, shooing the mosquitoes away with a fan. With the radio off, his loneliness seemed more intense.

'I told you,' Roque exclaimed with a certain joy at the prediction come true. 'Business has gone to hell.'

Damaso put a coin in the jukebox. The volume of the music and the machine's play of colors seemed to him a noisy proof of his loyalty. But he had the impression that Roque didn't notice it. Then he pulled up a seat and tried to console him with confused arguments which the proprietor demolished emotionlessly, to the careless rhythm of his fan.

'Nothing can be done about it,' he was saying. 'The baseball championship couldn't last forever.'

'But the balls may show up.'

'They won't show up.'

'The Negro couldn't have eaten them.'

'The police looked everywhere,' said Roque with an exasperating certainty. 'He threw them into the river.'

'A miracle could happen.'

'Forget your illusions, son,' replied Roque. 'Misfortune is like a snail. Do you believe in miracles?'

When he left the place, the movie hadn't yet ended. The loudspeaker's lengthy and broken dialogues resounded in the darkened town, and there was something temporary in the few houses which were still open. Damaso wandered a moment in the direction of the movie. Then he went to the dance hall.

The band was playing for a lone customer who was dancing with two women at once. The others, judiciously seated against the wall seemed to be waiting for the mail. Damaso sat down at a table, made a sign to the bartender to bring him a beer, and drank it from the bottle with brief pauses to breathe, observing as if through a glass the man who was dancing with the two women. He was shorter than they were.

At midnight the women who had been at the movies arrived, pursued by a group of men. Damaso's friend, who was with them, left the others and sat at his table.

Damaso didn't look at her. He had drunk half a dozen beers and kept staring at the man, who now was dancing with three women but without paying attention to them, diverted by the intricate movements of his own feet. He looked happy, and it was evident that he would have been even happier if, in addition to his legs and arms, he had had a tail.

'I don't like that guy,' said Damaso.

'Then don't look at him,' said the girl.

She ordered a drink from the bartender. The dance floor began to fill up with couples, but the man with the three women kept on as if he were alone in the hall. On one turn his eyes met Damaso's and he pressed an even greater effort into his dancing, and showed him a smile with his rabbit's teeth. Damaso stood his look without blinking, until the man got serious and turned his back.

'He thinks he's very happy,' said Damaso.

'He is very happy,' said the girl. 'Every time he comes to town, he picks up the bill for the music, like all the traveling salesmen.'

Damaso averted his eyes, turning them on her.

'Then go with him,' he said. 'Where there's enough for three, there's enough for four.'

Without replying she turned her face toward the dance floor, drinking with slow sips. The pale-yellow dress accented her shyness.

They danced the next set. When it was over, Damaso was smoldering. 'I'm dying of hunger,' the girl said, leading him by the arm toward the counter. 'You have to eat, too.' The happy man was coming in the opposite direction with the three women.

'Listen,' Damaso said to him.

The man smiled at him without stopping. Damaso let go of his companion's arm and blocked his path.

'I don't like your teeth.'

The man blanched, but kept smiling.

'Me neither,' he said.

Before the girl could stop it, Damaso punched him in the face and the man sat down in the middle of the dance floor. None of the customers interfered. The three women hugged Damaso around the waist, shouting, while his companion pushed him toward the back of the hall. The man got up, his face out of joint from the blow. He jumped like a monkey to the center of the dance floor and shouted:

'On with the music!'

Toward two o'clock the hall was almost empty, and the women without customers began to eat. It was hot. The girl brought a dish of rice with beans and fried meat to the table, and ate it all with a spoon. Damaso watched her in a sort of stupor. She held out a spoonful of rice to him.

'Open your mouth.'

Damaso lowered his chin to his chest and shook his head.

'That's for women,' he said. 'We men don't eat.'

He had to rest his hands on the table in order to stand up. When he regained his balance, the bartender was in front of him, arms crossed.

'It comes to nine-eighty,' he said. 'This party's not on the house.'

Damaso pushed him aside.

'I don't like queers,' he said.

The bartender grabbed him by the sleeve but, at a sign from the girl, let him pass, saying:

'You don't know what you're missing.'

Damaso stumbled outside. The mysterious sheen of the river beneath the moon opened a furrow of lucidity in his brain. But it closed immediately. When he saw the door to his room, on the other side of town, Damaso was certain that he had walked in his sleep. He shook his head. In a confused but urgent way he realized that from that moment on he had to watch every one of his movements. He pushed the door carefully to keep the hinges from creaking.

Ana felt him looking in the trunk. She turned toward the wall to avoid the light from the lamp, but then realized that her husband was not getting undressed. A flash of intuition made her sit up in bed. Damaso was next to the trunk, with the package of balls and the flashlight in his hand.

He put his forefinger on his lips.

Ana jumped out of bed. 'You're crazy,' she murmured, running toward the door. She shot the bolt quickly. Damaso put the flashlight in his pants pocket, together with the little knife and some sharpened files, and advanced toward her gripping the package under his arm. Ana leaned her back against the door.

'You won't leave here as long as I'm alive,' she said quietly.

Damaso tried to push her aside. 'Get away,' he said. Ana grabbed the doorjamb with both hands. They looked each other in the eye without blinking. 'You're an ass,' whispered Ana. 'What God gave you in your looks he took away from your brains.' Damaso grabbed her by the hair, twisted her wrist, and made her lower her head; with clenched teeth he said, 'I told you get away.' Ana looked at him out of the corner of her eye, like an ox under the yoke. For a moment she felt invulnerable to pain and stronger than her husband, but he kept twisting her hair until her tears choked her.

'You're going to kill the baby in my belly,' she said.

Damaso dragged, almost carried, her bodily to the bed. When he let her go, she jumped on his back, wrapped her legs and arms around him, and both of them fell on the bed. They had begun to get winded. 'I'll scream,' Ana whispered in his ear. 'If you move I'll scream.' Damaso snorted in rage, hitting her knees with the package of balls. Ana let out a cry and loosened her legs, but fastened herself to his waist to prevent him from reaching the door. Then she began to beg. 'I promise you I'll take them tomorrow myself,' she was saying. 'I'll put them back so no one will notice.' Nearer and nearer to the door, Damaso was hitting her hands with the balls. She would let him go for a moment to get over the pain. Then she would grab him again, and continue begging.

'I can say it was me,' she was saying. 'They can't put me in jail in my condition.'

Damaso shook her off. 'The whole town will see you,' Ana said. 'You're so dumb you don't realize there's a full moon.' She grabbed him again before he got the bolt open. Then, with closed eyes, she pummeled him in the neck and face, almost shouting, 'Animal, animal.' Damaso tried to ward off the blows and she clutched the bolt and took it out of his hands. She threw a blow at his head. Damaso dodged it and the bolt resounded on his shoulder bone as on a pane of glass.

'Bitch!' he shouted.

At that moment he wasn't concerned about not making noise. He hit her on the ear with the back of his fist, and felt the deep cry and heavy impact of her body against the wall, but he didn't look at her. He left the room without closing the door.

Ana stayed on the floor, stupefied by the pain, and waited

for something to happen in her abdomen. They called her from the other side of the wall in a voice which sounded as if it came from beyond the grave. She bit her lips to keep from crying. Then she got up and got dressed. It did not occur to her – as it had not the first time – that Damaso might still be outside the room, telling himself that the plan had failed and waiting for her to come outside shouting. She made the same mistake a second time: instead of pursuing her husband, she put on her shoes, closed the door, and sat down on the bed to wait.

Only when the door closed did Damaso understand that he couldn't go back. The clamor of dogs pursued him to the end of the street, but then there was a ghostly silence. He avoided the sidewalks, trying to escape his own steps, which sounded huge and alien in the sleeping town. He took no precautions until he was in the empty lot at the rear door of the pool hall.

This time he didn't have to make use of the flashlight. The door had been reinforced only at the point of the broken staple. They had taken out a piece of wood the size and shape of a brick, replaced it with new wood, and put the same staple back again. The rest was the same. Damaso pulled on the lock with his left hand, put the end of a file between the legs of the staple that had not been reinforced, and moved the file back and forth like a gearshift lever, with force but without violence, until the wood gave way in a plaintive explosion of rotted splinters. Before he pushed the door, he raised it into line to lessen the noise of its scraping on the bricks of the floor. He opened it just halfway. Finally he took off his shoes, slid them inside with the package of balls, and, crossing himself, entered the room flooded in moonlight.

Right in front of him there was a dark passageway crammed with bottles and empty boxes. Farther on, beneath the flood of light from the glass skylight, was the billiard table, and then the back of the cabinets, and finally the little tables and the chairs piled up against the back of the front door. Everything was the same as the first time, except the flood of moonlight and the crispness of the silence. Damaso, who until that moment had had to subdue his nervous system, felt a strange fascination.

This time he wasn't careful of the loose bricks. He blocked the door with his shoes and, after crossing the flood of light, lit the flashlight to look for the little box the balls belonged in behind the counter. He acted without caution. Moving the flashlight from left to right, he saw a pile of dusty jars, a pair of stirrups with spurs, a rolled-up shirt soiled with motor oil, and then the little box in the same spot where he had left it. But he didn't stop the beam of light until the end of the counter. There was the cat.

The animal looked at him without mystery, against the light. Damaso kept the light on him until he remembered with a slight shiver that he had never seen him in the place during the day. He moved the flash forward, saying, 'Scat,' but the animal remained impassive. Then there was a kind of silent detonation inside his head, and the cat disappeared completely from his memory. When he realized what was happening, he had already dropped the flashlight and was hugging the package of balls against his chest. The room was lit up.

'Well!'

He recognized Roque's voice. He stood up slowly, feeling a terrible fatigue in his kidneys. Roque approached from the rear of the room, in his underwear and with an iron bar in his hand, still dazzled by the brightness. There was a hammock hanging behind the bottles and the empty boxes, very near the spot Damaso had passed when he came in. This also was different from the first time.

When he was less than thirty feet away, Roque gave a little hop and got on his guard. Damaso hid the hand with the package behind him. Roque wrinkled his nose and thrust out his head, trying to recognize him without his glasses.

'You!' he exclaimed.

Damaso felt as if something infinite had ended at last. Roque lowered the bar and approached with his mouth open. Without glasses and without his false teeth, he looked like a woman.

'What are you doing here?'

'Nothing,' said Damaso

He changed his position with an imperceptible movement of his body.

'What do you have there?' asked Roque.

Damaso stepped back. 'Nothing,' he said. Roque reddened and began to tremble. 'What do you have there!' he shouted, stepping forward with the bar raised. Damaso gave him the package. Roque took it with his left hand, still on guard, and examined it with his fingers. Only then did he understand.

'It can't be,' he said.

He was so perplexed that he put the bar on the counter and seemed to forget Damaso while he was opening the package. He contemplated the balls silently.

'I came to put them back,' said Damaso.

'Of course,' said Roque.

Damaso felt limp. The alcohol had left him completely, and there was only a gravelly sediment left on his tongue, and a confused feeling of loneliness. 'So that was the miracle,' said Roque, wrapping up the package. 'I can't believe you could be so stupid.' When he raised his head, he had changed his expression.

'And the two hundred pesos?'

'There was nothing in the drawer,' said Damaso

Roque looked at him thoughtfully, chewing emptily, and then smiled. 'There was nothing,' he repeated several times. 'So there was nothing.' He grasped the bar again, saying:

'Well, we're going to tell the Mayor this story right now.'

Damaso dried the sweat of his hands on his pants.

'You know there was nothing.'

Roque kept smiling.

'There were two hundred pesos,' he said. 'And now they're going to take them out of your hide, not so much for being a thief as for being a fool.'

Balthazar's Marvelous Afternoon

The cage was finished. Balthazar hung it under the eave, from force of habit, and when he finished lunch everyone was already saying that it was the most beautiful cage in the world. So many people came to see it that a crowd formed in front of the house, and Balthazar had to take it down and close the shop.

'You have to shave,' Ursula, his wife, told him. 'You look like a Capuchin.'

'It's bad to shave after lunch,' said Balthazar.

He had two weeks' growth, short, hard, and bristly hair like the mane of a mule, and the general expression of a frightened boy. But it was a false expression. In February he was thirty; he had been living with Ursula for four years, without marrying her and without having children, and life had given him many reasons to be on guard but none to be frightened. He did not even know that for some people the cage he had just made was the most beautiful one in the world. For him, accustomed to making cages since childhood, it had been hardly any more difficult than the others.

'Then rest for a while,' said the woman. 'With that beard you can't show yourself anywhere.'

While he was resting, he had to get out of his hammock several times to show the cage to the neighbors. Ursula had paid little attention to it until then. She was annoyed because her husband had neglected the work of his carpenter's shop to devote himself entirely to the cage, and for two weeks had slept poorly, turning over and muttering incoherencies and he hadn't thought of shaving. But her annoyance dissolved in the face of the finished cage. When Balthazar woke up from his nap, she had ironed his pants and a shirt; she had put them on a chair near the hammock and had carried the cage to the dining table. She regarded it in silence.

'How much will you charge?' she asked.

'I don't know,' Balthazar answered. 'I'm going to ask for thirty pesos to see if they'll give me twenty.'

'Ask for fifty,' said Ursula. 'You've lost a lot of sleep in these two weeks. Furthermore, it's rather large. I think it's the biggest cage I've ever seen in my life.'

Balthazar began to shave.

'Do you think they'll give me fifty pesos?'

'That's nothing for Mr Chepe Montiel, and the cage is worth it,' said Ursula. 'You should ask for sixty.'

The house lay in the stifling shadow. It was the first week of April and the heat seemed less bearable because of the chirping of the cicadas. When he finished dressing, Balthazar opened the door to the patio to cool off the house, and a group of children entered the dining room.

The news had spread. Dr Octavio Giraldo, an old physician, happy with life but tired of his profession, thought about Balthazar's cage while he was eating lunch with his invalid wife. On the inside terrace, where they put the table on hot days, there were many flowerpots and two cages with canaries. His wife liked birds, and she liked them so much that she hated cats because they could eat them up. Thinking about her, Dr Giraldo went to see a patient that afternoon, and when he returned he went by Balthazar's house to inspect the cage.

There were a lot of people in the dining room. The cage was on display on the table: with its enormous dome of wire, three stories inside, with passageways and compartments especially for eating and sleeping and swings in the space set aside for the birds' recreation, it seemed like a small-scale model of a gigantic ice factory. The doctor inspected it carefully, without touching it, thinking that in effect the cage was better than its reputation, and much more beautiful than any he had ever dreamed of for his wife.

'This is a flight of the imagination,' he said. He sought out Balthazar among the group of people and, fixing his paternal eyes on him, added, 'You would have been an extraordinary architect.'

Balthazar blushed.

'Thank you,' he said.

'It's true,' said the doctor. He was smoothly and delicately fat, like a woman who had been beautiful in her youth, and he had delicate hands. His voice seemed like that of a priest speaking Latin. 'You wouldn't even need to put birds in it,' he said, making the cage turn in front of the audience's eyes as if he were auctioning it off. 'It would be enough to hang it in the trees so it could sing by itself.' He put it back on the table, thought a moment, looking at the cage, and said:

'Fine, then I'll take it.'

'It's sold,' said Ursula.

'It belongs to the son of Mr Chepe Montiel,' said Balthazar. 'He ordered it specially.'

The doctor adopted a respectful attitude.

'Did he give you the design?'

'No,' said Balthazar. 'He said he wanted a large cage, like this one, for a pair of troupials.'

The doctor looked at the cage.

'But this isn't for troupials.'

'Of course it is, Doctor,' said Balthazar, approaching the table. The children surrounded him. 'The measurements are carefully calculated,' he said, pointing to the different compartments with his forefinger. Then he struck the dome with his knuckles, and the cage filled with resonant chords.

'It's the strongest wire you can find, and each joint is soldered outside and in,' he said.

'It's even big enough for a parrot,' interrupted one of the children.

'That it is,' said Balthazar.

The doctor turned his head.

'Fine, but he didn't give you the design,' he said. 'He gave you no exact specifications, aside from making it a cage big enough for troupials. Isn't that right?'

'That's right,' said Balthazar.

'Then there's no problem,' said the doctor. 'One thing is a cage big enough for troupials, and another is this cage. There's no proof that this one is the one you were asked to make.'

'It's this very one,' said Balthazar, confused. 'That's why I made it.'

The doctor made an impatient gesture.

'You could make another one,' said Ursula, looking at her husband. And then, to the doctor: 'You're not in any hurry.'

'I promised it to my wife for this afternoon,' said the doctor.

'I'm very sorry, Doctor,' said Balthazar, 'but I can't sell you something that's sold already.'

The doctor shrugged his shoulders. Drying the sweat from his neck with a handkerchief, he contemplated the cage silently with the fixed, unfocused gaze of one who looks at a ship which is sailing away.

'How much did they pay you for it?'

Balthazar sought out Ursula's eyes without replying.

'Sixty pesos,' she said.

The doctor kept looking at the cage. 'It's very pretty.' He sighed. 'Extremely pretty.' Then, moving toward the door, he began to fan himself energetically, smiling, and the trace of that episode disappeared forever from his memory.

'Montiel is very rich,' he said.

In truth, José Montiel was not as rich as he seemed, but he would have been capable of doing anything to become so. A few blocks from there, in a house crammed with equipment, where no one had ever smelled a smell that couldn't be sold, he remained indifferent to the news of the cage. His wife, tortured by an obsession with death, closed the doors and windows after lunch and lay for two hours with her eyes opened to the shadow of the room, while José Montiel took his siesta. The clamor of many voices surprised her there. Then she opened the door to the living room and found a crowd in front of the house, and Balthazar with the cage in the middle of the crowd, dressed in white, freshly shaved, with that expression of decorous candor with which the poor approach the houses of the wealthy.

'What a marvelous thing!' José Montiel's wife exclaimed, with a radiant expression, leading Balthazar inside. 'I've never seen anything like it in my life,' she said, and added, annoyed by the crowd which piled up at the door:

'But bring it inside before they turn the living room into a grandstand.'

Balthazar was no stranger to José Montiel's house. On different occasions, because of his skill and forthright way of dealing, he had been called in to do minor carpentry jobs. But he never felt at ease among the rich. He used to think about them, about their ugly and argumentative wives, about their tremendous surgical operations, and he always experienced a feeling of pity. When he entered their houses, he couldn't move without dragging his feet.

'Is Pepe home?' he asked.

He had put the cage on the dining-room table.

'He's at school,' said José Montiel's wife. 'But he shouldn't be long,' and she added, 'Montiel is taking a bath.'

In reality, José Montiel had not had time to bathe. He was giving himself an urgent alcohol rub, in order to come out and see what was going on. He was such a cautious man that he slept without an electric fan so he could watch over the noises of the house while he slept.

'Adelaide!' he shouted. 'What's going on?'

'Come and see what a marvelous thing!' his wife shouted.

José Montiel, obese and hairy, his towel draped around his neck, appeared at the bedroom window.

'What is that?'

'Pepe's cage,' said Balthazar.

His wife looked at him perplexedly.

'Whose?'

'Pepe's,' replied Balthazar. And then, turning toward José Montiel, 'Pepe ordered it.'

Nothing happened at that instant, but Balthazar felt as if someone had just opened the bathroom door on him. José Montiel came out of the bedroom in his underwear.

'Pepe!' he shouted.

'He's not back,' whispered his wife, motionless.

Pepe appeared in the doorway. He was about twelve and had the same curved eyelashes and was as quietly pathetic as his mother.

'Come here,' José Montiel said to him. 'Did you order this?'

The child lowered his head. Grabbing him by the hair, José Montiel forced Pepe to look him in the eye.

'Answer me.'

The child bit his lip without replying.

'Montiel,' whispered his wife.

José Montiel let the child go and turned toward Balthazar in a fury. 'I'm very sorry, Balthazar,' he said. 'But you should have consulted me before going on. Only to you would it occur to contract with a minor.' As he spoke, his face recovered its serenity. He lifted the cage without looking at it and gave it to Balthazar.

'Take it away at once, and try to sell it to whomever you can,' he said. 'Above all, I beg you not to argue with me.' He patted him on the back and explained, 'The doctor has forbidden me to get angry.'

The child had remained motionless, without blinking, until Balthazar looked at him uncertainly with the cage in his hand. Then he emitted a guttural sound, like a dog's growl, and threw himself on the floor screaming.

José Montiel looked at him, unmoved, while the mother tried to pacify him. 'Don't even pick him up,' he said. 'Let him break his head on the floor, and then put salt and lemon on it so he can rage to his heart's content.' The child was shrieking tearlessly while his mother held him by the wrists.

'Leave him alone,' José Montiel insisted.

Balthazar observed the child as he would have observed the

death throes of a rabid animal. It was almost four o'clock. At that hour, at his house, Ursula was singing a very old song and cutting slices of onion.

'Pepe,' said Balthazar.

He approached the child, smiling, and held the cage out to him. The child jumped up, embraced the cage which was almost as big as he was, and stood looking at Balthazar through the wirework without knowing what to say. He hadn't shed one tear.

'Balthazar,' said José Montiel softly. 'I told you already to take it away.'

'Give it back,' the woman ordered the child.

'Keep it,' said Balthazar. And then, to José Montiel: 'After all, that's what I made it for.'

José Montiel followed him into the living room.

'Don't be foolish, Balthazar,' he was saying, blocking his path. 'Take your piece of furniture home and don't be silly. I have no intention of paying you a cent.'

'It doesn't matter,' said Balthazar. 'I made it expressly as a gift for Pepe. I didn't expect to charge anything for it.'

As Balthazar made his way through the spectators who were blocking the door, José Montiel was shouting in the middle of the living room. He was very pale his eyes were beginning to get red.

'Idiot!' he was shouting. 'Take your trinket out of here. The last thing we need is for some nobody to give orders in my house. Son of a bitch!'

In the pool hall, Balthazar was received with an ovation. Until that moment, he thought that he had made a better cage than ever before, that he'd had to give it to the son of José Montiel so he wouldn't keep crying, and that none of these things was particularly important. But then he realized that all of this had a certain importance for many people, and he felt a little excited.

'So they gave you fifty pesos for the cage.'

'Sixty,' said Balthazar.

'Score one for you,' someone said. 'You're the only one

who has managed to get such a pile of money out of Mr Chepe Montiel. We have to celebrate.'

They bought him a beer, and Balthazar responded with a round for everybody. Since it was the first time he had ever been out drinking, by dusk he was completely drunk, and he was talking about a fabulous project of a thousand cages, at sixty pesos each, and then of a million cages, till he had sixty million pesos. 'We have to make a lot of things to sell to the rich before they die,' he was saying, blind drunk. 'All of them are sick, and they're going to die. They're so screwed up they can't even get angry any more.' For two hours he was paying for the jukebox, which played without interruption. Everybody toasted Balthazar's health, good luck, and fortune, and the death of the rich, but at mealtime they left him alone in the pool hall.

Ursula had waited for him until eight, with a dish of fried meat covered with slices of onion. Someone had told her that her husband was in the pool hall, delirious with happiness, buying beers for everyone, but she didn't believe it, because Balthazar had never got drunk. When she went to bed, almost at midnight Balthazar was in a lighted room where there were little tables, each with four chairs, and an outdoor dance floor, where the plovers were walking around. His face was smeared with rouge, and since he couldn't take one more step, he thought he wanted to lie down with two women in the same bed. He had spent so much that he had had to leave his watch in pawn, with the promise to pay the next day. A moment later, spread-eagled in the street, he realized that his shoes were being taken off, but he didn't want to abandon the happiest day of his life. The women who passed on their way to five-o'clock Mass didn't dare look at him, thinking he was dead.

Montiel's Widow

When José Montiel died, everyone felt avenged except his widow; but it took several hours for everyone to believe that he had indeed died. Many continued to doubt it after seeing the corpse in the sweltering room, crammed along with pillows and linen sheets into a yellow coffin, with sides as rounded as a melon. He was very closely shaved, dressed in white, with patent-leather boots, and he looked so well that he had never seemed as alive as at that moment. It was the same Mr Chepe Montiel as was present every Sunday at eight-o'clock Mass, except that instead of his riding quirt he had a crucifix in his hands. It took screwing the lid on the coffin and walling him up in the showy family mausoleum for the whole town to become convinced that he wasn't playing dead.

After the burial, the only thing which seemed incredible to everyone except his widow was that José Montiel had died a natural death. While everyone had been hoping he would be shot in the back in an ambush, his widow was certain she would see him die an old man in his bed, having confessed, and painlessly, like a modern-day saint. She was mistaken in only a few details. José Montiel died in his hammock, the second of August, 1951, at two in the afternoon, as a result of a fit of anger which the doctor had forbidden. But his wife also was hoping that the whole town would attend the funeral and that the house would be too small to hold all the flowers. Nevertheless only the members of his own party and of his religious brotherhood attended, and the only wreaths they received were those from the municipal government. His son, from his consular post in Germany, and his two daughters, from Paris, sent three-page telegrams. One could see that they had written them standing up, with the plentiful ink of the telegraph office, and that they had torn up many telegram forms before finding twenty dollars' worth of words. None of them promised to come back. That night, at the age of sixty-two, while crying on the pillow upon which the head of the man who had made her happy had rested, the widow of Montiel knew for the first time the taste of resentment. I'll lock myself up forever, she was thinking. For me, it is as if they had put me in the same box as José Montiel. I don't want to know anything more about this world.

She was sincere, that fragile woman, lacerated by superstition, married at twenty by her parents' will to the only suitor they had allowed her to see at less than thirty feet; she had never been in direct contact with reality. Three days after they took her husband's body out of the house, she understood through her tears that she ought to pull herself together, but she could not find the direction of her new life. She had to begin at the beginning.

Among the innumerable secrets José Montiel had taken with him to the grave was the combination of the safe. The Mayor took on the problem. He ordered the safe put in the patio, against the wall, and two policemen fired their rifles at the lock. All morning long the widow heard from the bedroom the muffled reports successively ordered by the Mayor's shouts.

That's the last straw, she thought. Five years spent praying to God to end the shooting, and now I have to thank them for shooting in my house.

That day, she made a concerted effort to summon death, but no one replied. She was beginning to fall asleep when a tremendous explosion shook the foundations of the house. They had had to dynamite the safe.

Montiel's widow heaved a sigh. October was interminable with its swampy rains, and she felt lost, sailing without direction in the chaotic and fabulous hacienda of José

Montiel. Mr Carmichael, an old and diligent friend of the family, had taken charge of the estate. When at last she faced the concrete fact that her husband had died, Montiel's widow came out of the bedroom to take care of the house. She stripped it of all decoration, had the furniture covered in mourning colors, and put funeral ribbons on the portraits of the dead man which hung on all the walls. In the two months after the funeral, she had acquired the habit of biting her nails. One day – her eyes reddened and swollen from crying so much – she realized that Mr Carmichael was entering the house with an open umbrella.

'Close that umbrella, Mr Carmichael,' she told him. 'After all the misfortune we've had, all we need is for you to come into the house with your umbrella open.'

Mr Carmichael put the umbrella in the corner. He was an old Negro, with shiny skin, dressed in white, and with little slits made with a knife in his shoes to relieve the pressure of his bunions.

'It's only while it's drying.'

For the first time since her husband died, the widow opened the window.

'So much misfortune and, in addition, this winter,' she murmured biting her nails. 'It seems as though it will never clear up.'

'It won't clear up today or tomorow,' said the executor. 'Last night my bunions wouldn't let me sleep.'

She trusted the atmospheric predictions of Mr Carmichael's bunions. She contemplated the desolate little plaza, the silent houses whose doors did not open to witness the funeral of José Montiel, and then she felt desperate, with her nails, with her limitless lands, and with the infinite number of obligations which she inherited from her husband and which she would never manage to understand.

'The world is all wrong,' she said, sobbing.

Those who visited her in those days had many reasons to think she had gone mad. But she was never more lucid than then. Since before the political slaughter began, she had spent the sad October mornings in front of the window in her room, sympathizing with the dead and thinking that if God had not rested on Sunday He would have had time to finish the world properly. 'He should have used that day to tie up a few of the loose ends,' she used to say. 'After all, He had all eternity to rest.' The only difference, after the death of her husband, was that then she had a concrete reason for harboring such dark thoughts.

Thus, while Montiel's widow ate herself up in desperation, Mr Carmichael tried to prevent the shipwreck. Things weren't going well. Free of the threat of José Montiel, who had monopolized local business through terror, the town was taking reprisals. Waiting for the customers who never came, the milk went sour in the jugs lined up in the patio, and the honey spoiled in its combs, and the cheese fattened worms in the dark cabinets of the cheesehouse. In his mausoleum adorned with electric-light bulbs and imitation-marble arch-angels, José Montiel was paying for six years of murders and oppression. No one in the history of the country had got so rich in so short a time. When the first Mayor of the dictator-ship arrived in town, José Montiel was a discreet partisan of all regimes who had spent half of his life in his underwear seated in front of his rice mill. At one time he enjoyed a certain reputation as a lucky man, and a good believer, because he promised out loud to give the Church a life-size image of Saint Joseph if he won the lottery, and two weeks later he won himself a fat prize and kept his promise. The first time he was seen to wear shoes was when the new Mayor, a brutish, underhanded police sergeant, arrived with express orders to liquidate the opposition. José Montiel began by being his confidential informer. That modest businessman, whose fat man's quiet humor never awakened the least uneasiness, segregated his enemies into rich and poor. The police shot down the poor in the public square. The rich were given a period of twenty-four hours to get out of town. Planning the massacre, José Montiel was closeted together with the Mayor in his stifling office for days on end, while his wife was sympathizing with the dead. When the Mayor left the office, she would block her husband's way. 'That man is a murderer,' she would tell him. 'Use your influence with the government to get them to take that beast away; he's not going to leave a single human being in town alive.' And José Montiel, so busy those days, put her aside without really looking at her, saying, 'Don't be such a fool.' In reality, his business was not the killing of the poor but the expulsion of the rich. After the Mayor riddled their doors with gunfire and gave them their twenty-four hours to get out of town, José Montiel bought their lands and cattle from them for a price which he himself set. 'Don't be silly,' his wife told him. 'You'll ruin yourself helping them so that they won't die of hunger someplace else, and they will never thank you.' And José Montiel, who now didn't even have time to smile, brushed her aside, saying, 'Go to your kitchen and don't bother me so much.' At this rate, in less than a year the opposition was liquidated, and José Montiel was the richest and most powerful man in town. He sent his daughters to Paris, found a consular post in Germany for his son, and devoted himself to consolidating his empire. But he didn't live to enjoy even six years of his outrageous wealth.

After the first anniversary of his death, the widow heard the stairs creak only with the arrival of bad news. Someone always came at dusk. 'Again the bandits,' they used to say. 'Yesterday they made off with a herd of fifty heifers.' Motionless in her rocker, biting her nails, Montiel's widow fed on nothing but resentment.

'I told you José Montiel,' she was saying, talking to herself. 'This is an unappreciative town. You are still warm in your grave, and already everyone has turned their backs on us.'

No one came to the house again. The only human being whom she saw in those interminable months when it did not stop raining was the persistent Mr Carmichael, who never entered the house with his umbrella closed. Things were going no better. Mr Carmichael had written several letters to José Montiel's son. He suggested that it would be convenient if he came to take charge of affairs, and he even allowed himself to make some personal observations about the health of the widow. He always received evasive answers. At last, the son of José Montiel replied that frankly he didn't dare return for fear he would be shot. Then Mr Carmichael went up to the widow's bedroom and had to confess to her that she was ruined.

'Better that way,' she said. 'I'm up to here with cheese and flies. If you want, take what you need and let me die in peace.'

Her only contacts with the world, from then on, were the letters which she wrote to her daughters at the end of very month. 'This is a blighted town,' she told them. 'Stay there forever, and don't worry about me. I am happy knowing that you are happy.' Her daughters took turns answering her. Their letters were always happy, and one could see that they had been written in warm, well-lit places, and that the girls saw themselves reflected in many mirrors when they stopped to think. They didn't wish to return either. 'This is civiliz- ation,' they would say. 'There, on the other hand, it's not a good atmosphere for us. It's impossible to live in a country so savage that people are killed for political reasons.' Reading the letters, Montiel's widow felt better, and she nodded her head in agreement at every phrase.

On a certain occasion, her daughters wrote her about the butcher shops of Paris. They told her about the pink pigs that were killed there and then hung up whole in the doorways, decorated with wreaths and garlands of flowers. At the end of the letter, a hand different from her daughters' had added, 'Imagine! They put the biggest and prettiest carnation in the pig's ass.'

Reading that phrase, for the first time in two years Montiel's widow smiled. She went up to her bedroom without turning out the lights in the house and, before lying down, turned the electric fan over against the wall. Then, from the night-table drawer she took some scissors, a can of Band-Aids, and a rosary, and she bandaged the nail of her right thumb, which was irritated by her biting. Then she began to pray, but at the second mystery she put the rosary into her left hand, because she couldn't feel the beads through the bandage. For a moment she heard the vibration of distant thunder. Then she fell asleep with her head bent on her breast. The hand with the rosary fell to her side, and then she saw Big Mama in the patio, with a white sheet and a comb in her lap, squashing lice with her thumbnails. She asked her:

'When am I going to die?'

Big Mama raised her head.

'When the tiredness begins in your arm.'

One Day After Saturday

The trouble began in July, when Rebecca, an embittered widow who lived in an immense house with two galleries and nine bedrooms, discovered that the screens were torn as if they had been stoned from the street. She made the first discovery in her bedroom and thought that she must speak to Argenida, her servant and confidante since her husband died. Later, moving things around (for a long time Rebecca had done nothing but move things around), she noticed that not only the screens in her bedroom but those in all the rest of the house were torn, too. The widow had an academic sense of authority, inherited perhaps from her paternal great-grand-father, a creole who in the War of Independence had fought on the side of the Royalists and later made an arduous journey to Spain with the sole purpose of visiting the palace which Charles III built in San Ildefonso. So that when she discovered the state of the other screens, she thought no more about speaking to Argenida about it but, rather, put on her straw hat with the tiny velvet flowers and went to the town hall to make a report about the attack. But when she got there, she saw that the Mayor himself, shirtless, hairy, and with a solidity which seemed bestial to her, was busy repairing the town hall screens, torn like her own.

Rebecca burst into the dirty and cluttered office, and the first thing she saw was a pile of dead birds on the desk. But she was disconcerted, in part by the heat and in part by the indignation which the destruction of her screens had produced in her, so that she did not have time to shudder at the unheard-of spectacle of the dead birds on the desk. Nor was she scandalized by the evidence of authority degraded, at the top of a stairway, repairing the metal threads of the window with a roll of screening and a screwdriver. She was not thinking now of any other dignity than her own, mocked by her own screens, and her absorption prevented her even from connecting the windows of her house with those of the town hall. She planted herself with discreet solemnity two steps inside the door and, leaning on the long ornate handle of her parasol, said:

'I have to register a complaint.'

From the top of the stairway, the Mayor turned his head, flushed from the heat. He showed no emotion before the gratuitous presence of the widow in his office. With gloomy nonchalance he continued untacking the ruined screen, and asked from up above:

'What is the trouble?'

'The boys from the neighborhood broke my screens.'

The Mayor took another look at her. He examined her carefully, from the elegant little velvet flowers to her shoes the color of old silver, and it was as if he were seeing her for the first time in his life. He descended with great economy of movement, without taking his eyes off her, and when he reached the bottom, he rested one hand on his belt, motioned with the screwdriver toward the desk, and said:

'It's not the boys, Señora. It's the birds.'

And it was then that she connected the dead birds on the desk with the man at the top of the stairs, and with the broken screens of her bedrooms. She shuddered, imagining all the bedrooms in her house full of dead birds.

'The birds!' she exclaimed.

'The birds,' the Mayor concurred. 'It's strange you haven't noticed, since we've had this problem with the birds breaking windows and dying inside the houses for three days.'

When she left the town hall, Rebecca felt ashamed. And a little resentful of Argenida, who dragged all the town gossip into her house and who nevertheless had not spoken to her about the birds. She opened her parasol, dazzled by the brightness of an impending August, and while she walked along the stifling and deserted street she had the impression that the bedrooms of all the houses were giving off a strong and penetrating stench of dead birds.

This was at the end of July, and never in the history of the town had it been so hot. But the inhabitants, alarmed by the death of the birds, did not notice that. Even though the strange phenomenon had not seriously affected the town's activities, the majority were held in suspense by it at the beginning of August. A majority among whom was not numbered His Reverence, Anthony Isabel of the Holy Sacrament of the Altar Castañeda y Montero, the bland parish priest who, at the age of ninety-four, assured people that he had seen the devil on three occasions, and that nevertheless he had only seen two dead birds, without attributing the least importance to them. He found the first one in the sacristy, one Tuesday after Mass, and thought it had been dragged in there by some neighborhood cat. He found the other one on Wednesday, in the veranda of the parish house, and he pushed it with the point of his boot into the street, thinking, Cats shouldn't exist.

But on Friday, when he arrived at the railroad station, he found a third dead bird on the bench he chose to sit down on. It was like a lightning stroke inside him when he grabbed the body by its little legs; he raised it to eye level, turned it over, examined it, and thought astonishedly, Gracious, this is the third one I've found this week.

From that moment on he began to notice what was happening in the town, but in a very inexact way, for Father Anthony Isabel, in part because of his age and in part also because he swore he had seen the devil on three occasions (something which seemed to the town just a bit out of place), was considered by his parishioners as a good man, peaceful and obliging, but with his head habitually in the clouds. He noticed that something was happening with the birds, but even then he didn't believe that it was so important as to deserve a sermon. He was the first one who experienced the smell. He smelled it Friday night, when he woke up alarmed, his light slumber interrupted by a nauseating stench, but he didn't know whether to attribute it to a nightmare or to a new and original trick of the devil's to disturb his sleep. He sniffed all around him, and turned over in bed, thinking that that experience would serve him for a sermon. It could be, he thought, a dramatic sermon on the ability of Satan to infiltrate the human heart through any of the five senses.

When he strolled around the porch the next day before Mass, he heard someone speak for the first time about the dead birds. He was thinking about the sermon, Satan, and the sins which can be committed through the olfactory sense when he heard someone say that the bad nocturnal odor was due to the birds collected during the week; and in his head a confused hodgepodge of evangelical cautions, evil odors, and dead birds took shape. So that on Sunday he had to improvise a long paragraph on Charity which he himself did not understand very well, and he forgot forever about the relations between the devil and the five senses.

Nevertheless, in some very distant spot in his thinking, those experiences must have remained lurking. That always happened to him, not only in the seminary, more than seventy years before, but in a very particular way after he passed ninety. At the seminary, one very bright afternoon when there was a heavy downpour with no thunder, he was reading a selection from Sophocles in the original. When the rain was over, he looked through the window at the tired field, the newly washed afternoon, and forgot entirely about Greek theater and the classics, which he did not distinguish but, rather, called in a general way, 'the little ancients of old.' One rainless afternoon, perhaps thirty or forty years later, he was crossing the cobblestone plaza of a town which he was visiting and, without intending to, recited the stanza from Sophocles which he had been reading in the seminary. That same week, he had a long conversation about 'the little ancients of old' with the apostolic deputy, a talkative and impressionable old man, who was fond of certain complicated puzzles which he claimed to have invented and which became popular years later under the name of crosswords.

That interview permitted him to recover at one stroke all his old heartfelt love for the Greek classics. At Christmas of that year he received a letter. And if it were not for the fact that by that time he had acquired the solid prestige of being exaggeratedly imaginative, daring in his interpretations, and a little foolish in his sermons, on that occasion they would have made him a bishop.

But he had buried himself in the town long before the War of 1885, and at the time when the birds began dying in the bedrooms it had been a long while since they had asked for him to be replaced by a younger priest, especially when he claimed to have seen the devil. From that time on they began not paying attention to him, something which he didn't notice in a very clear way in spite of still being able to decipher the tiny characters of his breviary without glasses.

He had always been a man of regular habits. Small, insignificant, with pronounced and solid bones and calm gestures, and a soothing voice for conversation but too soothing for the pulpit. He used to stay in his bedroom until lunchtime daydreaming, carelessly stretched out in a canvas chair and wearing nothing but his long twill trousers with the bottoms tied at the ankles.

He didn't do anything except say Mass. Twice a week he sat in the confessional, but for many years no one confessed. He simply thought that his parishioners were losing the faith because of modern customs, and that's why he would have thought it a very opportune occurrence to have seen the devil on three occasions, although he knew that people gave very little credence to his words and although he was aware that he was not very convincing when he spoke about those experiences. For himself it would have been a surprise to discover that he was dead, not only during the last five years but also in those extraordinary moments when he found the first two birds. When he found the third, however, he came back to life a little, so that in the last few days he was thinking with appreciable frequency about the dead bird on the station bench.

He lived ten steps from the church in a small house without screens, with a veranda toward the street and two rooms which served as office and bedroom. He considered, perhaps in his moments of less lucidity, that it is possible to achieve happiness on earth when it is not very hot, and this idea made him a little confused. He liked to wander through meta-physical obstacle courses. That was what he was doing when he used to sit in the bedroom every morning, with the door ajar, his eyes closed and his muscles tensed. However, he himself did not realize that he had become so subtle in his thinking that for at least three years in his meditative moments he was no longer thinking about anything.

At twelve o'clock sharp a boy crossed the corridor with a sectioned tray which contained the same things every day: bone broth with a piece of yucca, white rice, meat prepared without onion, fried banana or a corn muffin, and a few lentils which Father Anthony Isabel of the Holy Sacrament of the Altar had never tasted.

The boy put the tray next to the chair where the priest sat, but the priest didn't open his eyes until he no longer heard steps in the corridor. Therefore, in town they thought that the Father took his siesta before lunch (a thing which seemed exceedingly nonsensical) when the truth was that he didn't even sleep normally at night.

Around that time his habits had become less complicated, almost primitive. He lunched without moving from his canvas chair, without taking the food from the tray, without using the dishes or the fork or the knife, but only the same spoon with which he drank his soup. Later he would get up, throw a little water on his head, put on his white soutane dotted with great square patches, and go to the railroad station precisely at the hour when the rest of the town was lying down for its siesta. He had been covering this route for several months, murmur-ing the prayer which he himself had made up the last time the devil had appeared to him.

One Saturday – nine days after the dead birds began to fall – Father Anthony Isabel of the Holy Sacrament of the Altar was going to the station when a dying bird fell at his feet, directly in front of Rebecca's house. A flash of intuition exploded in his head, and he realized that this bird, contrary to the others, might be saved. He took it in his hands and knocked at Rebecca's door at the moment when she was unhooking her bodice to take her siesta.

In her bedroom, the widow heard the knocking and instinctively turned her glance toward the screens. No bird had got into that bedroom for two days. But the screen was still torn. She had thought it a useless expense to have it repaired as long as the invasion of birds, which kept her nerves on edge, continued. Above the hum of the electric fan, she heard the knocking at the door and remembered with impatience that Argenida was taking a siesta in the bedroom at the end of the corridor. It didn't even occur to her to wonder who might be imposing on her at that hour. She hooked up her bodice again, pushed open the screen door, and walked the length of the corridor, stiff and straight, then crossed the living room crowded with furniture and decorative objects and, before opening the door, saw through the metal screen that there stood taciturn Father Anthony Isabel, with his eyes closed and a bird in his hands. Before she opened the door, he said, 'If we give him a little water and then put him under a dish, I'm sure he'll get well.' And when she opened the door, Rebecca thought she'd collapse from fear.

He didn't stay there for more than five minutes. Rebecca thought that it was she who had cut short the meeting. But in reality it had been the priest. If the widow had thought about it at that moment, she would have realized that the priest, in the thirty years he had been living in the town, had never stayed more than five minutes in her house. It seemed to him that amid the profusion of decorations in the living room the concupiscent spirit of the mistress of the house showed itself clearly, in spite of her being related, however distantly, but as everyone was aware, to the Bishop. Furthermore, there had been a legend (or a story) about Rebecca's family which surely, the Father thought, had not reached the episcopal palace, in spite of the fact that Colonel Aureliano Buendía, a cousin of the widow's whom she considered lacking in family affection, had once sworn that the Bishop had not come to the town in this century in order to avoid visiting his relation. In any case, be it history or legend, the truth was that Father Anthony Isabel of the Holy Sacrament of the Altar did not feel at ease in this house, whose only inhabitant had never shown any signs of piety and who confessed only once a year but always replied with evasive answers when he tried to pin her down about the puzzling death of her husband. If he was there now, waiting for her to bring him a glass of water to bathe a dying bird, it was the result of a chance occurrence which he was not responsible for.

While he waited for the widow to return, the priest, seated on a luxurious carved wooden rocker, felt the strange humidity of that house which had not become peaceful since the time when a pistol shot rang out, more than twenty years before, and José Arcadio Buendía, cousin of the colonel and of his own wife, fell face down amidst the clatter of buckles and spurs on the still-warm leggings which he had just taken off.

When Rebecca burst into the living room again, she saw Father Anthony Isabel seated in the rocker with an air of vagueness which terrified her.

'The life of an animal,' said the Father, 'is as dear to Our Lord as that of a man.'

As he said it, he did not remember José Arcadio Buendía. Nor did the widow recall him. But she was used to not giving any credence to the Father's words ever since he had spoken from the pulpit about the three times the devil had appeared to him. Without paying attention to him she took the bird in her hands, dipped him in the glass of water, and shook him afterward. The Father observed that there was impiety and carelessness in her way of acting, an absolute lack of consideration for the animal's life.

'You don't like birds,' he said softly but affirmatively.

The widow raised her eyelids in a gesture of impatience and hostility. 'Although I liked them once,' she said, 'I detest them now that they've taken to dying inside of our houses.'

'Many have died,' he said implacably. One might have thought that there was a great deal of cleverness in the tone of his voice.

'All of them,' said the widow. And she added, as she squeezed the animal with repugnance and placed him under the dish, 'And even that wouldn't bother me if they hadn't torn my screens.'

And it seemed to him that he had never known such hardness of heart. A moment later, holding the tiny and defenseless body in his own hand, the priest realized that it had ceased breathing. Then he forgot everything – the humidity of the house, the concupiscence, the unbearable smell of gunpowder on José Arcadio Buendía's body – and he realized the prodigious truth which had surrounded him since the beginning of the week. Right there, while the widow watched him leave the house with a menacing gesture and the dead bird in his hands, he witnessed the marvelous revelation that a rain of dead birds was falling over the town, and that he, the minister of God, the chosen one, who had known happiness when it had not been hot, had forgotten entirely about the Apocalypse.

That day he went to the station, as always, but he was not fully aware of his actions. He knew vaguely that something was happening in the world, but he felt muddled, dumb, unequal to the moment. Seated on the bench in the station, he tried to remember if there was a rain of dead birds in the Apocalypse, but he had forgotten it entirely. Suddenly he thought that his delay at Rebecca's house had made him miss the train, and he stretched his head up over the dusty and broken glass and saw on the clock in the ticket office that it was still twelve minutes to one. When he returned to the bench, he felt as if he were suffocating. At that moment he remembered it was Saturday. He moved his woven palm fan for a while, lost in his dark interior fog. Then he fretted over the buttons on his soutane and the buttons on his boots and over his long, snug, clerical trousers, and he noticed with alarm that he had never in his life been so hot.

Without moving from the bench he unbuttoned the collar of his soutane, took his handkerchief out of his sleeve, and wiped his flushed face, thinking, in a moment of illuminated pathos, that perhaps he was witnessing the unfolding of an earthquake. He had read that somewhere. Nevertheless the sky was clear: a transparent blue sky from which all the birds had mysteriously disappeared. He noticed the color and the transparency, but for a moment forgot about the dead birds. Now he was thinking about something else, about the possibility that a storm would break. Nevertheless the sky was diaphanous and tranquil, as if it were the sky over some other town, distant and different, where he had never felt the heat, and as if they were other eyes, not his own, which were looking at it. Then he looked toward the north, above the roofs of palms and rusted zinc, and saw the slow, silent, rhythmic blot of the buzzards over the dump.

For some mysterious reason, he relived at that moment the emotions he felt one Sunday in the seminary, shortly before taking his minor orders. The rector had given him permission to make use of his private library and he often stayed for hours and hours (especially on Sundays) absorbed in the reading of some yellowed books smelling of old wood, with annotations in Latin in the tiny, angular scrawl of the rector. One Sunday, after he had been reading for the whole day, the rector entered the room and rushed, shocked, to pick up a card which evidently had fallen from the pages of the book he was reading. He observed his superior's confusion with discreet indifference, but he managed to read the card. There was only one sentence, written in purple ink in a clean, straightforward hand: '*Madame Ivette est morte cette nuit.*' More than half a century later, seeing a blot of buzzards over a forgotten town, he remembered the somber expression of the rector seated in front of him, purple against the dusk, his breathing imperceptibly quickened.

Shaken by that association, he did not then feel the heat, but rather exactly the reverse, the sting of ice in his groin and in the soles of his feet. He was terrified without knowing what the precise cause of that terror was, tangled in a net of confused ideas, among which it was impossible to distinguish a nauseating sensation, from Satan's hoof stuck in the mud, from a flock of dead birds falling on the world, while he, Anthony Isabel of the Holy Sacrament of the Altar, remained indifferent to that event. Then he straightened up, raised an awed hand, as if to begin a greeting which was lost in the void, and cried out in horror, 'The Wandering Jew!'

At that moment the train whistled. For the first time in many years he did not hear it. He saw it pull into the station, surrounded by a dense cloud of smoke, and heard the rain of cinders against the sheets of rusted zinc. But that was like a distant and undecipherable dream from which he did not awaken completely until that afternoon, a little after four, when he put the finishing touches on the imposing sermon he would deliver on Sunday. Eight hours later, he was called to administer extreme unction to a woman.

With the result that the Father did not find out who arrived that afternoon on the train. For a long time he had watched the four cars go by, ramshackle and colorless, and he could not recall anyone's getting off to stay, at least in recent years. Before it was different, when he could spend a whole afternoon watching a train loaded with bananas go by; a hundred and forty cars loaded with fruit, passing endlessly until, well on toward nightfall, the last car passed with a man dangling a green lantern. Then he saw the town on the other side of the track – the lights were on now – and it seemed to him that, by merely watching the train pass, it had taken him to another town. Perhaps from that came his habit of being present at the station every day, even after they shot the workers to death and the banana plantations were finished, and with them the hundred-and-forty-car trains, and there was left only that yellow, dusty train which neither brought anyone nor took anyone away.

But that Saturday someone did come. When Father Anthony Isabel of the Holy Sacrament of the Altar left the station, a quiet boy with nothing particular about him except his hunger saw the priest from the window of the last car at the precise moment that he remembered he had not eaten since the previous day. He thought, If there's a priest, there must be a hotel. And he got off the train and crossed the street, which was blistered by the metallic August sun, and entered the cool shade of a house located opposite the station whence issued the sound of a worn gramophone record. His sense of smell, sharpened by his two-day-old hunger, told him that was the hotel. And he went in without seeing the sign 'HOTEL MACONDO,' a sign which he was never to read in his life.

The proprietress was more than five months pregnant. She was the color of mustard, and looked exactly as her mother had when her mother was pregnant with her. He ordered, 'Lunch, as quick as you can,' and she, not trying to hurry, served him a bowl of soup with a bare bone and some chopped green banana in it. At that moment the train whistled. Absorbed in the warm and healthful vapor of the soup, he calculated the distance which lay between him and the station, and immediately felt himself invaded by that confused sensation of panic which missing a train produces.

He tried to run. He reached the door, anguished, but he hadn't even taken one step across the threshold when he realized that he didn't have time to make the train. When he returned to the table, he had forgotten his hunger; he saw a girl next to the gramophone who looked at him pitifully, with the horrible expression of a dog wagging his tail. Then, for the first time that whole day, he took off his hat, which his mother had given him two months before, and lodged it between his knees while he finished eating. When he got up from the table, he didn't seem bothered by missing the train, or by the prospect of spending a weekend in a town whose name he would not take the trouble to find out. He sat down in a corner of the room, the bones of his back supported by a hard, straight chair, and stayed there for a long time, not listening to the records until the girl who was picking them out said:

'It's cooler on the veranda.'

He felt ill. It took an effort to start conversation with strangers. He was afraid to look people in the face, and when he had no recourse but to speak, the words came out different from the way he thought them. 'Yes,' he replied. And he felt a slight shiver. He tried to rock, forgetting that he was not in a rocker.

'The people who come here pull a chair to the veranda since it's cooler,' the girl said. And, listening to her, he realized how anxiously she wanted to talk. He risked a look at her just as she was winding up the gramophone. She seemed to have been sitting there for months, years perhaps, and she showed not the slightest interest in moving from that spot. She was winding up the gramophone but her life was concentrated on him. She was smiling.

'Thank you,' he said, trying to get up, to put some ease and spontaneity into his movements. The girl didn't stop looking at him. She said, 'They also leave their hats on the hook.'

This time he felt a burning in his ears. He shivered, thinking about her way of suggesting things. He felt uncomfortably shut in, and again felt his panic over the missed train. But at that moment the proprietress entered the room.

'What are you doing?' she asked.

'He's pulling a chair onto the veranda, as they all do,' the girl said.

He thought he perceived a mocking tone in her words.

'Don't bother,' said the proprietress. 'I'll bring you a stool.'

The girl laughed and he felt disconcerted. It was hot. An unbroken, dry heat, and he was sweating. The proprietress dragged a wooden stool with a leather seat to the veranda. He was about to follow her when the girl spoke again.

'The bad part of it is that the birds will frighten him,' she said.

He managed to see the harsh look when the proprietress turned her eyes on the girl. It was a swift but intense look.

'What you should do is be quiet,' she said, and turned smiling to him. Then he felt less alone and had the urge to speak.

'What was that she said?' he asked.

'That at this hour of the day dead birds fall onto the veranda,' the girl said.

'Those are just some notions of hers,' said the proprietress. She bent over to straighten a bouquet of artificial flowers on the little table in the middle of the room. There was a nervous twitch in her fingers.

'Notions of mine, no,' the girl said. 'You yourself swept two of them up the day before yesterday.'

The proprietress looked exasperatedly at her. The girl had a pitiful expression, and an obvious desire to explain everything until not the slightest trace of doubt remained.

'What is happening, sir, is that the day before yesterday some boys left two dead birds in the hall to annoy her, and then they told her that dead birds were falling from the sky. She swallows everything people tell her.'

He smiled. The explanation seemed very funny to him; he rubbed his hands and turned to look at the girl, who was observing him in anguish. The gramophone had stopped playing. The proprietress withdrew to the other room, and when he went toward the hall the girl insisted in a low voice:

'I saw them fall. Believe me. Everyone has seen them.'

And he thought he understood then her attachment to the gramophone, and the proprietress's exasperation. 'Yes,' he said sympathetically. And then, moving toward the hall: 'I've seen them, too.'

It was less hot outside, in the shade of the almond trees. He leaned the stool against the doorframe, threw his head back, and thought of his mother: his mother, exhausted, in her rocker, shooing the chickens with a long broomstick, while she realized for the first time that he was not in the house.

The week before, he could have thought that his life was a smooth straight string, stretching from the rainy dawn during the last civil war when he came into the world between the four mud-and-rush walls of a rural schoolhouse to that June morning on his twenty-second birthday when his mother approached his hammock and gave him a hat with a card: 'To my dear son, on his day.' At times he shook off the rustiness of his inactivity and felt nostalgic for school, for the blackboard and the map of a country overpopulated by the excrement of the flies, and for the long line of cups hanging on the wall under the names of the children. It wasn't hot there. It was a green, tranquil town, where chickens with ashen long legs entered the schoolroom in order to lay their eggs under the washstand. His mother then was a sad and uncommunicative woman. She would sit at dusk to take the air which had just filtered through the coffee plantations, and say, 'Manaure is the most beautiful town in the world.' And then, turning toward him, seeing him grow up silently in the hammock: 'When you are grown up you'll understand.' But he didn't understand anything. He didn't understand at fifteen, already too tall for his age and bursting with that insolent and reckless health which idleness brings. Until his twentieth birthday his life was not essentially different from a few changes of position in his hammock. But around that time his mother, obliged by her rheumatism, left the school she had served for eighteen years, with the result that they went to live in a two-room house with a huge patio, where they raised chickens with ashen legs like those which used to cross the schoolroom.

Caring for the chickens was his first contact with reality. And it had been the only one until the month of July, when his mother thought about her retirement and deemed her son wise enough to undertake to petition for it. He collaborated in an effective way in the preparation of the documents, and even had the necessary tact to convince the parish priest to change his mother's baptismal certificate by six months, since she still wasn't old enough to retire. On Thursday he received the final instructions, scrupulously detailing his mother's teaching experience, and he began the trip to the city with twelve pesos, a change of clothing, the file of documents, and an entirely rudimentary idea of the word 'retirement,' which he interpreted crudely as a certain sum of money which the government ought to give him so he could set himself up in pig breeding.

Dozing on the hotel veranda, dulled by the sweltering heat, he had not stopped to think about the gravity of his situation. He supposed that the mishap would be resolved the following day, when the train returned, so that now his only worry was to wait until Sunday to resume his trip and forget forever about this town where it was unbearably hot. A little before four, he fell into an uncomfortable and sluggish sleep, thinking while he slept that it was a shame not to have brought his hammock. Then it was that he realized everything, that he had forgotten his bundle of clothes and the documents for the retirement on the train. He woke up with a start, terrified, thinking of his mother, and hemmed in again by panic.

When he dragged his seat back to the dining room, the lights of the town had been lit. He had never seen electric lights, so he was very impressed when he saw the poor spotted bulbs of the hotel. Then he remembered that his mother had spoken to him about them, and he continued dragging the seat toward the dining room, trying to dodge the horseflies which were bumping against the mirrors like bullets. He ate without appetite, confused by the clear evidence of his situation, by the intense heat, by the bitterness of that loneliness which he was suffering for the first time in his life. After nine o'clock he was led to the back of the house to a wooden room papered with newspapers and magazines. At midnight he had sunk into a miasmic and feverish sleep while, five blocks away, Father Anthony Isabel of the Holy Sacrament of the Altar, lying face down on his cot, was thinking that the evening's experiences reinforced the sermon which he had prepared for seven in the morning. A little before twelve he had crossed the town to administer extreme unction to a woman, and he felt excited and nervous, with the result that he put the sacramental objects next to his cot and lay down to go over his sermon. He stayed that way for several hours, lying face down on the cot until he heard the distant call of a plover at dawn. Then he tried to get up, sat up painfully, stepped on the little bell, and fell headlong on the cold, hard floor of his room.

He had hardly regained consciousness when he felt the trembling sensation which rose up his side. At that instant he was aware of his entire weight: the weight of his body, his sins, and his age all together. He felt against his cheek the solidity of the stone floor which so often when he was preparing his sermons had helped him form a precise idea of the road which leads to Hell. 'Lord,' he murmured, afraid; and he thought, I shall certainly never be able to get up again.

He did not know how long he lay prostrate on the floor, not thinking about anything, without even remembering to pray for a good death. It was as if, in reality, he had been dead for a minute. But when he regained consciousness, he no longer felt pain or fear. He saw the bright ray beneath the door; he heard, far off and sad, the raucous noise of the roosters, and he realized that he was alive and that he remembered the words of his sermon perfectly.

When he drew back the bar of the door, dawn was breaking. He had ceased feeling pain, and it even seemed that the blow had unburdened him of his old age. All the goodness, the misconduct, and the sufferings of the town penetrated his heart when he swallowed the first mouthful of that air which was a blue dampness full of roosters. Then he looked around himself, as if to reconcile himself to the solitude, and saw, in the peaceful shade of the dawn, one, two, three dead birds on the veranda.

For nine minutes he contemplated the three bodies, thinking, in accord with his prepared sermon, that the birds' collective death needed some expiation. Then he walked to the other end of the corridor, picked up the three dead birds and returned to the pitcher, and one after the other threw the birds into the green, still water without knowing exactly the purpose of that action. Three and three are half a dozen, in one week, he thought, and a miraculous flash of lucidity told him that he had begun to experience the greatest day of his life.

At seven the heat began. In the hotel, the only guest was waiting for his breakfast. The gramophone girl had not yet got up. The proprietress approached, and at that moment it seemed as if the seven strokes of the clock's bell were sounding inside her swollen belly.

'So you missed the train,' she said in a tone of belated commiseration. And then she brought the breakfast: coffee with milk, a fried egg, and slices of green banana.

He tried to eat, but he wasn't hungry. He was alarmed that the heat had come on. He was sweating buckets. He was suffocating. He had slept poorly, with his clothes on, and now he had a little fever. He felt the panic again, and remembered his mother just as the proprietress came to the table to pick up the dishes, radiant in her new dress with the large green flowers. The proprietress's dress reminded him that it was Sunday.

'Is there a Mass?' he asked.

'Yes, there is,' the woman said. 'But it's just as if there weren't, because almost nobody goes. The fact is they haven't wanted to send us a new priest.'

'And what's wrong with this one?'

'He's about a hundred years old, and he's half crazy,' the woman said; she stood motionless, pensive, with all the dishes in one hand. Then she said, 'The other day, he swore from the pulpit that he had seen the devil, and since then no one goes to Mass.'

So he went to the church, in part because of desperation and in part out of curiosity to meet a person a hundred years old. He noticed that it was a dead town, with interminable, dusty streets and dark wooden houses with zinc roofs, which seemed uninhabited. That was the town on Sunday: streets without grass, houses with screens, and a deep, marvelous sky over a stifling heat. He thought that there was no sign there which would permit one to distinguish Sunday from any other day, and while he walked along the deserted street he remembered his mother: 'All the streets in every town lead inevitably to the church or the cemetery.' At that moment he came out into a small cobblestoned plaza with a whitewashed building that had a tower and a wooden weathercock on the top, and a clock which had stopped at ten after four.

Without hurrying he crossed the plaza, climbed the three steps of the atrium, and immediately smelled the odor of aged human sweat mixed with the odor of incense, and he went into the warm shade of the almost empty church.

Father Anthony Isabel of the Holy Sacrament of the Altar had just risen to the pulpit. He was about to begin the sermon when he saw a boy enter with his hat on. He saw him examining the almost empty temple with his large, serene, and clear eyes. He saw him sit down in the last pew, his head to one side and his hands on his knees. He noticed that he was a stranger to the town. He had been in town for thirty years, and he could have recognized any of its inhabitants just by his smell. Therefore, he knew that the boy who had just arrived was a stranger. In one intense, brief look, he observed that he was a quiet soul, and a little sad, and that his clothes were dirty and wrinkled. It's as if he had spent a long time sleeping in them, he thought with a feeling that was a combination of repugnance and pity. But then, seeing him in the pew, he felt his heart overflowing with gratitude, and he got ready to deliver what was for him the greatest sermon of his life. Lord, he thought in the meantime, please let him remember his hat so I don't have to throw him out of the temple. And he began his sermon.

At the beginning he spoke without realizing what he was saying. He wasn't even listening to himself. He hardly heard the clear and fluent melody which flowed from a spring dormant in his soul ever since the beginning of the world. He had the confused certainty that his words were flowing forth precisely, opportunely, exactly, in the expected order and place. He felt a warm vapor pressing his innards. But he also knew that his spirit was free of vanity, and that the feeling of pleasure which paralyzed his senses was not pride or defiance or vanity but, rather, the pure rejoicing of his spirit in Our Lord.

In her bedroom, Rebecca felt faint, knowing that within a few moments the heat would become impossible. If she had not felt rooted to the town by a dark fear of novelty, she would have put her odds and ends in a trunk with mothballs and would have gone off into the world, as her great-grandfather did, so she had been told. But she knew inside that she was destined to die in the town, amid those endless corridors and the nine bedrooms, whose screens she thought she would have replaced by translucent glass when the heat stopped. So she would stay there, she decided (and that was a decision she always took when she arranged her clothes in the closet), and she also decided to write 'My Eminent Cousin' to send them a young priest, so she could attend church again with her hat with the tiny velvet flowers, and hear a coherent Mass and sensible and edifying sermons again. Tomorrow is Monday, she thought, beginning to think once and for all about the salutation of the letter to the Bishop (a salutation which Colonel Buendía had called frivolous and disrespectful), when Argenida suddenly opened the screened door and shouted:

'Señora, people are saying that the Father has gone crazy in the pulpit!'

The widow turned a not characteristically withered and bitter face toward the door. 'He's been crazy for at least five years,' she said. And she kept on arranging her clothing, saying:

'He must have seen the devil again.'

'It's not the devil this time,' said Argenida.

'Then who?' Rebecca asked, prim and indifferent.

'Now he says that he saw the Wandering Jew.'

The widow felt her skin crawl. A multitude of confused ideas, among which she could not distinguish her torn screens, the heat, the dead birds, and the plague, passed through her head as she heard those words which she hadn't remembered since the afternoons of her distant girlhood: 'The Wandering Jew.' And then she began to move, enraged, icily, toward where Argenida was watching her with her mouth open.

'It's true,' Rebecca said in a voice which rose from the

depths of her being. 'Now I understand why the birds are dying off.'

Impelled by terror, she covered herself with a black embroidered shawl and, in a flash, crossed the long corridor and the living room stuffed with decorative objects, and the street door, and the two blocks to the church, where Father Anthony Isabel of the Holy Sacrament of the Altar, transfigured, was saying, 'I swear to you that I saw him. I swear to you that he crossed my path this morning when I was coming back from administering the holy unction to the wife of Jonas the carpenter. I swear to you that his face was blackened with the malediction of the Lord, and that he left a track of burning embers in his wake.'

His sermon broke off, floating in the air. He realized that he couldn't restrain the trembling of his hands, that his whole body was shaking, and that a thread of icy sweat was slowly descending his spinal column. He felt ill, feeling the trembling, and the thirst, and a violent wrenching in his gut, and a noise which resounded like the bass note of an organ in his belly. Then he realized the truth.

He saw that there were people in the church, and that Rebecca, pathetic, showy, her arms open, and her bitter, cold face turned toward the heavens, was advancing up the central nave. Confusedly he understood what was happening, and he even had enough lucidity to understand that it would have been vanity to believe that he was witnessing a miracle. Humbly he rested his trembling hands on the wooden edge of the pulpit and resumed his speech.

'Then he walked toward me,' he said. And this time he heard his own voice, convincing, impassioned. 'He walked toward me and he had emerald eyes, and shaggy hair, and the smell of a billy goat. And I raised my hand to reproach him in the name of Our Lord, and I said to him: "Halt, Sunday has never been a good day for sacrificing a lamb." '

When he finished, the heat had set in. That intense, solid, burning heat of that unforgettable August. But Father Anthony Isabel was no longer aware of the heat. He knew that there, at his back, the town was again humbled, speechless with his sermon, but he wasn't even pleased by that. He wasn't even pleased with the immediate prospect that the wine would relieve his ravaged throat. He felt uncomfortable and out of place. He felt distracted and he could not concentrate on the supreme moment of the sacrifice. The same thing had been happening to him for some time, but now it was a different distraction, because his thoughts were filled by a definite uneasiness. Then, for the first time in his life, he knew pride. And just as he had imagined and defined it in his sermons, he felt that pride was an urge the same as thirst. He closed the tabernacle energetically and said:

'Pythagoras.'

The acolyte, a child with a shaven and shiny head, godson of Father Anthony Isabel, who had named him, approached the altar.

'Take up the offering,' said the priest.

The child blinked, turned completely around, and then said in an almost inaudible voice, 'I don't know where the plate is.'

It was true. It had been months since an offering had been collected.

'Then go find a big bag in the sacristy and collect as much as you can,' said the Father.

'And what shall I say?' said the boy.

The Father thoughtfully contemplated his shaven blue skull, with its prominent sutures. Now it was he who blinked:

'Say that it is to expel the Wandering Jew,' he said, and he felt as he said it that he was supporting a great weight in his heart. For a moment he heard nothing but the guttering of the candles in the silent temple and his own excited and labored breathing. Then, putting his hand on the acolyte's shoulder, while the acolyte looked at him with his round eyes aghast, he said:

'Then take the money and give it to the boy who was alone at the beginning, and you tell him that it's from the priest, and that he should buy a new hat.'

Artificial Roses

Feeling her way in the gloom of dawn, Mina put on the sleeveless dress which the night before she had hung next to the bed, and rummaged in the trunk for the detachable sleeves. Then she looked for them on the nails on the wall, and behind the doors, trying not to make noise so as not to wake her blind grandmother, who was sleeping in the same room. But when she got used to the darkness, she noticed that the grandmother had got up, and she went into the kitchen to ask her for the sleeves.

'They're in the bathroom,' the blind woman said. 'I washed them yesterday afternoon.'

There they were, hanging from a wire with two wooden clothespins. They were still wet. Mina went back into the kitchen and stretched the sleeves out on the stones of the fireplace. In front of her, the blind woman was stirring the coffee, her dead pupils fixed on the stone border of the veranda, where there was a row of flowerpots with medicinal herbs.

'Don't take my things again,' said Mina. 'These days, you can't count on the sun.'

The blind woman moved her face toward the voice.

'I had forgotten that it was the first Friday,' she said.

After testing with a deep breath to see if the coffee was ready, she took the pot off the fire.

'Put a piece of paper underneath, because these stones are dirty,' she said.

Mina ran her index finger along the fireplace stones.

They were dirty, but with a crust of hardened soot which would not dirty the sleeves if they were not rubbed against the stones.

'If they get dirty you're responsible,' she said.

The blind woman had poured herself a cup of coffee. 'You're angry,' she said, pulling a chair toward the veranda. 'It's a sacrilege to take Communion when one is angry.' She sat down to drink her coffee in front of the roses in the patio. When the third call for Mass rang, Mina took the sleeves off the fireplace and they were still wet. But she put them on. Father Ángel would not give her Communion with a bare-shouldered dress on. She didn't wash her face. She took off the traces of rouge with a towel, picked up the prayer book and shawl in her room, and went into the street. A quarter of an hour later she was back.

'You'll get there after the reading of the gospel,' the blind woman said, seated opposite the roses in the patio.

Mina went directly to the toilet. 'I can't go to Mass,' she said. 'The sleeves are wet, and my whole dress is wrinkled.' She felt a knowing look follow her.

'First Friday and you're not going to Mass,' exclaimed the blind woman.

Back from the toilet, Mina poured herself a cup of coffee and sat down against the whitewashed doorway, next to the blind woman. But she couldn't drink the coffee.

'You're to blame,' she murmured, with a dull rancor, feeling that she was drowning in tears.

'You're crying,' the blind woman exclaimed.

She put the watering can next to the pots of oregano and went out into the patio, repeating, 'You're crying.' Mina put her cup on the ground before sitting up.

'I'm crying from anger,' she said. And added, as she passed next to her grandmother, 'You must go to confession because you made me miss the first-Friday Communion.'

The blind woman remained motionless, waiting for Mina to close the bedroom door. Then she walked to the end of the veranda. She bent over haltingly until she found the untouched cup in one piece on the ground. While she poured the coffee into the earthen pot, she went on:

'God knows I have a clear conscience.'

Mina's mother came out of the bedroom.

'Who are you talking to?' she asked.

'To no one,' said the blind woman. 'I've told you already that I'm going crazy.'

Ensconced in her room, Mina unbuttoned her bodice and took out three little keys which she carried on a safety pin. With one of the keys she opened the lower drawer of the armoire and took out a miniature wooden trunk. She opened it with another key. Inside there was a packet of letters written on colored paper, held together by a rubber band. She hid them in her bodice, put the little trunk in its place, and locked the drawer. Then she went to the toilet and threw the letters in.

'I thought you were at church,' her mother said when Mina came into the kitchen.

'She couldn't go,' the blind woman interrupted. 'I forgot that it was first Friday, and I washed the sleeves yesterday afternoon.'

'They're still wet,' murmured Mina.

'I've had to work hard these days,' the blind woman said.

'I have to deliver a hundred and fifty dozen roses for Easter,' Mina said.

The sun warmed up early. Before seven Mina set up her artificial-rose shop in the living room: a basket full of petals and wires, a box of crêpe paper, two pairs of scissors, a spool of thread, and a pot of glue. A moment later Trinidad arrived, with a pasteboard box under her arm, and asked her why she hadn't gone to Mass.

'I didn't have any sleeves,' said Mina.

'Anyone could have lent some to you,' said Trinidad.

She pulled over a chair and sat down next to the basket of petals.

'I was too late,' Mina said.

She finished a rose. Then she pulled the basket closer to

shirr the petals with the scissors. Trinidad put the pasteboard box on the floor and joined in the work.

Mina looked at the box.

'Did you buy shoes?' she asked.

'They're dead mice,' said Trinidad.

Since Trinidad was an expert at shirring petals, Mina spent her time making stems of wire wound with green paper. They worked silently without noticing the sun advance in the living room, which was decorated with idyllic prints and family photographs. When she finished the stems, Mina turned toward Trinidad with a face that seemed to end in something immaterial. Trinidad shirred with admirable neatness, hardly moving the petal tip between her fingers, her legs close together. Mina observed her masculine shoes. Trinidad avoided the look without raising her head, barely drawing her feet backward, and stopped working.

'What's the matter?' she said.

Mina leaned toward her.

'He went away,' she said.

Trinidad dropped the scissors in her lap.

'No.'

'He went away,' Mina repeated.

Trinidad looked at her without blinking. A vertical wrinkle divided her knit brows.

'And now?' she asked.

Mina replied in a steady voice.

'Now nothing.'

Trinidad said goodbye before ten.

Freed from the weight of her intimacy, Mina stopped her a moment to throw the dead mice into the toilet. The blind woman was pruning the rosebush.

'I'll bet you don't know what I have in this box,' Mina said to her as she passed.

She shook the mice.

The blind woman began to pay attention. 'Shake it again,' she said. Mina repeated the movement, but the blind woman could not identify the objects after listening for a third time with her index finger pressed against the lobe of her ear.

'They are the mice which were caught in the church traps last night,' said Mina.

When she came back, she passed next to the blind woman without speaking. But the blind woman followed her. When she got to the living room, Mina was alone next to the closed window, finishing the artificial roses.

'Mina,' said the blind woman. 'If you want to be happy, don't confess with strangers.'

Mina looked at her without speaking. The blind woman sat down in the chair in front of her and tried to help with the work. But Mina stopped her.

'You're nervous,' said the blind woman.

'Why didn't you go to Mass?' asked the blind woman.

'You know better than anyone.'

'If it had been because of the sleeves, you wouldn't have bothered to leave the house,' said the blind woman. 'Someone was waiting for you on the way who caused you some disappointment.'

Mina passed her hands before her grandmother's eyes, as if cleaning an invisible pane of glass.

'You're a witch,' she said.

'You went to the toilet twice this morning,' the blind woman said. 'You never go more than once.'

Mina kept making roses.

'Would you dare show me what you are hiding in the drawer of the armoire?' the blind woman asked.

Unhurriedly, Mina stuck the rose in the window frame, took the three little keys out of her bodice, and put them in the blind woman's hand. She herself closed her fingers.

'Go see with your own eyes,' she said.

The blind woman examined the little keys with her finger-tips.

'My eyes cannot see down the toilet.'

Mina raised her head and then felt a different sensation: she felt that the blind woman knew that she was looking at her.

'Throw yourself down the toilet if what I do is so interesting to you,' she said.

The blind woman ignored the interruption.

'You always stay up writing in bed until early morning,' she said.

'You yourself turn out the light,' Mina said.

'And immediately you turn on the flashlight,' the blind woman said. 'I can tell that you're writing by your breathing.'

Mina made an effort to stay calm. 'Fine,' she said without raising her head. 'And supposing that's the way it is. What's so special about it?'

'Nothing,' replied the blind woman. 'Only that it made you miss first-Friday Communion.'

With both hands Mina picked up the spool of thread, the scissors, and a fistful of unfinished stems and roses. She put it all in the basket and faced the blind woman. 'Would you like me to tell you what I went to do in the toilet, then?' she asked. They both were in suspense until Mina replied to her own question:

'I went to take a shit.'

The blind woman threw the three little keys into the basket. 'It would be a good excuse,' she murmured, going into the kitchen. 'You would have convinced me if it weren't the first time in your life I've ever heard you swear.' Mina's mother was coming along the corridor in the opposite direction, her arms full of bouquets of thorned flowers.

'What's going on?' she asked.

'I'm crazy,' said the blind woman. 'But apparently you haven't thought of sending me to the madhouse so long as I don't start throwing stones.'

Big Mama's Funeral

This is, for all the world's unbelievers, the true account of Big Mama, absolute sovereign of the Kingdom of Macondo, who lived for ninety-two years, and died in the odor of sanctity one Tuesday last September, and whose funeral was attended by the Pope.

Now that the nation, which was shaken to its vitals, has recovered its balance; now that the bagpipers of San Jacinto, the smugglers of Guajira, the rice planters of Sinú, the prostitutes of Caucamayal, the wizards of Sierpe, and the banana workers of Aracataca have folded up their tents to recover from the exhausting vigil and have regained their serenity, and the President of the Republic and his Ministers and all those who represented the public and supernatural powers on the most magnificent funeral occasion recorded in the annals of history have regained control of their estates; now that the Holy Pontiff has risen up to Heaven in body and soul; and now that it is impossible to walk around in Macondo because of the empty bottles, the cigarette butts, the gnawed bones, the cans and rags and excrement that the crowd which came to the burial left behind; now is the time to lean a stool against the front door and relate from the beginning the details of this national commotion, before the historians have a chance to get at it.

Fourteen weeks ago, after endless nights of poultices, mustard plasters, and leeches, and weak with the delirium of her death agony, Big Mama ordered them to seat her in her old rattan rocker so she could express her last wishes. It was the only thing she needed to do before she died. That morning, with the intervention of Father Anthony Isabel, she had put the affairs of her soul in order, and now she needed only to put her worldly affairs in order with her nine nieces and nephews, her sole heirs, who were standing around her bed. The priest, talking to himself and on the verge of his hundredth birthday, stayed in the room. Ten men had been needed to take him up to Big Mama's bedroom, and it was decided that he should stay there so they should not have to take him down and then take him up again at the last minute.

Nicanor, the eldest nephew, gigantic and savage, dressed in khaki and spurred boots, with a .38-caliber long-barreled revolver holstered under his shirt, went to look for the notary. The enormous two-story mansion, fragrant from molasses and oregano, with its dark apartments crammed with chests and the odds and ends of four generations turned to dust, had become paralyzed since the week before, in expectation of that moment. In the long central hall, with hooks on the walls where in another time butchered pigs had been hung and deer were slaughtered on sleepy August Sundays, the peons were sleeping on farm equipment and bags of salt, awaiting the order to saddle the mules to spread the bad news to the four corners of the huge hacienda. The rest of the family was in the living room. The women were limp, exhausted by the inheritance proceedings and lack of sleep; they kept a strict mourning which was the culmination of countless accumulated mournings. Big Mama's matriarchal rigidity had surrounded her fortune and her name with a sacramental fence, within which uncles married the daughters of their nieces, and the cousins married their aunts, and brothers their sisters-in-law, until an intricate mesh of consanguinity was formed, which turned procreation into a vicious circle. Only Magdalena, the youngest of the nieces, managed to escape it. Terrified by hallucinations, she made Father Anthony Isabel exorcise her, shaved her head, and renounced the glories and vanities of the world in the novitiate of the Mission District.

On the margin of the official family, and in exercise of the *jus primae noctis*, the males had fertilized ranches, byways, and settlements with an entire bastard line, which circulated among the servants without surnames, as godchildren, employees, favorites, and protégés of Big Mama.

The imminence of her death stirred the exhausting expectation. The dying woman's voice, accustomed to homage and obedience, was no louder than a bass organ pipe in the closed room, but it echoed in the most far-flung corners of the hacienda. No one was indifferent to this death. During this century, Big Mama had been Macondo's center of gravity, as had her brothers, her parents, and the parents of her parents in the past, in a dominance which covered two centuries. The town was founded on her surname. No one knew the origin, or the limits or the real value of her estate, but everyone was used to believing that Big Mama was the owner of the waters, running and still, of rain and drought, and of the district's roads, telegraph poles, leap years, and heat waves, and that she had furthermore a hereditary right over life and property. When she sat on her balcony in the cool afternoon air, with all the weight of her belly and authority squeezed into her old rattan rocker, she seemed, in truth, infinitely rich and powerful, the richest and most powerful matron in the world.

It had not occurred to anyone to think that Big Mama was mortal, except the members of her tribe, and Big Mama herself, prodded by the senile premonitions of Father Anthony Isabel. But she believed that she would live more than a hundred years, as did her maternal grandmother, who in the War of 1885 confronted a patrol of Colonel Aureliano Buendía's, barricaded in the kitchen of the hacienda. Only in April of this year did Big Mama realize that God would not grant her the privilege of personally liquidating, in an open skirmish, a horde of Federalist Masons.

During the first week of pain, the family doctor maintained her with mustard plasters and woolen stockings. He was a hereditary doctor, a graduate of Montpellier, hostile by philosophical conviction to the progress of his science, whom Big Mama had accorded the lifetime privilege of preventing the establishment in Macondo of any other doctors. At one time he covered the town on horseback, visiting the doleful, sick people at dusk, and Nature had accorded him the privilege of being the father of many another's children. But arthritis kept him stiff-jointed in bed, and he ended up attending to his patients without calling on them, by means of suppositions, messengers, and errands. Summoned by Big Mama, he crossed the plaza in his pajamas, leaning on two canes, and he installed himself in the sick woman's bedroom. Only when he realized that Big Mama was dying did he order a chest with porcelain jars labeled in Latin brought, and for three weeks he besmeared the dying woman inside and out with all sorts of academic salves, magnificent stimulants, and masterful suppositories. Then he applied bloated toads to the site of her pain, and leeches to her kidneys, until the early morning of that day when he had to face the dilemma of either having her bled by the barber or exorcised by Father Anthony Isabel.

Nicanor sent for the priest. His ten best men carried him from the parish house to Big Mama's bedroom, seated on a creaking willow rocker, under the mildewed canopy reserved for great occasions. The little bell of the Viaticum in the warm September dawn was the first notification to the inhabitants of Macondo. When the sun rose, the little plaza in front of Big Mama's house looked like a country fair.

It was like a memory of another era. Until she was seventy, Big Mama used to celebrate her birthday with the most prolonged and tumultuous carnivals within memory. Demijohns of rum were placed at the townspeople's disposal, cattle were sacrificed in the public plaza, and a band installed on top of a table played for three days without stopping. Under the dusty almond trees, where, in the first week of the century, Colonel Aureliano Buendía's troops had camped, stalls were set up which sold banana liquor, rolls, blood puddings, chopped fried meat, meat pies, sausage, yucca breads, crullers, buns, corn breads, puff pastes, *longanizas*, tripes, coconut nougats, rum toddies, along with all sorts of trifles, gewgaws, trinkets, and knicknacks, and cockfights and lottery tickets. In the midst of the confusion of the agitated mob, prints and scapularies with Big Mama's likeness were sold.

The festivities used to begin two days before and end on the day of her birthday, with the thunder of fireworks and a family dance at Big Mama's house. The carefully chosen guests and the legitimate members of the family, generously attended by the bastard line, danced to the beat of the old pianola which was equipped with the rolls most in style. Big Mama presided over the party from the rear of the hall in an easy chair with linen pillows, imparting discreet instructions with her right hand, adorned with rings on all her fingers. On that night the coming year's marriages were arranged, at times in complicity with the lovers, but almost always counseled by her own inspiration. To finish off the jubilation, Big Mama went out to the balcony, which was decorated with diadems and Japanese lanterns, and threw coins to the crowd.

That tradition had been interrupted, in part because of the successive mournings of the family and in part because of the political instability of the last few years. The new generations only heard stories of those splendid celebrations. They never managed to see Big Mama at High Mass, fanned by some functionary of the Civil Authority, enjoying the privilege of not kneeling, even at the moment of the elevation, so as not to ruin her Dutch-flounced skirt and her starched cambric petticoats. The old people remembered, like a hallucination out of their youth, the two hundred yards of matting which were laid down from the manorial house to the main altar the afternoon on which Maria del Rosario Castañeda y Montero attended her father's funeral and returned along the matted street endowed with a new and radiant dignity, turned into Big Mama at the age of twenty-two. That medieval vision belonged then not only to the family's past but also to the nation's past. Ever more indistinct and remote, hardly visible on her balcony, stifled by the geraniums on hot afternoons, Big Mama was melting into her own legend. Her authority was exercised through Nicanor. The tacit promise existed, formulated by tradition, that the day Big Mama sealed her will the heirs would declare three nights of public merrymaking. But at the same time it was known that she had decided not to express her last wishes until a few hours before dying, and no one thought seriously about the possibility that Big Mama was mortal. Only this morning, awakened by the tinkling of the Viaticum, did the inhabitants of Macondo become convinced not only that Big Mama was mortal but also that she was dying.

Her hour had come. Seeing her in her linen bed, bedaubed with aloes up to her ears, under the dust-laden canopy of Oriental crêpe, one could hardly make out any life in the thin respiration of her matriarchal breasts. Big Mama, who until she was fifty rejected the most passionate suitors, and who was well enough endowed by Nature to suckle her whole issue all by herself, was dying a virgin and childless. At the moment of extreme unction, Father Anthony Isabel had to ask for help in order to apply the oils to the palms of her hands, for since the beginning of her death throes Big Mama had had her fists closed. The attendance of the nieces was useless. In the struggle, for the first time in a week, the dying woman pressed against her chest the hand bejeweled with precious stones and fixed her colorless look on the nieces, saying, 'Highway robbers.' Then she saw Father Anthony Isabel in his liturgical habit and the acolyte with the sacramental implements, and with calm conviction she murmured, 'I am dying.' Then she took off the ring with the great diamond and gave it to Magdalena, the novice, to whom it belonged since she was the youngest heir. That was the end of a tradition: Magdalena had renounced her inheritance in favor of the Church.

At dawn, Big Mama asked to be left alone with Nicanor to impart her last instructions. For half an hour, in perfect command of her faculties, she asked about the conduct of her affairs. She gave special instructions about the disposition of her body, and finally concerned herself with the wake. 'You have to keep your eyes open,' she said. 'Keep everything of value under lock and key, because many people come to wakes only to steal.' A moment later, alone with the priest, she made an extravagant confession, sincere and detailed, and later on took Communion in the presence of her nieces and nephews. It was then that she asked them to seat her in her rattan rocker so that she could express her last wishes.

Nicanor had prepared, on twenty-four folios written in a very clear hand, a scrupulous account of her possessions. Breathing calmly, with the doctor and Father Anthony Isabel as witnesses, Big Mama dictated to the notary the list of her property, the supreme and unique source of her grandeur and authority. Reduced to its true proportions the real estate was limited to three districts, awarded by Royal Decree at the founding of the Colony; with the passage of time, by dint of intricate marriages of convenience, they had accumulated under the control of Big Mama. In that unworked territory, without definite borders, which comprised five townships and in which not one single grain had ever been sown at the expense of the proprietors, three hundred and fifty-two families lived as tenant farmers. Every year, on the eve of her name day, Big Mama exercised the only act of control which prevented the lands from reverting to the state: the collection of rent. Seated on the back porch of her house, she personally received the payment for the right to live on her lands, as for more than a century her ancestors had received it from the ancestors of the tenants. When the three-day collection was over, the patio was crammed with pigs, turkeys, and chickens, and with the tithes and first fruits of the land which were deposited there as gifts. In reality, that was the only harvest the family ever collected from a territory which had been dead since its beginnings, and which was calculated on first examination at a hundred thousand hectares. But historical circumstances had brought it about that within those boundaries the six towns of Macondo district should grow and prosper, even the county seat, so that no person who lived in a house had any property rights other than those which pertained to the house itself, since the land belonged to Big Mama, and the rent was paid to her, just as the government had to pay her for the use the citizens made of the streets.

On the outskirts of the settlements, a number of animals, never counted and even less looked after, roamed, branded on the hindquarters with the shape of a padlock. This hereditary brand, which more out of disorder than out of quantity had become familiar in distant districts where the scattered cattle, dying of thirst, strayed in summer, was one of the most solid supports of the legend. For reasons which no one had bothered to explain, the extensive stables of the house had progressively emptied since the last civil war, and lately sugar-cane presses, milking parlors, and a rice mill had been installed in them.

Aside from the items enumerated, she mentioned in her will the existence of three containers of gold coins buried somewhere in the house during the War of Independence, which had not been found after periodic and laborious excavations. Along with the right to continue the exploitation of the rented land, and to receive the tithes and first fruits and all sorts of extraordinary donations, the heirs received a chart kept up from generation to generation, and perfected by each generation, which facilitated the finding of the buried treasure.

Big Mama needed three hours to enumerate her earthly possessions. In the stifling bedroom the voice of the dying woman seemed to dignify in its place each thing named. When she affixed her trembling signature, and the witnesses affixed theirs below, a secret tremor shook the hearts of the crowds which were beginning to gather in front of the house, in the shade of the dusty almond trees of the plaza.

The only thing lacking then was the detailed listing of her immaterial possessions. Making a supreme effort – the same kind that her forebears made before they died to assure the dominance of their line – Big Mama raised herself up on her monumental buttocks, and in a domineering and sincere voice, lost in her memories, dictated to the notary this list of her invisible estate:

The wealth of the subsoil, the territorial waters, the colors of the flag, national sovereignty, the traditional parties, the rights of man, civil rights, the nation's leadership, the right of appeal, Congressional hearings, letters of recommendation, historical records, free elections, beauty queens, transcendental speeches, huge demonstrations, distinguished young ladies, proper gentlemen, punctilious military men, His Illustrious Eminence, the Supreme Court, goods whose importation was forbidden, liberal ladies, the meat problem, the purity of the language, setting a good example, the free but responsible press, the Athens of South America, public opinion, the lessons of democracy, Christian morality, the shortage of foreign exchange, the right of asylum, the Communist menace, the ship of state, the high cost of living, statements of political support.

She didn't manage to finish. The laborious enumeration cut off her last breath. Drowning in the pandemonium of abstract formulas which for two centuries had constituted the moral justification of the family's power, Big Mama emitted a loud belch and expired.

That afternoon the inhabitants of the distant and somber capital saw the picture of a twenty-year-old woman on the first page of the extra editions, and thought that it was a new beauty queen. Big Mama lived again the momentary youth of her photograph, enlarged to four columns and with needed retouching, her abundant hair caught up atop her skull with an ivory comb and a diadem on her lace collar. That image, captured by a street photographer who passed through Macondo at the beginning of the century, and kept in the newspaper's morgue for many years in the section of unidentified persons, was destined to endure in the memory of future generations. In the dilapidated buses, in the elevators at the Ministries, and in the dismal tearooms hung with pale decorations, people whispered with veneration and respect about the dead personage in her sultry, malarial region, whose name was unknown in the rest of the country a few hours before – before it had been sanctified by the printed word. A fine drizzle covered the passers-by with misgiving and mist. All the church bells tolled for the dead. The President of the Republic, taken by surprise by the news when on his way to the commencement exercises for the new cadets, suggested to the War Minister, in a note in his own hand on the back of the telegram, that he conclude his speech with a minute of silent homage to Big Mama.

The social order had been brushed by death. The President of the Republic himself, who was affected by urban feelings as if they reached him through a purifying filter, managed to perceive from his car in a momentary but to a certain extent brutal vision the silent consternation of the city. Only a few low cafés remained open; the Metropolitan Cathedral was readied for nine days of funeral rites. At the National Capitol, where the beggars wrapped in newspapers slept in the shelter of the Doric columns and the silent statues of dead Presidents, the lights of Congress were lit. When the President entered his office, moved by the vision of the capital in mourning, his Ministers were waiting for him dressed in funereal garb, standing, paler and more solemn than usual.

The events of that night and the following ones would later be identified as a historic lesson. Not only because of the Christian spirit which inspired the most lofty personages of public power, but also because of the abnegation with which dissimilar interests and conflicting judgments were conciliated in the common goal of burying the illustrious body. For many years Big Mama had guaranteed the social peace and political harmony of her empire, by virtue of the three trunks full of forged electoral certificates which formed part of her secret estate. The men in her service, her protégées and tenants, elder and younger, exercised not only their own rights of suffrage but also those of electors dead for a century. She exercised the priority of traditional power over transitory authority, the predominance of class over the common people, the transcendence of divine wisdom over human improvisation. In times of peace, her dominant will approved and disapproved canonries, benefices, and sinecures, and watched over the welfare of her associates, even if she had to resort to clandestine maneuvers or election fraud in order to obtain it. In troubled times, Big Mama contributed secretly for weapons for her partisans, but came to the aid of her victims in public. That patriotic zeal guaranteed the highest honors for her.

The President of the Republic had not needed to consult with his advisers in order to weigh the gravity of his responsibility. Between the Palace reception hall and the little paved patio which had served the viceroys as a *cochère*, there was an interior garden of dark cypresses where a Portuguese monk had hanged himself out of love in the last days of the Colony. Despite his noisy coterie of bemedaled officials, the President could not suppress a slight tremor of uncertainty when he passed that spot after dusk. But that night his trembling had the strength of a premonition. Then the full awareness of his historical destiny dawned on him, and he decreed nine days of national mourning, and posthumous honors for Big Mama at the rank befitting a heroine who had died for the fatherland on the field of battle. As he expressed it in the dramatic address which he delivered that morning to his compatriots over the national radio and television network, the Nation's Leader trusted that the funeral rites for Big Mama would set a new example for the world.

Such a noble aim was to collide nevertheless with certain grave inconveniences. The judicial structure of the country, built by remote ancestors of Big Mama, was not prepared for events such as those which began to occur. Wise Doctors of Law, certified alchemists of the statutes, plunged into hermeneutics and syllogisms in search of the formula which would permit the President of the Republic to attend the funeral. The upper strata of politics, the clergy, the financiers lived through entire days of alarm. In the vast semicircle of Congress, rarefied by a century of abstract legislation, amid oil paintings of National Heroes and busts of Greek thinkers, the vocation of Big Mama reached unheard-of proportions, while her body filled with bubbles in the harsh Macondo September. For the first time, people spoke of her and conceived of her without her rattan rocker, her afternoon stupors, and her mustard plasters, and they saw her ageless and pure, distilled by legend.

Interminable hours were filled with words, words, words, which resounded throughout the Republic, made prestigious by the spokesmen of the printed word. Until, endowed with a sense of reality in that assembly of aseptic lawgivers, the historic blahblahblah was interrupted by the reminder that Big Mama's corpse awaited their decision at 104° in the shade. No one batted an eye in the face of that eruption of common sense in the pure atmosphere of the written law. Orders were issued to embalm the cadaver, while formulas were adduced, viewpoints were reconciled, or constitutional amendments were made to permit the President to attend the burial.

So much had been said that the discussions crossed the borders, traversed the ocean, and blew like an omen through the pontifical apartments at Castel Gandolfo. Recovered from the drowsiness of the torpid days of August, the Supreme Pontiff was at the window watching the lake where the divers were searching for the head of a decapitated young girl. For the last few weeks, the evening newspapers had been concerned with nothing else, and the Supreme Pontiff could not be indifferent to an enigma located such a short distance from his summer residence. But that evening, in an unforeseen substitution, the newspapers changed the photographs of the possible victims for that of one single twenty-year-old woman, marked off with black margins. 'Big Mama,' exclaimed the Supreme Pontiff, recognizing instantly the hazy daguerreotype which many years before had been offered to him on the occasion of his ascent to the Throne of Saint Peter. 'Big Mama,' exclaimed in chorus the members of the College of Cardinals in their private apartments, and for the third time in twenty centuries there was an hour of confusion, chagrin, and bustle in the limitless empire of Christendom, until the Supreme Pontiff was installed in his long black limousine en route to Big Mama's fantastic and far-off funeral.

The shining peach orchards were left behind, the Via Appia Antica with warm movie stars tanning on terraces without as yet having heard any news of the commotion, and then the somber promontory of Castel Sant' Angelo on the edge of the

Tiber. At dusk the resonant pealing of St Peter's Basilica mingled with the cracked tinklings of Macondo. Inside his stifling tent across the tangled reeds and the silent bogs which marked the boundary between the Roman Empire and the ranches of Big Mama, the Supreme Pontiff heard the uproar of the monkeys agitated all night long by the passing of the crowds. On his nocturnal itinerary, the canoe had been filled with bags of yucca, stalks of green bananas, and crates of chickens, and with men and women who abandoned their customary pursuits to try their luck at selling things at Big Mama's funeral. His Holiness suffered that night, for the first time in the history of the Church, from the fever of insomnia and the torment of the mosquitoes. But the marvelous dawn over the Great Old Woman's domains, the primeval vision of the balsam apple and the iguana, erased from his memory the suffering of his trip and compensated him for his sacrifice.

Nicanor had been awakened by three knocks at the door which announced the imminent arrival of His Holiness. Death had taken possession of the house. Inspired by successive and urgent Presidential addresses, by the feverish controversies which had been silenced but continued to be heard by means of conventional symbols, men and congregations the world over dropped everything and with their presence filled the dark hallways, the jammed passageways, the stifling attics; and those who arrived later climbed up on the low walls around the church, the palisades, vantage points, timberwork, and parapets, where they accommodated themselves as best they could. In the central hall, Big Mama's cadaver lay mummifying while it waited for the momentous decisions contained in a quivering mound of telegrams. Weakened by their weeping, the nine nephews sat the wake beside the body in an ecstasy of reciprocal surveillance.

And still the universe was to prolong the waiting for many more days. In the city-council hall, fitted out with four leather stools, a jug of purified water, and a burdock hammock, the Supreme Pontiff suffered from a perspiring insomnia, diverting himself by reading memorials and administrative orders in the lengthy, stifling nights. During the day, he distributed Italian candy to the children who approached to see him through the window, and lunched beneath the hibiscus arbor with Father Anthony Isabel, and occasionally with Nicanor. Thus he lived for interminable weeks and months which were protracted by the waiting and the heat, until the day Father Pastrana appeared with his drummer in the middle of the plaza and read the proclamation of the decision. It was declared that Public Order was disturbed, ratatatat, and that the President of the Republic, ratatatat, had in his power the extraordinary prerogatives, ratatatat, which permitted him to attend Big Mama's funeral, ratatatat, tatatat, tatat, tatat.

The great day had arrived. In the streets crowded with carts, hawkers of fried foods, and lottery stalls, and men with snakes wrapped around their necks who peddled a balm which would definitively cure erysipelas and guarantee eternal life; in the mottled little plaza where the crowds had set up their tents and unrolled their sleeping mats, dapper archers cleared the Authorities' way. There they were, awaiting the supreme moment: the washerwomen of San Jorge, the pearl fighers from Cabo de la Vela, the fishermen from Ciénaga, the shrimp fishermen from Tasajera, the sorcerers from Mojajana, the salt miners from Manaure, the accordionists from Valledupar, the fine horsemen of Ayapel, the ragtag musicians from San Pelayo, the cock breeders from La Cueva, the improvisers from Sábanas de Bolívar, the dandies from Rebolo, the oarsmen of the Magdalena, the shysters from Monpox, in addition to those enumerated at the beginning of this chronicle, and many others. Even the veterans of Colonel Aureliano Buendía's camp – the Duke of Marlborough at their head, with the pomp of his furs and tiger's claws and teeth – overcame their centenarian hatred of Big Mama and those of her line and came to the funeral to ask the President of the Republic for the payment of their veteran's pensions which they had been waiting for for sixty years.

A little before eleven the delirious crowd which was sweltering in the sun, held back by an imperturbable élite force of warriors, decked out in embellished jackets and filigreed morions, emitted a powerful roar of jubilation. Dignified, solemn in their cutaways and top hats, the President of the Republic and his Ministers, the delegations from Parliament, the Supreme Court, the Council of State, the traditional parties and the clergy, and representatives of Banking, Commerce, and Industry made their appearance around the corner of the telegraph office. Bald and chubby, the old and ailing President of the Republic paraded before the astonished eyes of the crowds who had seen him inaugurated without knowing who he was and who only now could give a true account of his existence. Among the archbishops enfeebled by the gravity of their ministry, and the military men with robust chests armored with medals, the Leader of the Nation exuded the unmistakable air of power.

In the second rank, in a serene array of mourning crêpe, paraded the national queens of all things that have been or ever will be. Stripped of their earthly splendor for the first time, they marched by, preceded by the universal queen: the soybean queen, the green-squash queen, the banana queen, the meal yucca queen, the guava queen, the coconut queen, the kidney-bean queen, the 255-mile-long-string-of-iguana-eggs queen, and all the others who are omitted so as not to make this account interminable.

In her coffin draped in purple, separated from reality by eight copper turnbuckles, Big Mama was at that moment too absorbed in her formaldehyde eternity to realize the magnitude of her grandeur. All the splendor which she had dreamed of on the balcony of her house during her heat-induced insomnia was fulfilled by those forty-eight glorious hours during which all the symbols of the age paid homage to her memory. The Supreme Pontiff himself, who she in her delirium imagined floating above the gardens of the Vatican in a resplendent carriage, conquered the heat with a plaited palm fan, and honored with his Supreme Dignity the greatest funeral in the world.

Dazzled by the show of power, the common people did not

discern the covetous bustling which occurred on the rooftree of the house when agreement was imposed on the town grandees' wrangling and the catafalque was taken into the street on the shoulders of the grandest of them all. No one saw the vigilant shadow of the buzzards which followed the cortege through the sweltering little streets of Macondo, nor did they notice that as the grandees passed they left a pestilential train of garbage in the street. No one noticed that the nephews, godchildren, servants, and protégés of Big Mama closed the doors as soon as the body was taken out, and dismantled the doors, pulled the nails out of the planks, and dug up the foundations to divide up the house. The only thing which was not missed by anyone amid the noise of that funeral was the thunderous sigh of relief which the crowd let loose when fourteen days of supplications, exaltations, and dithyrambs were over, and the tomb was sealed with a lead plinth. Some of those present were sufficiently aware as to understand that they were witnessing the birth of a new era. Now the Supreme Pontiff could ascend to Heaven in body and soul, his mission on earth fulfilled, and the President of the Republic could sit down and govern according to his good judgment, and the queens of all things that have been or ever will be could marry and be happy and conceive and give birth to many sons, and the common people could set up their tents where they damn well pleased in the limitless domains of Big Mama, because the only one who could oppose them and had sufficient power to do so had begun to rot beneath a lead plinth. The only thing left then was for someone to lean a stool against the doorway to tell this story, lesson and example for future generations, so that not one of the world's disbelievers would be left who did not know the story of Big Mama, because tomorrow, Wednesday, the garbage men will come and will sweep up the garbage from her funeral, forever and ever.

A Very Old Man
with Enormous Wings

A TALE FOR CHILDREN

On the third day of rain they had killed so many crabs inside the house that Pelayo had to cross his drenched courtyard and throw them into the sea, because the newborn child had a temperature all night and they thought it was due to the stench. The world had been sad since Tuesday. Sea and sky were a single ash-gray thing and the sands of the beach, which on March nights glimmered like powdered light, had become a stew of mud and rotten shellfish. The light was so weak at noon that when Pelayo was coming back to the house after throwing away the crabs, it was hard for him to see what it was that was moving and groaning in the rear of the courtyard. He had to go very close to see that it was an old man, lying face down in the mud, who, in spite of his tremendous efforts, couldn't get up, impeded by his enormous wings.

Frightened by that nightmare, Pelayo ran to get Elisenda, his wife, who was putting compresses on the sick child, and he took her to the rear of the courtyard. They both looked at the fallen body with mute stupor. He was dressed like a ragpicker. There were only a few faded hairs left on his bald skull and very few teeth in his mouth, and his pitiful condition of a drenched great-grandfather had taken away any sense of grandeur he might have had. His huge buzzard wings, dirty and half-plucked, were forever entangled in the mud. They looked at him so long and so closely that Pelayo and Elisenda very soon overcame their surprise and in the end found him familiar. Then they dared speak to him, and he answered in an incomprehensible dialect with a strong sailor's voice. That was how they skipped over the inconvenience of the wings and quite intelligently concluded that he was a lonely castaway from some foreign ship wrecked by the storm. And yet, they called in a neighbor woman who knew everything about life and death to see him, and all she needed was one look to show them their mistake.

'He's an angel,' she told them. 'He must have been coming for the child, but the poor fellow is so old that the rain knocked him down.'

On the following day everyone knew that a flesh-and-blood angel was held captive in Pelayo's house. Against the judgment of the wise neighbor woman, for whom angels in those times were the fugitive survivors of a celestial conspiracy, they did not have the heart to club him to death. Pelayo watched over him all afternoon from the kitchen, armed with his bailiff's club, and before going to bed he dragged him out of the mud and locked him up with the hens in the wire chicken coop. In the middle of the night, when the rain stopped, Pelayo and Elisenda were still killing crabs. A short time afterward the child woke up without a fever and with a desire to eat. Then they felt magnanimous and decided to put the angel on a raft with fresh water and provisions for three days and leave him to his fate on the high seas. But when they went out into the courtyard with the first light of dawn, they found the whole neighborhood in front of the chicken coop having fun with the angel, without the slightest reverence, tossing him things to eat through the openings in the wire as if he weren't a supernatural creature but a circus animal.

Father Gonzaga arrived before seven o'clock, alarmed at the strange news. By that time onlookers less frivolous than those at dawn had already arrived and they were making all kinds of conjectures concerning the captive's future. The simplest among them thought that he should be named mayor of the world. Others of sterner mind felt that he should be promoted to the rank of five-star general in order to win all wars. Some visionaries hoped that he could be put to stud in order to implant on earth a race of winged wise men who could take charge of the universe. But Father Gonzaga, before becoming a priest, had been a robust woodcutter. Standing by the wire, he reviewed his catechism in an instant and asked them to open the door so that he could take a close look at that pitiful man who looked more like a huge decrepit hen among the fascinated chickens. He was lying in a corner drying his open wings in the sunlight among the fruit peels and breakfast leftovers that the early risers had thrown him. Alien to the impertinences of the world, he only lifted his antiquarian eyes and murmured something in his dialect when Father Gonzaga went into the chicken coop and said good morning to him in Latin. The parish priest had his first suspicion of an imposter when he saw that he did not understand the language of God or know how to greet His ministers. Then he noticed that seen close up he was much too human: he had an unbearable smell of the outdoors, the back side of his wings was strewn with parasites and his main feathers had been mistreated by terrestrial winds, and nothing about him measured up to the proud dignity of angels. Then he came out of the chicken coop and in a brief sermon warned the curious against the risks of being ingenuous. He reminded them that the devil had the bad habit of making use of carnival tricks in order to confuse the unwary. He argued that if wings were not the essential element in determining the difference between a hawk and an airplane, they were even less so in the recognition of angels. Nevertheless, he promised to write a letter to his bishop so that the latter would write to his primate so that the latter would write to the Supreme Pontiff in order to get the final verdict from the highest courts.

His prudence fell on sterile hearts. The news of the captive angel spread with such rapidity that after a few hours the courtyard had the bustle of a marketplace and they had to call in troops with fixed bayonets to disperse the mob that was about to knock the house down. Elisenda, her spine all twisted from sweeping up so much marketplace trash, then got the idea of fencing in the yard and charging five cents admission to see the angel.

The curious came from far away. A traveling carnival arrived with a flying acrobat who buzzed over the crowd several times, but no one paid any attention to him because his wings were not those of an angel but, rather, those of a sidereal bat. The most unfortunate invalids on earth came in search of health: a poor woman who since childhood had been counting her heartbeats and had run out of numbers; a Portuguese man who couldn't sleep because the noise of the stars disturbed him; a sleepwalker who got up at night to undo the things he had done while awake; and many others with less serious ailments. In the midst of that shipwreck disorder that made the earth tremble, Pelayo and Elisenda were happy with fatigue, for in less than a week they had crammed their rooms with money and the line of pilgrims waiting their turn to enter still reached beyond the horizon.

The angel was the only one who took no part in his own act. He spent his time trying to get comfortable in his borrowed nest, befuddled by the hellish heat of the oil lamps and sacramental candles that had been placed along the wire. At first they tried to make him eat some mothballs, which, according to the wisdom of the wise neighbor woman, were the food prescribed for angels. But he turned them down, just as he turned down the papal lunches that the penitents brought him, and they never found out whether it was because he was an angel or because he was an old man that in the end he ate nothing but eggplant mush. His only supernatural virtue seemed to be patience. Especially during the first days, when the hens pecked at him, searching for the stellar parasites that proliferated in his wings, and the cripples pulled out feathers to touch their defective parts with, and even the most merciful threw stones at him, trying to get him to rise so they could see him standing. The only time they succeeded in arousing him was when they burned his side with an iron for branding steers, for he had been motionless for so many hours that they thought he was dead. He awoke with a start, ranting in his hermetic language and with tears in his eyes, and he flapped his wings a couple of times, which brought on a whirlwind of chicken dung and lunar dust and a gale of panic that did not seem to be of this world. Although many thought that his reaction had been one not of rage but of pain, from then on they were careful not to annoy him, because the majority understood that his passivity was not that of a hero taking his ease but that of a cataclysm in repose.

Father Gonzaga held back the crowd's frivolity with formulas of maidservant inspiration while awaiting the arrival of a final judgment on the nature of the captive. But the mail from Rome showed no sense of urgency. They spent their time finding out if the prisoner had a navel, if his dialect had any connection with Aramaic, how many times he could fit on the head of a pin, or whether he wasn't just a Norwegian with wings. Those meager letters might have come and gone until the end of time if a providential event had not put an end to the priest's tribulations.

It so happened that during those days, among so many other carnival attractions, there arrived in town the traveling show of the woman who had been changed into a spider for having disobeyed her parents. The admission to see her was not only less than the admission to see the angel, but people were permitted to ask her all manner of questions about her absurd state and to examine her up and down so that no one would ever doubt the truth of her horror. She was a frightful tarantula the size of a ram and with the head of a sad maiden. What was most heartrending, however, was not her outlandish shape but the sincere affliction with which she recounted the details of her misfortune. While still practically a child she had sneaked out of her parents' house to go to a dance, and while she was coming back through the woods after having danced all night without permission, a fearful thunderclap rent the sky in two and through the crack came the lightning bolt of brimstone that changed her into a spider. Her only nourishment came from the meatballs that charitable souls chose to toss into her mouth. A spectacle like that, full of so much human truth and with such a fearful lesson, was bound to defeat without even trying that of a haughty angel who scarcely deigned to look at mortals. Besides, the few miracles attributed to the angel showed a certain mental disorder, like the blind man who didn't recover his sight but grew three new teeth, or the paralytic who didn't get to walk but almost won the lottery, and the leper whose sores sprouted sunflowers. Those consolation miracles, which were more like mocking fun, had already ruined the angel's reputation when the woman who had been changed into a spider finally crushed him completely. That was how Father Gonzaga was cured forever of his insomnia and Pelayo's courtyard went back to being as empty as during the time it had rained for three days and crabs walked through the bedrooms.

The owners of the house had no reason to lament. With the money they saved they built a two-story mansion with balconies and gardens and high netting so that crabs wouldn't get in during the winter, and with iron bars on the windows so that angels wouldn't get in. Pelayo also set up a rabbit warren close to town and gave up his job as bailiff for good, and Elisenda bought some satin pumps with high heels and many dresses of iridescent silk, the kind worn on Sunday by the most desirable women in those times. The chicken coop was the only thing that didn't receive any attention. If they washed it down with creolin and burned tears of myrrh inside it every so often, it was not in homage to the angel but to drive away the dungheap stench that still hung everywhere like a ghost and was turning the new house into an old one. At first, when the child learned to walk, they were careful that he did not get too close to the chicken coop. But then they began to lose their fears and got used to the smell, and before the child got his second teeth he'd gone inside the chicken coop to play, where the wires were falling apart. The angel was no less standoffish with him than with other mortals, but he tolerated the most ingenious infamies with the patience of a dog who had no illusions. They both came down with chicken-pox at the same time. The doctor who took care of the child couldn't resist the temptation to listen to the angel's heart, and he found so much whistling in the heart and so many sounds in his kidneys that it seemed impossible for him to be alive. What surprised him most, however, was the logic of his wings. They seemed so natural on that completely human organism that he couldn't understand why other men didn't have them too.

When the child began school it had been some time since the sun and rain had caused the collapse of the chicken coop. The angel went dragging himself about here and there like a stray dying man. They would drive him out of the bedroom with a broom and a moment later find him in the kitchen. He seemed to be in so many places at the same time that they grew to think that he'd been duplicated, that he was reproducing himself all through the house, and the exasperated and unhinged Elisenda shouted that it was awful living in that hell full of angels. He could scarcely eat and his antiquarian eyes had also become so foggy that he went about bumping into posts. All he had left were the bare cannulae of his last feathers. Pelayo threw a blanket over him and extended him the charity of letting him sleep in the shed, and only then did they notice that he had a temperature at night, and was delirious with the tongue twisters of an old Norwegian. That was one of the few times they became alarmed, for they thought he was going to die and not even the wise neighbor woman had been able to tell them what to do with dead angels.

And yet he not only survived his worst winter, but seemed improved with the first sunny days. He remained motionless for several days in the farthest corner of the courtyard, where no one would see him, and at the beginning of December some large, stiff feathers began to grow on his wings, the feathers of a scarecrow, which looked more like another misfortune of decrepitude. But he must have known the reason for those changes, for he was quite careful that no one should notice them, that no one should hear the sea chanteys that he sometimes sang under the stars. One morning Elisenda was cutting some bunches of onions for lunch when a wind that seemed to come from the high seas blew into the kitchen.

Then she went to the window and caught the angel in his first attempts at flight. They were so clumsy that his fingernails opened a furrow in the vegetable patch and he was on the point of knocking the shed down with the ungainly flapping that slipped on the light and couldn't get a grip on the air. But he did manage to gain altitude. Elisenda let out a sigh of relief, for herself and for him, when she saw him pass over the last houses, holding himself up in some way with the risky flapping of a senile vulture. She kept watching him even when she was through cutting the onions and she kept on watching until it was no longer possible for her to see him, because then he was no longer an annoyance in her life but an imaginary dot on the horizon of the sea.

The Sea of Lost Time

Toward the end of January the sea was growing harsh, it was beginning to dump its heavy garbage on the town, and a few weeks later everything was contaminated with its unbearable mood. From that time on the world wasn't worth living in, at least until the following December, so no one stayed awake after eight o'clock. But the year Mr Herbert came the sea didn't change, not even in February. On the contrary, it became smoother and more phosphorescent and during the first nights of March it gave off a fragrance of roses.

Tobías smelled it. His blood attracted crabs and he spent half the night chasing them off his bed until the breeze rose up again and he was able to sleep. During his long moments of lying awake he learned how to distinguish all the changes in the air. So that when he got a smell of roses he didn't have to open up the door to know that it was a smell from the sea.

He got up late. Clotilde was starting a fire in the courtyard. The breeze was cool and all the stars were in place, but it was hard to count them down to the horizon because of the lights from the sea. After having his coffee, Tobías could still taste a trace of night on his palate.

'Something very strange happened last night,' he remembered.

Clotilde, of course, had not smelled it. She slept so heavily that she didn't even remember her dreams.

'It was a smell of roses,' Tobías said, 'and I'm sure it came from the sea.'

'I don't know what roses smell like,' said Clotilde.

She could have been right. The town was arid, with a hard soil furrowed by saltpeter, and only occasionally did someone bring a bouquet of flowers from outside to cast into the sea where they threw their dead.

'It's the smell that drowned man from Guacamayal had,' Tobías said.

'Well,' Clotilde said, smiling 'if it was a good smell, then you can be sure it didn't come from this sea.'

It really was a cruel sea. At certain times, when the nets brought in nothing but floating garbage, the streets of the town were still full of dead fish when the tide went out. Dynamite only brought the remains of old shipwrecks to the surface.

The few women left in town, like Clotilde, were boiling up with bitterness. And like her, there was old Jacob's wife, who got up earlier than usual that morning, put the house in order, and sat down to breakfast with a look of adversity.

'My last wish,' she said to her husband, 'is to be buried alive.'

She said it as if she were on her deathbed, but she was sitting across the table in a dining room with windows through which the bright March light came pouring in and spread throughout the house. Opposite her, calming his peaceful hunger, was old Jacob, a man who had loved her so much and for so long that he could no longer conceive of any suffering that didn't start with his wife.

'I want to die with the assurance that I'll be laid beneath the ground like proper people,' she went on. 'And the only way to be sure of it is to go around asking people to do me the blessed charity of burying me alive.'

'You don't have to ask anybody,' old Jacob said with the greatest of calm. 'I'll put you there myself.'

'Let's go, then,' she said, 'because I'm going to die before very long.'

Old Jacob looked her over carefully. Her eyes were the only thing still young. Her bones had become knotted up at the joints and she had the same look of a plowed field which, when it came right down to it, she had always had.

'You're in better shape than ever,' he told her.

'Last night I caught a smell of roses,' she sighed.

'Don't pay it any mind,' old Jacob said to assure her. 'Things like that are always happening to poor people like us.'

'Nothing of the sort,' she said. 'I've always prayed that I'd know enough ahead of time when death would come so I could die far away from this sea. A smell of roses in this town can only be a message from God.'

All that old Jacob could think of was to ask for a little time to put things in order. He'd heard tell that people don't die when they ought to but when they want to, and he was seriously worried by his wife's premonition. He even wondered whether, when the moment came, he'd be up to burying her alive.

At nine o'clock he opened the place where he used to have a store. He put two chairs and a small table with the checkerboard on it by the door and he spent all morning playing opponents who happened by. From his house he looked at the ruined town, the shambles of a town with the traces of former colors that had been nibbled away by the sun and a chunk of sea at the end of the street.

Before lunch, as always, he played with Don Máximo Gómez. Old Jacob couldn't imagine a more humane opponent than a man who had survived two civil wars intact and had only sacrificed an eye in the third. After losing one game on purpose, he held him back for another.

'Tell me one thing, Don Máximo,' he asked him then. 'Would you be capable of burying your wife alive?'

'Certainly,' Don Máximo Gómez answered. 'You can believe me when I say that my hand wouldn't even tremble.'

Old Jacob fell into a surprised silence. Then, after letting himself be despoiled of his best pieces, he sighed:

'Well, the way it looks, Petra is going to die.'

Don Máximo Gómez didn't change his expression. 'In that case,' he said, 'there's no reason to bury her alive.' He gobbled up two pieces and crowned a king. Then he fastened an eye wet with sad waters on his opponent.

'What's she got?'

'Last night,' old Jacob explained, 'she caught a smell of roses.'

'Then half the town is going to die,' Don Máximo Gómez said. 'That's all they've been talking about this morning.'

It was hard for old Jacob to lose again without offending him. He brought in the table and chairs, closed up the shop, and went about everywhere looking for someone who had caught the smell. In the end only Tobías was sure. So he asked him please to stop by his place, as if by chance, and tell his wife about it.

Tobías did as he was told. At four o'clock, all dressed up in his Sunday best, he appeared on the porch where the wife had spent all afternoon getting old Jacob's widower's outfit together.

He had come up so quietly that the woman was startled.

'Mercy,' she exclaimed. 'I thought it was the archangel Gabriel.'

'Well, you can see it's not,' Tobías said. 'It's only me and I've come to tell you something.'

She adjusted her glasses and went back to work.

'I know what it's all about,' she said.

'I bet you don't,' Tobías said.

'You caught the smell of roses last night.'

'How did you know?' Tobías asked in desolation.

'At my age,' the woman said, 'there's so much time left over for thinking that a person can become a regular prophet.'

Old Jacob, who had his ear pressed against the partition wall in the back of the store, stood up in shame.

'You see, woman,' he shouted through the wall. He made a turn and appeared on the porch. 'It wasn't what you thought it was after all.'

'This boy has been lying,' she said without raising her head. 'He didn't smell anything.'

'It was around eleven o'clock,' Tobías said. 'I was chasing crabs away.'

The woman finished mending a collar.

'Lies,' she insisted. 'Everybody knows you're a tricker.' She bit the thread with her teeth and looked at Tobías over her glasses.

'What I can't understand is why you went to the trouble to put Vaseline on your hair and shine your shoes just to come and be so disrespectful to me.'

From then on Tobías began to keep watch on the sea. He hung his hammock up on the porch by the yard and spent the night waiting, surprised by the things that go on in the world while people are asleep. For many nights he could hear the desperate scrawling of the crabs as they tried to claw-climb up the supports of the house, until so many nights went by that they got tired of trying. He came to know Clotilde's way of sleeping. He discovered how her fluty snores became more high-pitched as the heat grew more intense until they became one single languid note in the torpor of July.

At first Tobías kept watch on the sea the way people who know it well do, his gaze fixed on a single point of the horizon. He watched it change color. He watched it turn out its lights and become frothy and dirty and toss up its refuse-laden belches when great rainstorms agitated its digestion. Little by little he learned to keep watch the way people who know it better do, not even looking at it but unable to forget about it even in his sleep.

Old Jacob's wife died in August. She died in her sleep and they had to cast her, like everyone else, into a flowerless sea. Tobías kept on waiting. He had waited so long that it was becoming his way of being. One night, while he was dozing in his hammock, he realized that something in the air had changed. It was an intermittent wave, like the time a Japanese ship had jettisoned a cargo of rotten onions at the harbor mouth. Then the smell thickened and was motionless until dawn. Only when he had the feeling that he could pick it up in his hands and exhibit it did Tobías leap out of his hammock and go into Clotilde's room. He shook her several times.

'Here it is,' he told her.

Clotilde had to brush the smell away like a cobweb in order to get up. Then she fell back down on her tepid sheets.

'God curse it,' she said.

Tobías leaped toward the door, ran into the middle of the street, and began to shout. He shouted with all his might, took a deep breath and shouted again, and then there was a silence and he took a deeper breath, and the smell was still on the sea. But nobody answered. Then he went about knocking on doors from house to house, even on houses that had no owners, until his uproar got entwined with that of the dogs and he woke everybody up.

Many of them couldn't smell it. But others, especially the old ones, went down to enjoy it on the beach. It was a compact fragrance that left no chink for any odor of the past. Some, worn out from so much smelling, went back to their houses. Most of the people stayed to finish their night's sleep on the beach. By dawn the smell was so pure that it was a pity even to breathe it.

Tobías slept most of the day. Clotilde caught up with him at siesta time and they spent the afternoon frolicking in bed without even closing the door to the yard. First they did it like earthworms, then like rabbits, and finally like turtles, until the world grew sad and it was dark again. There was still a trace of roses in the air. Sometimes a wave of music reached the bedroom.

'It's coming from Catarino's,' Clotilde said. 'Someone must have come to town.'

Three men and a woman had come. Catarino thought that others might come later and he tried to fix his gramophone. Since he couldn't do it, he asked Pancho Aparecido, who did all kinds of things because he'd never owned anything, and besides, he had a box of tools and a pair of intelligent hands.

Catarino's place was a wooden building set apart and facing the sea. It had one large room with benches and small tables, and several bedrooms in the rear. While they watched Pancho Aparecido working, the three men and the woman drank in silence, sitting at the bar and yawning in turn.

The gramophone worked well after several tries. When they heard the music, distant but distinct, the people stopped chatting. They looked at one another and for a moment had nothing to say, for only then did they realize how old they had become since the last time they'd heard music.

Tobías found everybody still awake after nine o'clock. They were sitting in their doorways listening to Catarino's old records, with the same look of childish fatalism of people watching an eclipse. Every record reminded them of someone who had died, the taste of food after a long illness, or something they'd had to do the next day many years ago which never got done because they'd forgotten.

The music stopped around eleven o'clock. Many people went to bed, thinking it was going to rain because a dark cloud hung over the sea. But the cloud descended, floated for a while on the surface, and then sank into the water. Only the stars remained above. A short while later, the breeze went out from the town and came back with a smell of roses.

'Just what I told you, Jacob,' Don Máximo Gómez exclaimed. 'Here it is back with us again. I'm sure now that we're going to smell it every night.'

'God forbid,' old Jacob said. 'That smell is the only thing in life that's come too late for me.'

They'd been playing checkers in the empty store without paying any attention to the records. Their memories were so ancient that there weren't records old enough to stir them up.

'For my part, I don't believe much of anything about this,' Don Máximo Gómez said. 'After so many years of eating dust, with so many women wanting a little yard to plant flowers in, it's not strange that a person should end up smelling things like this and even thinking it's all true.'

'But we can smell it with our own noses,' old Jacob said.

'No matter,' said Don Máximo Gómez. 'During the war, when the revolution was already lost, we'd wanted a general so bad that we saw the Duke of Marlborough appear in flesh and blood. I saw him with my own eyes, Jacob.'

It was after midnight. When he was alone, old Jacob closed his store and took his lamp to the bedroom. Through the window, outlined against the glow of the sea, he saw the crag from which they threw their dead.

'Petra,' he called in a soft voice.

She couldn't hear him. At that moment she was floating along almost on the surface of the water beneath a radiant noonday sun on the Bay of Bengal. She'd lifted her head to look through the water, as through an illuminated showcase, at a huge ocean liner. But she couldn't see her husband, who at that moment on the other side of the world was starting to hear Catarino's gramophone again.

'Just think,' old Jacob said. 'Barely six months ago they thought you were crazy and now they're the ones making a festival out of the smell that brought on your death.'

He put out the light and got into bed. He wept slowly with that graceless little whimper old people have, but soon he fell asleep.

'I'd get away from this town if I could,' he sobbed as he tossed. 'I'd go straight to hell or anywhere else if I could only get twenty pesos together.'

From that night on and for several weeks, the smell remained on the sea. It impregnated the wood of the houses, the food, and the drinking water, and there was nowhere to escape the odor. A lot of people were startled to find it in the vapors of their own shit. The men and the woman who had come to Catarino's place left one Friday, but they were back on Saturday with a whole mob. More people arrived on Sunday. They were in and out of everywhere like ants, looking for something to eat and a place to sleep, until it got to be impossible to walk the streets.

More people came. The women who had left when the town died came back to Catarino's. They were fatter and wore heavier make-up, and they brought the latest records, which didn't remind anyone of anything. Some of the former inhabitants of the town returned. They'd gone off to get filthy rich somewhere else and they came back talking about their fortunes but wearing the same clothes they'd left with. Music and side shows arrived, wheels of chance, fortunetellers and gunmen and men with snakes coiled about their necks who were selling the elixir of eternal life. They kept on coming for many weeks, even after the first rains had come and the sea became rough and the smell disappeared.

A priest arrived among the last. He walked all over, eating bread dipped in light coffee, and little by little, he banned everything that had come before him: games of chance, the new music and the way it was danced, and even the recent custom of sleeping on the beach. One evening, at Melchor's house, he preached a sermon about the smell of the sea.

'Give thanks to heaven, my children,' he said, 'for this is the smell of God.'

Someone interrupted him.

'How can you tell, Father? You haven't smelled it yet.'

'The Holy Scriptures,' he said, 'are quite explicit in regard to this smell. We are living in a chosen village.'

Tobías went about back and forth in the festival like a sleepwalker. He took Clotilde to see what money was. They made believe they were betting enormous sums at roulette, and then they figured things up and felt extremely rich with all the money they could have won. But one night not just they, the whole multitude occupying the town, saw more money in one place than they could possibly have imagined.

That was the night Mr Herbert arrived. He appeared suddenly, set up a table in the middle of the street, and on top of the table placed two large trunks brimful with bank notes. There was so much money that no one noticed it at first, because they couldn't believe it was true. But when Mr Herbert started ringing a little bell, the people had to believe him, and they went over to listen.

'I'm the richest man in the world,' he said. 'I've got so much money I haven't got room to keep it any more. And besides, since my heart's so big that there's no room for it in my chest,

I have decided to travel the world over solving the problems of mankind.'

He was tall and ruddy. He spoke in a loud voice and without any pauses, and simultaneously he waved about a pair of lukewarm, languid hands that always looked as if they'd just been shaved. He spoke for fifteen minutes and rested. Then he rang the little bell and began to speak again. Halfway through his speech, someone in the crowd waved a hat and interrupted him.

'Come on, mister, don't talk so much and start handing out the money.'

'Not so fast,' Mr Herbert replied. 'Handing out money with no rhyme or reason, in addition to being an unfair way of doing things, doesn't make any sense at all.'

With his eyes he located the man who had interrupted him, and motioned him to come forward. The crowd let him through.

'On the other hand,' Mr Herbert went on, 'this impatient friend of ours is going to give us a chance to explain the most equitable system of the distribution of wealth.' He reached out a hand and helped him up.

'What's your name?'

'Patricio.'

'All right, Patricio,' Mr Herbert said. 'Just like everybody else, you've got some problem you haven't been able to solve for some time.'

Patricio took off his hat and confirmed it with a nod.

'What is it?'

'Well, my problem is this,' Patricio said. 'I haven't got any money.'

'How much do you need?'

'Forty-eight pesos.'

Mr Herbert gave an exclamation of triumph. 'Forty-eight pesos,' he repeated. The crowd accompanied him in clapping.

'Very well, Patricio,' Mr Herbert went on. 'Now, tell us one thing: what can you do?'

'Lots of things.'

'Decide on one,' Mr Herbert said. 'The thing you do best.'

'Well,' Patricio said, 'I can do birds.'

Applauding a second time, Mr Herbert turned to the crowd.

'So, then, ladies and gentlemen, our friend Patricio, who does an extraordinary job at imitating birds, is going to imitate forty-eight different birds and in that way he will solve the great problem of his life.'

To the startled silence of the crowd, Patricio then did his birds. Sometimes whistling, sometimes with his throat, he did all known birds and finished off the figure with others that no one was able to identify. When he was through, Mr Herbert called for a round of applause and gave him forty-eight pesos.

'And now,' he said, 'come up one by one. I'm going to be here until tomorrow at this time solving problems.'

Old Jacob learned about the commotion from the comments of people walking past his house. With each bit of news his heart grew bigger and bigger until he felt it burst.

'What do you think about this gringo?' he asked.

Don Máximo Gómez shrugged his shoulders. 'He must be a philanthropist.'

'If I could only do something,' old Jacob said, 'I could solve my little problem right now. It's nothing much: twenty pesos.'

'You play a good game of checkers,' Don Máximo Gómez said.

Old Jacob appeared not to have paid any attention to him, but when he was alone, he wrapped up the board and the box of checkers in a newspaper and went off to challenge Mr Herbert. He waited until midnight for his turn. Finally Mr Herbert had them pack up his trunks and said good-bye until the next morning.

He didn't go off to bed. He showed up at Catarino's place with the men who were carrying his trunks and the crowd followed him all the way there with their problems. Little by little, he went on solving them, and he solved so many that finally, in the store, the only ones left were the women and some men with their problems already solved. And in the back of the room there was a solitary woman fanning herself slowly with a cardboard advertisement.

'What about you?' Mr Herbert shouted at her. 'What's your problem?'

The woman stopped fanning herself.

'Don't try to get me mixed up in your fun, mister gringo,' she shouted across the room. 'I haven't got any kind of problem and I'm a whore because it comes out of my balls.'

Mr Herbert shrugged his shoulders. He went on drinking his cold beer beside the open trunks, waiting for other problems. He was sweating. A while later, a woman broke away from the group that was with her at the table and spoke to him in a low voice. She had a five-hundred-peso problem.

'How would you split that up?' Mr Herbert asked her.

'By five.'

'Just imagine,' Mr Herbert said. 'That's a hundred men.'

'It doesn't matter,' she said. 'If I can get all that money together they'll be the last hundred men of my life.'

He looked her over. She was quite young, fragile-boned, but her eyes showed a simple decision.

'All right,' Mr Herbert said. 'Go into your room and I'll start sending each one with his five pesos to you.'

He went to the street door and rang his little bell.

At seven o'clock in the morning Tobías found Catarino's place open. All the lights were out. Half asleep and puffed up with beer, Mr Herbert was controlling the entry of men into the girl's room.

Tobías went in too. The girl recognized him and was surprised to see him in her room.

'You too?'

'They told me to come in,' Tobías said. 'They gave me five pesos and told me not to take too long.'

She took the soaked sheet off the bed and asked Tobías to hold the other end. It was as heavy as canvas. They squeezed it, twisting it by the ends, until it got its natural weight back. They turned the mattress over and the sweat came out the other side. Tobías did things as best he could. Before leaving he put the five pesos on the pile of bills that was growing high beside the bed.

'Send everybody you can,' Mr Herbert suggested to him. 'Let's see if we can get this over with before noon.'

The girl opened the door a crack and asked for a cold beer. There were still several men waiting.

'How many left?' she asked.

'Sixty-three,' Mr Herbert answered.

Old Jacob followed him about all day with his checkerboard. His turn came at nightfall and he laid out his problem and Mr Herbert accepted. They put two chairs and a small table on top of the big table in the middle of the street, and old Jacob made the first move. It was the last play he was able to premeditate. He lost.

'Forty pesos,' Mr Herbert said, 'and I'll give you a handicap of two moves.'

He won again. His hands barely touched the checkers. He played blindfolded, guessing his opponent's moves, and still won. The crowd grew tired of watching. When old Jacob decided to give up, he was in debt to the tune of five thousand seven hundred forty-two pesos and twenty-three cents.

He didn't change his expression. He jotted down the figure on a piece of paper he had in his pocket. Then he folded up the board, put the checkers in their box, and wrapped everything in the newspaper.

'Do with me what you will,' he said, 'but let me have these things. I promise you that I will spend the rest of my life getting all that money together.'

Mr Herbert looked at his watch.

'I'm terribly sorry,' he said. 'Your time will be up in twenty minutes.' He waited until he was sure that his opponent hadn't found the solution. 'Don't you have anything else to offer?'

'My honor.'

'I mean,' Mr Herbert explained, 'something that changes color when a brush daubed with paint is passed over it.'

'My house,' old Jacob said as if he were solving a riddle. 'It's not worth much, but it is a house.'

That was how Mr Herbert took possession of old Jacob's house. He also took possession of the houses and property of others who couldn't pay their debts, but he called for a week of music, fireworks, and acrobats and he took charge of the festivities himself.

It was a memorable week. Mr Herbert spoke of the miraculous destiny of the town and he even sketched out the city of the future, great glass buildings with dance floors on top. He showed it to the crowd. They looked in astonishment, trying to find themselves among the pedestrians painted in Mr Herbert's colors, but they were so well dressed that they couldn't recognize themselves. It pained them to be using him so much. They laughed at the urge they'd had to cry back in October and they kept on living in the midst of hope until Mr Herbert rang his little bell and said the party was over. Only then did he get some rest.

'You're going to die from that life you lead,' old Jacob said.

'I've got so much money that there's no reason for me to die,' Mr Herbert said.

He flopped onto his bed. He slept for days on end, snoring like a lion, and so many days went by that people grew tired of waiting on him. They had to dig crabs to eat. Catarino's new records got so old that no one could listen to them any more without tears, and he had to close his place up.

A long time after Mr Herbert had fallen asleep, the priest knocked on old Jacob's door. The house was locked from the inside. As the breathing of the man asleep had been using up the air, things had lost their weight and were beginning to float about.

'I want to have a word with him,' the priest said.

'You'll have to wait,' said old Jacob.

'I haven't got much time.'

'Have a seat, Father, and wait,' old Jacob repeated. 'And please talk to me in the meantime. It's been a long time since I've known what's been going on in the world.'

'People have all scattered,' the priest said. 'It won't be long before the town will be the same as it was before. That's the only thing that's new.'

'They'll come back when the sea smells of roses again,' old Jacob said.

'But meanwhile, we've got to sustain the illusions of those who stay with something,' the priest said. 'It's urgent that we start building the church.'

'That's why you've come to see Mr Herbert,' old Jacob said.

'That's right,' said the priest. 'Gringos are very charitable.'

'Wait a bit, then, Father,' old Jacob said. 'He might just wake up.'

They played checkers. It was a long and difficult game which lasted several days, but Mr Herbert didn't wake up.

The priest let himself be confused by desperation. He went all over with a copper plate asking for donations to build the church, but he didn't get very much. He was getting more and more diaphanous from so much begging, his bones were starting to fill with sounds, and one Sunday he rose two hands above the ground, but nobody noticed it. Then he packed his clothes in one suitcase and the money he had collected in another and said good-bye forever.

'The smell won't come back,' he said to those who tried to dissuade him. 'You've got to face up to the fact that the town has fallen into mortal sin.'

When Mr Herbert woke up the town was the same as it had been before. The rain had fermented the garbage the crowds had left in the streets and the soil was as arid and hard as a brick once more.

'I've been asleep a long time,' Mr Herbert said, yawning.

'Centuries,' said old Jacob.

'I'm starving to death.'

'So is everybody else,' old Jacob said. 'There's nothing to do but to go to the beach and dig for crabs.'

Tobías found him scratching in the sand, foaming at the mouth, and he was surprised to discover that when rich people were starving they looked so much like the poor. Mr Herbert didn't find enough crabs. At nightfall he invited Tobías to come look for something to eat in the depths of the sea.

'Listen,' Tobías warned him, 'only the dead know what's down inside there.'

'Scientists know too,' Mr Herbert said. 'Beneath the sea of the drowned there are turtles with exquisite meat on them. Get your clothes off and let's go.'

They went. At first they swam straight along and then down very deep to where the light of the sun stopped and then the light of the sea, and things were visible only in their own light. They passed by a submerged village with men and women on horseback turning about a musical kiosk. It was a splendid day and there were brightly colored flowers on the terraces.

'A Sunday sank at about eleven o'clock in the morning,' Mr Herbert said. 'It must have been some cataclysm.'

Tobías turned off toward the village, but Mr Herbert signaled him to keep going down.

'There are roses there,' Tobías said. 'I want Clotilde to know what they are.'

'You can come back another time at your leisure,' Mr Herbert said. 'Right now I'm dying of hunger.'

He went down like an octopus, with slow, slinky strokes of his arms. Tobías, who was trying hard not to lose sight of him, thought that it must be the way rich people swam. Little by little, they were leaving the sea of common catastrophes and entering the sea of the dead.

There were so many of them that Tobías thought that he'd never seen as many people on earth. They were floating motionless, face up, on different levels, and they all had the look of forgotten souls.

'They're very old dead,' Mr Herbert said. 'It's taken them centuries to reach this state of repose.'

Farther down, in the waters of the more recent dead, Mr Herbert stopped. Tobías caught up with him at the instant that a very young woman passed in front of them. She was floating on her side, her eyes open, followed by a current of flowers.

Mr Herbert put his finger to his lip and held it there until the last of the flowers went by.

'She's the most beautiful woman I've ever seen in all my life,' he said.

'She's old Jacob's wife,' Tobías said. 'She must be fifty years younger, but that's her. I'm sure of it.'

'She's done a lot of traveling,' Mr Herbert said. 'She's carrying behind her flowers from all the seas of the world.'

They reached bottom. Mr Herbert took a few turns over earth that looked like polished slate. Tobías followed him. Only when he became accustomed to the half light of the depths did he discover that the turtles were there. There were thousands of them, flattened out on the bottom, so motionless they looked petrified.

'They're alive,' Mr Herbert said, 'but they've been asleep for millions of years.'

He turned one over. With a soft touch he pushed it upward and the sleeping animal left his hands and continued drifting up. Tobías let it pass by. Then he looked toward the surface and saw the whole sea upside down.

'It's like a dream,' he said.

'For your own good,' Mr Herbert said, 'don't tell anyone about it. Just imagine the disorder there'd be in the world if people found out about these things.'

It was almost midnight when they got back to the village. They woke up Clotilde to boil some water. Mr Herbert butchered the turtle, but it took all three of them to chase and kill the heart a second time as it bounced out into the courtyard while they were cutting the creature up. They ate until they couldn't breathe any more.

'Well, Tobías,' Mr Herbert then said, 'we've got to face reality.'

'Of course.'

'And reality says,' Mr Herbert went on, 'that the smell will never come back.'

'It will come back.'

'It won't come back,' Clotilde put in, 'among other reasons because it never really came. It was you who got everybody all worked up.'

'You smelled it yourself,' Tobías said.

'I was half dazed that night,' Clotilde said. 'But right now I'm not sure about anything that has to do with this sea.'

'So I'll be on my way,' Mr Herbert said. 'And,' he added, speaking to both of them, 'you should leave too. There are too many things to do in the world for you to be starving in this town.'

He left. Tobías stayed in the yard counting the stars down to the horizon and he discovered that there were three more since last December. Clotilde called him from the bedroom, but he didn't pay any attention.

'Come here, you dummy,' Clotilde insisted. 'It's been years since we did it like rabbits.'

Tobías waited a long time. When he finally went in, she had fallen asleep. He half woke her, but she was so tired that they both got things mixed up and they were only able to do it like earthworms.

'You're acting like a boob,' Clotilde said grouchily. 'Try to think about something else.'

'I am thinking about something else.'

She wanted to know what it was and he decided to tell her on the condition that she wouldn't repeat it. Clotilde promised.

'There's a village at the bottom of the sea,' Tobías said, 'with little white houses with millions of flowers on the terraces.'

Clotilde raised her hands to her head.

'Oh, Tobías,' she exclaimed. 'Oh, Tobías, for the love of God, don't start up with those things again.'

Tobías didn't say anything else. He rolled over to the edge of the bed and tried to go to sleep. He couldn't until dawn, when the wind changed and the crabs left him in peace.

The Handsomest Drowned Man in the World

A TALE FOR CHILDREN

The first children who saw the dark and slinky bulge approaching through the sea let themselves think it was an enemy ship. Then they saw it had no flags or masts and they thought it was a whale. But when it washed up on the beach, they removed the clumps of seaweed, the jellyfish tentacles, and the remains of fish and flotsam, and only then did they see it was a drowned man.

They had been playing with him all afternoon, burying him in the sand and digging him up again, when someone chanced to see them and spread the alarm in the village. The men who carried him to the nearest house noticed that he weighed more than any dead man they had ever known, almost as much as a horse, and they said to each other that maybe he'd been floating too long and the water had got into his bones. When they laid him on the floor they said he'd been taller than all other men because there was barely enough room for him in the house, but they thought that maybe the ability to keep on growing after death was part of the nature of certain drowned men. He had the smell of the sea about him and only his shape gave one to suppose that it was the corpse of a human being, because the skin was covered with a crust of mud and scales.

They did not even have to clean off his face to know that the dead man was a stranger. The village was made up of only twenty-odd wooden houses that had stone courtyards with no flowers and which were spread about on the end of a desert-like cape. There was so little land that mothers always went about with the fear that the wind would carry off their children and the few dead that the years had caused among them had to be thrown off the cliffs. But the sea was calm and bountiful and all the men fitted into seven boats. So when they found the drowned man they simply had to look at one another to see that they were all there.

That night they did not go out to work at sea. While the men went to find out if anyone was missing in neighboring villages, the women stayed behind to care for the drowned man. They took the mud off with grass swabs, they removed the underwater stones entangled in his hair, and they scraped the crust off with tools used for scaling fish. As they were doing that they noticed that the vegetation on him came from faraway oceans and deep water and that his clothes were in tatters, as if he had sailed through labyrinths of coral. They noticed too that he bore his death with pride, for he did not have the lonely look of other drowned men who came out of the sea or that haggard, needy look of men who drowned in rivers. But only when they finished cleaning him off did they become aware of the kind of man he was and it left them breathless. Not only was he the tallest, strongest, most virile, and best built man they had ever seen, but even though they were looking at him there was no room for him in their imagination.

They could not find a bed in the village large enough to lay him on nor was there a table solid enough to use for his wake. The tallest men's holiday pants would not fit him, nor the fattest ones' Sunday shirts, nor the shoes of the one with the biggest feet. Fascinated by his huge size and his beauty, the women then decided to make him some pants from a large piece of sail and a shirt from some bridal brabant linen so that he could continue through his death with dignity. As they sewed, sitting in a circle and gazing at the corpse between stitches, it seemed to them that the wind had never been so steady nor the sea so restless as on that night and they supposed that the change had something to do with the dead man. They thought that if that magnificent man had lived in the village, his house would have had the widest doors, the highest ceiling, and the strongest floor, his bedstead would have been made from a midship frame held together by iron bolts, and his wife would have been the happiest woman. They thought that he would have had so much authority that he could have drawn fish out of the sea simply by calling their names and that he would have put so much work into his land that springs would have burst forth from among the rocks so that he would have been able to plant flowers on the cliffs. They secretly compared him to their own men, thinking that for all their lives theirs were incapable of doing what he could do in one night, and they ended up dismissing them deep in their hearts as the weakest, meanest, and most useless creatures on earth. They were wandering through that maze of fantasy when the oldest woman, who as the oldest had looked upon the drowned man with more compassion than passion, sighed:

'He has the face of someone called Esteban.'

It was true. Most of them had only to take another look at him to see that he could not have any other name. The more stubborn among them, who were the youngest, still lived for a few hours with the illusion that when they put his clothes on and he lay among the flowers in patent leather shoes his name might be Lautaro. But it was a vain illusion. There had not been enough canvas, the poorly cut and worse sewn pants were too tight, and the hidden strength of his heart popped the buttons on his shirt. After midnight the whistling of the wind died down and the sea fell into its Wednesday drowsiness. The silence put an end to any last doubts: he was Esteban. The women who had dressed him, who had combed his hair, had cut his nails and shaved him were unable to hold back a shudder of pity when they had to resign themselves to his being dragged along the ground. It was then that they understood how unhappy he must have been with that huge body since it bothered him even after death. They could see him in life, condemned to going through doors sideways, cracking his head on crossbeams, remaining on his feet during visits, not knowing what to do with his soft, pink, sea lion hands while the lady of the house looked for her most resistant chair and begged him, frightened to death, sit here, Esteban, please, and he, leaning against the wall, smiling, don't bother, ma'am, I'm fine where I am, his heels raw and his back roasted from having done the same thing so many times whenever he paid a visit, don't bother, ma'am, I'm fine where I am, just to avoid the embarrassment of breaking up the chair, and never knowing perhaps that the ones who said don't go, Esteban, at least wait till the coffee's ready, were the ones who later on would whisper the big boob finally left, how nice, the handsome fool has gone. That was what the women were thinking beside the body a little before dawn. Later, when they covered his face with a handkerchief so that the light would not bother him, he looked so forever dead, so defenseless, so much like their men that the first furrows of tears opened in their hearts. It was one of the younger ones who began the weeping. The others, coming to, went from sighs to wails, and the more they sobbed the more they felt like weeping, because the drowned man was becoming all the more Esteban for them, and so they wept so much, for he was the most destitute, most peaceful, and most obliging man on earth, poor Esteban. So when the men returned with the news that the drowned man was not from the neighboring villages either, the women felt an opening of jubilation in the midst of their tears.

'Praise the Lord,' they sighed, 'he's ours!'

The men thought the fuss was only womanish frivolity. Fatigued because of the difficult nighttime inquiries, all they wanted was to get rid of the bother of the newcomer once and for all before the sun grew strong on that arid, windless day. They improvised a litter with the remains of foremasts and gaffs, tying it together with rigging so that it would bear the weight of the body until they reached the cliffs. They wanted to tie the anchor from a cargo ship to him so that he would sink easily into the deepest waves, where fish are blind and divers die of nostalgia, and bad currents would not bring him back to shore, as had happened with other bodies. But the more they hurried, the more the women thought of ways to waste time. They walked about like startled hens, pecking with the sea charms on their breasts, some interfering on one side to put a scapular of the good wind on the drowned man, some on the other side to put a wrist compass on him, and after a great deal of *get away from there, woman, stay out of the way, look, you almost made me fall on top of the dead man*, the men began to feel mistrust in their livers and started grumbling about why so many main-altar decorations for a stranger, because no matter how many nails and holy-water jars he had on him, the sharks would chew him all the same, but the women kept piling on their junk relics, running back and forth, stumbling, while they released in sighs what they did not in tears, so that the men finally exploded with *since when has there ever been such a fuss over a drifting corpse, a drowned nobody, a piece of cold Wednesday meat*. One of the women, mortified by so much lack of care, then removed the handkerchief from the dead man's face and the men were left breathless too.

He was Esteban. It was not necessary to repeat it for them, to recognize him. If they had been told Sir Walter Raleigh, even they might have been impressed with his gringo accent, the macaw on his shoulder, his cannibal-killing blunderbuss, but there could be only one Esteban in the world and there he was, stretched out like a sperm whale, shoeless, wearing the pants of an undersized child, and with those stony nails that had to be cut with a knife. They only had to take the handkerchief off his face to see that he was ashamed, that it was not his fault that he was so big or so heavy or so handsome, and if he had known that this was going to happen, he would have looked for a more discreet place to drown in, seriously, I even would have tied the anchor off a galleon around my neck and staggered off a cliff like someone who doesn't like things in order not to be upsetting people now with this Wednesday dead body, as you people say, in order not to be bothering anyone with this filthy piece of cold meat that doesn't have anything to do with me. There was so much truth in his manner that even the most mistrustful men, the ones who felt the bitterness of endless nights at sea fearing that their women would tire of dreaming about them and begin to dream of drowned men, even they and others who were harder still shuddered in the marrow of their bones at Esteban's sincerity.

That was how they came to hold the most splendid funeral they could conceive of for an abandoned drowned man. Some women who had gone to get flowers in the neighboring villages returned with other women who could not believe what they had been told, and those women went back for more flowers when they saw the dead man, and they brought more and more until there were so many flowers and so many people that it was hard to walk about. At the final moment it pained them to return him to the waters as an orphan and they chose a father and mother from among the best people, and aunts and uncles and cousins, so that through him all the inhabitants of the village became kinsmen. Some sailors who heard the weeping from a distance went off course and people heard of one who had himself tied to the mainmast, remembering ancient fables about sirens. While they fought for the privilege of carrying him on their shoulders along the steep escarpment by the cliffs, men and women became aware for the first time of the desolation of their streets, the dryness of their courtyards, the narrowness of their dreams as they faced the splendor and beauty of their drowned man. They let him go without an anchor so that he could come back if he wished and whenever he wished, and they all held their breath for the fraction of centuries the body took to fall into the abyss. They did not need to look at one another to realize that they were no longer all present, that they would never be. But they also knew that everything would be different from then on, that their houses would have wider doors, higher ceilings, and stronger floors so that Esteban's memory could go everywhere without bumping into beams and so that no one in the future would dare whisper the big boob finally died, too bad, the handsome fool has finally died, because they were going to paint their house fronts gay colors to make Esteban's memory eternal and they were going to break their backs digging for springs among the stones and planting flowers on the cliffs so that in future years at dawn the passengers on great liners would awaken, suffocated by the smell of gardens on the high sea, and the captain would have to come down from the bridge in his dress uniform, with his astrolabe, his pole star, and his row of war medals and, pointing to the promontory of roses on the horizon, he would say in fourteen languages, look there, where the wind is so peaceful now that it's gone to sleep beneath the beds, over there, where the sun's so bright that the sunflowers don't know which way to turn, yes, over there, that's Esteban's village.

Death Constant Beyond Love

Senator Onésimo Sánchez had six months and eleven days to go before his death when he found the woman of his life. He met her in Rosal del Virrey, an illusory village which by night was the furtive wharf for smugglers' ships, and on the other hand, in broad daylight looked like the most useless inlet on the desert, facing a sea that was arid and without direction and so far from everything no one would have suspected that someone capable of changing the destiny of anyone lived there. Even its name was a kind of joke, because the only rose in that village was being worn by Senator Onésimo Sánchez himself on the same afternoon when he met Laura Farina.

It was an unavoidable stop in the electoral campaign he made every four years. The carnival wagons had arrived in the morning. Then came the trucks with the rented Indians who were carried into the towns in order to enlarge the crowds at public ceremonies. A short time before eleven o'clock, along with the music and rockets and jeeps of the retinue, the ministerial automobile, the color of strawberry soda, arrived. Senator Onésimo Sánchez was placid and weatherless inside the air-conditioned car, but as soon as he opened the door he was shaken by a gust of fire and his shirt of pure silk was soaked in a kind of light-colored soup and he felt many years older and more alone than ever. In real life he had just turned forty-two, had been graduated from Göttingen with honors as a metallurgical engineer, and was an avid reader, although without much reward, of badly translated Latin classics. He was married to a radiant German woman who had given him five children and they were all happy in their home, he the happiest of all until they told him, three months before, that he would be dead forever by next Christmas.

While the preparations for the public rally were being completed, the senator managed to have an hour alone in the house they had set aside for him to rest in. Before he lay down he put in a glass of drinking water the rose he had kept alive all across the desert, lunched on the diet cereals that he took with him so as to avoid the repeated portions of fried goat that were waiting for him during the rest of the day, and he took several analgesic pills before the time prescribed so that he would have the remedy ahead of the pain. Then he put the electric fan close to the hammock and stretched out naked for fifteen minutes in the shadow of the rose, making a great effort at mental distraction so as not to think about death while he dozed. Except for the doctors, no one knew that he had been sentenced to a fixed term, for he had decided to endure his secret all alone, with no change in his life, not because of pride but out of shame.

He felt in full control of his will when he appeared in public again at three in the afternoon, rested and clean, wearing a pair of coarse linen slacks and a floral shirt, and with his soul sustained by the anti-pain pills. Nevertheless, the erosion of death was much more pernicious than he had supposed, for as he went up onto the platform he felt a strange disdain for those who were fighting for the good luck to shake his hand, and he didn't feel sorry as he had at other times for the groups of barefoot Indians who could scarcely bear the hot saltpeter coals of the sterile little square. He silenced the applause with a wave of his hand, almost with rage, and he began to speak without gestures, his eyes fixed on the sea, which was sighing with heat. His measured, deep voice had the quality of calm water, but the speech that had been memorized and ground out so many times had not occurred to him in the nature of telling the truth, but, rather, as the opposite of a fatalistic pronouncement by Marcus Aurelius in the fourth book of his *Meditations*.

'We are here for the purpose of defeating nature,' he began, against all his convictions. 'We will no longer be foundlings in our own country, orphans of God in a realm of thirst and bad climate, exiles in our own land. We will be different people, ladies and gentlemen, we will be a great and happy people.'

There was a pattern to his circus. As he spoke his aides threw clusters of paper birds into the air and the artificial creatures took on life, flew about the platform of planks, and went out to sea. At the same time, other men took some prop trees with felt leaves out of the wagons and planted them in the saltpeter soil behind the crowd. They finished by setting up a cardboard façade with make-believe houses of red brick that had glass windows, and with it they covered the miserable real-life shacks.

The senator prolonged his speech with two quotations in Latin in order to give the farce more time. He promised rainmaking machines, portable breeders for table animals, the oils of happiness which would make vegetables grow in the saltpeter and clumps of pansies in the window boxes. When he saw that his fictional world was all set up, he pointed to it. 'That's the way it will be for us, ladies and gentlemen,' he shouted. 'Look! That's the way it will be for us.'

The audience turned around. An ocean liner made of painted paper was passing behind the houses and it was taller than the tallest houses in the artificial city. Only the senator himself noticed that since it had been set up and taken down and carried from one place to another the superimposed cardboard town had been eaten away by the terrible climate and that it was almost as poor and dusty as Rosal del Virrey.

For the first time in twelve years, Nelson Farina didn't go to greet the senator. He listened to the speech from his hammock amidst the remains of his siesta, under the cool bower of a house of unplaned boards which he had built with the same pharmacist's hands with which he had drawn and quartered his first wife. He had escaped from Devil's Island and appeared in Rosal del Virrey on a ship loaded with innocent macaws, with a beautiful and blasphemous black woman he had found in Paramaribo and by whom he had a daughter. The woman died of natural causes a short while later and she didn't suffer the fate of the other, whose pieces had fertilized her own cauliflower patch, but was buried whole and with her Dutch name in the local cemetery. The daughter had inherited her color and her figure along with her father's yellow and astonished eyes, and he had good reason to imagine that he was rearing the most beautiful woman in the world.

Ever since he had met Senator Onésimo Sánchez during his first electoral campaign, Nelson Farina had begged for his help in getting a false identity card which would place him beyond the reach of the law. The senator, in a friendly but firm way, had refused. Nelson Farina never gave up, and for several years, every time he found the chance, he would repeat his request with a different recourse. But this time he stayed in his hammock, condemned to rot alive in that burning den of buccaneers. When he heard the final applause, he lifted his head, and looking over the boards of the fence, he saw the back side of the farce: the props for the buildings, the framework of the trees, the hidden illusionists who were pushing the ocean liner along. He spat without rancor.

'*Merde,*' he said. '*C'est le Blacamán de la politique.*'

After the speech, as was customary, the senator took a walk through the streets of the town in the midst of the music and the rockets and was besieged by the townspeople, who told him their troubles. The senator listened to them good-naturedly and he always found some way to console everybody without having to do them any difficult favors. A woman up on the roof of a house with her six youngest children managed to make herself heard over the uproar and the fireworks.

'I'm not asking for much, Senator,' she said. 'Just a donkey to haul water from Hanged Man's Well.'

The senator noticed the six thin children. 'What became of your husband?' he asked.

'He went to find his fortune on the island of Aruba,' the woman answered good-humoredly, 'and what he found was a foreign woman, the kind that put diamonds on their teeth.'

The answer brought on a roar of laughter.

'All right,' the senator decided, 'you'll get your donkey.'

A short while later an aide of his brought a good pack donkey to the woman's house and on the rump it had a campaign slogan written in indelible paint so that no one would ever forget that it was a gift from the senator.

Along the short stretch of street he made other, smaller gestures, and he even gave a spoonful of medicine to a sick man who had had his bed brought to the door of his house so he could see him pass. At that last corner, through the boards of the fence, he saw Nelson Farina in his hammock, looking ashen and gloomy, but nonetheless the senator greeted him, with no show of affection.

'Hello, how are you?'

Nelson Farina turned in his hammock and soaked him in the sad amber of his look.

'*Moi, vous savez,*' he said.

His daughter came out into the yard when she heard the greeting. She was wearing a cheap, faded Guajiro Indian robe, her head was decorated with colored bows, and her face was painted as protection against the sun, but even in that state of disrepair it was possible to imagine that there had never been another so beautiful in the whole world. The senator was left breathless. 'I'll be damned!' he breathed in surprise. 'The Lord does the craziest things!'

That night Nelson Farina dressed his daughter up in her best clothes and sent her to the senator. Two guards armed with rifles who were nodding from the heat in the borrowed house ordered her to wait on the only chair in the vestibule.

The senator was in the next room meeting with the important people of Rosal del Virrey, whom he had gathered together in order to sing for them the truths he had left out of his speeches. They looked so much like all the ones he always met in all the towns in the desert that even the senator himself was sick and tired of that perpetual nightly session. His shirt was soaked with sweat and he was trying to dry it on his body with the hot breeze from an electric fan that was buzzing like a horse fly in the heavy heat of the room.

'We, of course, can't eat paper birds,' he said. 'You and I know that the day there are trees and flowers in this heap of goat dung, the day there are shad instead of worms in the water holes, that day neither you nor I will have anything to do here, do I make myself clear?'

No one answered. While he was speaking, the senator had torn a sheet off the calendar and fashioned a paper butterfly out of it with his hands. He tossed it with no particular aim into the air current coming from the fan and the butterfly flew about the room and then went out through the half-open door. The senator went on speaking with a control aided by the complicity of death.

'Therefore,' he said, 'I don't have to repeat to you what you already know too well: that my reelection is a better piece of business for you than it is for me, because I'm fed up with stagnant water and Indian sweat, while you people, on the other hand, make your living from it.'

Laura Farina saw the paper butterfly come out. Only she saw it because the guards in the vestibule had fallen asleep on the steps, hugging their rifles. After a few turns, the large lithographed butterfly unfolded completely, flattened against the wall, and remained stuck there. Laura Farina tried to pull it off with her nails. One of the guards, who woke up with the applause from the next room, noticed her vain attempt.

'It won't come off,' he said sleepily. 'It's painted on the wall.'

Laura Farina sat down again when the men began to come out of the meeting. The senator stood in the doorway of the room with his hand on the latch, and he only noticed Laura Farina when the vestibule was empty.

'What are you doing here?'

'*C'est de la part de mon père,*' she said.

The senator understood. He scrutinized the sleeping guards, then he scrutinized Laura Farina, whose unusual beauty was even more demanding than his pain, and he resolved then that death had made his decision for him.

'Come in,' he told her.

Laura Farina was struck dumb standing in the doorway to the room: thousands of bank notes were floating in the air, flapping like the butterfly. But the senator turned off the fan and the bills were left without air and alighted on the objects in the room.

'You see,' he said, smiling, 'even shit can fly.'

Laura Farina sat down on a schoolboy's stool. Her skin was smooth and firm, with the same color and the same solar density as crude oil, her hair was the mane of a young mare, and her huge eyes were brighter than the light. The senator followed the thread of her look and finally found the rose, which had been tarnished by the saltpeter.

'It's a rose,' he said.

'Yes,' she said with a trace of perplexity. 'I learned what they were in Riohacha.'

The senator sat down on an army cot, talking about roses as he unbuttoned his shirt. On the side where he imagined his heart to be inside his chest he had a corsair's tattoo of a heart pierced by an arrow. He threw the soaked shirt to the floor and asked Laura Farina to help him off with his boots.

She knelt down facing the cot. The senator continued to scrutinize her, thoughtfully, and while she was untying the laces he wondered which one of them would end up with the bad luck of that encounter.

'You're just a child,' he said.

'Don't you believe it,' she said. 'I'll be nineteen in April.'

The senator became interested.

'What day?'

'The eleventh,' she said.

The senator felt better. 'We're both Aries,' he said. And smiling, he added:

'It's the sign of solitude.'

Laura Farina wasn't paying attention because she didn't know what to do with the boots. The senator, for his part, didn't know what to do with Laura Farina, because he wasn't used to sudden love affairs and, besides, he knew that the one at hand had its origins in indignity. Just to have some time to think, he held Laura Farina tightly between his knees, embraced her about the waist, and lay down on his back on the cot. Then he realized that she was naked under her dress, for her body gave off the dark fragrance of an animal of the woods, but her heart was frightened and her skin disturbed by a glacial sweat.

'No one loves us,' he sighed.

Laura Farina tried to say something, but there was only enough air for her to breathe. He laid her down beside him to help her, he put out the light and the room was in the shadow of the rose. She abandoned herself to the mercies of her fate. The senator caressed her slowly, seeking her with his hand, barely touching her, but where he expected to find her, he came across something iron that was in the way.

'What have you got there?'

'A padlock,' she said.

'What in hell!' the senator said furiously and asked what he knew only too well. 'Where's the key?'

Laura Farina gave a breath of relief.

'My papa has it,' she answered. 'He told me to tell you to send one of your people to get it and to send along with him a written promise that you'll straighten out his situation.'

The senator grew tense. 'Frog bastard,' he murmured indignantly. Then he closed his eyes in order to relax and he met himself in the darkness. *Remember*, he remembered, *that whether it's you or someone else, it won't be long before you'll be dead and it won't be long before your name won't even be left.*

He waited for the shudder to pass.

'Tell me one thing,' he asked then. 'What have you heard about me?'

'Do you want the honest-to-God truth?'

'The honest-to-God truth.'

'Well,' Laura Farina ventured, 'they say you're worse than

the rest because you're different.'

The senator didn't get upset. He remained silent for a long time with his eyes closed, and when he opened them again he seemed to have returned from his most hidden instincts.

'Oh, what the hell,' he decided. 'Tell your son of a bitch of a father that I'll straighten out his situation.'

'If you want, I can go get the key myself,' Laura Farina said. The senator held her back.

'Forget about the key,' he said, 'and sleep awhile with me. It's good to be with someone when you're so alone.'

Then she laid his head on her shoulder with her eyes fixed on the rose. The senator held her about the waist, sank his face into woods-animal armpit, and gave in to terror. Six months and eleven days later he would die in that same position, debased and repudiated because of the public scandal with Laura Farina and weeping with rage at dying without her.

The Last Voyage
of the Ghost Ship

Now they're going to see who I am, he said to himself in his strong new man's voice, many years after he had first seen the huge ocean liner without lights and without any sound which passed by the village one night like a great uninhabited palace, longer than the whole village and much taller than the steeple of the church, and it sailed by in the darkness toward the colonial city on the other side of the bay that had been fortified against buccaneers, with its old slave port and the rotating light, whose gloomy beams transfigured the village into a lunar encampment of glowing houses and streets of volcanic deserts every fifteen seconds, and even though at that time he'd been a boy without a man's strong voice but with his mother's permission to stay very late on the beach to listen to the wind's night harps, he could still remember, as if still seeing it, how the liner would disappear when the light of the beacon struck its side and how it would reappear when the light had passed, so that it was an intermittent ship sailing along, appearing and disappearing, toward the mouth of the bay, groping its way like a sleepwalker for the buoys that marked the harbor channel until something must have gone wrong with the compass needle, because it headed toward the shoals, ran aground, broke up, and sank without a single sound, even though a collision against the reefs like that should have produced a crash of metal and the explosion of engines that would have frozen with fright the soundest-sleeping dragons in the prehistoric jungle that began with the last streets of the village and ended on the other side of the world, so that he himself thought it was a dream, especially the next day, when he saw the radiant fishbowl of the bay, the disorder of colors of the Negro shacks on the hills above the harbor, the schooners of the smugglers from the Guianas loading their cargoes of innocent parrots whose craws were full of diamonds, he thought, I fell asleep counting the stars and I dreamed about that huge ship, of course, he was so convinced that he didn't tell anyone nor did he remember the vision again until the same night in the following March when he was looking for the flash of dolphins in the sea and what he found was the illusory liner, gloomy, intermittent, with the same mistaken direction as the first time, except that then he was so sure he was awake that he ran to tell his mother and she spent three weeks moaning with disappointment, because your brain's rotting away from doing so many things backward, sleeping during the day and going out at night like a criminal, and since she had to go to the city around that time to get something comfortable where she could sit and think about her dead husband, because the rockers on her chair had worn out after eleven years of widowhood, she took advantage of the occasion and had the boatman go near the shoals so that her son could see what he really saw in the glass of the sea, the lovemaking of manta rays in a springtime of sponges, pink snappers and blue corvinas diving into the other wells of softer waters that were there among the waters, and even the wandering hairs of victims of drowning in some colonial shipwreck, no trace of sunken liners or anything like it, and yet he was so pigheaded that his mother promised to watch with him the next March, absolutely, not knowing that the only thing absolute in her future now was an easy chair from the days of Sir Francis Drake which she had bought at an auction in a Turk's store, in which she sat down to rest that same night, sighing, oh, my poor Olofernos, if you could only see how nice it is to think about you on this velvet lining and this brocade from the casket of a queen, but the more she brought back the memory of her dead husband, the more the blood in her heart bubbled up and turned to chocolate, as if instead of sitting down she were running, soaked from chills and fevers and her breathing full of earth, until he returned at dawn and found her dead in the easy chair, still warm, but half rotted away as after a snakebite, the same as happened afterward to four other women before the murderous chair was thrown into the sea, far away where it wouldn't bring evil to anyone, because it had been used so much over the centuries that its faculty for giving rest had been used up, and so he had to grow accustomed to his miserable routine of an orphan who was pointed out by everyone as the son of the widow who had brought the throne of misfortune into the village, living not so much from public charity as from the fish he stole out of boats, while his voice was becoming a roar, and not remembering his visions of past times anymore until another night in March when he chanced to look seaward and suddenly, good Lord, there it is, the huge asbestos whale, the behemoth beast, come see it, he shouted madly, come see it, raising such an uproar of dogs' barking and women's panic that even the oldest men remembered the frights of their great-grandfathers and crawled under their beds, thinking that William Dampier had come back, but those who ran into the street didn't make the effort to see the unlikely apparatus which at that instant was lost again in the east and raised up in its annual disaster, but they covered him with blows and left him so twisted that it was then he said to himself, drooling with rage, now they're going to see who I am, but he took care not to share his determination with anyone, but spent the whole year with the fixed idea, now they're going to see who I am, waiting for it to be the eve of the apparition once more in order to do what he did, which was steal a boat, cross the bay, and spend the evening waiting for his great moment in the inlets of the slave port, in the human brine of the Caribbean, but so absorbed in his adventure that he didn't stop as he always did in front of the Hindu shops to look at the ivory mandarins carved from the whole tusk of an elephant, nor did he make fun of the Dutch Negroes in their orthopedic veloci-pedes, nor was he frightened as at other times of the copper skinned Malayans, who had gone around the world enthralled by the chimera of a secret tavern where they sold roast filets of Brazilian women, because he wasn't aware of anything until night came over him with all the weight of the stars and the jungle exhaled a sweet fragrance of gardenias and rotten salamanders, and there he was, rowing in the stolen boat toward the mouth of the bay, with the lantern out so as not to alert the customs police, idealized every fifteen seconds by the green wing flap of the beacon and turned human once more by the darkness, knowing that he was getting close to the buoys that marked the harbor channel, not only because its oppressive glow was getting more intense, but because the breathing of the water was becoming sad, and he rowed like that, so wrapped up in himself, that he didn't know where the fearful shark's breath that suddenly reached him came from or why the night became dense, as if the stars had suddenly died, and it was because the liner was there, with all of its inconceivable size, Lord, bigger than any other big thing in the world and darker than any other dark thing on land or sea, three hundred thousand tons of shark smell passing so close to the boat that he could see the seams of the steel precipice, without a single light in the infinite portholes, without a sigh from the engines, without a soul, and carrying its own circle of silence with it, its own dead air, its halted time, its errant sea in which a whole world of drowned animals floated, and suddenly it all disappeared with the flash of the beacon and for an instant it was the diaphanous Caribbean once more, the March night, the everyday air of the pelicans, so he stayed alone among the buoys, not knowing what to do, asking himself, startled, if perhaps he wasn't dreaming while he was awake, not just now but the other times too, but no sooner had he asked himself than a breath of mystery snuffed out the buoys, from the first to the last, so that when the light of the beacon passed by the liner appeared again and now its compasses were out of order, perhaps not even knowing what part of the ocean sea it was in, groping for the invisible channel but actually heading for the shoals, until he got the overwhelming revelation that that misfortune of the buoys was the last key to the enchantment and he lighted the lantern in the boat, a tiny red light that had no reason to alarm anyone in the watchtowers but which would be like a guiding sun for the pilot, because, thanks to it, the liner corrected its course and passed into the main gate of the channel in a maneuver of lucky resurrection, and then all the lights went on at the same time so that the boilers wheezed again, the stars were fixed in their places, and the animal corpses went to the bottom, and there was a clatter of plates and a fragrance of laurel sauce in the kitchens, and one could hear the pulsing of the orchestra on the moon decks and the throbbing of the arteries of high-sea lovers in the shadows of the staterooms, but he still carried so much leftover rage in him that he would not let himself be confused by emotion or be frightened by the miracle, but said to himself with more decision than ever, now they're going to see who I am, the cowards, now they're going to see, and instead of turning aside so that the colossal machine would not charge into him, he began to row in front of it, because now they really are going to see who I am, and he continued guiding the ship with the lantern until he was so sure of its obedience that he made it change course from the direction of the docks once more, took it out of the invisible channel, and led it by the halter as if it were a sea lamb toward the lights of the sleeping village, a living ship, invulnerable to the torches of the beacon, that no longer made it invisible but made it aluminum every fifteen seconds, and the crosses of the church, the misery of the houses, the illusion began to stand out, and still the ocean liner followed behind him, following his will inside of it, the captain asleep on his heart side, the fighting bulls in the snow of their pantries, the solitary patient in the infirmary, the orphan water of its cisterns, the unredeemed pilot who must have mistaken the cliffs for the docks, because at that instant the great roar of the whistle burst forth, once, and he was soaked with the downpour of steam that fell on him, again, and the boat belonging to someone else was on the point of capsizing, and again, but it was too late, because there were the shells of the shoreline, the stones of the streets, the doors of the disbelievers, the whole village illuminated by the lights of the fearsome liner itself, and he barely had time to get out of the way to make room for the cataclysm, shouting in the midst of the confusion, there it is, you cowards, a second before the huge steel cask shattered the ground and one could hear the neat destruction of ninety thousand five hundred champagne glasses breaking, one after the other, from stem to stern, and then the light came out and it was no longer a March dawn but the noon of a radiant Wednesday, and he was able to give himself the pleasure of watching the disbelievers as with open mouths they contemplated the largest ocean liner in this world and the other aground in front of the church, whiter than anything, twenty times taller than the steeple and some ninety-seven times longer than the village, with its name engraved in iron letters, *Halálcsillag*, and the ancient and languid waters of the seas of death dripping down its sides.

Blacamán the Good,
Vendor of Miracles

From the first Sunday I saw him he reminded me of a bullring mule, with his white suspenders that were backstitched with gold thread, his rings with colored stones on every finger, and his braids of jingle bells, standing on a table by the docks of Santa María del Darién in the middle of the flasks of specifics and herbs of consolation that he prepared himself and hawked through the towns along the Caribbean with his wounded shout, except that at that time he wasn't trying to sell any of that Indian mess but was asking them to bring him a real snake so that he could demonstrate on his own flesh an antidote he had invented, the only infallible one, ladies and gentlemen, for the bites of serpents, tarantulas, and centipedes plus all manner of poisonous mammals. Someone who seemed quite impressed by his determination managed to get a bushmaster of the worst kind somewhere (the snake that kills by poisoning the respiration) and brought it to him in a bottle, and he uncorked it with such eagerness that we all thought he was going to eat it, but as soon as the creature felt itself free it jumped out of the bottle and struck him on the neck, leaving him right then and there without any wind for his oratory and with barely enough time to take the antidote, and the vest-pocket pharmacist tumbled down into the crowd and rolled about on the ground, his huge body wasted away as if he had nothing inside of it, but laughing all the while with all of his gold teeth. The hubbub was so great that a cruiser from the north that had been docked there for twenty years on a goodwill mission declared a quarantine so that the snake

poison wouldn't get on board, and the people who were
sanctifying Palm Sunday came out of church with their blessed
palms, because no one wanted to miss the show of the
poisoned man, who had already begun to puff up with the air
of death and was twice as fat as he'd been before, giving off a
froth of gall through his mouth and panting through his pores,
but still laughing with so much life that the jingle bells tinkled
all over his body. The swelling snapped the laces of his
leggings and the seams of his clothes, his fingers grew purple
from the pressure of the rings, he turned the color of venison
in brine, and from his rear end came a hint of the last
moments of death, so that everyone who had seen a person
bitten by a snake knew that he was rotting away before dying
and that he would be so crumpled up that they'd have to pick
him up with a shovel to put him into a sack, but they also
thought that even in his sawdust state he'd keep on laughing.
It was so incredible that the marines came up on deck to take
colored pictures of him with long-distance lenses, but the
women who'd come out of church blocked their intentions by
covering the dying man with a blanket and laying blessed
palms on top of him, some because they didn't want the
soldiers to profane the body with their Adventist instruments,
others because they were afraid to continue looking at that
idolater who was ready to die dying with laughter, and others
because in that way perhaps his soul at least would not be
poisoned. Everybody had given him up for dead when he
pushed aside the palms with one arm, still half-dazed and not
completely recovered from the bad moment he'd had, but he
set the table up without anyone's help, climbed on it like a
crab once more, and there he was again, shouting that his
antidote was nothing but the hand of God in a bottle, as we
had all seen with our own eyes, but it only cost two cuartillos
because he hadn't invented it as an item for sale but for the
good of all humanity, and as soon as he said that, ladies and
gentlemen, I only ask you not to crowd around, there's
enough for everybody.

They crowded around, of course, and they did well to do

so, because in the end there wasn't enough for everybody. Even the admiral from the cruiser bought a bottle, convinced by him that it was also good for the poisoned bullets of anarchists, and the sailors weren't satisfied with just taking colored pictures of him up on the table, pictures they had been unable to take of him dead, but they had him signing autographs until his arm was twisted with cramps. It was getting to be night and only the most perplexed of us were left by the docks when with his eyes he searched for someone with the look of an idiot to help him put the bottles away, and naturally he spotted me. It was like the look of destiny, not just mine, but his too, for that was more than a century ago and we both remember it as if it had been last Sunday. What happened was that we were putting his circus drugstore into that trunk with purple straps that looked more like a scholar's casket, when he must have noticed some light inside of me that he hadn't seen in me before, because he asked me in a surly way who are you, and I answered that I was an orphan on both sides whose papa hadn't died, and he gave out with laughter that was louder than what he had given with the poison and then he asked me what do you do for a living, and I answered that I didn't do anything except stay alive, because nothing else was worth the trouble, and still weeping with laughter he asked me what science in the world do you most want to learn, and that was the only time I answered the truth without any fooling, I wanted to be a fortune-teller, and then he didn't laugh again but told me as if thinking out loud that I didn't need much for that because I already had the hardest thing to learn, which was my face of an idiot. That same night he spoke to my father and for one real and two cuartillos and a deck of cards that foretold adultery he bought me forevermore.

That was what Blacamán was like, Blacamán the Bad, because I'm Blacamán the Good. He was capable of convincing an astronomer that the month of February was nothing but a herd of invisible elephants, but when his good luck turned on him he became a heart-deep brute. In his days of glory he had been an embalmer of viceroys, and they say that he gave them faces with such authority that for many years they went on governing better than when they were alive, and that no one dared bury them until he gave them back their dead-man look, but his prestige was ruined by the invention of an endless chess game that drove a chaplain mad and brought on two illustrious suicides, and so he was on the decline, from an interpreter of dreams to a birthday hypnotist, from an extractor of molars by suggestion to a marketplace healer; therefore, at the time we met, people were already looking at him askance, even the freebooters. We drifted along with our trick stand and life was an eternal uncertainty as we tried to sell escape suppositories that turned smugglers transparent, furtive drops that baptized wives threw into the soup to instill the fear of God in Dutch husbands, and anything you might want to buy of your own free will, ladies and gentlemen, because this isn't a command, it's advice, and, after all, happiness isn't an obligation either. Nevertheless, as much as we died with laughter at his witticisms, the truth is that it was quite hard for us to manage enough to eat, and his last hope was founded on my vocation as a fortune-teller. He shut me up in the sepulchral trunk disguised as a Japanese and bound with starboard chains so that I could attempt to foretell what I could while he disemboweled the grammar book looking for the best way to convince the world of my new science, and here, ladies and gentlemen, you have this child tormented by Ezequiel's glowworms, and those of you who've been standing there with faces of disbelief, let's see if you dare ask him when you're going to die, but I was never able even to guess what day it was at that time, so he gave up on me as a soothsayer because the drowsiness of digestion disturbs your prediction gland, and after whacking me over the head for good luck, he decided to take me to my father and get his money back. But at that time he happened to find a practical application for the electricity of suffering, and he set about building a sewing machine that ran connected by cupping glasses to the part of the body where there was a pain. Since I spent the night moaning over the whacks he'd given me to conjure away misfortune, he had to keep me on as the one who could test his invention, and so our return was delayed and he was getting back his good humor until the machine worked so well that it not only sewed better than a novice nun but also embroidered birds or astromelias according to the position and intensity of the pain. That was what we were up to, convinced of our triumph over bad luck, when the news reached us that in Philadelphia the commander of the cruiser had tried to repeat the experiment with the antidote and that he'd been changed into a glob of admiral jelly in front of his staff.

He didn't laugh again for a long time. We fled through Indian passes and the more lost we became, the clearer the news reached us that the marines had invaded the country under the pretext of exterminating yellow fever and were going about beheading every inveterate or eventual potter they found in their path, and not only the natives, out of precaution, but also the Chinese, for distraction, the Negroes, from habit, and the Hindus, because they were snake charmers, and then they wiped out the flora and fauna and all the mineral wealth they were able to because their specialists in our affairs had taught them that the people along the Caribbean had the ability to change their nature in order to confuse gringos. I couldn't understand where that fury came from or why we were so frightened until we found ourselves safe and sound in the eternal winds of La Guajira, and only then did he have the courage to confess to me that his antidote was nothing but rhubarb and turpentine and that he'd paid a drifter two cuartillos to bring him that bushmaster with all the poison gone. We stayed in the ruins of a colonial mission, deluded by the hope that some smugglers would pass, because they were men to be trusted and the only ones capable of venturing out under the mercurial sun of those salt flats. At first we ate smoked salamanders and flowers from the ruins and we still had enough spirit to laugh when we tried to eat his boiled leggings, but finally we even ate the water cobwebs from the cisterns and only then did we realize how much we missed the world. Since I didn't know of any recourse against death at that time, I simply lay down to wait for it where it would hurt me least, while he was delirious remembering a woman who was so tender that she could pass through walls just by sighing, but that contrived recollection was also a trick of his genius to fool death with lovesickness. Still, at the moment we should have died, he came to me more alive than ever and spent the whole night watching over my agony, thinking with such great strength that I still haven't been able to tell whether what was whistling through the ruins was the wind or his thoughts, and before dawn he told me with the same voice and the same determination of past times that now he knew the truth, that I was the one who had twisted up his luck again, so get your pants ready, because the same way as you twisted it up for me, you're going to straighten it out.

That was when I lost the little affection I had for him. He took off the last rags I had on, rolled me up in some barbed wire, rubbed rock salt on the sores, put me in brine from my own waters, and hung me by the ankles for the sun to flay me, and he kept on shouting that all that mortification wasn't enough to pacify his persecutors. Finally he threw me to rot in my own misery inside the penance dungeon where the colonial missionaries regenerated heretics, and with the perfidy of a ventriloquist, which he still had more than enough of, he began to imitate the voices of edible animals, the noises of ripe beets, and the sound of fresh springs so as to torture me with the illusion that I was dying of indigence in the midst of paradise. When the smugglers finally supplied him, he came down to the dungeon to give me something to eat so that I wouldn't die, but then he made me pay for that charity by pulling out my nails with pliers and filing my teeth down with a grindstone, and my only consolation was the wish that life would give me time and the good fortune to be quit of so much infamy with even worse martyrdoms. I myself was surprised that I could resist the plague of my own putrefaction and he kept throwing the leftovers of his meals onto me and tossed pieces of rotten lizards and hawks into the corners so that the air of the dungeon would end up poisoning me. I don't know how much time had passed when he brought me the carcass of a rabbit in order to show me that he preferred throwing it away to rot rather than giving it to me to eat, but my patience only went so far and all I had left was rancor, so I grabbed the rabbit by the ears and flung it against the wall with the illusion that it was he and not the animal that was going to explode, and then it happened, as if in a dream. The rabbit not only revived with a squeal of fright, but came back to my hands, hopping through the air.

That was how my great life began. Since then I've gone through the world drawing the fever out of malaria victims for two pesos, visioning blind men for four-fifty, draining the water from dropsy victims for eighteen, putting cripples back together for twenty pesos if they were that way from birth, for twenty-two if they were that way because of an accident or a brawl, for twenty-five if they were that way because of wars, earthquakes, infantry landings, or any other kind of public calamity, taking care of the common sick at wholesale according to a special arrangement, madmen according to their theme, children at half price, and idiots out of gratitude, and who dares say that I'm not a philanthropist, ladies and gentlemen, and now, yes, sir, commandant of the twentieth fleet, order your boys to take down the barricades and let suffering humanity pass, lepers to the left, epileptics to the right, cripples where they won't get in the way, and there in the back the least urgent cases, only please don't crowd in on me because then I won't be responsible if the sicknesses get all mixed up and people are cured of what they don't have, and keep the music playing until the brass boils, and the rockets firing until the angels burn, and the liquor flowing until ideas are killed, and bring on the wenches and the acrobats, the butchers and the photographers, and all at my expense, ladies and gentlemen, for here ends the evil fame of the Blacamáns and the universal tumult starts. That's how I go along putting them to sleep with the techniques of a congressman in case my judgment fails and some turn out worse than they were before on me. The only thing I don't do is revive the dead, because as soon as they open their eyes they're murderous with rage at the one who disturbed their state, and when it's all done, those who don't commit suicide die again of disillusionment. At first I was pursued by a group of wise men investigating the legality of my industry, and when they were convinced, they threatened me with the hell of Simon Magus and recommended a life of penitence so that I could get to be a saint, but I answered them, with no disrespect for their authority, that it was precisely along those lines that I had started. The truth is that I'd gain nothing by being a saint after being dead, an artist is what I am, and the only thing I want is to be alive so I can keep going along at donkey level in this six-cylinder touring car I bought from the marines' consul, with this Trinidadian chauffeur who was a baritone in the New Orleans pirates' opera, with my genuine silk shirts, my Oriental lotions, my topaz teeth, my flat straw hat, and my bicolored buttons, sleeping without an alarm clock, dancing with beauty queens, and leaving them hallucinated with my dictionary rhetoric, and with no flutter in my spleen if some Ash Wednesday my faculties wither away, because in order to go on with this life of a minister, all I need is my idiot face, and I have more than enough with the string of shops I own from here to beyond the sunset, where the same tourists who used to go around collecting from us through the admiral, now go stumbling after my autographed pictures, almanacs with my love poetry, medals with my profile, bits of my clothing, and all of that without the glorious plague of spending all day and all night sculpted in equestrian marble and shat on by swallows like the fathers of our country.

It's a pity that Blacamán the Bad can't repeat this story so that people will see that there's nothing invented in it. The last time anyone saw him in this world he'd lost even the studs of his former splendor, and his soul was a shambles and his bones in disorder from the rigors of the desert, but he still had enough jingle bells left to reappear that Sunday on the docks of Santa María del Darién with his eternal sepulchral trunk, except that this time he wasn't trying to sell any antidotes, but was asking in a voice cracking with emotion for the marines to shoot him in a public spectacle so that he could demonstrate on his own flesh the life-restoring properties of this supernatural creature, ladies and gentlemen, and even though you have more than enough right not to believe me after suffering so long from my evil tricks as a deceiver and falsifier, I swear on the bones of my mother that this proof today is nothing from the other world, merely the humble truth, and in case you have any doubts left, notice that I'm not laughing now the way I used to, but holding back a desire to cry. How convincing he must have been, unbuttoning his shirt, his eyes drowning with tears, and giving himself mule kicks on his heart to indicate the best place for death, and yet the marines didn't dare shoot, out of fear that the Sunday crowd would discover their loss of prestige. Someone who may not have forgotten the blacamanipulations of past times managed, no one knew how, to get and bring him in a can enough *barbasco* roots to bring to the surface all the corvinas in the Caribbean, and he opened it with great desire, as if he really was going to eat them, and, indeed, he did eat them, ladies and gentlemen, but please don't be moved or pray for the repose of my soul, because this death is nothing but a visit. That time he was so honest that he didn't break into operatic death rattles, but got off the table like a crab, looked on the ground for the most worthy place to lie down after some hesitation, and from there he looked at me as he would have at a mother and exhaled his last breath in his own arms, still holding back his manly tears all twisted up by the tetanus of eternity. That was the only time, of course, that my science failed me. I put him in that trunk of premonitory size where there was room for him laid out. I had a requiem mass sung for him which cost me fifty four-peso doubloons, because the officiant was dressed in gold and there were also three seated bishops. I had the mausoleum of an emperor built for him on a hill exposed to the best seaside weather, with a chapel just for him and an iron plaque on which there was written in Gothic capitals HERE LIES BLACAMÁN THE DEAD, BADLY CALLED THE BAD, DECEIVER OF MARINES AND VICTIM OF SCIENCE, and when those honors were sufficient for me to do justice to his virtues, I began to get my revenge for his infamy, and then I revived him inside the armored tomb and left him there rolling about in horror. That was long before the fire ants devoured Santa María del Darién, but the mausoleum is still intact on the hill in the shadow of the dragons that climb up to sleep in the Atlantic winds, and every time I pass through here I bring him an automobile load of roses and my heart pains with pity for his virtues, but then I put my ear to the plaque to hear him weeping in the ruins of the crumbling trunk and if by chance he has died again, I bring him back to life once more, for the beauty of the punishment is that he will keep on living in his tomb as long as I'm alive, that is, forever.

The Incredible and Sad Tale
of Innocent Eréndira
and Her Heartless Grandmother

Eréndira was bathing her grandmother when the wind of her misfortune began to blow. The enormous mansion of moon-like concrete lost in the solitude of the desert trembled down to its foundations with the first attack. But Eréndira and her grandmother were used to the risks of the wild nature there, and in the bathroom decorated with a series of peacocks and childish mosaics of Roman baths they scarcely paid any attention to the caliber of the wind.

The grandmother, naked and huge in the marble tub, looked like a handsome white whale. The granddaughter had just turned fourteen and was languid, soft-boned, and too meek for her age. With a parsimony that had something like sacred rigor about it, she was bathing her grandmother with water in which purifying herbs and aromatic leaves had been boiled, the latter clinging to the succulent back, the flowing metal-colored hair, and the powerful shoulders which were so mercilessly tattooed as to put sailors to shame.

'Last night I dreamt I was expecting a letter,' the grandmother said.

Eréndira, who never spoke except when it was unavoidable, asked:

'What day was it in the dream?'

'Thursday.'

'Then it was a letter with bad news,' Eréndira said, 'but it will never arrive.'

When she had finished bathing her grandmother, she took her to her bedroom. The grandmother was so fat that she could only walk by leaning on her granddaughter's shoulder or on a staff that looked like a bishop's crosier, but even during her most difficult efforts the power of an antiquated grandeur was evident. In the bedroom, which had been furnished with an excessive and somewhat demented taste, like the whole house, Eréndira needed two more hours to get her grandmother ready. She untangled her hair strand by strand, perfumed and combed it, put an equatorially flowered dress on her, put talcum powder on her face, bright red lipstick on her mouth, rouge on her cheeks, musk on her eyelids, and mother-of-pearl polish on her nails, and when she had her decked out like a larger than life-size doll, she led her to an artificial garden with suffocating flowers that were like the ones on the dress, seated her in a large chair that had the foundation and the pedigree of a throne, and left her listening to elusive records on a phonograph that had a speaker like a megaphone.

While the grandmother floated through the swamps of the past, Eréndira busied herself sweeping the house, which was dark and motley, with bizarre furniture and statues of invented Caesars, chandeliers of teardrops and alabaster angels, a gilded piano, and numerous clocks of unthinkable sizes and shapes. There was a cistern in the courtyard for the storage of water carried over many years from distant springs on the backs of Indians, and hitched to a ring on the cistern wall was a broken-down ostrich, the only feathered creature who could survive the torment of that accursed climate. The house was far away from everything, in the heart of the desert, next to a settlement with miserable and burning streets where the goats committed suicide from desolation when the wind of misfortune blew.

That incomprehensible refuge had been built by the grandmother's husband, a legendary smuggler whose name was Amadís, by whom she had a son whose name was also Amadís and who was Eréndira's father. No one knew either the origins or the motivations of that family. The best known version in the language of the Indians was that Amadís the father had rescued his beautiful wife from a house of prostitution in the Antilles, where he had killed a man in a knife fight, and that he had transplanted her forever in the impunity of the desert. When the Amadíses died, one of melancholy fevers and the other riddled with bullets in a fight over a woman, the grandmother buried their bodies in the courtyard, sent away the fourteen barefoot servant girls, and continued ruminating on her dreams of grandeur in the shadows of the furtive house, thanks to the sacrifices of the bastard granddaughter whom she had reared since birth.

Eréndira needed six hours just to set and wind the clocks. The day when her misfortune began she didn't have to do that because the clocks had enough winding left to last until the next morning, but on the other hand, she had to bathe and overdress her grandmother, scrub the floors, cook lunch, and polish the crystalware. Around eleven o'clock, when she was changing the water in the ostrich's bowl and watering the desert weeds around the twin graves of the Amadíses, she had to fight off the anger of the wind, which had become unbearable, but she didn't have the slightest feeling that it was the wind of her misfortune. At twelve o'clock she was wiping the last champagne glasses when she caught the smell of broth and had to perform the miracle of running to the kitchen without leaving a disaster of Venetian glass in her wake.

She just managed to take the pot off the stove as it was beginning to boil over. Then she put on a stew she had already prepared and took advantage of a chance to sit down and rest on a stool in the kitchen. She closed her eyes, opened them again with an unfatigued expression, and began pouring the soup into the tureen. She was working as she slept.

The grandmother had sat down alone at the head of a banquet table with silver candlesticks set for twelve people. She shook her little bell and Eréndira arrived almost immediately with the steaming tureen. As Eréndira was serving the soup, her grandmother noticed the somnambulist look and passed her hand in front of her eyes as if wiping an invisible pane of glass. The girl didn't see the hand. The grandmother followed her with her look and when Eréndira turned to go back to the kitchen, she shouted at her:

'Eréndira!'

Having been awakened all of a sudden, the girl dropped the tureen onto the rug.

'That's all right, child,' grandmother said to her with assuring tenderness. 'You fell asleep while you were walking about again.'

'My body has that habit,' Eréndira said by way of an excuse.

Still hazy with sleep, she picked up the tureen, and tried to clean the stain on the rug.

'Leave it,' her grandmother dissuaded her. 'You can wash it this afternoon.'

So in addition to her regular afternoon chores, Eréndira had to wash the dining room rug, and she took advantage of her presence at the washtub to do Monday's laundry as well, while the wind went around the house looking for a way in. She had so much to do that night came upon her without her realizing it, and when she put the dining room rug back in its place it was time to go to bed.

The grandmother had been fooling around on the piano all afternoon, singing the songs of her times to herself in a falsetto, and she had stains of musk and tears on her eyelids. But when she lay down on her bed in her muslin nightgown, the bitterness of fond memories returned.

'Take advantage of tomorrow to wash the living room rug too,' she told Eréndira. 'It hasn't seen the sun since the days of all the noise.'

'Yes, Grandmother,' the girl answered.

She picked up a feather fan and began to fan the implacable matron, who recited the list of night-time orders to her as she sank into sleep.

'Iron all the clothes before you go to bed so you can sleep with a clear conscience.'

'Yes, Grandmother.'

'Check the clothes closets carefully, because moths get hungrier on windy nights.'

'Yes, Grandmother.'

'With the time you have left, take the flowers out into the courtyard so they can get a breath of air.'

'Yes, Grandmother.'

'And feed the ostrich.'

She had fallen asleep but she was still giving orders, for it was from her that the granddaughter had inherited the ability to be alive still while sleeping. Eréndira left the room without making any noise and did the final chores of the night, still replying to the sleeping grandmother's orders.

'Give the graves some water.'

'Yes, Grandmother.'

'And if the Amadíses arrive, tell them not to come in,' the grandmother said, 'because Porfirio Galán's gang is waiting to kill them.'

Eréndira didn't answer her any more because she knew that the grandmother was getting lost in her delirium, but she didn't miss a single order. When she finished checking the window bolts and put out the last lights, she took a candlestick from the dining room and lighted her way to her bedroom as the pauses in the wind were filled with the peaceful and enormous breathing of her sleeping grandmother.

Her room was also luxurious, but not so much as her grandmother's, and it was piled high with the rag dolls and wind-up animals of her recent childhood. Overcome by the barbarous chores of the day, Eréndira didn't have the strength to get undressed and she put the candlestick on the night table and fell onto the bed. A short while later the wind of her misfortune came into the bedroom like a pack of hounds and knocked the candle over against the curtain.

At dawn, when the wind finally stopped, a few thick and scattered drops of rain began to fall, putting out the last embers and hardening the smoking ashes of the mansion. The people in the village, Indians for the most part, tried to rescue the remains of the disaster: the charred corpse of the ostrich, the frame of the gilded piano, the torso of a statue. The grandmother was contemplating the residue of her fortune with an impenetrable depression. Eréndira, sitting between the two graves of the Amadíses, had stopped weeping. When the grandmother was convinced that very few things remained intact among the ruins, she looked at her granddaughter with sincere pity.

'My poor child,' she sighed. 'Life won't be long enough for you to pay me back for this mishap.'

She began to pay it back that very day, beneath the noise of the rain, when she was taken to the village storekeeper, a skinny and premature widower who was quite well known in the desert for the good price he paid for virginity. As the grandmother waited undauntedly, the widower examined Eréndira with scientific austerity: he considered the strength of her thighs, the size of her breasts, the diameter of her hips. He didn't say a word until he had some calculation of what she was worth.

'She's still quite immature,' he said then. 'She has the teats of a bitch.'

Then he had her get on a scale to prove his decision with figures. Eréndira weighed ninety pounds.

'She isn't worth more than a hundred pesos,' the widower said.

The grandmother was scandalized.

'A hundred pesos for a girl who's completely new!' she almost shouted. 'No, sir, that shows a great lack of respect for virtue on your part.'

'I'll make it a hundred and fifty,' the widower said.

'This girl caused me damages amounting to more than a million pesos,' the grandmother said. 'At this rate she'll need two hundred years to pay me back.'

'You're lucky that the only good feature she has is her age,' the widower said.

The storm threatened to knock the house down, and there were so many leaks in the roof that it was raining almost as much inside as out. The grandmother felt all alone in a world of disaster.

'Just raise it to three hundred,' she said.

'Two hundred and fifty.'

Finally they agreed on two hundred and twenty pesos in cash and some provisions. The grandmother then signaled Eréndira to go with the widower and he led her by the hand to the back room as if he were taking her to school.

'I'll wait for you here,' the grandmother said.

'Yes, Grandmother,' said Eréndira.

The back room was a kind of shed with four brick columns, a roof of rotted palm leaves, and an adobe wall three feet high, through which outdoor disturbances got into the building. Placed on top of the adobe wall were pots with cacti and other plants of aridity. Hanging between two columns and flapping like the free sail of a drifting sloop was a faded hammock. Over the whistle of the storm and the lash of the water one could hear distant shouts, the howling of far-off animals, the cries of a shipwreck.

When Eréndira and the widower went into the shed they had to hold on so as not to be knocked down by a gust of rain which left them soaked. Their voices could not be heard but their movements became clear in the roar of the squall. At the widower's first attempt, Eréndira shouted something inaudible and tried to get away. The widower answered her without any voice, twisted her arm by the wrist, and dragged her to the hammock. She fought him off with a scratch on the face and shouted in silence again, but he replied with a solemn slap which lifted her off the ground and suspended her in the air for an instant with her long Medusa hair floating in space. He grabbed her about the waist before she touched ground again, flung her into the hammock with a brutal heave, and held her down with his knees. Eréndira then succumbed to terror, lost consciousness, and remained as if fascinated by the moonbeams from a fish that was floating through the storm air, while the widower undressed her, tearing off her clothes with a methodical clawing, as if he were pulling up grass, scattering them with great tugs of color that waved like streamers and went off with the wind.

When there was no other man left in the village who could pay anything for Eréndira's love, her grandmother put her on a truck to go where the smugglers were. They made the trip on the back of the truck in the open, among sacks of rice and buckets of lard and what had been left by the fire: the headboard of the viceregal bed, a warrior angel, the scorched throne, and other pieces of useless junk. In a trunk with two crosses painted in broad strokes they carried the bones of the Amadíses.

The grandmother protected herself from the sun with a tattered umbrella and it was hard for her to breathe because of the torment of sweat and dust, but even in that unhappy state she kept control of her dignity. Behind the pile of cans and sacks of rice Eréndira paid for the trip and the cartage by making love for twenty pesos a turn with the truck's loader. At first her system of defense was the same as she had used against the widower's attack, but the loader's approach was different, slow and wise, and he ended up taming her with tenderness. So when they reached the first town after a deadly journey, Eréndira and the loader were relaxing from good love behind the parapet of cargo. The driver shouted to the grandmother:

'Here's where the world begins.'

The grandmother observed with disbelief the miserable and solitary streets of a town somewhat larger but just as sad as the one they had abandoned.

'It doesn't look like it to me,' she said.

'It's mission country,' the driver said.

'I'm not interested in charity, I'm interested in smugglers,' said the grandmother.

Listening to the dialogue from behind the load, Eréndira dug into a sack of rice with her finger. Suddenly she found a string, pulled on it, and drew out a necklace of genuine pearls. She looked at it amazed, holding it between her fingers like a dead snake, while the driver answered her grandmother.

'Don't be daydreaming, ma'am. There's no such thing as smugglers.'

'Of course not,' the grandmother said. 'I've got your word for it.'

'Try to find one and you'll see,' the driver bantered. 'Everybody talks about them, but no one's ever seen one.'

The loader realized that Eréndira had pulled out the necklace and hastened to take it away from her and stick it back into the sack of rice. The grandmother, who had decided to stay in spite of the poverty of the town, then called to her granddaughter to help her out of the truck. Eréndira said good-bye to the loader with a kiss that was hurried but spontaneous and true.

The grandmother waited, sitting on her throne in the middle of the street, until they finished unloading the goods. The last item was the trunk with the remains of the Amadíses.

'This thing weighs as much as a dead man,' said the driver, laughing.

'There are two of them,' the grandmother said, 'so treat them with the proper respect.'

'I bet they're marble statues.' The driver laughed again.

He put the trunk with bones down carelessly among the singed furniture and held out his open hand to the grandmother.

'Fifty pesos,' he said.

'Your slave has already paid on the right-hand side.'

The driver looked at his helper with surprise and the latter made an affirmative sign. The driver then went back to the cab, where a woman in mourning was riding, in her arms a baby who was crying from the heat. The loader, quite sure of himself, told the grandmother:

'Eréndira is coming with me, if it's all right by you. My intentions are honorable.'

The girl intervened, surprised:

'I didn't say anything!'

'The idea was all mine,' the loader said.

The grandmother looked him up and down, not to make

him feel small but trying to measure the true size of his guts.

'It's all right by me,' she told him, 'provided you pay me what I lost because of her carelessness. It's eight hundred seventy-two thousand three hundred fifteen pesos, less the four hundred and twenty which she's already paid me, making it eight hundred seventy-one thousand eight hundred ninety-five.'

The truck started up.

'Believe me, I'd give you that pile of money if I had it,' the loader said seriously. 'The girl is worth it.'

The grandmother was pleased with the boy's decision.

'Well, then, come back when you have it, son,' she answered in a sympathetic tone. 'But you'd better go now, because if we figure out accounts again you'll end up owing me ten pesos.'

The loader jumped onto the back of the truck and it went off. From there he waved good-bye to Eréndira, but she was still so surprised that she didn't answer him.

In the same vacant lot where the truck had left them, Eréndira and her grandmother improvised a shelter to live in from sheets of zinc and the remains of Oriental rugs. They laid two mats on the ground and slept as well as they had in the mansion until the sun opened holes in the ceiling and burned their faces.

Just the opposite of what normally happened, it was the grandmother who busied herself that morning fixing up Eréndira. She made up her face in the style of sepulchral beauty that had been the vogue in her youth and touched her up with artificial fingernails and an organdy bow that looked like a butterfly on her head.

'You look awful,' she admitted, 'but it's better that way: men are quite stupid when it comes to female matters.'

Long before they saw them they both recognized the sound of two mules walking on the flint of the desert. At a command from her grandmother, Eréndira lay down on the mat the way an amateur actress might have done at the moment when the curtain was about to go up. Leaning on her bishop's crosier, the grandmother went out of the shelter and sat down on the throne to wait for the mules to pass.

The mailman was coming. He was only twenty years old, but his work had aged him, and he was wearing a khaki uniform, leggings, a pith helmet, and had a military pistol on his cartridge belt. He was riding a good mule and leading by the halter another, more timeworn one, on whom the canvas mailbags were piled.

As he passed by the grandmother he saluted her and kept on going, but she signaled him to look inside the shelter. The man stopped and saw Eréndira lying on the mat in her posthumous make-up and wearing a purple-trimmed dress.

'Do you like it?' the grandmother asked.

The mailman hadn't understood until then what the proposition was.

'It doesn't look bad to someone who's been on a diet,' he said, smiling.

'Fifty pesos,' the grandmother said.

'Boy, you're asking a mint!' he said. 'I can eat for a whole month on that.'

'Don't be a tightwad,' the grandmother said. 'The airmail pays even better than being a priest.'

'I'm the domestic mail,' the man said. 'The airmail man travels in a pickup truck.'

'In any case, love is just as important as eating,' the grandmother said.

'But it doesn't feed you.'

The grandmother realized that a man who lived from what other people were waiting for had more than enough time for bargaining.

'How much have you got?' she asked him.

The mailman dismounted, took some chewed-up bills from his pocket, and showed them to the grandmother. She snatched them up all together with a rapid hand just as if they had been a ball.

'I'll lower the price for you,' she said, 'but on one condition:

that you spread the word all around.'

'All the way to the other side of the world,' the mailman said. 'That's what I'm for.'

Eréndira, who had been unable to blink, then took off her artificial eyelashes and moved to one side of the mat to make room for the chance boyfriend. As soon as he was in the shelter, the grandmother closed the entrance with an energetic tug on the sliding curtain.

It was an effective deal. Taken by the words of the mailman, men came from very far away to become acquainted with the newness of Eréndira. Behind the men came gambling tables and food stands, and behind them all came a photographer on a bicycle, who, across from the encampment, set up a camera with a mourning sleeve on a tripod and a backdrop of a lake with listless swans.

The grandmother, fanning herself on her throne, seemed alien to her own bazaar. The only thing that interested her was keeping order in the line of customers who were waiting their turn and checking the exact amount of money they paid in advance to go in to Eréndira. At first she had been so strict that she refused a good customer because he was five pesos short. But with the passage of months she was assimilating the lessons of reality and she ended up letting people in who completed their payment with religious medals, family relics, wedding rings, and anything her bite could prove was bona-fide gold even if it didn't shine.

After a long stay in that first town, the grandmother had sufficient money to buy a donkey, and she went off into the desert in search of places more propitious for the payment of the debt. She traveled on a litter that had been improvised on top of the donkey and she was protected from the motionless sun by the half-spoked umbrella that Eréndira held over her head. Behind them walked four Indian bearers with the remnants of the encampment: the sleeping mats, the restored throne, the alabaster angel, and the trunks with the remains of the Amadíses. The photographer followed the caravan on his bicycle, but never catching up, as if he were going to a different festival.

Six months had passed since the fire when the grandmother was able to get a complete picture of the business.

'If things go on like this,' she told Eréndira, 'you will have paid me the debt inside of eight years, seven months, and eleven days.'

She went back over her calculations with her eyes closed, fumbling with the seeds she was taking out of a cord pouch where she also kept the money, and she corrected herself:

'All that, of course, not counting the pay and board of the Indians and other minor expenses.'

Eréndira, who was keeping in step with the donkey, bowed down by the heat and dust, did not reproach her grandmother for her figures, but she had to hold back her tears.

'I've got ground glass in my bones,' she said.

'Try to sleep.'

'Yes, Grandmother.'

She closed her eyes, took in a deep breath of scorching air, and went on walking in her sleep.

A small truck loaded with cages appeared, frightening goats in the dust of the horizon, and the clamor of the birds was like a splash of cool water for the Sunday torpor of San Miguel del Desierto. At the wheel was a corpulent Dutch farmer, his skin splintered by the outdoors, and with a squirrel-colored mustache he had inherited from some great-grandfather. His son Ulises, who was riding in the other seat, was a gilded adolescent with lonely maritime eyes and with the appearance of a furtive angel. The Dutchman noticed a tent in front of which all the soldiers of the local garrison were awaiting their turn. They were sitting on the ground, drinking out of the same bottle, which passed from mouth to mouth, and they had almond branches on their heads as if camouflaged for combat. The Dutchman asked in his language:

'What the devil can they be selling there?'

'A woman,' his son answered quite naturally. 'Her name is Eréndira.'

'How do you know?'

'Everybody in the desert knows,' Ulises answered.

The Dutchman stopped at the small hotel in town and got out. Ulises stayed in the truck. With agile fingers he opened a briefcase that his father had left on the seat, took out a roll of bills, put several in his pocket, and left everything just the way it had been. That night, while his father was asleep, he climbed out the hotel window and went to stand in line in front of Eréndira's tent.

The festivities were at their height. The drunken recruits were dancing by themselves so as not to waste the free music, and the photographer was taking night-time pictures with magnesium papers. As she watched over her business, the grandmother counted the bank notes in her lap, dividing them into equal piles and arranging them in a basket. There were only twelve soldiers at that time, but the evening line had grown with civilian customers. Ulises was the last one.

It was the turn of a soldier with a woeful appearance. The grandmother not only blocked his way but avoided contact with his money.

'No, son,' she told him. 'You couldn't go in for all the gold in the world. You bring bad luck.'

The soldier, who wasn't from those parts, was puzzled.

'What do you mean?'

'You bring down the evil shadows,' the grandmother said. 'A person only has to look at your face.'

She waved him off with her hand, but without touching him, and made way for the next soldier.

'Go right in, handsome,' she told him good-naturedly, 'but don't take too long, your country needs you.'

The soldier went in but he came right out again because Eréndira wanted to talk to her grandmother. She hung the basket of money on her arm and went into the tent, which wasn't very roomy, but which was neat and clean. In the back, on an army cot, Eréndira was unable to repress the trembling in her body, and she was in sorry shape, all dirty with soldier sweat.

'Grandmother,' she sobbed, 'I'm dying.'

The grandmother felt her forehead and when she saw she had no fever, she tried to console her.

'There are only ten soldiers left,' she said.

Eréndira began to weep with the shrieks of a frightened animal. The grandmother realized then that she had gone beyond the limits of horror and, stroking her head, she helped her calm down.

'The trouble is that you're weak,' she told her. 'Come on, don't cry any more, take a bath in sage water to get your blood back into shape.'

She left the tent when Eréndira was calmer and she gave the soldier waiting his money back. 'That's all for today,' she told him. 'Come back tomorrow and I'll give you the first place in line.' Then she shouted to those lined up:

'That's all, boys. Tomorrow morning at nine.'

Soldiers and civilians broke ranks with shouts of protest. The grandmother confronted them, in a good mood but brandishing the devastating crosier in earnest.

'You're an inconsiderate bunch of slobs!' she shouted. 'What do you think the girl is made of, iron? I'd like to see you in her place. You perverts! You shitty bums!'

The men answered her with even cruder insults, but she ended up controlling the revolt and stood guard with her staff until they took away the snack tables and dismantled the gambling stands. She was about to go back into the tent when she saw Ulises, as large as life, all by himself in the dark and empty space where the line of men had been before. He had an unreal aura about him and he seemed to be visible in the shadows because of the very glow of his beauty.

'You,' the grandmother asked him. 'What happened to your wings?'

'The one who had wings was my grandfather,' Ulises answered in his natural way, 'but nobody believed it.'

The grandmother examined him again with fascination. 'Well, I do,' she said. 'Put them on and come back tomorrow.' She went into the tent and left Ulises burning where he stood.

Eréndira felt better after her bath. She had put on a short, lace-trimmed slip and she was drying her hair before going to bed, but she was still making an effort to hold back her tears. Her grandmother was asleep.

Behind Eréndira's bed, very slowly, Ulises' head appeared. She saw the anxious and diaphanous eyes, but before saying anything she rubbed her head with the towel in order to prove that it wasn't an illusion. When Ulises blinked for the first time, Eréndira asked him in a very low voice:

'Who are you?'

Ulises showed himself down to his shoulders. 'My name is Ulises,' he said. He showed her the bills he had stolen and added:

'I've got money.'

Eréndira put her hands on the bed, brought her face close to that of Ulises, and went on talking to him as if in a kindergarten game.

'You were supposed to get in line,' she told him.

'I waited all night long,' Ulises said.

'Well, now you have to wait until tomorrow,' Eréndira said. 'I feel as if someone had been beating me on the kidneys.'

At that instant the grandmother began to talk in her sleep.

'It's going on twenty years since it rained last,' she said. 'It was such a terrible storm that the rain was all mixed in with sea water, and the next morning the house was full of fish and snails and your grandfather Amadís, may he rest in peace, saw a glowing manta ray floating through the air.'

Ulises hid behind the bed again. Eréndira showed an amused smile.

'Take it easy,' she told him. 'She always acts kind of crazy when she's asleep, but not even an earthquake can wake her up.'

Ulises reappeared. Eréndira looked at him with a smile that was naughty and even a little affectionate and took the soiled sheet off the mattress.

'Come,' she said. 'Help me change the sheet.'

Then Ulises came from behind the bed and took one end of

the sheet. Since the sheet was much larger than the mattress, they had to fold it several times. With every fold Ulises drew closer to Eréndira.

'I was going crazy wanting to see you,' he suddenly said. 'Everybody says you're very pretty and they're right.'

'But I'm going to die,' Eréndira said.

'My mother says that people who die in the desert don't go to heaven but to the sea,' Ulises said.

Eréndira put the dirty sheet aside and covered the mattress with another, which was clean and ironed.

'I never saw the sea,' she said.

'It's like the desert but with water,' said Ulises.

'Then you can't walk on it.'

'My father knew a man who could,' Ulises said, 'but that was a long time ago.'

Eréndira was fascinated but she wanted to sleep.

'If you come very early tomorrow you can be first in line,' she said.

'I'm leaving with my father at dawn,' said Ulises.

'Won't you be coming back this way?'

'Who can tell?' Ulises said. 'We just happened along now because we got lost on the road to the border.'

Eréndira looked thoughtfully at her sleeping grandmother.

'All right,' she decided. 'Give me the money.'

Ulises gave it to her. Eréndira lay down on the bed but he remained trembling where he was: at the decisive moment his determination had weakened. Eréndira took him by the hand to hurry him up and only then did she notice his tribulation. She was familiar with that fear.

'Is it the first time?' she asked him.

Ulises didn't answer but he smiled in desolation. Eréndira became a different person.

'Breathe slowly,' she told him. 'That's the way it always is the first time. Afterwards you won't even notice.'

She laid him down beside her and while she was taking his clothes off she was calming him maternally.

'What's your name?'

'Ulises.'

'That's a gringo name,' Eréndira said.

'No, a sailor name.'

Eréndira uncovered his chest, gave a few little orphan kisses, sniffed him.

'It's like you were made of gold all over,' she said, 'but you smell of flowers.'

'It must be the oranges,' Ulises said.

Calmer now, he gave a smile of complicity.

'We carry a lot of birds along to throw people off the track,' he added, 'but what we're doing is smuggling a load of oranges across the border.'

'Oranges aren't contraband,' Eréndira said.

'These are,' said Ulises. 'Each one is worth fifty thousand pesos.'

Eréndira laughed for the first time in a long while.

'What I like about you,' she said, 'is the serious way you make up nonsense.'

She had become spontaneous and talkative again, as if Ulises's innocence had changed not only her mood but her character. The grandmother, such a short distance away from misfortune, was still talking in her sleep.

'Around those times, at the beginning of March, they brought you home,' she said. 'You looked like a lizard wrapped in cotton. Amadís, your father, who was young and handsome, was so happy that afternoon that he sent for twenty carts loaded with flowers and arrived strewing them along the street until the whole village was gold with flowers like the sea.'

She ranted on with great shouts and with a stubborn passion for several hours. But Ulises couldn't hear her because Eréndira had loved him so much and so truthfully that she loved him again for half price while her grandmother was raving and kept on loving him for nothing until dawn.

A group of missionaries holding up their crucifixes stood shoulder to shoulder in the middle of the desert. A wind as fierce as the wind of misfortune shook their burlap habits and their rough beards and they were barely able to stand on their feet. Behind them was the mission, a colonial pile of stone with a tiny belfry on top of the harsh whitewashed walls.

The youngest missionary, who was in charge of the group, pointed to a natural crack in the glazed clay ground.

'You shall not pass beyond this line!' he shouted.

The four Indian bearers carrying the grandmother in a litter made of boards stopped when they heard the shout. Even though she was uncomfortable sitting on the planks of the litter and her spirit was dulled by the dust and sweat of the desert, the grandmother maintained her haughtiness intact. Eréndira was on foot. Behind the litter came a file of eight Indians carrying the baggage and at the very end the photographer on his bicycle.

'The desert doesn't belong to anyone,' the grandmother said.

'It belongs to God,' the missionary said, 'and you are violating his sacred laws with your filthy business.'

The grandmother then recognized the missionary's peninsular usage and diction and avoided a head-on confrontation so as not to break her head against his intransigence. She went back to being herself.

'I don't understand your mysteries, son.'

The missionary pointed at Eréndira.

'That child is underage.'

'But she's my granddaughter.'

'So much the worse,' the missionary replied. 'Put her under our care willingly or we'll have to seek recourse in other ways.'

The grandmother had not expected them to go so far.

'All right, if that's how it is.' She surrendered in fear. 'But sooner or later I'll pass, you'll see.'

Three days after the encounter with the missionaries, the grandmother and Eréndira were sleeping in a village near the mission when a group of stealthy, mute bodies, creeping along like an infantry patrol, slipped into the tent. They were six Indian novices, strong and young, their rough cloth habits seeming to glow in the moonlight. Without making a sound they cloaked Eréndira in a mosquito netting, picked her up without waking her, and carried her off wrapped like a large, fragile fish caught in a lunar net.

There were no means left untried by the grandmother in an attempt to rescue her granddaughter from the protection of the missionaries. Only when they had all failed, from the most direct to the most devious, did she turn to the civil authority, which was vested in a military man. She found him in the courtyard of his home, his chest bare, shooting with an army rifle at a dark and solitary cloud in the burning sky. He was trying to perforate it to bring on rain, and his shots were furious and useless, but he did take the necessary time out to listen to the grandmother.

'I can't do anything,' he explained to her when he had heard her out. 'The priests, according to the concordat, have the right to keep the girl until she comes of age. Or until she gets married.'

'Then why do they have you here as mayor?' the grandmother asked.

'To make it rain,' was the mayor's answer.

Then, seeing that the cloud had moved out of range, he interrupted his official duties and gave his full attention to the grandmother.

'What you need is someone with a lot of weight who will vouch for you,' he told her. 'Someone who can swear to your moral standing and your good behavior in a signed letter. Do you know Senator Onésimo Sánchez?'

Sitting under the naked sun on a stool that was too narrow for her astral buttocks, the grandmother answered with a solemn rage:

'I'm just a poor woman all alone in the vastness of the desert.'

The mayor, his right eye twisted from the heat, looked at her with pity.

'Then don't waste your time, ma'am,' he said. 'You'll rot in hell.'

She didn't rot, of course. She set up her tent across from the mission and sat down to think, like a solitary warrior besieging a fortified city. The wandering photographer, who knew her quite well, loaded his gear onto the carrier of his bicycle and was ready to leave all alone when he saw her in the full sun with her eyes fixed on the mission.

'Let's see who gets tired first,' the grandmother said, 'they or I.'

'They've been here for three hundred years and they can still take it,' the photographer said. 'I'm leaving.'

Only then did the grandmother notice the loaded bicycle.

'Where are you going?'

'Wherever the wind takes me,' the photographer said, and he left. 'It's a big world.'

The grandmother sighed.

'Not as big as you think, you ingrate.'

But she didn't move her head in spite of her anger so as not to lose sight of the mission. She didn't move it for many, many days of mineral heat, for many, many nights of wild winds, for all the time she was meditating and no one came out of the mission. The Indians built a lean-to of palm leaves beside the tent and hung their hammocks there, but the grandmother stood watch until very late, nodding on her throne and chewing the uncooked grain in her pouch with the invincible laziness of a resting ox.

One night a convoy of slow covered trucks passed very close to her and the only lights they carried were wreaths of colored bulbs which gave them the ghostly size of sleep-walking altars. The grandmother recognized them at once because they were just like the trucks of the Amadíses. The last truck in the convoy slowed, stopped, and a man got out of the cab to adjust something in back. He looked like a replica of the Amadíses, wearing a hat with a turned-up brim, high boots, two crossed cartridge belts across his chest, an army rifle, and two pistols. Overcome by an irresistible temptation, the grandmother called to the man.

'Don't you know who I am?' she asked him.

The man lighted her pitilessly with a flashlight. For an instant he studied the face worn out by vigil, the eyes dim from fatigue, the withered hair of the woman who, even at her age, in her sorry state, and with that crude light on her face, could have said that she had been the most beautiful woman in the world. When he examined her enough to be sure that he had never seen her before, he turned out the light.

'The only thing I know for sure is that you're not the Virgin of Perpetual Help.'

'Quite the contrary,' the grandmother said with a very sweet voice. 'I'm the Lady.'

The man put his hand to his pistol out of pure instinct.

'What lady?'

'Big Amadís's.'

'Then you're not of this world,' he said, tense. 'What is it you want?'

'For you to help me rescue my granddaughter, Big Amadís's granddaughter, the daughter of our son Amadís, held captive in that mission.'

The man overcame his fear.

'You knocked on the wrong door,' he said. 'If you think we're about to get mixed up in God's affairs, you're not the one you say you are, you never knew the Amadíses, and you haven't got the whoriest notion of what smuggling's all about.'

Early that morning the grandmother slept less than before. She lay awake pondering things, wrapped in a wool blanket while the early hour got her memory all mixed up and the repressed raving struggled to get out even though she was awake, and she had to tighten her heart with her hand so as not to be suffocated by the memory of a house by the sea with great red flowers where she had been happy. She remained that way until the mission bell rang and the first lights went on in the windows and the desert became saturated with the smell of the hot bread of matins. Only then did she abandon her fatigue, tricked by the illusion that Eréndira had got up and was looking for a way to escape and come back to her.

Eréndira, however, had not lost a single night's sleep since they had taken her to the mission. They had cut her hair with pruning shears until her head was like a brush, they put a hermit's rough cassock on her and gave her a bucket of whitewash and a broom so that she could whitewash the stairs every time someone went up or down. It was mule work because there was an incessant coming and going of muddied missionaries and novice carriers, but Eréndira felt as if every day were Sunday after the fearsome galley that had been her bed. Besides, she wasn't the only one worn out at night, because that mission was dedicated to fighting not against the devil but against the desert. Eréndira had seen the Indian novices bulldogging cows in the barn in order to milk them, jumping up and down on planks for days on end in order to press cheese, helping a goat through a difficult birth. She had seen them sweat like tanned stevedores hauling water from the cistern, watering by hand a bold garden that other novices cultivated with hoes in order to plant vegetables in the flintstone of the desert. She had seen the earthly inferno of the ovens for baking bread and the rooms for ironing clothes. She had seen a nun chase a pig through the courtyard, slide along holding the runaway animal by the ears, and roll in a mud puddle without letting go until two novices in leather aprons helped her get it under control and one of them cut its throat with a butcher knife as they all became covered with blood and mire. In the isolation ward of the infirmary she had seen tubercular nuns in their nightgown shrouds, waiting for God's last command as they embroidered bridal sheets on the terraces while the men preached in the desert. Eréndira was living in her shadows and discovering other forms of beauty and horror that she had never imagined in the narrow world of her bed, but neither the coarsest nor the most persuasive of the novices had managed to get her to say a word since they had taken her to the mission. One morning, while she was preparing the whitewash in her bucket, she heard string music that was like a light even more diaphanous than the light of the desert. Captivated by the miracle, she peeped into an immense and empty salon with bare walls and large windows through which the dazzling June light poured in and remained still, and in the center of the room she saw a very beautiful nun whom she had never seen before playing an Easter oratorio on the clavichord. Eréndira listened to the music without blinking, her heart hanging by a thread, until the lunch bell rang. After eating, while she whitewashed the stairs with her reed brush, she waited until all the novices had finished going up and coming down, and she was alone, with no one to hear her, and then she spoke for the first time since she had entered the mission.

'I'm happy,' she said.

So that put an end to the hopes the grandmother had that Eréndira would run away to rejoin her, but she maintained her granite siege without having made any decision until Pentecost. During that time the missionaries were combing the desert in search of pregnant concubines in order to get them married. They traveled all the way to the most remote settlements in a broken-down truck with four well-armed soldiers and a chest of cheap cloth. The most difficult part of that Indian hunt was to convince the women, who defended themselves against divine grace with the truthful argument that men, sleeping in their hammocks with legs spread, felt they had the right to demand much heavier work from legitimate wives than from concubines. It was necessary to seduce them with trickery, dissolving the will of God in the syrup of their own language so that it would seem less harsh to them, but even the most crafty of them ended up being convinced by a pair of flashy earrings. The men, on the other hand, once the women's acceptance had been obtained, were routed out of their hammocks with rifle butts, bound, and hauled away in the back of the truck to be married by force.

For several days the grandmother saw the little truck loaded with pregnant Indian women heading for the mission, but she failed to recognize her opportunity. She recognized it on Pentecost Sunday itself, when she heard the rockets and the ringing of the bells and saw the miserable and merry crowd that was going to the festival, and she saw that among the crowds there were pregnant women with the veil and crown of a bride holding the arms of their casual mates, whom they would legitimize in the collective wedding.

Among the last in the procession a boy passed, innocent of heart, with gourd-cut Indian hair and dressed in rags, carrying an Easter candle with a silk bow in his hand. The grandmother called him over.

'Tell me something, son,' she asked with her smoothest voice. 'What part do you have in this affair?'

The boy felt intimidated by the candle and it was hard for him to close his mouth because of his donkey teeth.

'The priests are going to give me my first communion,' he said.

'How much did they pay you?'

'Five pesos.'

The grandmother took a roll of bills from her pouch and the boy looked at them with surprise.

'I'm going to give you twenty,' the grandmother said. 'Not for you to make your first communion, but for you to get married.'

'Who to?'

'My granddaughter.'

So Eréndira was married in the courtyard of the mission in her hermit's cassock and a silk shawl that the novices gave her, and without even knowing the name of the groom her grandmother had bought for her. With uncertain hope she withstood the torment of kneeling on the saltpeter ground, the goat-hair stink of the two hundred pregnant brides, the punishment of the Epistle of Saint Paul hammered out in Latin under the motionless and burning sun, because the missionaries had found no way to oppose the wile of that unforeseen marriage, but had given her a promise as a last attempt to keep her in the mission. Nevertheless, after the ceremony in the presence of the apostolic prefect, the military mayor who shot at the clouds, her recent husband, and her impassive grandmother, Eréndira found herself once more under the spell that had dominated her since birth. When they asked her what her free, true, and definitive will was, she didn't even give a sigh of hesitation.

'I want to leave,' she said. And she clarified things by pointing at her husband. 'But not with him, with my grandmother.'

Ulises had wasted a whole afternoon trying to steal an orange from his father's grove, because the older man wouldn't take his eyes off him while they were pruning the sick trees, and his mother kept watch from the house. So he gave up his plan, for that day at least, and grudgingly helped his father until they had pruned the last orange trees.

The extensive grove was quiet and hidden, and the wooden house with a tin roof had copper grating over the windows and a large porch set on pilings, with primitive plants bearing intense flowers. Ulises' mother was on the porch sitting back in a Viennese rocking chair with smoked leaves on her temples to relieve her headache, and her full-blooded-Indian look followed her son like a beam of invisible light to the most remote corners of the orange grove. She was quite beautiful, much younger than her husband, and not only did she still wear the garb of her tribe, but she knew the most ancient secrets of her blood.

When Ulises returned to the house with the pruning tools, his mother asked him for her four o'clock medicine, which was on a nearby table. As soon as he touched them, the glass and the bottle changed color. Then, out of pure play, he touched a glass pitcher that was on the table beside some tumblers and the pitcher also turned blue. His mother observed him while she was taking her medicine and when she was sure that it was not a delirium of her pain, she asked him in the Guajiro Indian language:

'How long has that been happening to you?'

'Ever since we came back from the desert,' Ulises said, also in Guajiro. 'It only happens with glass things.'

In order to demonstrate, one after the other he touched the

glasses that were on the table and they all turned different colors.

'Those things happen only because of love,' his mother said. 'Who is it?'

Ulises didn't answer. His father, who couldn't understand the Guajiro language, was passing by the porch at that moment with a cluster of oranges.

'What are you two talking about?' he asked Ulises in Dutch.

'Nothing special,' Ulises answered.

Ulises' mother didn't know any Dutch. When her husband went into the house, she asked her son in Guajiro:

'What did he say?'

'Nothing special,' Ulises answered.

He lost sight of his father when he went into the house, but he saw him again through a window of the office. The mother waited until she was alone with Ulises and then repeated:

'Tell me who it is.'

'It's nobody,' Ulises said.

He answered without paying attention because he was hanging on his father's movements in the office. He had seen him put the oranges on top of the safe when he worked out the combination. But while he was keeping an eye on his father, his mother was keeping an eye on him.

'You haven't eaten any bread for a long time,' she observed.

'I don't like it.'

The mother's face suddenly took on an unaccustomed liveliness. 'That's a lie,' she said. 'It's because you're lovesick and people who are lovesick can't eat bread.' Her voice, like her eyes, had passed from entreaty to threat.

'It would be better if you told me who it was,' she said, 'or I'll make you take some purifying baths.'

In the office the Dutchman opened the safe, put the oranges inside, and closed the armored door. Ulises moved away from the window then and answered his mother impatiently.

'I already told you there wasn't anyone,' he said. 'If you don't believe me, ask Papa.'

The Dutchman appeared in the office doorway lighting his

sailor's pipe and carrying his threadbare Bible under his arm. His wife asked him in Spanish:

'Who did you meet in the desert?'

'Nobody,' her husband answered, a little in the clouds. 'If you don't believe me, ask Ulises.'

He sat down at the end of the hall and sucked on his pipe until the tobacco was used up. Then he opened the Bible at random and recited spot passages for almost two hours in flowing and ringing Dutch.

At midnight Ulises was still thinking with such intensity that he couldn't sleep. He rolled about in his hammock for another hour, trying to overcome the pain of memories until the very pain gave him the strength he needed to make a decision. Then he put on his cowboy pants, his plaid shirt, and his riding boots, jumped through the window, and fled from the house in the truck loaded with birds. As he went through the groves he picked the three ripe oranges he had been unable to steal that afternoon.

He traveled across the desert for the rest of the night and at dawn he asked in towns and villages about the whereabouts of Eréndira, but no one could tell him. Finally they informed him that she was traveling in the electoral campaign retinue of Senator Onésimo Sánchez and that on that day he was probably in Nueva Castilla. He didn't find him there but in the next town and Eréndira was no longer with him, for the grandmother had managed to get the senator to vouch for her morality in a letter written in his own hand, and with it she was going about opening the most tightly barred doors in the desert. On the third day he came across the domestic mailman and the latter told him what direction to follow.

'They're heading toward the sea,' he said, 'and you'd better hurry because the goddamned old woman plans to cross over to the island of Aruba.'

Following that direction, after half a day's journey Ulises spotted the broad, stained tent that the grandmother had bought from a bankrupt circus. The wandering photographer had come back to her, convinced that the world was really not as large as he had thought, and he had set up his idyllic backdrops near the tent. A band of brass-blowers was captivating Eréndira's clientele with a taciturn waltz.

Ulises waited for his turn to go in, and the first thing that caught his attention was the order and cleanliness of the inside of the tent. The grandmother's bed had recovered its viceregal splendor, the statue of the angel was in its place beside the funerary trunk of the Amadíses, and in addition, there was a pewter bathtub with lion's feet. Lying on her new canopied bed, Eréndira was naked and placid, irradiating a childlike glow under the light that filtered through the tent. She was sleeping with her eyes open. Ulises stopped beside her, the oranges in his hand, and he noticed that she was looking at him without seeing him. Then he passed his hand over her eyes and called her by the name he had invented when he wanted to think about her:

'Arídnere.'

Eréndira woke up. She felt naked in front of Ulises, let out a squeak, and covered herself with the sheet up to her neck.

'Don't look at me,' she said. 'I'm horrible.'

'You're the color of an orange all over,' Ulises said. He raised the fruits to her eyes so that she could compare. 'Look.'

Eréndira uncovered her eyes and saw that indeed the oranges did have her color.

'I don't want you to stay now,' she said.

'I only came to show you this,' Ulises said. 'Look here.'

He broke open an orange with his nails, split it in two with his hands, and showed Eréndira what was inside: stuck in the heart of the fruit was a genuine diamond.

'These are the oranges we take across the border,' he said.

'But they're living oranges!' Eréndira exclaimed.

'Of course.' Ulises smiled. 'My father grows them.'

Eréndira couldn't believe it. She uncovered her face, took the diamond in her fingers and contemplated it with surprise.

'With three like these we can take a trip around the world,' Ulises said.

Eréndira gave him back the diamond with a look of disappointment. Ulises went on:

'Besides, I've got a pickup truck,' he said. 'And besides that ... Look!'

From underneath his shirt he took an ancient pistol.

'I can't leave for ten years,' Eréndira said.

'You'll leave,' Ulises said. 'Tonight, when the white whale falls asleep, I'll be outside there calling like an owl.'

He made such a true imitation of the call of an owl that Eréndira's eyes smiled for the first time.

'It's my grandmother,' she said.

'The owl?'

'The whale.'

They both laughed at the mistake, but Eréndira picked up the thread again.

'No one can leave for anywhere without my grandmother's permission.'

'There's no reason to say anything.'

'She'll find out in any case,' Eréndira said. 'She can dream things.'

'When she starts to dream that you're leaving we'll already be across the border. We'll cross over like smugglers,' Ulises said.

Grasping the pistol with the confidence of a movie gunfighter, he imitated the sounds of the shots to excite Eréndira with his audacity. She didn't say yes or no, but her eyes gave a sigh and she sent Ulises away with a kiss. Ulises, touched, whispered:

'Tomorrow we'll be watching the ships go by.'

That night, a little after seven o'clock, Eréndira was combing her grandmother's hair when the wind of her misfortune blew again. In the shelter of the tent were the Indian bearers and the leader of the brass band, waiting to be paid. The grandmother finished counting out the bills on a chest she had within reach, and after consulting a ledger she paid the oldest of the Indians.

'Here you are,' she told him. 'Twenty pesos for the week,

less eight for meals, less three for water, less fifty cents on account for the new shirts, that's eight fifty. Count it.'

The oldest Indian counted the money and they all withdrew with a bow.

'Thank you, white lady.'

Next came the leader of the band. The grandmother consulted her ledger and turned to the photographer, who was trying to repair the bellows of his camera with wads of gutta-percha.

'What's it going to be?' she asked him. 'Will you or won't you pay a quarter of the cost of the music?'

The photographer didn't even raise his head to answer.

'Music doesn't come out in pictures.'

'But it makes people want to have their pictures taken,' the grandmother answered.

'On the contrary,' said the photographer. 'It reminds them of the dead and then they come out in the picture with their eyes closed.'

The bandleader intervened.

'What makes them close their eyes isn't the music,' he said. 'It's the lightning you make taking pictures at night.'

'It's the music,' the photographer insisted.

The grandmother put an end to the dispute. 'Don't be a cheapskate,' she said to the photographer. 'Look how well things have been going for Senator Onésimo Sánchez and it's thanks to the musicians he has along.' Then, in a harsh tone, she concluded:

'So pay what you ought to or go follow your fortune by yourself. It's not right for that poor child to carry the whole burden of expenses.'

'I'll follow my fortune by myself,' the photographer said. 'After all, an artist is what I am.'

The grandmother shrugged her shoulders and took care of the musician. She handed him a bundle of bills that matched the figure written in her ledger.

'Two hundred and fifty-four numbers,' she told him. 'At fifty cents apiece, plus thirty-two on Sundays and holidays at sixty cents apiece, that's one hundred fifty-six twenty.'

The musician wouldn't accept the money.

'It's one hundred eighty-two forty,' he said. 'Waltzes cost more.'

'Why is that?'

'Because they're sadder,' the musician said.

The grandmother made him take the money.

'Well, this week you'll play us two happy numbers for each waltz I owe you for and we'll be even.'

The musician didn't understand the grandmother's logic, but he accepted the figures while he unraveled the tangle. At that moment the fearsome wind threatened to uproot the tent, and in the silence that it left in its wake, outside, clear and gloomy, the call of an owl was heard.

Eréndira didn't know what to do to disguise her upset. She closed the chest with the money and hid it under the bed, but the grandmother recognized the fear in her hand when she gave her the key. 'Don't be frightened,' she told her. 'There are always owls on windy nights.' Still she didn't seem so convinced when she saw the photographer go out with the camera on his back.

'Wait till tomorrow if you'd like,' she told him. 'Death is on the loose tonight.'

The photographer had also noticed the call of the owl, but he didn't change his intentions.

'Stay, son,' the grandmother insisted. 'Even if it's just because of the liking I have for you.'

'But I won't pay for the music,' the photographer said.

'Oh, no,' the grandmother said. 'Not that.'

'You see?' the photographer said. 'You've got no love for anybody.'

The grandmother grew pale with rage.

'Then beat it!' she said. 'You lowlife!'

She felt so outraged that she was still venting her rage on him while Eréndira helped her go to bed. 'Son of an evil mother,' she muttered. 'What does that bastard know about anyone else's heart?' Eréndira paid no attention to her, because the owl was calling her with tenacious insistence during the pauses in the wind and she was tormented by uncertainty. The grandmother finally went to bed with the same ritual that had been *de rigueur* in the ancient mansion, and while her granddaughter fanned her she overcame her anger and once more breathed her sterile breath.

'You have to get up early,' she said then, 'so you can boil the infusion for my bath before the people get here.'

'Yes, Grandmother.'

'With the time you have left, wash the Indians' dirty laundry and that way we'll have something else to take off their pay next week.'

'Yes, Grandmother,' Eréndira said.

'And sleep slowly so that you won't get tired, because tomorrow is Thursday, the longest day of the week.'

'Yes, Grandmother.'

'And feed the ostrich.'

'Yes, Grandmother,' Eréndira said.

She left the fan at the head of the bed and lighted two altar candles in front of the chest with their dead. The grandmother, asleep now, was lagging behind with her orders.

'Don't forget to light the candles for the Amadíses.'

'Yes, Grandmother.'

Eréndira knew then that she wouldn't wake up, because she had begun to rave. She heard the wind barking about the tent, but she didn't recognize it as the wind of her misfortune that time either. She looked out into the night until the owl called again and her instinct for freedom in the end prevailed over her grandmother's spell.

She hadn't taken five steps outside the tent when she came across the photographer, who was lashing his equipment to the carrier of his bicycle. His accomplice's smile calmed her down.

'I don't know anything,' the photographer said, 'I haven't seen anything, and I won't pay for the music.'

He took his leave with a blessing for all. Then Eréndira ran toward the desert, having decided once and for all, and she was swallowed up in the shadows of the wind where the owl was calling.

That time the grandmother went to the civil authorities at once. The commandant of the local detachment leaped out of his hammock at six in the morning when she put the senator's letter before his eyes. Ulises' father was waiting at the door.

'How in hell do you expect me to know what it says!' the commandant shouted. 'I can't read.'

'It's a letter of recommendation from Senator Onésimo Sánchez,' the grandmother said.

Without further questions, the commandant took down a rifle he had near his hammock and began to shout orders to his men. Five minutes later they were all in a military truck flying toward the border against a contrary wind that had erased all trace of fugitives. The commandant rode in the front seat beside the driver. In back were the Dutchman and the grandmother, with an armed policeman on each running board.

Close to town they stopped a convoy of trucks covered with waterproof canvases. Several men who were riding concealed in the rear raised the canvas and aimed at the small vehicle with machine guns and army rifles. The commandant asked the driver of the first truck how far back they had passed a farm truck loaded with birds.

The driver started up before he answered.

'We're not stool pigeons,' he said indignantly, 'we're smugglers.'

The commandant saw the sooty barrels of the machine guns pass close to his eyes and he raised his arms and smiled.

'At least,' he shouted at them, 'you could have the decency not to go around in broad daylight.'

The last truck had a sign on its rear bumper: I THINK OF YOU, ERÉNDIRA.

The wind became drier as they headed north and the sun was fiercer than the wind. It was hard to breathe because of the heat and dust inside the closed-in truck.

The grandmother was the first to spot the photographer: he

was pedaling along in the same direction in which they were flying, with no protection against the sun except for a handkerchief tied around his head.

'There he is.' She pointed. 'He was their accomplice, the lowlife.'

The commandant ordered one of the policemen on the running board to take charge of the photographer.

'Grab him and wait for us here,' he said. 'We'll be right back.'

The policeman jumped off the running board and shouted twice for the photographer to halt. The photographer didn't hear him because of the wind blowing in the opposite direction. When the truck went on, the grandmother made an enigmatic gesture to him, but he confused it with a greeting, smiled, and waved. He didn't hear the shot. He flipped into the air and fell dead on top of his bicycle, his head blown apart by a rifle bullet, and he never knew where it came from.

Before noon they began to see feathers. They were passing by in the wind and they were feathers from young birds. The Dutchman recognized them because they were from his birds, plucked out by the wind. The driver changed direction, pushed the gas pedal to the floor, and in half an hour they could make out the pickup truck on the horizon.

When Ulises saw the military vehicle appear in the rearview mirror, he made an effort to increase the distance between them, but the motor couldn't do any better. They had traveled with no sleep and were done in from fatigue and thirst. Eréndira, who was dozing on Ulises' shoulder, woke up in fright. She saw the truck that was about to overtake them and with innocent determination she took the pistol from the glove compartment.

'It's no good,' Ulises said. 'It used to belong to Sir Francis Drake.'

She pounded it several times and threw it out the window. The military patrol passed the broken-down truck loaded with birds plucked by the wind, turned sharply, and cut it off.

*

It was around that time that I came to know them, their moment of greatest splendor, but I wouldn't look into the details of their lives until many years later when Rafael Escalona, in a song, revealed the terrible ending of the drama and I thought it would be good to tell the tale. I was traveling about selling encyclopedias and medical books in the province of Riohacha. Álvaro Cepeda Samudio, who was also traveling in the region, selling beer-cooling equipment, took me through the desert towns in his truck with the intention of talking to me about something and we talked so much about nothing and drank so much beer that without knowing when or where we crossed the entire desert and reached the border. There was the tent of wandering love under hanging canvas signs: ERÉNDIRA IS BEST; LEAVE AND COME BACK — ERÉNDIRA WAITS FOR YOU; THERE'S NO LIFE WITHOUT ERÉNDIRA. The endless wavy line composed of men of diverse races and ranks looked like a snake with human vertebrae dozing through vacant lots and squares, through gaudy bazaars and noisy marketplaces, coming out of the streets of that city, which was noisy with passing merchants. Every street was a public gambling den, every house a saloon, every doorway a refuge for fugitives. The many undecipherable songs and the shouted offerings of wares formed a single roar of panic in the hallucinating heat.

Among the throng of men without a country and sharpers was Blacamán the Good, up on a table and asking for a real serpent in order to test an antidote of his invention on his own flesh. There was the woman who had been changed into a spider for having disobeyed her parents, who would let herself be touched for fifty cents so that people would see there was no trick, and she would answer questions of those who might care to ask about her misfortune. There was an envoy from the eternal life who announced the imminent coming of the fearsome astral bat, whose burning brimstone breath would overturn the order of nature and bring the mysteries of the sea to the surface.

The one restful backwater was the red-light district, reached only by the embers of the urban din. Women from the four quadrants of the nautical rose yawned with boredom in the abandoned cabarets. They had slept their siestas sitting up, unawakened by people who wanted them, and they were still waiting for the astral bat under the fans that spun on the ceilings. Suddenly one of them got up and went to a balcony with pots of pansies that overlooked the street. Down there the row of Eréndira's suitors was passing.

'Come on,' the woman shouted at them. 'What's that one got that we don't have?'

'A letter from a senator,' someone shouted.

Attracted by the shouts and the laughter, other women came out onto the balcony.

'The line's been like that for days,' one of them said. 'Just imagine, fifty pesos apiece.'

The one who had come out first made a decision:

'Well, I'm going to go find out what jewel that seven-month baby has got.'

'Me too,' another said. 'It'll be better than sitting here warming our chairs for free.'

On the way others joined them and when they got to Eréndira's tent they made up a rowdy procession. They went in without any announcement, used pillows to chase away the man they found spending himself as best he could for his money, and they picked up Eréndira's bed and carried it out into the street like a litter.

'This is an outrage!' the grandmother shouted. 'You pack of traitors, you bandits!' And then, turning to the men in line: 'And you, you sissies, where do you keep your balls, letting this attack against a poor defenseless child go on? Damned fags!'

She kept on shouting as far as her voice would carry, distributing whacks with her crosier against all who came within reach, but her rage was inaudible amongst the shouts and mocking whistles of the crowd.

Eréndira couldn't escape the ridicule because she was prevented by the dog chain that the grandmother used to hitch her to a slat of the bed ever since she had tried to run away.

But they didn't harm her. They exhibited her on the canopied altar along the noisiest streets like the allegorical passage of the enchained penitent and finally they set her down like a catafalque in the center of the main square. Eréndira was all coiled up, her face hidden, but not weeping, and she stayed that way under the terrible sun in the square, biting with shame and rage at the dog chain of her evil destiny until someone was charitable enough to cover her with a shirt.

That was the only time I saw them, but I found out that they had stayed in that border town under the protection of the public forces until the grandmother's chests were bursting and then they left the desert and headed toward the sea. Never had such opulence been seen gathered together in that realm of poor people. It was a procession of ox-drawn carts on which cheap replicas of the paraphernalia lost in the disaster of the mansion were piled, not just the imperial busts and rare clocks, but also a secondhand piano and a Victrola with a crank and the records of nostalgia. A team of Indians took care of the cargo and a band of musicians announced their triumphal arrival in the villages.

The grandmother traveled on a litter with paper wreaths, chomping on the grains in her pouch, in the shadow of a church canopy. Her monumental size had increased, because under her blouse she was wearing a vest of sailcloth in which she kept the gold bars the way one keeps cartridges in a bandoleer. Eréndira was beside her, dressed in gaudy fabrics and with trinkets hanging, but with the dog chain still on her ankle.

'You've got no reason to complain,' her grandmother had said to her when they left the border town. 'You've got the clothes of a queen, a luxurious bed, a musical band of your own, and fourteen Indians at your service. Don't you think that's splendid?'

'Yes, Grandmother.'

'When you no longer have me,' the grandmother went on, 'you won't be left to the mercy of men because you'll have your own home in an important city. You'll be free and happy.'

It was a new and unforeseen vision of the future. On the other hand, she no longer spoke about the original debt, whose details had become twisted and whose installments had grown as the costs of the business became more complicated. Still Eréndira didn't let slip any sigh that would have given a person a glimpse of her thoughts. She submitted in silence to the torture of the bed in the saltpeter pits, in the torpor of the lakeside towns, in the lunar craters of the talcum mines, while her grandmother sang the vision of the future to her as if she were reading cards. One afternoon, as they came out of an oppressive canyon, they noticed a wind of ancient laurels and they caught snatches of Jamaica conversations and felt an urge to live and a knot in their hearts. They had reached the sea.

'There it is,' the grandmother said, breathing in the glassy light of the Caribbean after half a lifetime of exile. 'Don't you like it?'

'Yes, Grandmother.'

They pitched the tent there. The grandmother spent the night talking without dreaming and sometimes she mixed up her nostalgia with clairvoyance of the future. She slept later than usual and awoke relaxed by the sound of the sea. Nevertheless, when Eréndira was bathing her she again made predictions of the future and it was such a feverish clairvoyance that it seemed like the delirium of a vigil.

'You'll be a noble lady,' she told her. 'A lady of quality, venerated by those under your protection and favored and honored by the highest authorities. Ships' captains will send you postcards from every port in the world.'

Eréndira wasn't listening to her. The warm water perfumed with oregano was pouring into the bathtub through a tube fed from outside. Eréndira picked it up in a gourd, impenetrable, not even breathing, and poured it over her grandmother with one hand while she soaped her with the other.

'The prestige of your house will fly from mouth to mouth from the string of the Antilles to the realm of Holland,' the grandmother was saying. 'And it will be more important than the presidential palace, because the affairs of government will be discussed there and the fate of the nation will be decided.'

Suddenly the water in the tube stopped. Eréndira left the tent to find out what was going on and saw the Indian in charge of pouring water into the tube chopping wood by the kitchen.

'It ran out,' the Indian said. 'We have to cool more water.'

Eréndira went to the stove, where there was another large pot with aromatic herbs boiling. She wrapped her hands in a cloth and saw that she could lift the pot without the help of the Indian.

'You can go,' she told him. 'I'll pour the water.'

She waited until the Indian had left the kitchen. Then she took the boiling pot off the stove, lifted it with great effort to the height of the tube, and was about to pour the deadly water into the conduit to the bathtub when the grandmother shouted from inside the tent:

'Eréndira!'

It was as if she had seen. The granddaughter, frightened by the shout, repented at the last minute.

'Coming, Grandmother,' she said. 'I'm cooling off the water.'

That night she lay thinking until quite late while her grandmother sang in her sleep, wearing the golden vest. Eréndira looked at her from her bed with intense eyes that in the shadows resembled those of a cat. Then she went to bed like a person who had drowned, her arms on her breast and her eyes open, and she called with all the strength of her inner voice:

'Ulises!'

Ulises woke up suddenly in the house on the orange plantation. He had heard Eréndira's voice so clearly that he was looking for her in the shadows of the room. After an instant of reflection, he made a bundle of his clothing and shoes and left the bedroom. He had crossed the porch when his father's voice surprised him:

'Where are you going?'

Ulises saw him blue in the moonlight.

'Into the world,' he answered.

'This time I won't stop you,' the Dutchman said. 'But I warn you of one thing: wherever you go your father's curse will follow you.'

'So be it,' said Ulises.

Surprised and even a little proud of his son's resolution, the Dutchman followed him through the orange grove with a look that slowly began to smile. His wife was behind him with her beautiful Indian woman's way of standing. The Dutchman spoke when Ulises closed the gate.

'He'll be back,' he said, 'beaten down by life, sooner than you think.'

'You're so stupid,' she sighed. 'He'll never come back.'

On that occasion Ulises didn't have to ask anyone where Eréndira was. He crossed the desert hiding in passing trucks, stealing to eat and sleep and stealing many times for the pure pleasure of the risk until he found the tent in another seaside town which the glass buildings gave the look of an illuminated city and where resounded the nocturnal farewells of ships weighing anchor for the island of Aruba. Eréndira was asleep chained to the slat and in the same position of a drowned person on the beach from which she had called him. Ulises stood looking at her for a long time without waking her up, but he looked at her with such intensity that Eréndira awoke. Then they kissed in the darkness, caressed each other slowly, got undressed wearily, with a silent tenderness and a hidden happiness that was more than ever like love.

At the other end of the tent the sleeping grandmother gave a monumental turn and began to rant.

'That was during the time the Greek ship arrived,' she said. 'It was a crew of madmen who made the women happy and didn't pay them with money but with sponges, living sponges that later on walked about the houses moaning like patients in a hospital and making the children cry so that they could drink the tears.'

She made a subterranean movement and sat up in bed.

'That was when he arrived, my God,' she shouted, 'stronger, taller, and much more of a man than Amadís.'

Ulises, who until then had not paid any attention to the raving, tried to hide when he saw the grandmother sitting up in bed. Eréndira calmed him.

'Take it easy,' she told him. 'Every time she gets to that part she sits up in bed, but she doesn't wake up.'

Ulises leaned on her shoulder.

'I was singing with the sailors that night and I thought it was an earthquake,' the grandmother went on. 'They all must have thought the same thing because they ran away shouting, dying with laughter, and only he remained under the starsong canopy. I remember as if it had been yesterday that I was singing the song that everyone was singing those days. Even the parrots in the courtyard sang it.'

Flat as a mat, as one can sing only in dreams, she sang the lines of her bitterness:

> *Lord, oh, Lord, give me back the innocence I had*
> *So I can feel his love all over again from the start.*

Only then did Ulises become interested in the grandmother's nostalgia.

'There he was,' she was saying, 'with a macaw on his shoulder and a cannibal-killing blunderbuss, the way Guatarral arrived in the Guianas, and I felt his breath of death when he stood opposite me and said: "I've been around the world a thousand times and seen women of every nation, so I can tell you on good authority that you are the haughtiest and the most obliging, the most beautiful woman on earth."'

She lay down again and sobbed on her pillow. Ulises and Eréndira remained silent for a long time, rocked in the shadows by the sleeping old woman's great breathing. Suddenly Eréndira, without the slightest quiver in her voice, asked:

'Would you dare to kill her?'

Taken by surprise, Ulises didn't know what to answer.

'Who knows,' he said. 'Would you dare?'

'I can't,' Eréndira said. 'She's my grandmother.'

Then Ulises looked once more at the enormous sleeping body as if measuring the quantity of life and decided:

'For you I'd be capable of anything.'

Ulises bought a pound of rat poison, mixed it with whipped cream and raspberry jam, and poured that fatal cream into a piece of pastry from which he had removed the original filling. Then he put some thicker cream on top, smoothing it with a spoon until there was no trace of his sinister maneuver, and he completed the trick with seventy-two little pink candles.

The grandmother sat up on her throne waving her threatening crosier when she saw him come into the tent with the birthday cake.

'You brazen devil!' she shouted. 'How dare you set foot in this place?'

Ulises hid behind his angel face.

'I've come to ask your forgiveness,' he said, 'on this day, your birthday.'

Disarmed by his lie, which had hit its mark, the grandmother had the table set as if for a wedding feast. She sat Ulises down on her right while Eréndira served them, and after blowing out the candles with one devastating gust, she cut the cake into two equal parts. She served Ulises.

'A man who knows how to get himself forgiven has earned half of heaven,' she said. 'I give you the first piece, which is the piece of happiness.'

'I don't like sweet things,' he said. 'You take it.'

The grandmother offered Eréndira a piece of cake. She took it into the kitchen and threw it in the garbage.

The grandmother ate the rest all by herself. She put whole pieces into her mouth and swallowed them without chewing, moaning with delight and looking at Ulises from the limbo of her pleasure. When there was no more on her plate she also ate what Ulises had turned down. While she was chewing the last bit, with her fingers she picked up the crumbs from the tablecloth and put them into her mouth.

She had eaten enough arsenic to exterminate a whole generation of rats. And yet she played the piano and sang until midnight, went to bed happy, and was able to have a normal sleep. The only thing new was a rocklike scratch in her breathing.

Eréndira and Ulises kept watch over her from the other bed, and they were only waiting for her death rattle. But the voice was as alive as ever when she began to rave.

'I went crazy, my God, I went crazy!' she shouted. 'I put two bars on the bedroom door so he couldn't get in; I put the dresser and table against the door and the chairs on the table, and all he had to do was give a little knock with his ring for the defenses to fall apart, the chairs to fall off the table by themselves, the table and dresser to separate by themselves, the bars to move out of their slots by themselves.'

Eréndira and Ulises looked at her with growing surprise as the delirium became more profound and dramatic and the voice more intimate.

'I felt I was going to die, soaked in the sweat of fear, begging inside for the door to open without opening, for him to enter without entering, for him never to go away but never to come back either so I wouldn't have to kill him!'

She went on repeating her drama for several hours, even the most intimate details, as if she had lived it again in her dream. A little before dawn she rolled over in bed with a movement of seismic accommodation and the voice broke with the imminence of sobs.

'I warned him and he laughed,' she shouted. 'I warned him again and he laughed again, until he opened his eyes in terror, saying, 'Agh, queen! Agh, queen!' and his voice wasn't coming out of his mouth but through the cut the knife had made in his throat.'

Ulises, terrified at the grandmother's fearful evocation, grabbed Eréndira's hand.

'Murdering old woman!' he exclaimed.

Eréndira didn't pay any attention to him because at that instant dawn began to break. The clocks struck five.

'Go!' Eréndira said. 'She's going to wake up now.'

'She's got more life in her than an elephant,' Ulises exclaimed. 'It can't be!'

Eréndira cut him with a knifing look.

'The whole trouble,' she said, 'is that you're no good at all for killing anybody.'

Ulises was so affected by the crudeness of the reproach that he left the tent. Eréndira kept on looking at the sleeping grandmother with her secret hate, with the rage of her frustration, as the sun rose and the bird air awakened. Then the grandmother opened her eyes and looked at her with a placid smile.

'God be with you, child.'

The only noticeable change was a beginning of disorder in the daily routine. It was Wednesday, but the grandmother wanted to put on a Sunday dress, decided that Eréndira would receive no customers before eleven o'clock, and asked her to paint her nails garnet and give her a pontifical coiffure.

'I never had so much of an urge to have my picture taken,' she exclaimed.

Eréndira began to comb her grandmother's hair, but as she drew the comb through the tangles a clump of hair remained between the teeth. She showed it to her grandmother in alarm. The grandmother examined it, pulled on another clump with her fingers, and another bush of hair was left in her hand. She threw it on the ground, tried again and pulled out a larger lock. Then she began to pull her hair with both hands, dying with laughter, throwing the handfuls into the air with an incomprehensible jubilation until her head looked like a peeled coconut.

Eréndira had no more news of Ulises until two weeks later when she caught the call of the owl outside the tent. The grandmother had begun to play the piano and was so absorbed in her nostalgia that she was unaware of reality. She had a wig of radiant feathers on her head.

Eréndira answered the call and only then did she notice the wick that came out of the piano and went on through the underbrush and was lost in the darkness. She ran to where Ulises was, hid next to him among the bushes, and with tight hearts they both watched the little blue flame that crept along the wick, crossed the dark space, and went into the tent.

'Cover your ears,' Ulises said.

They both did, without any need, for there was no explosion. The tent lighted up inside with a radiant glow, burst in silence, and disappeared in a whirlwind of wet powder. When Eréndira dared enter, thinking that her grandmother was dead, she found her with her wig singed and her nightshirt in tatters, but more alive than ever, trying to put out the fire with a blanket.

Ulises slipped away under the protection of the shouts of the Indians, who didn't know what to do, confused by the grandmother's contradictory orders. When they finally managed to conquer the flames and get rid of the smoke, they were looking at a shipwreck.

'It's like the work of the evil one,' the grandmother said. 'Pianos don't explode just like that.'

She made all kinds of conjectures to establish the causes of the new disaster, but Eréndira's evasions and her impassive attitude ended up confusing her. She couldn't find the slightest crack in her granddaughter's behavior, nor did she consider the existence of Ulises. She was awake until dawn, threading suppositions together and calculating the loss. She slept little and poorly. On the following morning, when Eréndira took the vest with the gold bars off her grandmother, she found fire blisters on her shoulders and raw flesh on her breast. 'I had good reason to be turning over in my sleep,' she said as Eréndira put egg whites on the burns. 'And besides, I had a strange dream.' She made an effort at concentration to evoke the image until it was as clear in her memory as in the dream.

'It was a peacock in a white hammock,' she said.

Eréndira was surprised but she immediately assumed her everyday expression once more.

'It's a good sign,' she lied. 'Peacocks in dreams are animals with long lives.'

'May God hear you,' the grandmother said, 'because we're back where we started. We have to begin all over again.'

Eréndira didn't change her expression. She went out of the tent with the plate of compresses and left her grandmother with her torso soaked in egg white and her skull daubed with mustard. She was putting more egg whites into the plate under the palm shelter that served as a kitchen when she saw Ulises' eyes appear behind the stove as she had seen them the first time behind her bed. She wasn't startled, but told him in a weary voice:

'The only thing you've managed to do is increase my debt.'

Ulises' eyes clouded over with anxiety. He was motionless, looking at Eréndira in silence, watching her crack the eggs with a fixed expression of absolute disdain, as if he didn't exist. After a moment the eyes moved, looked over the things in the kitchen, the hanging pots, the strings of annatto, the carving knife. Ulises stood up, still not saying anything, went in under the shelter, and took down the knife.

Eréndira didn't look at him again, but when Ulises left the shelter she told him in a very low voice:

'Be careful, because she's already had a warning of death. She dreamed about a peacock in a white hammock.'

The grandmother saw Ulises come in with the knife, and making a supreme effort, she stood up without the aid of her staff and raised her arms.

'Boy!' she shouted. 'Have you gone mad?'

Ulises jumped on her and plunged the knife into her naked breast. The grandmother moaned, fell on him, and tried to strangle him with her powerful bear arms.

'Son of a bitch,' she growled. 'I discovered too late that you have the face of a traitor angel.'

She was unable to say anything more because Ulises managed to free the knife and stab her a second time in the side. The grandmother let out a hidden moan and hugged her attacker with more strength. Ulises gave her a third stab, without pity, and a spurt of blood, released by high pressure, sprinkled his face: it was oily blood, shiny and green, just like mint honey.

Eréndira appeared at the entrance with the plate in her hand and watched the struggle with criminal impassivity.

Huge, monolithic, roaring with pain and rage, the grandmother grasped Ulises' body. Her arms, her legs, even her hairless skull were green with blood. Her enormous bellows-breathing, upset by the first rattles of death, filled the whole area. Ulises managed to free his arm with the weapon once more, opened a cut in her belly, and an explosion of blood soaked him in green from head to toe. The grandmother tried to reach the open air which she needed in order to live now and fell face down. Ulises got away from the lifeless arms and without pausing a moment gave the vast fallen body a final thrust.

Eréndira then put the plate on a table and leaned over her grandmother, scrutinizing her without touching her. When she was convinced that she was dead her face suddenly acquired all the maturity of an older person which her twenty years of misfortune had not given her. With quick and precise movements she grabbed the gold vest and left the tent.

Ulises remained sitting by the corpse, exhausted by the fight, and the more he tried to clean his face the more it was daubed with that green and living matter that seemed to be flowing from his fingers. Only when he saw Eréndira go out with the gold vest did he become aware of his state.

He shouted to her but got no answer. He dragged himself to the entrance to the tent and he saw Eréndira starting to run along the shore away from the city. Then he made a last effort to chase her, calling her with painful shouts that were no longer those of a lover but of a son, yet he was overcome by the terrible drain of having killed a woman without anybody's help. The grandmother's Indians caught up to him lying face down on the beach, weeping from solitude and fear.

Eréndira had not heard him. She was running into the wind, swifter than a deer, and no voice of this world could stop her.

292 · Gabriel García Márquez

Without turning her head she ran past the saltpeter pits, the talcum craters, the torpor of the shacks, until the natural science of the sea ended and the desert began, but she still kept on running with the gold vest beyond the arid winds and the never-ending sunsets and she was never heard of again nor was the slightest trace of her misfortune ever found.

GABRIEL GARCÍA MÁRQUEZ

ONE HUNDRED YEARS OF SOLITUDE

'Dazzling' *The New York Times*

'Márquez is a spellbinder' *Spectator*

When the eccentric José Arcadio Buendía starts his life anew by establishing the South American settlement of Macondo he becomes obsessed with new inventions brought to him by a band of gypsies. It is left to his wife, Úrsula, to protect the family from lingering ghosts, alchemy, a plague of insomnia, civil war, and incessant rain. Only a few of the Buendía household have time to escape their chaotic life to wonder about the indecipherable manuscript left by José Arcadio's mysterious gypsy friend Melquíades. And only one of them can reveal its hidden message …

GABRIEL GARCÍA MÁRQUEZ

LOVE IN THE TIME OF CHOLERA

'An exquisite writer, wise, compassionate and extremely funny' *Sunday Telegraph*

On the Caribbean coast at the dawn of the twentieth century hopeless romantic Florentino Ariza falls passionately for beautiful Fermina Daza – but tragically his love is rejected. Instead Fermina marries distinguished Dr Juvenal, while Florentino can only forget her in the arms of other women. Yet fifty one years, nine months and four days later, Florentino has another chance to profess his enduring love for Fermina when her husband unexpectedly dies in a bizarre accident. Can a love over half a century old remain unrequited?

GABRIEL GARCÍA MÁRQUEZ

CHRONICLE OF A DEATH FORETOLD

'A tour de force of moral and emotional complexity' Angela Carter, *Guardian*

Santiago Nasar is brutally murdered in a small town by two brothers. All the townspeople knew it was going to happen – including the victim. But nobody did anything to prevent the killing. Twenty-seven years later, a man arrives in town to try and piece together the truth from the contradictory testimonies of the townsfolk. To at last understand what happened to Santiago, and why …

GABRIEL GARCÍA MÁRQUEZ

If you enjoyed this book, there are several ways you can read more by the same author and make sure you get the inside track on all Penguin books.

Order any of the following titles direct:

0141019425	LIVING TO TELL THE TALE	7.99

'A treasure trove, a thrilling miracle of a book' *The Times*

0140267832	NEWS OF A KIDNAPPING	8.99

'A story only a writer of Marquez's stature could tell so brilliantly'
  Mail on Sunday

0140157506	IN EVIL HOUR	7.99

'Belongs to the very best category of his work' *Financial Times*

0140230963	STRANGE PILGRIMS	8.99

'A fascinating and memorable addition to the canon' William Boyd

0140157492	NO ONE WRITES TO THE COLONEL	7.99

'An exquisite writer' Mary Wesley, *Sunday Telegraph*

*Visit www.penguin.com and find out first about forthcoming titles, read
exclusive material and author interviews, and enter exciting competitions.
You can also browse through thousands of Penguin books and buy online.*

IT'S NEVER BEEN EASIER TO READ MORE WITH PENGUIN